Staffordshire Library and Information Services
Please return or renew by the last date shown

Hednesford

2/6/22 .

If not required by other readers, this item may be
renewed in person, by post or telephone, online or by
email. To renew, either the book or ticket are required

24 Hour Renewal Line
0845 33 00 740

063/16

Staffordshire
County Council

FAREWELL TO BURRACOMBE

The day that Hilary and David have been waiting for has finally arrived and as the church bells ring out for the arrival of the bride, everyone's fingers are crossed for the day to go without a hitch. There's more love in the air as planning continues for both Dottie and Joe's and Frances and James's nuptials. There's nothing like a wedding to bring the village together. Times are changing in Burracombe and as young and old embark on new adventures it's time to say goodbye. But with friends like these, a goodbye is rarely for ever, so instead we'll say a very fond farewell.

FAREWELL TO BURRACOMBE

FAREWELL TO BURRACOMBE

by

Lilian Harry

Magna Large Print Books
Long Preston, North Yorkshire,
BD23 4ND, England.

British Library Cataloguing in Publication Data.

A catalogue record of this book is
available from the British Library

ISBN   978-0-7505-4475-7

First published in Great Britain in 2016 by Orion Books,
an imprint of The Orion Publishing Group Ltd.

Published in Large Print 2017 by arrangement with
The Orion Publishing Group Ltd.

Magna Large Print is an imprint of Library Magna Books Ltd.

Printed and bound in Great Britain by
T.J. (International) Ltd., Cornwall, PL28 8RW

To all my readers, past, present and future, who have supported me so loyally over the years. I have met some of you, corresponded with others and always been aware of your presence in my life. I wish you all a fond farewell, but never a final one. We may yet pay more visits to Burracombe together.

Acknowledgements

I would like to acknowledge, with grateful thanks, the help and support I have received over my writing career from publishers, editors, copy editors, artists and all those many other people who may stay in the background but who work so hard to make my books both good to read and attractive on the shelves.

And, speaking of shelves, I would like to thank all the booksellers who have had enough faith in me to stock my books, and the libraries who have kept me at the top of the loans figures for so long.

Lastly, my very special thanks go to my literary agent, Caroline Sheldon, who has been a friend and help to me for over twenty-five years. Without her there might never have been a Lilian Harry!

Chapter One

September 1955

'Today of all days!' Basil Harvey lamented, wringing his hands. 'Why couldn't it have kept going for just one more day? It will spoil *everything*.'

'Not everything,' Felix Copley tried to console him. 'The reception will go just as planned. It's just the service...' His voice faded as he caught Basil's eye. Although now a vicar in his own right, he still felt very much a curate when he was in the Burracombe church. 'I'm sorry,' he added humbly. 'Of course the marriage service is the most important part of the day. But not having the organ won't affect Hilary and David getting married.'

'And how is the bride going to feel, entering the church to a deathly silence instead of Wagner's "Wedding March"?' Basil enquired coldly. 'It will start everything off on the wrong foot. And it's too late to get a piano or any other musical instrument – unless you can suddenly produce a violin from under your cassock?'

Felix thought briefly of suggesting the village skiffle group, but decided against it. He looked plaintively at Dorothy Doidge, the organist, a tall, thin sixty-year-old who was bending this way and that between them like a willow sapling in a breeze, and almost in tears. 'Is there really no

15

hope of getting a tune out of it?'

Miss Doidge shook her head mournfully. 'I've been trying all morning. I came early for a last rehearsal and it wouldn't give a single note. I knew it was failing, of course–'

'We all did,' Basil interrupted. 'That's why we've been raising money for the repairs. But we're barely halfway there and I hoped and prayed that it would last a little while longer. To let us down *today...*' He looked ready to burst into tears himself, his round, rosy face crumpled like a baby's.

'Well, it's no use bemoaning something we can't put right,' Felix said briskly. 'We've got about five minutes before David arrives and a quarter of an hour before Hilary's due. We've got to make a decision.'

'*What* decision? I can't see that there's anything to decide. We don't have an organ and that's all there is to it. At least we have the bells,' Basil added as a sudden clamour broke out overhead. 'It will sound from outside as if we're celebrating a marriage, even if it's more like a funeral inside. And for dear *Hilary*, too! It's such a *shame*.'

'But not a disaster,' Felix said firmly. 'Look, we've got a good choir. I can sing tenor, and James Raynor has a fine baritone voice, not to mention Alf Coker's bass. The congregation will all join in, I'm sure, and if we all put our hearts into it we can make a sound as fine as any organ.' He caught Miss Doidge's eye. '*Almost* as fine.'

Basil stared at him. 'What are you talking about? Sing the "Wedding March"? It doesn't have any words!'

'But it has a *tune*,' Felix said. 'And it's a tune

16

everyone knows. We can *hum* it. Honestly, it will sound quite wonderful.' As long as nobody sang the unofficial words, *Here comes the bride, all fat and wide* ... he thought, but it was best not to put that idea into Basil's head. 'Look, if you agree, I'll go into the church now and tell them – nearly everyone's there already – and we'll have a quick rehearsal.' He saw the wavering look on the vicar's face. 'I really can't think of any other solution,' he said persuasively.

'But there are the *hymns*,' Basil said, despairing again. 'And she's coming out to Mendelssohn ... are they really up to humming that as well?'

'I'm sure they will be,' Felix assured him, trying to keep the doubt from his own voice. 'Everyone will be in the swing of it by then. And the happy couple will hardly notice. I know I didn't notice the organ at all when Stella and I got married.' He caught Dorothy Doidge's eye again. 'Well, you know bridegrooms never do notice things like that. Anyway, it's the entrance that's most important. If the worst comes to the worst, we can all just clap as they come out of the vestry, and we'll ask Ted Tozer to start the bells ringing then instead of waiting until they're at the church door.' He pulled up the sleeve of his surplice to glance at his watch. 'But we really do need to decide now, if I'm going to explain it to the congregation and do a quick run-through.' He gazed at Basil in entreaty and the vicar gave way.

'Very well. It seems we have no choice. But if you're not happy with your rehearsal, please don't do it. I can't have the whole thing degenerate into a farce.'

'Of course not,' Felix said, and escaped into the church.

Basil and Miss Doidge looked at each other.

'I'm really very sorry,' the organist said, twisting her long fingers together. 'I've been worried about it for some time but I did think it had a few more services left in it. If only we'd known sooner. I blame myself entirely.' A tear ran down her bony nose and Basil patted her arm.

'You mustn't upset yourself, my dear lady. Nothing can be done about it now, and we must just hope that Felix's idea works. He's quite right: we do have a fine choir and there are plenty of good voices in the congregation. Why don't you go on in now and add your own voice? The more the better, you know.'

Miss Doidge sniffed, nodded and hurried in to find a seat at the back. The church was already crowded with friends and relatives of the Napier family, old acquaintances from the squire's army days, and David Hunter's relatives and friends from Derby, as well as many of the villagers and estate tenants. Those who couldn't get in were thronging the village green by the lychgate which led to the churchyard, and the doors of the Bell Inn, where Bernie and Rose had done a roaring lunchtime trade, stood wide open. The sound of the bells added a joyous note to the festive atmosphere and the excitement mounted as the onlookers waited for the car which would bring the bride the short distance from Burracombe Barton.

'And about time too,' they told each other. 'Poor Miss Hilary's waited a long time for this day. Us thought her would never find the right man to wed, but he's come along at last and they do make a lovely couple ... and 'tis a bonus, him being the new village doctor, ready for when Dr Latimer retires. Made his mark already, he has. Look, here he comes now. Don't he look handsome, in that grey top hat and all?'

David Hunter arrived in his own car with his best man, a friend from his army days whom Hilary had also known when she and David had first met in Egypt during the war. They drew up by the green and crossed the grass beneath the great oak tree, waving and smiling at the well-wishers. Basil stood by the church door, watching them with dread in his heart. He could hear Felix's voice inside, explaining what had happened, and there was a murmur as the congregation realised what he was asking them to do. Oh, I do hope this is going to work, Basil thought again. Of all the days, and with all these grand people here to witness our humiliation... Not even to be able to play the 'Wedding March'...

'Why, Basil, whatever's the matter?' David Hunter exclaimed, stopping in front of him. 'You look as if you've all the troubles in the world on your shoulders. Has something gone wrong?' A sudden fear quickened his voice. 'Hilary's all right, isn't she? She hasn't changed her mi–'

'No, no, nothing like that,' Basil said hastily. Really, when you thought about what *could* have gone wrong, perhaps Felix was right and the failure of the church organ wasn't such a catastrophe after all. He explained as quickly as he could and David's expression relaxed. He even

19

began to smile.

'They're going to *hum* it? Why, that's marvellous!' David turned to his best man. 'Have you ever heard of anything so inspired, Adam? I told you Burracombe was a very special village.'

'I hope everyone else will think so,' Basil said dubiously. 'I wouldn't be surprised if Colonel Napier doesn't have another heart attack when he walks into the church with Hilary on his arm to hear the whole congregation humming like a swarm of bees.'

'He'll understand,' David said robustly. 'Don't worry about it. Come on, Adam, we'd better go in and join in the rehearsal. Not that I'll be able to hum a note myself. I'll be too overcome at seeing my bride walking up the aisle to join me at last.'

The two men walked through the big door, receiving hardly a glance from the congregation who were gazing transfixed at Felix, standing at the chancel steps. He had evidently just finished his explanation and was in the act of lifting both arms as if to conduct an orchestra, so that his surplice billowed around him and he looked like an enormous white butterfly. He lowered his wings and looked anxiously at the bridegroom, speaking quietly as the two approached.

'Has Basil explained?'

'He's told us all about it. I think it's a marvellous idea. Adam here used to sing in the church choir at Sandhurst and in the regiment, so he'll be able to join in. I'm afraid I can't promise myself, but then I've got a voice like a crow anyway.'

'I know that isn't true,' Felix said. 'But it's a relief to know you're not upset. It's just Hilary and her father I have to worry about now.'

'Hilary won't mind a bit. She might break down in giggles, of course.'

'I hope not. She'll start everyone else off if she does that – including me, except that mine will be more hysteria than amusement. I can't imagine her father finding it funny, though.'

'He'll know it's not deliberate and you're doing your best,' David reassured him. 'Anyway, weren't you just going to have a quick rehearsal? You'd better buck up – Hilary's notoriously punctual.'

'Even on her wedding day?' his best man murmured as they took their seats in the front pew.

'Even more so on her wedding day,' David muttered back, and glanced behind him. He caught a glimpse of coloured dresses fluttering in the porch and knew that the bridesmaids – Hilary's two cousins, Catherine and Sylvia, her sister-in-law Maddy and best friend, Val Ferris – had arrived. So if Stephen, Hilary's brother, who had driven them there in the big Aston Martin, had managed to arrive on time, he was quite sure that Hilary would not be even a minute late.

Everyone seemed to be here now and Felix was lifting his arms again, beating time with both hands and counting softly to three. At the last count he began to hum and, to David's surprise, the choir and entire congregation joined in, at very nearly the right moment, with an only faintly ragged version of Wagner's 'Wedding March'. It sounded rather effective, he thought, and turned to grin at his best man.

'What are you smiling at?' Adam demanded. 'You're meant to be nervous. You were like a cat

21

on hot bricks until we got here.'

'I was afraid the car would break down or the church disappear overnight. I was so sure something would go wrong, I couldn't think of anything else. But now it has, and it was only the organ, so I know it will all be all right.' He beamed. 'My beautiful bride will be here at any minute, and in half an hour's time, she'll be my wife. And then nothing can ever go wrong again.'

Adam looked quizzically at him. Perhaps this, he thought, was not the moment to remind his friend that life just wasn't like that, and it was often when it appeared to be at its sunniest that the storm clouds would gather out of nowhere. After all, people were entitled to enjoy their perfect moment on their wedding day. And even before the perfect moment arrived, they still had to get through Hilary's arrival at the church – with her father, Colonel Napier, who, Adam knew, wasn't a man to take a small matter like the church organ breaking down as lightly as David appeared to be doing.

I hope he doesn't have a fit or a heart attack at the church door, Adam thought. That really would spoil Hilary and David's perfect day.

As she stood in her bedroom at the Barton, Hilary was outwardly calm; but inside she felt as if she were about to give birth to a litter of kittens. She turned in front of the cheval mirror, twisting her body to glimpse the train that swept in a foam of satin and lace around her feet. The dress itself was a slender column that fitted her perfectly; it had a collar that stood around her neck with a glitter of crystals which matched the

22

sparkling earrings that almost brushed it. Her rich brown hair was piled on top of her head, and the sparkle echoed in the tiny diamond tiara that had been her mother's.

'You look absolutely beautiful,' Val said in awed tones as she made one last adjustment and then stood back to see the final effect. 'David will think he's died and gone to heaven.'

'You're sure it's not overdone?' Hilary asked anxiously. 'I don't want to look like a Christmas tree.'

'You don't look a bit like a Christmas tree,' Maddy assured her. 'A beautifully wrapped present, perhaps!' She giggled as Hilary blushed. 'Honestly, Hil, you look wonderful. And what do you think of your bridesmaids? Come along, girls, line up to be inspected!' She stood at mock attention and the other three formed a line beside her, arms held stiffly at their sides and heads facing forward, their eyes unblinking, as Hilary turned towards them. She laughed at their stern expressions.

'Stop fooling about, all of you! This is a solemn occasion and nothing is to go wrong.' She glanced at the gold wristwatch that had been David's wedding present to her. 'Come on – we'll be late if we don't hurry.'

She swept out of the room, impervious to Maddy's murmuring protest that it was a bride's privilege to be late, and stood at the top of the stairs. Then, just for a moment, she paused, realising that this was the last time she would leave that bedroom as a single woman. When she and David returned from their honeymoon in Venice, they would move into the big room that had once been occupied by her mother and father but for years now had only been used for visitors. Gilbert himself had suggested this, for he preferred his room at the back of the house, and while they were away, a new bathroom was to be installed next door, so that they would be entirely private. From now on, the room Hilary had had since she was a child would become David's study.

It's all going to be different, she thought. I knew it would be, of course, and I'm happy about the changes – very happy indeed. But even good changes take a little getting used to.

She looked down the broad curve of the stairs into the hallway, to see her father looking up at her, and hoped that he, too, would embrace the changes that were to come.

Gilbert, arrayed in his best morning suit, with his grey silk topper under his arm, had come out of the drawing room and was standing at the foot of the stairs to welcome his only daughter on her wedding day.

They all seemed to have waited a long time for this day to come. If the war had not taken her first fiancé, Henry, Hilary would have been married for years by now and probably would have three or four children. Even after Henry's death, she could very easily have found someone else to marry – she was an attractive young woman, from a good family, with plenty of connections – yet somehow it had never happened. It wasn't for lack of effort on Gilbert's part, but she had never shown any interest in the sons of any of his friends and gradually they had all drifted away and married other girls. But now, at last, she had found someone for herself: a man he liked and approved of – a doctor who had seen army service during the war, who had been married and widowed, and who would be of benefit to the village of Burracombe. And while David Hunter was never likely to want to manage the estate, Hilary had, when Stephen had made it clear that he had no interest in taking on the task, proved herself more than capable of being able to do it and seemed to want to continue. This was something that would never have happened if she had married and gone to live somewhere else in Devon. She might even have gone to live further afield, and Gilbert would have lost her company and help for all these years.

These thoughts, so typical of Gilbert Napier, passed through his mind as he stood waiting for his daughter to appear, but they were swiftly followed by others. For Gilbert had learned, through the past few years of illness and change, to value more than background, wealth and social position. He had learned to value more human qualities and the happiness and contentment that they could bring. Where once he had wanted a 'good marriage' for his daughter, he now desired her happiness more than anything else in the world, and he knew that of all the men she could have chosen to be her husband, David Hunter was the one most likely to give it to her.

The door at the top of the stairs opened and, in a cloud of pearly white that seemed to shimmer in the light cast by the sunlight streaming through the open door, his daughter Hilary appeared, with the soft blue shadow of her bridesmaids behind her. She stood perfectly still for a moment, gazing down at him, and as their eyes met he felt a sudden unexpected lump in his throat and the heat of tears in his eyes. He frowned, shook his head a little and blinked them away, then stepped forward, his hands held out towards her as she came slowly down the sweep of the stairs.

'My dear,' he said huskily, 'you look beautiful. David is a very lucky man. I shall be proud to give you into his keeping.'

'They're here,' Basil hissed as the two silver cars drew up at the lychgate. He twisted his hands together again in an agony of dread. 'Oh dear... Stephen, tell Felix I've changed my mind – we *can't* ask the congregation to hum the "Wedding March". The colonel will never understand. Quickly, my dear chap, *please*... Oh my goodness...'

'It's too late,' Stephen Napier said, grinning. 'They've got the bit between their teeth now.' He tilted his head as the murmur of the congregation sounded through the open door. 'I'll tell Felix they're coming and he'll make sure they start just as the bells stop ringing and Hilary comes through the door.' He reached out his hand and patted Basil's arm. 'Don't worry, Mr Harvey. It'll all be fine, you'll see.'

He vanished into the dim interior and Basil gazed after him despairingly, then quickly re-arranged his features into a welcoming smile.

Hilary was out of the car now, assisted by Val and Maddy, who were carefully gathering the long train in their arms to carry it up the gravel path. The other two bridesmaids came behind them and Gilbert walked beside his daughter to the door where they all paused to make the final adjustments. The bells were ringing the last few changes of their peal, ready to stop the moment Ted was given the signal, and within the church itself there was an expectant hush.

Hilary gave Basil a shaky smile and slipped her arm through her father's.

'I think we're all ready,' she said softly, and then turned to her father. 'Thank you for everything, Dad. You've been a wonderful father.'

Gilbert blinked again and cleared his throat. Nervously, Basil began to speak, to warn them of the change that would accompany their entrance, but Gilbert waved him to silence.

'No more to be said now. We're as ready as ever we will be. Let's get on with it.' He pushed at the church door and it moved slowly open.

'But I must...' Basil whispered in a desperate squeak. 'There's something you–' The clamour of the bells ceased and his voice trembled to a halt. With a sense of imminent doom, he stepped in front of Hilary and her father and as the bridesmaids took up their positions behind, he preceded them into the church.

Gilbert stopped abruptly.

'What in heaven's name...? What on earth has happened to the organ?'

His voice was low but forceful. Hilary stared around her. She saw Felix waiting at the chancel steps, his expression unnaturally solemn. She saw David and his best man standing by the front pew, their eyes fixed firmly ahead. She saw the entire congregation, their faces rigid with the

27

effort to restrain their smiles, their lips pressed together as if ... as if–

'Why!' she gasped, and her own smile broke out unfettered. 'Father, they're *humming!* They're humming the "Wedding March"! The organ must have given up at last.'

'*Whaat?*' Gilbert's voice was still low, but there was a touch of disbelief in it, and more than a touch of annoyance. 'You mean to say that today of *all* days–'

Basil turned his head. 'We couldn't think what else to do. Felix said it would all right, and by the time I decided against it, it was too late to–'

'But it sounds wonderful,' Hilary whispered. 'It's a lovely idea.' She squeezed her father's arm. 'Come on, Dad, what are you waiting for? Take me up the aisle. I thought you couldn't wait to marry me off!'

Gilbert pulled himself together. Looking neither to left nor right, he stepped forward and proceeded purposefully towards the altar steps. The humming, with which Felix had managed to create a surprising depth of harmony, continued as they walked and when Hilary saw her groom turn to welcome her to his side, her smile was radiant. Gilbert stepped back and David took her hand, looking deep into her eyes.

'Hello, darling,' he murmured, and as she whispered her own hello in return the humming faded to a silence that left only birdsong drifting through the open door and Basil, relief adding to the joy in his voice, turned to face them and began the words of the marriage service.

'Dearly beloved, we are gathered here together...'

Chapter Two

'Thank goodness it worked,' Felix said. 'I was terrified everyone would get the giggles and ruin it.'

'I was terrified *you'd* get the giggles.' Stella smiled, lifting her own glass of orange juice to touch his of champagne. 'But you did really well, getting them to do it. It's a good job you had time to rehearse.'

'It must never happen again,' Basil said. 'It went very well this time, but who knows whether another congregation would be large enough to make such a good job of it – or so willing to try? It's obvious that the organ must now be considered out of action and something urgent must be done about its repair. But how are we to manage in the meantime?'

'Oh, that's easy,' Joyce Warren said, coming up to them as they stood by the drawing-room window of Burracombe Barton. 'You can borrow our grand piano.'

Basil stared at her. 'Your grand piano? But surely you don't want to move that over to the church?'

'Why ever not? It can stand in the south transept. It's got a lovely tone.'

'Yes, but it's a valuable instrument, and the church is left unlocked all day. It would be terrible if anything happened to it.'

'What could happen to it in Burracombe? You're not telling me you don't trust your own congregation, Basil!'

'Of course I do. But you never know who else might be about. Visitors...' His pink face was flushed with agitation. 'It would be such a responsibility.'

Joyce shook her head at him. 'No more than the organ itself is, or any of the other artefacts in the church. And the lid can be locked. Really, Basil, I'd be delighted to see our piano in the church and to hear it playing every Sunday. It doesn't get nearly enough use these days.'

'But that's another thing! Who would play it? I'm not sure that dear Dorothy Doidge would. She's a very good organist, of course, but a grand piano – I just don't know if she's quite capable...' He floundered into silence and Joyce took pity on him.

'Of course she's quite capable. Anyone who can play an organ can manage a piano, surely. In any case, Henry's a fine pianist and he'd be only too pleased to step in if needed. Wouldn't you, Henry?' She turned to her husband, who had just joined the little group.

'Wouldn't I what?' He listened as his wife told him of her offer. 'Well, of course, if you'd like me to. I wouldn't like to tread on Miss Doidge's toes, though. You must ask her if she needs my help first.'

'I will.' Basil was clearly relieved at being able to shelve the problem for the time being, but Felix wasn't ready to let it go so easily.

'Whatever you decide, you need to do it soon,' he remarked. 'You've got your normal services tomorrow and people might find it rather tiring

30

to hum their way through an entire Matins. And there's another wedding coming up.'

'So there is – Joe and Dottie's. But that's not for another three weeks. You're right about tomorrow, though, and kind though your offer is, Mrs Warren, we certainly can't think of moving your grand piano by eleven o'clock tomorrow morning.'

'You can bring our harmonium, though,' Ted Tozer butted in, and they all turned to him in surprise. 'That's what I came over to say, vicar. Mother told me to tell you, you're welcome to use that for as long as you needs, and she'll play it for you too if Dorothy Doidge ain't up to it. Not that it would be any trouble to her, after playing the church organ, but it do be a bit temperamental at times. And Tom and me could get it over and set it up first thing in the morning, all ready for morning service.'

'That would be a great help,' Basil said in relief. 'Just for the time being, anyway.' He drew in a deep breath, smiled round at them all and took a large sip of his champagne. 'And now that's settled, let's enjoy the rest of this happy day. I think Colonel Napier wants us to join the guests in the marquee.'

The rest of the villagers, having gathered outside the church to see Hilary arrive and then leave again on the arm of her new husband, drifted away in the September sunshine talking of the event.

'She did look lovely in that beautiful frock,' Aggie Madge sighed. 'And so happy, too. She looked as if the sun was shining right out of her.'

'Well, she's got the money for it,' Ivy Sweet

31

commented, and then as the others turned to her in indignation, added defensively, 'I mean, anyone can look nice in frocks made in London by smart dressmakers. Not that Miss Hilary's not a good-looking young woman, I didn't mean that. But you got to admit, if she'd left it to Dottie Friend to make the frock...' Her voice trailed away and became more feeble. 'I didn't mean nothing by it.'

'No, but you said it just the same,' Aggie said coldly. 'That's your trouble, Ivy, always got summat sharp to say about everything. You knows as well as I do that Dottie's got a lot of experience in dressmaking and she'd have made just as good a job of it, if she hadn't had that stroke. I hear she's doing her own wedding costume anyway, and I dare say it will be just as good. And us shouldn't be saying Miss Hilary no more,' she added. 'She's Mrs Hunter now and entitled to her proper married name.'

'Mrs *Napier* Hunter,' Nancy Pettifer corrected her. 'That's what our Patsy told us she was going to be called. So the Napier name don't die out.'

The others were diverted from their annoyance with Ivy Sweet. They paused on their way down the church path and stared at her. 'But wasn't young Rob going to take the name?' someone asked. 'I thought the colonel wanted him to be in charge of the whole estate when he grows up.'

'You're behind the times, then,' Nancy said. 'That wasn't no more than a flash in the pan. His mother put a stop to it, said she wanted him back in France. Miss Hilary – *Mrs Napier Hunter* – wanted to go on running the estate, with Mr Kellaway helping her and I reckon the colonel saw she was making a good job of it and settled for that. Good job too, if you ask me – you don't know what that French tacker would have done if it had been left to him. He could have split the whole place up and sold us off wholesale, for all us knows.'

'Well, that won't happen now,' Aggie Madge said comfortably. 'Burracombe looks safe for a good few years yet and us got a new doctor as a bonus! I reckon it's all turned out better than anyone could have wished for. Mind you, us haven't seen the last of young Rob and his mother. They came over for the wedding after all, and very smart she looked too, in her Paris hat.'

'They're still family,' Nancy pointed out. 'She was married to the colonel's son in the war, and Rob's his grandson. You can't get away from that.'

The others nodded thoughtfully. Marianne's unexpected arrival two years earlier with her son, who looked so much like Gilbert Napier's elder son Baden, lost at Dunkirk, had caused a stir throughout the village, and it had seemed for some time that the inheritance would pass to him. But it all seemed to have been settled eventually, although none of them knew the details, and Rob, who had for a few weeks attended the nearby Kelly College, had gone home to France. The squire's experiment in trying to turn him into an English schoolboy had failed, and nobody except Gilbert himself had been sorry. And even Gilbert's disappointment had diminished as he accepted at last that his daughter could run the estate as well as any man, and would stay at Burracombe, living in the Barton, after her marriage.

'I don't believe us've got much to fear from them, all the same,' Jacob Prout pronounced, holding the lychgate open for Jessie Friend and her sister to pass through. 'Miss Hilary – and you needn't look at me like that, Nancy Pettifer, she'll always be Miss Hilary to me, and to most of us, I reckon – will keep the reins in her hands, even when she've got a quiverful of little 'uns round her feet.'

'A quiverful!' Ivy said with a sharp little laugh. 'She needs to be getting on with that pretty smartish! She's no spring chicken, when all's said and done.'

'And there you go again!' Nancy exclaimed in exasperation. 'Always got to pass some remark.' She shook her head. 'I hope you'll be able to keep your opinions to yourself in the Bell tonight, that's all, or Bernie will be asking your George to take you back home again.'

Ivy flushed scarlet and turned on her heel. 'It's not me, Nancy Pettifer, it's you always taking things the wrong way. I'm as pleased as anyone else that Miss Hilary's found a man at last and going to be happy, and I hope she do have a family of her own, and I don't see anything wrong with that. It's only what we all hope.'

'Yes, it is, but it's the way you say things. Like "found a man *at last*" and "no spring chicken" – there wasn't no need for that. Aggie's right, you're too sharp.' Nancy hesitated, then went on more quietly, 'Let's leave it there, anyway. This is meant to be a happy day and the colonel's paid for us all to have a party in the Bell tonight and I reckon us all wants to enjoy it, with no argufying.

So let's say no more about it.'

'Suits me,' Ivy said. 'Since I never meant to give offence in the first place.' She gave Nancy a look. 'I'll see you later, then, I dare say.'

'That's right. All in our glad rags.' Nancy smiled. 'Maybe you can get your George to sing that song of his.'

'Try and stop him!' someone observed, and they all laughed. 'And Jacob will say some poetry. It'll be a real good old-fashioned Burracombe party.'

'It will too,' Nancy said quietly to her husband Jack as they walked back to their cottage. 'If only Ivy can keep her remarks to herself. She do have a way of making everything sound nasty.'

'I don't think she even knows she's doing it,' Jack said. 'And I thought she seemed a bit better just lately. She's not nearly so sharp in the pub. Sort of softer, somehow.'

'I thought that too. She seemed a bit different after that trip to London she and George had, after the summer fair. But folk like Ivy don't change overnight. I reckon she's got a long way to go before she stops making acid remarks and we ought to be used to it by now.'

'And maybe we should be used to Ivy,' he said. 'Give her the benefit of the doubt, like. Anyway, never mind that for the minute. We've got our Bob bringing his new lady friend to tea tomorrow and I dare say you'll be wanting to spring-clean the whole house to impress her!'

Ivy walked back to the bakery alone, burning with a resentment that was more than half annoyance at her own actions. Why was it that whatever she

35

said seemed to set other people against her? Since the events of the summer fair, she'd felt different, softer towards her neighbours, many of whom she had known all her life. She'd finally admitted to herself and George the truth of what had happened to her during the war, and faced the consequences, and somehow it had released a tight spring inside her, a coil of guilt and fear that had made her defensive towards everything and everybody. She'd thought everyone would have seen this difference and start to treat her differently in turn, but somehow it hadn't happened. Somehow, she still managed to offend them with her remarks. She was beginning to think it wasn't worth trying any longer.

'What's the matter, Ive?' George asked when she came through the kitchen door. 'Didn't the wedding go off well after all?'

'It was all right.' She shrugged off her jacket impatiently. 'Apart from the organ breaking down and everyone having to hum the "Wedding March". You'd think that might have spoilt it – it would, if it had been anyone else's wedding – but no, Felix Copley got them all singing as good as a choir at the Albert Hall and you'd have thought it was meant.' She sat down at the kitchen table, her shoulders drooping. 'Some people always get things going well for them. My dad would have said if they fell down a sewer they'd come up smelling of violets.'

'Here, come on, Ive.' George pulled a chair round the table and sat down beside her, his arm across her thin shoulders. 'That's no way to go on. You know we all wish Miss Hilary and her man well. What's really the matter? Has someone said summat to upset you?'

She shook her head. 'It's the other way about, George. It don't matter what I say, someone takes it wrong. I don't mean to be nasty, and I don't reckon I say anything but what they're all thinking anyway, but there's always someone to take me up on it. I don't know why I bother, really I don't. I'm better off keeping myself to myself like I've always done. I'm never going to be friends with Burracombe folk, and that's all there is to it.'

'Don't say that. You grew up with half of them, and so did I. We were all friends together in the old days, weren't we? And now you're working at the Bell a few evenings a week, you need to be able to give and take a bit of ribbing. You got on all right in Horrabridge, after all.'

'That was different,' she said, turning a dull red. 'I didn't know them like I know Burracombe folk. Anyway, those days are gone. I dunno if I want to go on working at the Bell, George. The customers are all right when it's just the men, I can talk to them; it's the women that seem to bring out the worst in me. People like Nancy Pettifer and Alice Tozer.'

'Well, they don't go in the pub much,' George said. 'Only on special occasions like New Year's Eve or a do like tonight. I don't know what you're worrying about, Ive. It's not as if you've ever got on with Alice, after all.'

'No, I haven't.' Ivy allowed herself to remember for an instant the day when she had first met Alice, back in 1918 when she'd arrived as a maid at the Tozers' farm, to work for Minnie Tozer.

She'd seen immediately the way Minnie's son, Ted, who was nearly half promised to Ivy herself at that time, had looked at Alice, and so Ivy had set out to get rid of the unwelcome newcomer. But she'd failed and had to turn instead to George Sweet, who had been following her about like a faithful puppy for months. And it hadn't turned out badly, she had to admit. George had been a good husband, better than she deserved, and a good father to Barry.

'I should forget about it,' George advised now, and she had to think for a moment to realise what he meant. 'I don't suppose it's you who always gets your words out wrong. Some of the others might be wishing they hadn't spoke sharp to you. As for the pub, if Bernie and Rose are satisfied with your work and you're happy to go on with it, you just carry on. I've seen you there and once you're behind the bar you're a different woman. It's as if you feel safe to be yourself then.'

'Yes, it is,' Ivy said slowly. 'I never thought of it like that before, George, but you're right. I'd miss it if I didn't go, I know that.' She got up from the table. 'I'd better see about getting tea ready. Our Barry will be in soon and he'll be starving hungry as usual. Where did he say he was going?'

'Getting conkers, I think,' George said vaguely. 'I told him it was a bit early for them, we don't get many hereabouts till October, but he said if he couldn't get any he'd go blackberrying instead. There's plenty of them about.'

'That'd be more useful. I could make a blackberry and apple crumble for tomorrow.' Ivy opened the larder door. 'Rose was telling me there

38

was going to be quite a spread at the pub tonight so we won't want much to eat now. I'll do Barry some beans on toast when he comes in.' She hesitated. 'Does he seem all right to you, George? About – you know – his granny in Poland? I've never been sure he took in what we told him.'

'He's not really old enough to understand,' George said. 'And being a boy... A girl might have been more interested – might have thought it were romantic, like, and made up all kinds of stories about being a princess and God knows what. I reckon we should think ourselves lucky Barry don't seem too interested at the moment. He could be asking a lot of questions we don't know how to answer.'

Ivy stood still for a moment, her jacket in her hand ready to hang up behind the staircase door. She looked at George and then laid her hand on his shoulder, her face softening.

'You're a good man, George,' she said a little huskily. 'I don't know as I deserve you. There's plenty would have chucked their wives out for doing what I did.'

'And what good would that have done?' he asked, his plump, florid face turning a deeper red than ever. 'You'd have gone off out of the village and I'd have lost my wife and the baby. And it was wartime, too. I don't know what you'd have done – had to go and work in a munitions factory, like as not, and put the little tacker in one of those day nurseries. I don't see how I could have let that happen.'

'Well, plenty would,' she repeated. 'And I've only realised just lately how lucky I was. Not that it seems to stop me being a bit sharp, just the same,' she added despondently. 'I don't seem able to help it.'

George laughed. 'I know, Ive, and I don't take it to heart. You were always a bit quick to speak up even as a girl, and you're not going to change now. You just go on being yourself and we'll rub along same as usual. Anyway, I can hear our Barry coming up the path now – you'd better get his tea ready and put your glad rags on, and then it'll be time for us to go round to the Bell and enjoy ourselves. It's a happy day for Burracombe – let's make the most of it.'

Chapter Three

'Do you realise,' Travis Kellaway said to his wife, wiping his breakfast plate clean with the last corner of fried bread, 'that this is the first time I've been left completely in charge, for more than a day or two, since I came to work at the Burracombe estate?'

'And if you think you're in charge now, you're being wildly optimistic,' Jennifer replied, wiping Molly's face with a damp flannel before lifting her down from her high chair. 'There you are, my pretty, go and play with your bricks and don't throw them at Tavy. That dog is too placid for her own good,' she added as the Jack Russell followed the toddler out of the kitchen. 'One of these days Molly's going to meet a dog who won't put up with having its ears pulled and dolls' bonnets strapped on its head.' She poured him another cup of tea. 'But going back to being in charge, is the colonel really going to stand aside and let you run the estate all on your own? I can't see it happening myself.'

Travis chuckled. 'No, I don't suppose he will. You're right, I'll have less authority with Hilary away than I do with her around. She does let me do more and more these days, especially since David came along. And when she's got two or three little ones like our Molly to take up her time, she'll probably hand over completely. But Colonel Napier' – he shook his head – 'since Dr Latimer gave him the all-clear, he thinks he's a young man again.'

'Perhaps having Stephen and Maddy home from Cyprus will take his mind off the estate for a bit,' Jennifer said hopefully, but Travis shook his head.

'Stephen's got to go back to the RAF hospital this week, and Maddy's going too. They're renting a cottage for her to stay in while he's still having treatment. It was rotten luck, losing an arm. He's a good pilot, too, by all accounts. It will almost certainly put paid to his plans to go to Canada and start up an air-freight service.'

'Thank goodness he wasn't killed,' Jennifer said soberly. 'The colonel's already lost one son. To lose Stephen as well could have brought on another heart attack.'

Travis put down his cup and pushed back his chair. 'I must be off. I won't be home at dinner time today – I've got to go over to that chap at Brentor to see about some steers he's thinking of

41

selling. If they look a good buy, I'll snap them up, otherwise they'll be going to Tavistock for the cattle market on Goose Fair Day. I'll have dinner there – his wife likes to see a different face now and again.'

'I'll take Molly down to the village to see Jacob, then,' Jennifer said. 'He'll probably be working in the churchyard. I'll take him the rest of the casserole we had yesterday and pop into Mr Foster's for some Cokers for dinner tomorrow.' She meant the sausages made by the village butcher, which everyone said were the size of the blacksmith Alf Coker's fingers.

Travis nodded. 'I'll just go and say goodbye to Molly.' He went to the door to look through to the living room. 'Er ... did you mean them to have that pile of magazines to play with?'

'Magazines?' Jennifer jumped up. 'Oh, *Molly!* And Tavy, too! Look what you've done! I was saving those to give to Patsy Pettifer for her mother. Now they're all in tatters. Honestly – you're both old enough to know better!' She stared in dismay at the shreds of several copies of *Woman Own* and Travis chuckled, scooped up his daughter for a kiss and departed.

Jennifer stood in the doorway, gazing at the devastation. Both dog and toddler gazed back, identical expressions in their brown eyes, their heads tilted enquiringly to one side as if to say, 'You seem upset. Is there anything we can do to help?' She bent to gather up the wreckage and scolded them both but her heart wasn't in it. It was my fault, she thought, for leaving the magazines in reach. And I'd rather be here, living with

42

Travis in this lovely cottage in the woods with a baby and a little dog than where I was a few years ago – in a back street in Plymouth with nothing but memories of an unhappy marriage.

It was hard to imagine anything going wrong in her life now.

Jacob Prout was cutting the churchyard grass when Jennifer appeared, pushing Molly in her pram with Tavy running alongside. His own dog, Scruff, pottering about between the gravestones, made a rush at them as they came through the lychgate, and the two dogs bounded off together to search for rabbits in the high Devon bank that surrounded the graveyard. Molly clamoured to get out of the pram and Jennifer lifted her down to scamper over to the old man.

'Grandpa! It's me!'

'So it is,' he said, his face creased with smiles. 'I thought 'twas a little angel come to raise me up to heaven!' He brushed his hands down his trousers and swung her into the air.

Jennifer laughed. 'You get more poetic every day, Jacob. And you wouldn't call her an angel if you saw what she and that dog got up to this morning.' She told him about the magazines.

'Well, maybe they shouldn't have been left lying about,' he said, but Jennifer shook her head.

'They've got to learn to leave things alone, both of them. So what's the vicar decided to do about the church organ, do you know?'

Jacob rolled his eyes. 'What a to-do that were! I thought Squire would have a fit, taking his daughter up the aisle to everyone humming the

43

"Wedding March". As it turned out, he took it pretty well and it were vicar more likely to have a heart attack. And as for Miss Hilary – Mrs Napier Hunter, as we've got to call her now if I can ever get my tongue round it – she looked ready to burst out laughing. I never saw nothing like it. But at least it's made us take the organ fund seriously. We've just been playing about at raising money up till now, as fast as we raised a bit there always seemed to be summat else wanting the money.'

'There's always something to spend money on,' Jennifer said. 'Jacob, I've got a casserole in the pram, left over from yesterday. There's enough for two – two and a little one – so if you like, I'll take it round to the cottage now and pop it in your oven. Then we can share it when you've finished here and I've done my shopping.'

Jacob beamed. 'Proper job. And you can leave the little maid here with her grandpa. I'll see she comes to no harm, the dear of her.'

Jennifer lifted her basket from the pram and crossed the village green towards Jacob's cottage. He wasn't really Molly's grandfather but Jennifer had met him when she had first come to Burracombe in search of her own father and discovered that he and her mother had been sweethearts. Had it not been for that search, she would never have come to Burracombe and never have met Travis, and Jacob would, in turn, have been a lonelier man.

'Where in the world are you?' a voice accosted her. 'Miles away, by the look of it!'

'Dottie!' Jennifer stopped as the older woman waved to her from the side of the green. 'How are

44

you? Recovered from the party on Saturday night?'

The older woman chuckled. 'Joe made me go home early. Said I've got to take care of myself to be ready for our own wedding. I still can't believe I'm getting married, at my age!'

'Go on, you're not as old as all that.' They fell into step along the road. 'I'm glad you're not going to America straight away.'

'No, we decided to stay here for the winter. Joe's like a mother hen, don't want me travelling until I'm completely over that bit of a stroke I had and he says the weather will be better for the crossing in spring. We're going to have a couple of weeks in Cornwall for our honeymoon – that trip we went on to Perranporth with Ted and Alice at the beginning of the month was so good, we thought we'd go back and see a bit more of the area. And by the time we get back from that, it'll be Harvest Supper and then we'll all be thinking about Christmas. I don't know where the time goes,' she ended a little breathlessly.

'Nor do I. It seems hardly any time since Molly was a tiny baby and now she's fifteen months old and running about. And yet, I can hardly remember what it was like not to have her.'

'Will you be thinking of having another one, for company for the little maid? I always think it's nice to have them close together in age.'

Jennifer blushed and laughed. 'Well, who knows?'

Dottie gave her a quick look. 'You don't mean–?'

'Well, not as far as I know. But – well, it could be just an ordinary tummy upset but I've felt a bit queasy in the mornings this past week. It's nothing very much, mind, so don't say anything to anyone, will you?'

'I won't say a word,' Dottie promised. 'But I hope you're right. And Jacob will be like a dog with two tails. I dare say you'd like a little boy this time.'

'Travis would, I think. I would too, but two little girls would be lovely. Really, all we want is for it to be healthy. That's if there is one,' she added hastily. 'It's really too soon to tell yet.'

'Tell me as soon as you know for sure,' Dottie said. She thought for a moment. 'Let's see, if you're feeling sick now, you could be nearly two months gone, and that means the little dear would be born around the end of April. That's a lovely time to have a baby.'

'Goodness, you are getting ahead!' Jennifer laughed. 'Honestly, Dottie, it could just be a false alarm.' She was half regretting she'd mentioned it at all. There was something in the air of Burracombe that seemed to catch at the slightest hint of rumour and turn it into common knowledge. She remembered the time when she and Travis had got engaged – without telling anyone their intentions, they had gone to a jeweller's shop in Tavistock to buy the ring and someone had seen them there, with the result that by the time they returned to the village everyone had known not only that they were engaged but also that they had fixed the date of the wedding. Even more irritatingly, they'd got it right!

Still, Dottie wasn't a gossip and had too much to think about with her own wedding on the horizon

46

to bother mentioning that Jennifer Kellaway had felt a bit queasy one morning.

'It's a shame you never had children, Dottie,' Jennifer said. 'You'd have made a wonderful mother, and grandmother too.'

'I had Maddy as a maid, though,' Dottie reminded her. 'She was just like my own little girl when she lived with me. Still is, for all that she's grown up and is a married woman now.'

Jennifer smiled, then pursed her lips. 'It's so sad that Stephen's lost his arm. They've only been married a few months. I wonder what they'll do now. I suppose they'll come back to Burracombe to live.'

Dottie shook her head. 'Not from what they were saying after the wedding. Stephen's still set on making his own life and he's never been that interested in the estate. Talking of going to Canada, they were, just like nothing had happened.'

'Really? But surely he won't be able to fly, with only one arm.' Jennifer opened her mouth to say more, then remembered her own thoughts about village gossip and stopped. Instead, she smiled and took the brake off the pram. 'I mustn't stay here chatting – I've got a casserole to put in the oven for Jacob. He's got Molly "helping" him in the churchyard so he'll need a good dinner! And when I've done that, I need to go the butcher for some Cokers.'

They parted and Dottie went on her way to the village butcher's shop. She too wanted some Cokers, for Joe's dinner. He was dividing his time now between his brother's farmhouse and Dottie's cottage but once they were married he would move in with her.

It'll be a bit different for him, living in a tiny cottage instead of the big farmhouse or that lovely home he's got in America, Dottie thought, a small frown appearing between her brows. I hope he won't find it too cramped. It's all very well, this idea of living half the year in America and half in Burracombe, but it's a big change for both of us, and change is harder at our time of life.

Sudden panic swept over her and she stopped dead in the middle of the street. Was it really sensible to be marrying her childhood sweetheart after all these years? Crossing the Atlantic four times a year – twice one way, twice the other ... not so much *spending* half the year in Burracombe, as *missing* the other half – never being here in spring when the snowdrops were like white icing under the hedges, the primroses a blanket of gold covering the Devon banks and the bluebells like patches of fallen sky in the woods. Nor in the summer, when the gorse and heather flung a cape of gold and purple fit for a king over the swooping moor, when the gardens were full of roses and the blackberries glowed like jewels on the bramble bushes... Never, ever, seeing any of that again.

I can't do it, she thought, her hands clutching the handle of her wicker basket. I can't leave all this and go to America.

She put one hand to her heart and drew in a sudden, sharp breath of pain.

I can't marry Joe...

Joe was helping his brother with the milking. Even though he'd left the farm nearly forty years earlier, he'd soon settled back into the old ways and milking had been one of his favourite jobs as a boy. Sitting on the little three-legged stool, with your head pressed against a cow's warm flank, feeling her steady breathing as you squeezed her teats to make the milk flow, was a job you couldn't hurry, and each cow had her own personality. That, his father used to say, was when you really got to know your animals. You could tell in a minute if there was something wrong, if she wasn't feeling up to the mark that day. You could see if she didn't want to let her milk down or if she wasn't making as much, which usually indicated a problem either with the cow or with the pasture. It gave you time with each animal, time you'd never otherwise have.

'I know what Father used to tell us,' Joe remarked as they sent the cows out of the parlour and started to wash down, 'but I gotta say I'm surprised you've never moved on to machines. Nobody in the States milks by hand and the beasts don't seem to suffer any.'

Ted screwed up his face. 'Tom's been on at me about that. Says we could have a bigger herd and produce more milk, but you've got to have the pasture and I'm not sure we could do it. We've got to make enough hay for the winter feed too. I reckon we'd need another couple of fields at least to make it work. And – I dunno, Joe, I reckon I'd miss the hand milking. I know it's a chore but you still got to keep to the same routine, even if you do use a machine, and I can't see as you can get to know your beasts so well. And *they* get to know *us* – that's the important part. Come any trouble at calving time, and they trust us to help 'em.'

They finished scrubbing the parlour walls and floor, leaving it clean for afternoon milking when it would all have to be done again, and went indoors for a late breakfast. Ted usually made a pot of tea in the morning when he first got up and fried up a couple of strips of bacon to put between two slices of bread, just to keep him going through the milking, as he would say, and then Alice would cook him a proper breakfast when he came in. Eggs, more bacon, tomatoes and mushrooms in season, baked beans, fried bread or potato – that was what a man needed after two or three hours outside with the cows. Tom would be there too, and now Joe, and their cousin, Norman, would come in too if he'd helped with the morning milking. In winter especially, when it was still only just getting light outside and the puddles were frozen and the air icy cold, the farmhouse kitchen with its smells of bacon and fried bread was a warm and welcoming place.

Now, although dawn was breaking a little later each day, the sky was light by six and the sun was well up when the two brothers pushed open the kitchen door. Alice was standing at the range, tending a huge cast-iron frying pan, and Minnie was taking plates out of the warm bottom oven and putting them on the table. The kettle came to the boil just as Ted pulled off his leather jacket and hung it on the row of hooks by the door.

'There you are,' Alice said, as if Ted's appearance in the kitchen at this hour came as a surprise. 'Your breakfast's just ready. It's a fine morning. I heard on the wireless it's going to hold for a few days.'

'That's good. We'll be able to get on with–' The ringing of the telephone interrupted him and he went to answer it, while Alice began to dish up fried potatoes, sausages and eggs. Joe sat down at the table and she set a plateful in front of him, then slid Ted's back into the oven to keep hot.

A moment or two later he came back into the kitchen, his face suddenly lined and grey.

Minnie, now seated in her rocking chair by the fire with her knitting, looked at him in alarm. 'Why, Ted, whatever be the matter? You look as if you've seen a ghost.'

Alice, who had bent to take his plate out of the oven, turned quickly. 'What is it?' She stared at her husband. 'Bad news?'

Ted sat down heavily. 'It was Joe's eldest girl. Telephoning from America.' His eyes met Alice's and his mouth worked as if he hardly knew what to say.

The others gazed at him and Alice put the hot plate on the table, her hands shaking. 'It – it's not our Jackie?' Her voice sharpened. 'It is, isn't it? Our Jackie...' The family laughed at her for always thinking that something terrible would happen to her youngest daughter, in America, but she could see from Ted's face that this time she was right. 'What is it?' she demanded. 'What's happened to her?'

'There've been an accident,' he said shakily. 'A car – automobile, she said, but that just means car, don't it? I didn't catch what happened, I'm not sure they knows for certain, but it went off

51

the road and down a bank.'

'Oh, no...' Alice whispered, her hand at her throat, while Minnie sat forward in her chair, her wrinkled hands gripping the knitting. 'Is she – Ted, don't tell me she's–'

'She's in hospital,' he said quickly. 'She was hurt, but they don't know how bad it was, not yet. A broken leg – ribs too – and maybe summat inside but it's too soon to tell.' He paused, then added in a bewildered tone, as if he could scarcely believe his own words, 'It was Bryce driving, and – and it seems he was killed. Killed outright, she said.'

'Killed? Bryce? Oh, *Ted...'* Tears overflowed down Alice's cheeks and she sat down suddenly while Minnie gave a little cry of distress. 'Our little Jackie. Oh, the poor, poor maid. Hurt in a car accident and lost the man she was going to marry! And her all those thousands of miles away from her family...' She covered her face with her hands and rocked back and forth for a few moments, then took in a deep, shuddering breath and raised her head. 'We'll have to go over there, Ted. We'll have to go – as soon as it can possibly be arranged.'

Chapter Four

'But how, Mum?' Val asked when she heard the news. 'You haven't even got passports. And there's the tickets for the ship – they're dreadfully expensive and you might have to wait for a passage. It could take weeks and Jackie will probably be better by then. I don't see—'

'And I don't see how you can raise objections at all,' Alice snapped. She had run down to Jed's Cottage, as it was still called, as soon as breakfast was over, her head in a whirl. 'I'd have thought you'd have a bit more sympathy for your sister, Val. Obviously, we can't be there in five minutes but the maid will want her mother just the same. She's lost her sweetheart as well as broken her leg, in case you've forgotten already. And we don't even know how much worse it could be. Unconscious, Elaine said she was when she phoned us. How will the poor dear feel when she comes to, all alone and away from her family? As for the cost, that don't matter – your father and me have always put a bit by for a rainy day. And your Uncle Joe'll help with getting the tickets and everything. He knows what to do.'

Val helped Christopher spoon porridge into his mouth. 'I'm sorry, Mum. I didn't mean to be awkward. It's just come as a shock – and you running in like that, all of a dither, you frightened me. I thought it was something serious.'

'It *is* something serious!'

'I mean, with Granny or Dad, or maybe one of the children.' She sighed. 'Please, Mum, don't take everything I say the wrong way. I know you're upset – I am too. It's awful to think of Jackie hurt and unhappy. But she does have family in America – our cousins and Uncle Joe when he's there – and they'll look after her until you can get there, and you know Luke and me'll do all we can to help. Now look, there's tea in the pot – pour yourself a cup while Chris finishes his breakfast, and tell me all you know.'

'I'm having porridge,' Christopher said importantly. He waved his spoon and a small blob of porridge flew off and landed on the table.

Alice nodded distractedly. 'I know, lovey, and look what you're doing with it. There's not that much more to tell,' she went on, calming down and doing as Val said. 'They were off somewhere together on holiday, apparently – and *that's* something your father and I would never have allowed, her going away with a man on her own, even if they were engaged – and there was some sort of accident. That's all we know. Joe's girl Elaine it was who rang us up, and she didn't know no more herself. She and her hubby Earl – outlandish sort of name – were going straight off to wherever Jackie is, and I can't even tell you that. It could be hundreds of miles away. They were talking about going to California for this holiday, right over on the other side of America.' Alice stared into her cup and a tear splashed into the tea. 'Val, I feel so *helpless*. My youngest, not even twenty yet, in hospital with a broken leg over on the other side of the world, and I can't even put my finger on the map to see where she is. She could be on the moon, for all the difference it makes. And you're right, it'll be weeks before we can get there. I don't even know how to *start* making such a journey.'

'Well, Uncle Joe will help with all that,' Val said reassuringly. 'Thank goodness he and Dottie are still here and not gone off on their honeymoon. And the wedding's still over two weeks–'

'The wedding!' Alice cried. 'My stars above, I hadn't even *thought* about the wedding! How can we go before that? And they're planning a week in Perranporth too. I was depending on them being in Burracombe when we go. Tom and Joanna can't be left to manage on their own with me and your father away.'

'They won't be on their own. We'll all rally round. Norman won't mind putting a few more hours in with the milking, and I can do a bit too. I'll go up every day to give Jo a hand with the meals and the hens and everything. You don't have to worry about all that, Mum.'

'It's not knowing that's the worst,' Alice said fretfully. 'I don't know how long it will take to get passports and book our passage and even when we get to New York we've got to go to Corning, and she might not even be back there. She might still be wherever she is now, in some hospital in the middle of nowhere. And what are their hospitals like anyway? Will they have all the proper equipment and all that? Some of these films our Tom goes to see at the pictures–'

'They're Westerns, Mum,' Val said with a grin. 'They're set a hundred years ago as it is. It's America, not darkest Africa. They're probably more up to date than we are.'

Alice looked at her doubtfully. 'Do you really think so?'

'I know they are. And if you're looking at films to prove it, think of that one you and Dad went to see backalong – *Rear Window*. The man in that had a broken leg and he was going to be all right. Jackie will be too.'

'She still needs her mother with her,' Alice said.

'Of course she does! And you'll be there, just as

soon as you can be, and with nothing to worry about here.' Val spooned the last bit of porridge into Christopher's mouth and wiped his face with a damp flannel. 'You just tell us what to do and we'll do it. Is there anything you need today? Shall I come back home with you?'

Alice shook her head and got up. 'We haven't even begun to think about it all yet. I were that flummoxed, I left the men eating their breakfasts and just ran down to tell you straight away. I'd better go back now and see what they've decided.' She bent to tickle her grandson under his chin. 'I'm sorry, my little dear, Granny's had hardly a word to say to you this morning, and you eating your porridge up so good, too. You come up and see me later on and we might have some more news. Elaine said she'd ring us up again when she'd been to the hospital. Where's Luke today? Out painting?'

'No, he's gone to London. He'll be there all week.' Val lifted her son from his high chair and set him on the floor. 'There you are, Chris. Go and play with your bricks.'

'Build a castle,' he said and marched over to the cardboard box of toys that was kept behind Luke's armchair. 'Build Granny a castle to live in.'

'That's right. The dear of him...' But Val could see that her mother's mind was far away, somewhere in America with her other daughter. Her voice trembled. 'Oh, *Val*... She's my *baby*.'

'I know, Mum, I know.' Val put her arms round the shaking body. 'There, there. Don't cry. Everything will be all right.'

'She's so far away,' Alice wept. 'We can't even

speak to her.'

'I'm sure you could,' Val said. 'Hospitals do have telephones, you know.'

'But we don't know the number, and it's so complicated, making calls to other countries...' She shook her head fretfully, then burst out, 'We never wanted her to go, you know, me and your father. We knew all along something would happen. We should have put our feet down hard when she first started to talk about it – it's all our fault for letting her have so much rein.'

'You couldn't do anything about it. She threatened to leave home anyway and if she'd done that, she wouldn't even have had Uncle Joe and his family to keep an eye on her.'

'I mean, when she was little. Always self-willed she was, and we let her get away with too much. If we had been firmer, then–'

'Well, it's no use thinking of all that now,' Val said. 'Anyway, I think you're wrong. Jackie was always Jackie and she wasn't going to be any different whatever you did. In fact, I think she'd have been worse. As it is, you've brought her up to be sensible and most girls of her age can manage quite well on their own. We had to during the war, after all.'

'Yes, you did, and you're not telling me it didn't lead to trouble then, either,' Alice said tersely, and Val bit her lip, wishing for the hundredth time that she had never confessed to her mother that she had given birth to a baby while on her way back from Egypt. Poor little Johnny had been born too early and had never lived, and only Hilary Napier and a few other VAD nurses had known about it – even Luke, the baby's father, had not known, for he and Val had parted by then and not met again until he came to Burracombe by chance a few years ago. Some secrets are better never told, she thought, and some are definitely better never told to your mother!

'Well, I'm sure Jackie's been sensible,' she said peaceably. 'And she's the one we've got to think about now. She's lost her fiancé as well as broken her leg and the sooner you can be with her the better.'

Alice nodded and turned to go. 'I'll go and tell Dottie what's happened. She'll need to know why Joe don't go down to the cottage this morning, though I dare say he'll want to go as soon as he can, with her still not properly back on her feet. Oh, why does everything have to happen at once?'

She hurried away along the village street, worry in every line of her body. Val watched her for a moment, then sighed and went back indoors where Christopher was carefully setting coloured wooden bricks on top of each other. Reassuring as she had tried to be, she was daunted herself by the enormity of the journey facing her parents. Neither had ever been abroad before and although Joe would be able to help he would not be going with them. He had his wedding and new life with Dottie to think of, and although Dottie was recovering well from her stroke she wouldn't be fit to travel for quite a while.

Val was suddenly swept with loneliness. I'm upset too, she thought, starting the washing-up. Jackie's my sister, my baby sister, and she's hurt and unhappy thousands of miles away and there's nothing I can do to help her. And nobody will give a thought to how I feel about it. I'm the one who's always expected to be strong.

She stood still, her hands plunged into the hot soapy water, and a tear trickled down the side of her nose. I want Luke, she thought. I want my husband here with me, to put his arms around me and tell me it'll be all right, like I told Mum. I know I said I'd be happy with him spending one week a month at the gallery in London, and I suppose most of the time I am – but when something goes wrong I need him here with me, to turn to. Isn't that what marriage is supposed to be about?

'So Joe won't be down till later on,' Alice finished. 'He asked me to drop in and tell you what's happened. But you can come back up to the farm with me now, if you'd rather.'

'Only if I can do something to help,' Dottie said. 'You don't want another body up there, getting under your feet.' She hesitated and bent to stroke Alfred, who was as usual a slumbering mound of black fur on her armchair. 'I need to have a private word with him anyway. I'll stop here, and see him when I see him. I've got a few jobs I can be getting on with.'

Alice looked at her curiously. 'Is everything all right, Dottie? You're not feeling poorly, are you? Because if you are, I'll send Joe down straight away.'

'Of course I'm not poorly. You know what Dr Latimer said – I'm getting over that silly bit of a stroke as if it never happened. You don't have to worry about me, Alice.'

59

'I'm glad to hear it. Only you seem a bit – well, as if you've got something on your mind.' Alice waited a moment, but Dottie said nothing. 'So if you're sure there's nothing you need, I'll be getting back.'

'That's right. You've got a lot to think about, you and Ted. But you know if there's anything I can do while you're away – or before you go – you've only got to say. That's what friends are for, and we've always been friends.'

'More than friends soon,' Alice said. 'We'll be as good as sisters in less than three weeks.'

Dottie lifted her head at last and Alice stared at her in dismay. 'Dottie! Whatever is it? You look as pale as a ghost. You *are* feeling poorly! Now, you just push that dratted cat off the chair and sit down. Do you want me to go for the doctor?'

Dottie shook her head but did as she was told, shoving the protesting Alfred off the chair and taking his place. She bit her lip but Alice could see the tears in her eyes and she pulled one of the kitchen chairs over and seated herself beside Dottie so that she could put her arm around the shaking shoulders. 'I could see something was wrong the minute I came in, only I was too taken up with my own news. What is it, Dottie? You and Joe have surely never fallen out?'

'Not yet,' Dottie sniffed, feeling up her sleeve for her hanky. 'But I reckon we're just about to.'

'I don't understand. What's happened? He's never said a word to us about anything being wrong.'

'He don't know yet. Oh, Alice, I'm sorry, I never meant to let it out, especially when you're so upset over Jackie. Don't take no notice. You've got too much to worry about – you go back to the farm and let me and Joe sort out our own problems.'

'Well, I will, if that's what you want,' Alice said doubtfully. 'But if you ask me, it's a family problem too, and I don't like to leave you like this. Why don't you tell me anyway, now you've started? I won't interfere, if you don't want me to.'

Dottie said nothing for a minute or two, then she looked up at Alice and gave her a wavering smile. 'You'll tell me I'm being foolish, I know. But – well, Alice, it just came over me yesterday afternoon, right in the middle of the village street. I was on my way to get some Cokers and was looking around me, thinking about Burracombe and all the things that go on here, and about all the spring flowers – snowdrops and primroses and violets and such – and the hawthorn blossom in May – and the heather and gorse on the moors – and how me and Joe are going to be away half the year, *every* year, and miss so much... And, well, I just felt I couldn't do it. I can't face leaving it all behind, knowing that some of it I'll never see again because we'll always be away that time of year. And it's the people, too – the old folk maybe passing on, that I'll never see again, and the babies that'll be born and be months old before I see their dear little faces. I just can't do it, Alice, and I can't ask Joe to give up his own home, neither. We've left it too late. And somehow, I got to tell him.'

Alice stared at her in dismay. 'You're not going to call off the wedding?'

'What else can I do? I love Joe and I know he loves me, but it's just not going to work out. I don't see any other way round it.'

'Dottie, you can't do that! Give up the man you love all for the sake of a few spring flowers? It don't make sense. It would break Joe's heart.'

'It's not just flowers – it's *everything*. Everything that means home to me.'

'*Joe* should be what means home to you,' Alice said firmly. 'It's not as if you're leaving the village for ever. A few months each year, that's all. And if you'd gone with him all that time ago, when you were young and starting out in life, you'd have been away for years. You'd only ever have come back for a visit, like Joe has himself. Think of it in that way – you've had years more of Burracombe and now you've got Joe again. You're a lucky, lucky woman, Dottie Friend!'

Her tone as she ended was quite severe and Dottie looked at her in surprise. 'I suppose you're right, looking at it like that. All the same...' She shook her head again. 'Oh, Alice, I dunno what to think. I'm all in a muddle.'

'You need to talk to Joe. I know what *he'll* think.' Alice stood up. 'Are you going to be all right here on your own for a bit? Only I must go back to the farm and see what Ted's decided.'

'You go. I'm all right.' Dottie stood up too and put her hand on Alice's arm. 'You're a good friend, Alice, putting aside your own troubles to listen to my silliness. You just remember, now, anything you want me to do, you let me know right away. And you won't say anything to Joe about this, will you?'

'Of course I won't.' Alice kissed her cheek. 'You talk to him yourself. You'll find a way round it together. Just don't forget I'm looking forward to having you for a sister. I've never had one before and I'm not likely to get another!'

Chapter Five

'Passports are the first thing,' Joe said. 'You can apply for them through the Post Office and you need to have your photographs taken. You don't need one of your own, Alice, you can go on Ted's. We'd better get started on that straight away.'

'Will Jessie have the forms in?' Alice asked anxiously. 'It might be better to go into Tavi and get them there. We'll have to go to the studio for our photos anyway. And how are we going to arrange the fares for the ship?'

'I'll see to it,' Joe reassured her. 'And look, if you want Dottie and me to come with you, I'm sure she wouldn't mind. We meant to stay here for the winter but we could easily change our plans. I reckon she'd be all right on the journey now, especially if you were there too.' He looked at his brother. 'On the other hand, you might want me to stay here – Tom'll be glad of some help around the place.'

Alice thought of Dottie and her sudden panic. She shook her head. 'We'll think about that later. The main thing is to get Ted and me over there with our Jackie as soon as we can do it. But if you really don't mind helping us make the arrangements, Joe...'

'Sure I will. You've got enough to do here, organising the farm and family.'

'Speaking of which,' Ted said, getting up from the table, 'I ought to be leaving now. Tom's gone with Norman up to Top Field to look at the sheep and I've got to see to those steers. It would happen now, right at a busy time.'

'It's always a busy time, from what I remember,' Joe said wryly. 'But I'll give you a hand when I've made a start on this. And I need to go down and see Dottie, as well.'

Once again, Alice thought of Dottie's doubts. I wish I could warn him, she thought. But she'd promised to say nothing, and it was Dottie's business after all. She and Joe must sort it out for themselves.

She sighed. She'd got up that morning, same as usual, still thinking about Hilary's wedding a few days ago, and within a couple of hours the world seemed to have turned upside down. It's to be hoped nothing else goes wrong, she thought, though it always seemed that if one problem came through the door half a dozen others followed. And it wasn't hard to see what they would be this time.

Suppose Dottie really did decide she couldn't marry Joe? What would that do to him? How could he stay on in Burracombe, even to help Tom on the farm while they were away, knowing he could bump into her at any moment? It wouldn't be fair on either of them. I wish he'd never proposed in the first place, she thought wretchedly. They were all right as they were, just staying friends. Oh, why did everything have to be so *complicated?*

But it was Jackie who mattered most now. Jackie, lying in some hospital bed thousands of miles away, hurt and bereaved and with nobody of her own beside her. The rest could sort themselves out. All Alice wanted was to be with her youngest child, her baby, looking after her the way she always had and maybe even bringing her home again.

That's what we'll do, she thought. We'll bring her home again, Ted and me, home where she belongs.

Ivy Sweet had been helping George set out the day's baking in the shop window when Alice hurried past. She watched for a moment, then turned to her husband.

'Did you see that? A face on her like she's lost a pound and found sixpence, and never even gave us a glance. I wonder what's the matter?'

'Looked like she'd been to see Dottie Friend,' George said. 'I hope there's nothing wrong there. 'Twould be a shame if Dottie took a turn for the worse, with her own wedding just round the corner.'

Ivy shook her head. 'Someone would have gone for the doctor. Alice was on her way home. You don't suppose it's Joe, do you? Had an accident on the farm? But then you'd think Dottie would be going up there too.' She stood for a moment biting the side of her thumb. 'I'd go and offer to help if I didn't think Alice Tozer would snap my head off.'

George laid his hand on her arm. 'Best wait awhile, Ive. You don't know that there is anything wrong, really – Alice just might not be feeling too

65

well, touch of biliousness or something. She might even have been to the doctor herself.'

'I suppose so. Anyway, if I go up there, they'll only think I'm being nosy. Anyone else, it'd be neighbourly, but Alice Tozer wouldn't give me the credit.' She set out a batch of cottage loaves. 'I dunno, George. I do try to be a good neighbour, but it always goes wrong. I'm better off keeping meself to meself, same as I've always done.'

George smiled. 'Come on, Ive. You haven't even passed a word with Alice, so how can you say it's gone wrong? All I'm saying is, just wait a bit and see if there's any help needed before you offer it. Anyway, aren't you working at the Bell this dinner time? If there's anything amiss, no doubt you'll hear it there. Norman Tozer usually goes in for a pint and he'll know, if anyone does.' He looked out along the village street. 'Customer coming, Ive. Will you see to her while I go back to the bakery? Those saffron buns should be ready to come out of the oven now.'

The customer was Jennifer Kellaway, carrying a basket. Ivy went behind the counter and wished her good morning, then waited enquiringly.

'Hello, Ivy. Could I have one of your nice cottage loaves, please? I'm having my dinner with Jacob and he likes the top as a roll to go with his stew.'

Ivy took one of the cottage loaves from the window. 'There you are. Still warm from the oven.' She hesitated. 'I don't suppose you saw Alice Tozer on your way here, did you?'

Jennifer shook her head. 'Haven't seen anyone this morning, only Jacob. Oh, and Dottie, but that was earlier, when I was taking the casserole to his

66

cottage. Why, did you want her for something?'

'No, no – only she went past here a few minutes ago looking as if the sky'd fallen in. I wondered if there was anything wrong. Did Dottie say anything?'

'No, but we were talking about other things.' Jennifer coloured faintly. 'Anyway, she might not have seen Alice then. It was quite a bit earlier.' She put the loaf into her basket and gave Ivy the money. 'I'd better go now. Jacob likes his dinner at twelve and I've left Molly and Tavy in the churchyard with him. Thanks, Ivy.'

She turned and went out of the shop, wondering why Ivy was so concerned about Alice. As far as Jennifer knew, the two had always been at daggers drawn. Probably just nosiness, she thought, and then turned her mind to the question Ivy herself had asked. Was there something really amiss at the Tozers' farm? Had old Minnie been taken ill, or Joanna and Tom's daughter, baby Heather? Perhaps I'll call in on my way home after dinner, she thought, and see if there's anything I can do.

The question was, as George had foreseen, answered in the Bell Inn at dinner time. Ivy was behind the bar pulling a pint of ale for Jack Pettifer when Ted's cousin Norman came in, his face alight with news. Ivy gave him a quick look, then pretended not to be interested.

'You look as if you've got summat on your mind, Norm,' Jack said, lifting his glass to his lips and sucking off the froth. 'What be going on? I hope there's no trouble up at the farm.'

'Well, there is and there isn't,' Norman said.

'Usual, please, Ivy.' He waited, while she drew back the pump handle 'Thanks.' He fished in his pocket for coins, enjoying his moment of mystery, then sucked off the foam as Jack had done. 'It's trouble all right, but not at the farm itself.'

The others watched impatiently. 'Well, come on – out with it,' Jack said at last. 'We only get an hour for dinner, and my Nancy'll have mine on the table in fifteen minutes. I don't have time for one of your long stories.'

'And I've only come in for a half of bitter,' Jacob Prout added. 'My Jennifer's brought me some dinner and she'll be getting it out of the oven any minute.'

'It's their Jackie,' Norman said, realising he had stretched it out as far as he could. 'Been in an accident, she has, somewhere over there in America. Broken leg, maybe even worse, by all accounts, and her chap that she was supposed to be engaged to, killed.'

The others stared at him. 'Killed?' Bernie Nethercott echoed, pausing in the act of drawing a pint for Alf Coker. 'And young Jackie badly hurt? Why, that's terrible.'

Norman nodded. 'Alice is in a rare old taking about it, I can tell you. Talking about going over there, soon as it can be arranged, and she's not even got a passport yet.'

'Alice Tozer?' Ivy said. 'Going to America, all on her own? But she's never been further than the Isle of Wight.'

'Not on her own, no. Ted'll go too, stands to reason. And Joe's talking about going as well, him and Dottie, instead of stopping in Burracombe for the winter like they'd meant. Only he's not too sure because he might be more use here, giving Tom and me a hand, with Ted being away.' Norman shook his head. 'They're all of a doodah up there, I can tell you. He hadn't even been down to see Dottie Friend when I come away for me lunch, so I dunno what she thinks about it.'

'And no more should you,' Rose Nethercott said sharply, coming in with a tray of hot pasties for the men who didn't go home for their dinner. 'That's their business and 'tis for them to sort out between them and then tell the rest of us, if they want us to know.'

Norman gave her an indignant look. 'There's no need to be so quick off the mark, Rose. I was only answering a question.'

'Yes, and adding a bit of your own to the answer. That's how gossip starts and gossip can hurt a lot of feelings when 'tis something serious like this.'

'You're right there,' Jacob said bitterly. 'I remember when my Jennifer and Travis were getting engaged and some busybody spotted them in Tavi and had 'em setting the date for the wedding before they got home that afternoon. And then when they was expecting little Molly half the village knew before–'

'I don't think Norman meant to gossip,' Bernie intervened peaceably. 'We're just concerned for the poor maid, that's all, and the more we know the more we can offer to help, if help's needed.'

Norman nodded righteously. 'And it seems to me they *will* need it, what with Ted leaving the farm for Tom to manage on his own, and Joanna with two little ones and old Minnie to look after.

Not that me and my Annie won't do all we can, being family and everything.'

'Well, there's nothing anyone can do until we know what's what,' Jack said, finishing his pint quickly. 'I'd better be getting home. I dare say Nancy'll be wanting to go up to the farm to offer whatever help they need as soon as she hears about it. Reckon the whole village'll be beating a path to the Tozers' door when the news gets about.'

'I don't doubt it,' Rose said, taking his empty tankard. 'It might be as well to wait till tomorrow, all the same. Like Norman said, they got a lot to think about and they won't want a crowd pushing through the door before they've had time to take it in theirselves. You tell 'em we're all here ready to give a hand if they want it, Norman, that's the best way.'

'I will,' he said, mollified. 'Thanks, Rose. I'd better be going now anyway. It's cottage pie today and I like it hot straight from the oven.'

The men drifted away, some carrying tankards and pasties to the benches outside. Left alone, the Nethercotts and Ivy looked at each other.

'That's a bit of bad news,' Ivy said, putting the corner of her tea towel to her eye. 'Poor little maid. I thought when I saw Alice Tozer scurrying past the shop this morning with her head down there was something wrong. I'd have gone out to ask, only I knew she'd take it the wrong way and say I was being nosy.'

Rose sighed. 'You were probably right, Ivy, though I can't see why you have to speak as if it's a grievance, since it never even happened. Anyway, the important thing is that the Tozers have got trouble and it behoves the rest of us to do what Burracombe folk always do, and rally round. I just think it's best to hold back a bit first, that's all. Let 'em get used to it and sort out what to do and sleep on it, and then it'll be time for the rest of us to come forward. They know we're here and ready to do whatever's asked.'

'Don't suppose they'll ask me, all the same,' Ivy muttered under her breath. She finished washing glasses and dried her hands. 'If that's all for this afternoon, I'll be on me way. George has asked me to go and get a few things in Tavi this afternoon and I want to catch the half past two bus.' She pulled her coat around her shoulders. 'I'll see you this evening.'

'All right, Ivy.' Bernie watched her go and shook his head. 'She'll never change. And that's summat we got to talk about, Rose. Do we keep her on permanent or not? It was only meant to be while Dottie was poorly but things have changed since then and it's obvious Dottie's not going to come back to work here, even when she is better. Joe Tozer won't want his wife behind the bar, specially when they've only got a few months at a time in the village.'

'I've been thinking the same. Ivy's a good barmaid and knows the work, but she do have a sharp tongue and it puts folk off. Dottie was always so bright and cheery, she was a proper asset. But Ivy's face is enough to turn milk sour sometimes.'

'She seemed to get along all right in Horrabridge,' Bernie pointed out. 'And you don't need to look at me like that, Rose! You know what I mean. But when I saw Lenny at the Victuallers meeting a week or so back he said she always got on fine with the customers, never gave them the rough edge of her tongue there.'

'Maybe it's because she hadn't grown up and lived side by side with them,' Rose said thoughtfully. 'People here don't always give her a chance. She's right, you know – they take her up on her words even when she don't mean to be nasty. And I got to admit she do seem to be trying her best. She never said a word out of place just now about the Tozers, and she seemed really upset about poor young Jackie.' She paused. 'I did wonder if something happened, back in the summer. You know there was that chap hanging around asking about her, and I'm sure as anything I spotted him at the Summer Fair. And then there was that holiday she and George took young Barry on just after, to London. There was something going on, I'm sure of it.'

'Well, whatever it was, she's not going to tell us, and we don't want any talk starting.' Bernie wiped a damp cloth down the bar. 'All we got to decide is whether to offer her the job permanent. We don't even know if she wants it, but we ought to sort it out because if she don't, we need to look for someone else.'

Rose picked up a glass and polished it, her brow furrowed. 'It's whether we can work with her, day in, day out, too, Bernie. That's what it comes down to. What do you think?'

He stood for a moment chewing his lip. Then he said, 'If you're of the same mind, Rose, I reckon we ought to give her a chance. She's been here a few weeks now and never given real cause to complain. Like you say, it's six of one and half a dozen of the other and as long as she don't drive customers away I don't see why she shouldn't stay.'

'That's how I feel,' Rose said. 'But there's another thing. I'm not sure she wants to work all the hours we need. She's helping George in the shop a lot more now, and she got young Barry to think of. Why don't we look for someone else, part-time, someone more like Dottie, perhaps, or a younger woman who wants a bit of pin money? She and Ivy could work turn and turn about and if Ivy don't suit, or takes umbrage at something and walks out, we wouldn't be left in the lurch.'

'That's a good idea.' Bernie went to lock the door. 'There's bound to be plenty hereabouts who'd like some extra money. All we got to do is put up a notice and they'll come flocking!'

Chapter Six

The news of Jackie Tozer's accident, once released in the Bell, spread like wildfire round the village. Jacob told Jennifer over the casserole she had brought and her face creased with dismay and tears came to her eyes.

'Jacob, that's awful! Poor Jackie. I can't think of anything worse, and to happen when she was so far from home too. Will Alice and Ted be able to go over, d'you think?'

'Norman reckons so, but they ain't even got

passports and I don't know how long it takes to get one. They're going to Tavistock this afternoon to get the forms, and maybe even to Plymouth to see about the travel arrangements. I can't see them getting over there sooner than two or three weeks, though, with the best will in the world.'

'Neither can I. Alice must be frantic. I'll call in on the way back and see if there's anything I can do to help. Oh no – if they're going to Plymouth, they won't be there, will they? But Joanna will, and Minnie. They might know if there's anything I can do.' She spooned mashed-up casserole into Molly's open mouth.

'I reckon all any of us can do is take the burden off them a bit,' he said, chewing on a piece of beef. 'Help out with a few of the jobs around the farm. And young Joanna might be glad of a hand with the little ones.'

'That's a good idea. I could have Heather over to play with Molly, or, go and fetch Robin from school. I'll offer anyway, and see if there's anything else I can do.' She bit her lip, tears coming again. 'Oh, Jacob, I can't bear to think of Jackie all alone and in such trouble. We got on so well when she lived with me in Plymouth while she was working at the hotel. We were almost like sisters. And she was my bridesmaid. I wish I could go and see her too.'

Jacob stared at her. 'You're never thinking of going all the way to America! Whatever would Travis say, and what about little Molly here?'

'No, of course I'm not. I just wish I could.' She persuaded Molly to swallow some cabbage, then took another mouthful herself and laid down her knife and fork. 'I can't eat any more. Have you finished, Jacob, or do you want another helping? There's apple pie for afters, and I brought some of my own clotted cream.'

'Proper job,' he said, pushing over his plate. 'And you have some too. Don't do no good starving ourselves just because of some bad news. That's when we needs our health and strength most. And while I think of it, there's someone else who might need a bit of company while you're down in the village, and that's Dottie. Norman was saying Joe hadn't managed to get down to see her this morning and if he's going into Plymouth with Ted and Alice this afternoon, she's not going to see much of him at all today. You might do more good slipping in to see her than going to the farm.'

'Yes, I might. Does she even know? I bumped into her on my way here and she never said a word then.'

Jacob nodded. 'Alice ran down to tell her. Must have been after you saw her. But I don't suppose she stopped long, and if Joe gets there at all this afternoon, it'll be only for a few minutes, to see she's all right. You drop in straight after you leave her, maid, and don't worry about the clearing up, neither. I'll do that later on.'

'There's some casserole left, and plenty of pie. I was going to leave it for you, but—'

'Take that as well. I know she's doing a bit of cooking now, but it won't do her no harm to have summat brought in for her. She's done it often enough for others.'

'The man in the travel office was really good,'

Alice said later that evening as the family sat round the supper table. 'Helped us fill in the passport application – I don't need one of my own, I can go on Ted's – and said he'd make sure it got done quick because of special circumstances. He reckoned we could have it back in a fortnight so he booked us tickets on a ship going from Southampton on October the thirteenth.'

'So you'll be here for Joe and Dottie's wedding,' Val said. She turned to smile at Dottie, who had come for supper, despite having not only Jennifer's casserole in her larder but also the Cokers she had bought that morning as well. Joe, who had managed to get in to see her at last after returning from Plymouth, had persuaded her that she must be there, as part of the family, and she hadn't had the heart to refuse even though she felt like an intruder. She wasn't proper family, nor ever would be now, Dottie thought, returning Val's smile rather wanly. 'And you won't have to bring the day forward like Uncle Joe wanted,' Val went on. 'I don't blame you, either – I wouldn't have wanted to rush my wedding day!'

'I don't know why not,' Joe said, putting his arm round Dottie's waist and giving her a squeeze. 'I'd marry Dottie tomorrow, if she'd only just say the word.'

'Leave the poor soul alone,' Minnie reprimanded him. 'You're just frightened she'll have second thoughts, that's your trouble. And I'm sure we would all understand if she did!' Her eyes twinkled at Dottie. 'Though I hope you don't – I had you earmarked as my daughter-in-law over thirty-five years ago, and I reckon I've waited long enough now for the wedding.'

Dottie felt her colour rise. She stared at her plate, then looked at Joe. I ought to tell him straight out, she thought miserably, and not let them all go on like this. But how can I, in front of everyone? It's got to be private. And it's got to be tonight.

'Joe,' she said a little desperately, so that only he could hear, 'can we go back to my cottage as soon as supper's done? There's something I need to talk to you about. Something important.'

'Why, sure, honey, if that's what you want.' He lifted his voice above the chatter about Ted's and Alice's plans for their journey. 'Dottie's feeling a bit tired, so you folks won't mind if we cut along now, will you? Guess we'll have a cup of tea there before I come back.'

'You go on, my pretty,' Alice said to Dottie. 'It's been a long day for all of us and no wonder you're looking so worn out, waiting for news all day. I'm feeling a bit done in myself, to tell the truth, but I'll be down in the morning to see you and tell you if there's any more news. Elaine said she'd telephone again but with the time difference I can't sort out whether it's teatime or the middle of the night!'

Joe helped Dottie on with her coat and they left amidst a chorus of goodbyes. The dusk had gathered almost to full darkness now and the stars were prickling the sky. They walked down the track in silence, and it was not until they were in Dottie's cottage that he said, 'What's on your mind, Dottie? I know there's something, so you'd better tell me. Whatever it is, I'm sure it's nothing we can't sort out together.'

Dottie stopped and looked up at him. She saw the grey, crinkled hair that had once been a rich chestnut, the strong, square face that had once been smooth and young, now corrugated with the years that had passed, and her heart seemed to turn over. For a moment, she hated herself for what she was about to do. The words trembled on her lips and she knew that once spoken they could not be taken back; yet they had to be said.

'Oh, Joe,' she said at last, in a voice filled with misery. 'I don't know what you're going to say to me. I won't blame you if you never want to speak to me again. I won't blame Ted or Alice or anyone in your family if they never wants to lay eyes on me after this. But – Joe, I can't marry you.' The words fell like cold stones into the soft ripples of a stream. 'It's not that I don't love you, I always have done, but it's like I said before – we're too old. *I'm* too old. Too old to uproot myself and live two lives in two different places – two different worlds. I can't do it, Joe. I can't leave Burracombe. I'll never be truly happy and I'll never be myself again, and I'm sorry. I'm so, *so* sorry...'

'It's bad news about young Jackie Tozer,' Gilbert Napier said, receiving a sherry from Basil Harvey. He had been invited to the vicarage for dinner and had been glad to accept. With Hilary and David away on honeymoon, the Barton seemed an empty, lonely house. 'She used to be our parlourmaid, you remember. Bright little thing. Hilary told her time and again that she could do better for herself, encouraged her to get that job at the

Duke of Cornwall Hotel, but I don't think Alice and Ted were best pleased about it at the time.'

'I don't think they were,' Basil agreed. 'They wanted her to stay in Burracombe, close at hand. But young women are different these days, Gilbert. They're not content to settle down to marriage in their early twenties and spend the rest of their lives raising a family as girls of our generation were. It's the war, I suppose – women came out of the kitchen and did all manner of jobs once reserved for men, and it unsettled them.'

'The older women didn't seem to mind, though,' Gilbert pointed out. 'They seemed happy enough to go back where they belonged. It's the younger ones, and their daughters, who have got itchy feet. Look at mine – never seemed to settle after it was all over. First she wanted to be an air stewardess, then she insisted on taking over the estate – I thought she'd never marry. Thank goodness she's found a good man now and they'll be staying in Burracombe, so the next generation will grow up here. And maybe once Stephen's recovered properly from losing his arm, he and young Madeleine will come back to their roots. It could all work out well in the end. But that's not what I wanted to talk to you about, Basil.'

Constance Bellamy arrived then, shuffling off her decrepit old coat and handing it to Grace Harvey along with an untidy bunch of chrysanthemums and a bag of apples from her garden. She too accepted a glass of sherry and sat down on the sofa, looking like a weathered little garden gnome beside the squire's bulk.

'I'd have brought you some apples too, Gilbert,'

79

she remarked in her unexpectedly gruff voice, 'but I thought you'd probably got more than enough in your own orchards. I'm overrun with the things this year. I'll have to take some along to Sam Endacott to make cider.'

'It's certainly been a good year,' Basil agreed, not mentioning that the tree in his own garden was bowed down with fruit. 'And Grace has been out in the fields picking blackberries, too, so you can probably guess what we're having for pudding.' He turned to Gilbert. 'Was there something special you wanted to discuss, then? Do you want to get it over with now, or wait until afterwards?'

'Might as well be now. There's nothing private about it and I dare say Constance will be interested too.' Gilbert put down his glass and pushed back his mane of white hair. 'It's about the church organ.'

'Ah, yes.' Basil had been fearing this. 'I really can't apologise enough. I feel very much at fault. To break down on Hilary's wedding day, of all days. You were very forbearing about it, Gilbert, and I'm very grateful, but it must have been most annoying for you. And to have Felix browbeating your guests into humming the "Wedding March"...' His rosy face grew pinker with every word and Constance broke in.

'Heavens above, Basil, you'll be in tears any minute. It wasn't that bad, and I don't think anyone could say that Felix did any browbeating. Seemed to me they all rather enjoyed it.'

Basil gave her a grateful glance but Gilbert Napier moved his hand impatiently. 'That's as maybe, and I'm glad to see you've got the Warrens' grand piano in place now, as a substitute. But it won't do for long. For one thing, the environment's not good for such an instrument – too cold, and with winter coming on it'll probably get damp as well. And for another, the church needs – and should have – its own organ. Now, how's the fund-raising getting along?'

'Well, we're not quite halfway. But we have received some quite substantial donations since the wedding – one came in this morning. People have been very kind.'

'Not quite halfway. And you've been raising money for how long?'

'Something over two years,' Basil said apologetically.

'Well, good God, man!' Gilbert recollected that he was talking to a vicar and masked his words with a cough. 'I mean, for goodness' sake – it'll take another two or three years before we can afford the repairs needed. A complete overhaul, I think you said?'

'I'm afraid so. It should have been carried out before the war but of course nothing could be done for the duration, and it's taken the country much longer than anyone expected to get back on its feet since the war ended.'

'Feeding starving Europe,' Constance muttered.

'And then we had to do those repairs to the north wall, which were really quite urgent, and it just got left. But now that we've got the bit between our teeth – and since it really is, as you say, imperative that we do it as quickly as possible, I'm sure we–'

'Stop waffling, Basil,' Gilbert ordered. 'Listen

81

to me. You've got almost half the money. I'd like to make it up to the full amount.'

The vicar's face turned crimson. He stared at the colonel, his mouth open and his eyes filling now with real tears. He tried to speak but could emit no more than a faint squeak. He looked at Miss Bellamy for help but she merely twinkled at him.

'I – I can't believe what you're saying,' he managed at last. 'It's going to cost hundreds of pounds. Don't you want to see the estimate first? It's in my desk.' He scrambled to his feet, but Gilbert lifted his hand again and he paused, half out of his chair, his eyes blinking.

'I know what the estimate is. You told me weeks ago. I only wish I'd taken you up on it at the time. If anyone's at fault, Basil, I think I am.'

'Of course not! How could you be? Please – you mustn't make any promises until we've fully discussed – let me go and fetch–'

'Basil, sit *down!*' the squire snapped, and Basil dropped back to his seat, looking more than ever like a terrified white rabbit. 'If I say I'm at fault, then so I am.' He turned and glowered at the old lady by his side, who was pressing her lips firmly together and shaking gently. 'I hope you're not laughing at me, Constance.'

'Perish the thought, Gilbert.' She met his gaze and let her smile break out, turning her brown face into a thousand tiny wrinkles. 'Oh, come on, you silly man – stop being so pompous. You're frightening poor Basil out of his wits.'

'Don't talk such nonsense!' he snapped. 'And nobody but you would dare call me a silly man.' But his manner was softer as he turned back to the

82

vicar. 'Sorry. Didn't mean to snap. It's just that – well, I've been thinking for some time about a memorial of some kind for my son, Baden, you know. I put in that stained-glass window for my wife, and I was considering something similar, but it seems to me that an organ would be more use. What do you think?' His last words were uttered almost humbly and Basil recovered himself.

'I think it would be a wonderful memorial, and most fitting. Baden used to play the old organ occasionally, didn't he? He was a musical boy as well as a fine soldier.'

'Yes.' It was Gilbert now who seemed hesitant. 'Got that from his mother, of course. I should have done it years ago, but as you say – the war got in the way, went on for a long time after he was lost at Dunkirk, and somehow since then there always seemed too much else to be done. And I could never quite make up my mind what was most fitting. But now I've decided, and I'd like to see it accomplished as soon possible. Get a firm quotation and let me know how much money you've got already, and I'll make up the shortfall. No further argument.' He fixed Basil with such a stern, gimlet stare that the vicar quailed again. 'Understood?'

'Understood,' Basil said in a quivering voice. Then he stood up and came over to the sofa, his hand held out for the colonel to shake. 'I can't thank you enough. I'm more grateful than I can say, and I know all my parishioners will feel the same. It's immensely kind of you.'

The door opened and Grace Harvey looked in.

'I thought I heard loud voices. Is everything all right?'

Her husband turned to her, his face beaming. 'It's more than all right, my dear. Gilbert has just given me the most wonderful, marvellous news.'

Chapter Seven

'Dottie!' Joe exclaimed. 'What are you saying? What in heaven's name do you mean?'

'Just what I say, Joe.' Now that she had spoken, her misery had deepened yet there was a tiny thread of relief that at last it was out. 'I've been wanting to tell you all day, ever since I first realised, but what with the news about poor Jackie and everyone being at sixes and sevens—'

'Wait a minute,' he broke in, putting his hands on her shoulders. 'Are you telling me this only came to you today? It's not something that's been building up?'

'No. It was this morning, only with all that's happened today it feels more like weeks ago. I was walking back from the village with the Cokers – they were meant for tea today and they're in the larder, we'd better have them tomorrow – and I suddenly thought about all I'd be missing, spending half the year in America for the rest of my life.' She looked up at him and tears filled her eyes. 'I know it's wrong, Joe, putting Burracombe before you, and I really don't mean it that way, but it would be like tearing out half my heart. I think the world of you, you know that – but I wouldn't be myself any more. And if I wasn't the same, you might find you didn't think so much of me after all, and – well, it just wouldn't work, Joe, and I don't want to make you unhappy, not at this time of life.'

Joe stared at her. She could feel his big hands, warm and strong, covering her shoulders. She felt the tears overflow and roll down her cheeks and she saw the pain in his eyes and found that she couldn't look at him any more. She stared down at her feet, her eyes blurred by her tears, and wished she had never spoken.

'I'm sorry, Joe. I've hurt you all over again, and I never meant to.'

'Well, how did you think I was going to feel?' he demanded, and she flinched at his tone. He spoke again, more softly. 'I'm sorry, Dottie, I don't mean to speak roughly, but it's come as a shock. The wedding's due in less than three weeks – we've even talked about bringing it forward from then – and you spring this on me.' He took a deep breath and released her shoulders, pushing both hands through his hair. 'I feel like I did the first time you turned me down, all those years ago. Don't tell me I've got to go through all that again, Dottie. Please.'

'It's upsetting for me too, Joe,' she said. 'I don't want to hurt you, and it'll break my heart to see you go away again and know it really is all over. But–'

'Then why do it? Why break both our hearts? And when you say it'll all be over, it really will be, Dottie. Because I'll never come back to Burracombe again if you're not beside me as my wife. Seeing you here in your cottage – bustling about the village – I just couldn't.'

'But your mother – you *can't* say you'll never come back to see her.' She shook her head. 'Don't hold that over me, Joe.'

'I'm not,' he said quietly. 'At least, I don't mean to.' He turned away and stared out of the window. Dottie pulled her hanky from the sleeve of her cardigan and wiped her eyes. She was trembling.

Joe spoke again, his back still turned. 'You said you'd got Cokers for tea. You said we'd better have them tomorrow. Dottie' – he wheeled round so suddenly that she jumped – 'you haven't thought properly about this at all. How can we go on as usual, with me coming here for half my meals and you coming up to the farm for the others, if it's all broken off?' He came over and laid his hands on her shoulders again, more gently this time. 'This isn't how people of our age go on, sweetheart,' he said. 'We talk things over. We share our worries and problems. That's what Ted and Alice do. It's what I used to do with Eleanor. Isn't it what *we'd* do if we were married?'

'Well – yes, of course it is. But–'

'But we're not married,' he said quietly. 'That's what you were going to say, isn't it? Dottie, you're still thinking like a girl – like the girl who first sent me away when we were too green to know how to live. But we've both grown up since then and we know that if we've got a problem, we talk it over together and see if we can find a solution. And we may not be married now but we will be in a couple of weeks' time, and as far as I can see, that means we do the same now. Talk about it.' He paused and added. 'I've got a right to have my say, Dottie. It's my life you're playing with, as well as yours.'

'Joe, I'm not playing.'

'I know,' he said. 'You're serious. But I've still got a right to have my say. So why don't I make us both a cup of tea and we'll sit down and have a proper talk, just like grown-up married folk do. It'll be good practice for when we're husband and wife.'

She gazed at him and a reluctant smile tugged at the corners of her mouth. 'You don't give up easy, do you, Joe?'

'No, I don't,' he said a trifle grimly. 'I did once, a long time ago, but I don't aim to do it again. I don't see there's any problem here that can't be sorted out, hon. In fact, I don't see any problem here at all.'

'It's marvellous,' Basil chattered on as Grace served them all with steak and kidney pie, mashed potato, carrots and cabbage. 'I'll ring the repairers first thing in the morning. I hope they can do it quickly. Just think, we might even have it up and running again for Christmas! Wouldn't that be simply wonderful? To hear our very own organ, sounding out its beautiful notes with not a single grunt or wheeze, on Christmas morning! "Hark! The Herald Angels Sing", "O Come, All Ye Faithful" – it's going to be simply splendid.'

'Don't get too excited, Basil,' Constance warned him. 'It's nearly the end of September now. They might not even be able to start before Christmas.'

'Constance is right,' Gilbert said, 'It's more likely to be January before it's done. They have to take the whole thing apart and put it back together again, not to mention the actual repairs. It's a big job.'

'They may not even be able to start it as soon as that,' Grace pointed out. 'I don't expect we're the only church needing organ repairs. There are probably a lot of churches like ours, who have been held up by the war and then we've had all these years of getting back on our feet. Fund-raising's been almost impossible for most parishes.'

Basil looked crestfallen. 'I suppose you're right. But it's ten years since the war ended – we can surely look forward to better times now. Rationing's over, rebuilding is well under way, and living standards are rising generally. People will not only want their churches to be in good heart, but they'll also be able to afford to contribute more towards them.'

'That's a new Conservative government for you,' Gilbert commented. 'Thank goodness the country's seen sense at last. I anticipate great things from Anthony Eden. A natural successor to Churchill, in my opinion.'

Basil said nothing. He seldom discussed politics but had often told Grace that he believed Jesus would have been a Socialist. To Basil's mind, all his sermons pointed towards this, with their emphasis on the poor, meek and lowly, and his own simple life. He was aware that such sentiments would not go down well with such parishioners as Gilbert Napier, so, without being hypocritical, he kept discreetly silent in private but made sure he preached what Christ had said when he next stood in the pulpit.

'It will be good to see them continuing to develop the Welfare State,' he said. 'A national health service and an old-age pension people can live on were sorely needed. We can lead the world in such benefits.'

'I've always looked after my tenants and workers,' Gilbert said with a touch of indignation. 'And so have all the other landowners of my acquaintance.'

'I know you have. We've been extremely lucky in Burracombe to have such a benevolent squire. But it's not the case everywhere, I'm afraid, and in any case, not all landowners, or indeed other employers, are in a position to be so generous. A national, government-run scheme takes the burden from their shoulders and allows us all to contribute.' He realised that he was being drawn into the sort of discussion he preferred to avoid and so he turned to his wife. 'Is there any more cabbage, my dear?'

Grace, who knew that he disliked cabbage and only ate it because he was too polite to refuse it when they had guests, knew that he had requested it now out of desperation. Wickedly, she served him a large second helping and offered her guests more pie. Gilbert refused reluctantly, saying that Charles Latimer had advised him not to eat too much pastry, and Constance declared that she had had 'an elegant sufficiency'. They all waited while Basil struggled through his pile of greenery and Grace changed the subject by asking if they were looking forward to Dottie Friend's wedding.

'I most certainly am,' Constance declared. 'Getting on for forty years too late, but better late than never. Silly girl should never have refused him in the first place.'

'Well, I imagine the village must be rather glad she did,' Basil observed, swallowing the last forkful and gratefully relinquishing his plate. 'Dottie's been a leading light here all these years. I know she spent some time in London, working as a dresser in the theatre, but as soon as she came back before the war she seemed to settle straight back into village life and since then she's given her all. Burracombe would be a poorer place without her.'

'That's true,' Gilbert said. 'Foster mother to my young daughter-in-law, too. We've a lot to thank Dottie for. She'll be sorely missed when she goes.'

'But at least we'll know she'll always come back,' Constance said. 'Though it's not the sort of life I'd find comfortable myself– forever upping sticks to cross the Atlantic, with a home on either side. I just hope she'll take to it. I don't think I could!'

'I dunno about you,' Ted said as he and Alice got ready for bed that night, 'but it seemed to me as if Dottie weren't quite herself at teatime.'

'Not herself?' Alice pulled her nightgown over her head and sat at the dressing table to brush her hair. She remembered her conversation with Dottie, and the doubts her friend had suddenly expressed. I almost forgot about that, she thought with dismay. Poor Dottie – she must have thought I didn't care. But with all the worry about Jackie, and with her and Joe sitting there looking just the same as ever and him so fond of her, it went clean out of my mind.

That poor woman, she thought, brushing

fiercely. I've let her down proper, and her as near a sister as I'm ever going to have.

She glanced in the mirror at Ted, wondering whether to mention it now, and decided not to. Least said soonest mended, and it was for the couple themselves to say when they'd made up their own minds. Joe might talk Dottie round anyway, and no more said. And what was the point of upsetting Ted even more than he was already?

'Well, she's still not properly over that stroke she had. It's bound to have taken it out of her, and she was as upset as the rest of us about Jackie.'

'I know, but ... it struck me there was summat else on her mind. I'm surprised you didn't notice it yourself, Alice. You're usually the one telling me I don't see these things.'

'Maybe because there was nothing to see. Anyway, if there was something on her mind, 'twas probably to do with the wedding, and her and Joe's sorting it out now. He should be back pretty soon, so you can ask him yourself.'

'I can't do that. 'Tis for him and her to set to rights between them.' Ted set the alarm clock for five and got into bed. 'You'll brush the hair right out of your head if you goes at it like that.'

Alice laid down her brush and turned to him. 'Oh, Ted, I can't stop thinking about Jackie. Our poor little maid, lying in some hospital all those thousands of miles away and nobody of her own beside her. It's so cruel.'

Ted got out of bed and came over to her. He bent to put his arms around her and she rested her face against him.

'We'll get over there as soon as we can,' he said.

'The tickets are booked and the travel man said the passports would come through in good time. We'll be with our Jackie before you know it.'

'Three weeks,' she said. 'Three weeks at least. And all that time she'll be on her own. It's *now* she needs us, Ted, not in three weeks' time.'

'I know, maid. But there's nothing we can do about that. And we got a lot to arrange here anyway. Joe says he and Dottie will stop here in the farmhouse, to help as much as they can.'

'And that's another thing. Wouldn't it be better if they came along too? Joe could take us about and show us what's what, and I'd like to have Dottie with me. A woman I know and feel comfortable with. We've never even *met* Joe's girls. I know Dottie got on with them all right, when she went over before, but I'd feel happier if there was going to be someone there we already knew.'

'We know Russell. He was here for weeks when he and Joe came before. He'll look after us, Alice. Look.' Ted drew her over to the bed and sat down beside her. 'We can't make things any different from how they be. We've got to work with what the situation is, not how we'd like it to be.'

'If 'twas how we'd *like* it to be, Jackie wouldn't be in hospital at all,' Alice snapped. 'If 'twas how we'd *like* it to be, she'd be home here with us, as she should be, as she *would* be, if your brother hadn't enticed her to America with his tales. And Dottie too – I tell you, Ted, he'd have the whole village over there if he had his way!'

'Now that's just silly talk, Alice, and you know it,' Ted said sternly. 'I know it's because you're upset and worried, and so am I, but that don't mean we got to lose sight of reason. And all I'm saying is that 'tis no good blaming Joe or wishing things was different. They're as they are and that's what we got to deal with. Now, isn't it?'

'I know, Ted, I know,' she said miserably. 'And I'm not blaming Joe, not really. He's been a tower of strength. I don't know what we'd have done today without him, and I'm glad we'll still be here for the wedding.' She wiped her eyes with the sleeve of her nightgown. 'You don't really think there was anything wrong with Dottie earlier on, do you? You don't suppose she's having second thoughts?' She was on the brink of telling him of Dottie's panic that morning, even though she had promised to say nothing.

'My stars, I hope not! I don't know what it would do to our Joe if she turned him down now. No, I dare say it was just some little hitch in the wedding arrangements. Or else I was imagining it. Anyway, unless Joe tells us something to the contrary, we'd better forget it. We got enough to think about in the next couple of weeks without making up trouble.'

They got into bed and Alice turned out the lamp. Ted slid his arm beneath her shoulders and she turned towards him, laying her head against his shoulder. For a few minutes they were quiet, then she said, 'You're a good man, Ted. You always manage to make me feel a bit better. But I shan't feel right now until I'm beside our Jackie again and can see for myself how she is. I don't reckon either of us will.'

'No,' he said. 'We won't. But we'll talk to Elaine again tomorrow. She'll know more then, and remember that every day gets us a day closer to seeing her.'

'And by then,' Alice said drowsily, 'Joe and Dottie will be wed. I'm glad we'll be here to celebrate that.'

Chapter Eight

Basil was still floating on air when he opened the vicarage door the next morning to find Joe and Dottie standing on the top step.

'Why, you're early birds!' he exclaimed, standing back to usher them in. 'And looking so serious, too. I hope it's not more bad news about Jackie.'

'No, it's not that,' Joe said, letting Dottie go first. 'But it's something we need to talk to you about.'

Basil directed them into the front room which served as his office, and pulled out chairs in the bay window. He waited until they were seated, then took his own seat and looked at them enquiringly.

'It's just that things have changed a bit in the past day or two,' Joe began slowly, with a glance at Dottie. 'It's partly hearing about Jackie, but it's not only that. See, we've got a bit of a problem and we want your advice.'

'Well, of course I'm only too willing to help, if you think I can,' Basil said, a little anxiously, 'It's not too serious a problem, I hope?'

'Depends on how you look at it, I reckon. I don't

know if you've heard, vicar, but me and Dottie were pretty close, a long while back, when we were youngsters. Walking out, it was called then. Pretty nearly engaged, we were, and I reckoned it was all sewn up and certain – all over bar the shouting, as my brother would say. Only I never thought there'd be much shouting between Dottie and me. Happy as sandboys, I reckoned we'd be if we married. But when push came to shove, Dottie thought otherwise. I wanted to go to the States, you see, but she couldn't bring herself to leave Burracombe, and there seemed to be no way round it. So I went off and after a bit I found my Eleanor and married her, and we had a good marriage and three fine youngsters. But that's all over now; Eleanor's been gone a few years and when I came back and found Dottie was still single, all the old feelings came welling up inside me. I thought – well, why not see if we can make a go of it after all? And after a bit, Dottie came to see it too, though I had to do a bit of persuading, mind you!'

'Yes, I understand all that,' Basil said, rather bewildered now. 'I already know most of the story. And now your wedding is fixed for two weeks' time, so it's a happy ending.' A dreadful thought struck him and he looked from one to the other. 'At least – I hope it's a happy ending! You're not having second thoughts, are you?'

'Well, that's just it,' Joe said. 'Dottie told me yesterday that she was doing just that. She felt the same way all over again – couldn't bear to think of missing half of every year in Burracombe. And the same half, too! It's either winter or summer, autumn or spring, and it's breaking her heart.' Joe

95

leaned forward, his hands on his knees. 'I can't do that to her, vicar. I can't break her heart all over again, and she don't want to break mine, neither. And that's why we've come to see you.'

Basil stared at them in distress. His joy over the organ faded. 'Do you mean to say you're not getting married after all? Don't tell me you want to call off the wedding!'

Gilbert Napier started his morning well pleased with himself. Basil's excitement and gratitude over the proposal for the organ had been all he could have wished for, and Grace had been equally delighted. Constance Bellamy had congratulated him and offered to donate an entire set of new music sheets to replace the rather tattered ones that Dorothy Doidge had been making do with for so long. She suggested that the Mothers' Union might like to embroider a new altar cloth to use when the organ was rededicated. The evening had been taken up with joyous plans and Gilbert had gone home glowing with an aura of satisfaction.

He finished his breakfast and went to the estate office at the back of the house. Travis was already there, working on some papers, and he looked up with a smile.

'You look particularly cheerful, colonel.'

'I am,' Gilbert said, and told him the news. 'The vicar hardly knew where to put himself, he was so pleased.'

'He must be overjoyed. How long will the repairs take?'

'He's going to set things in motion this morning, so he'll be able to find out then, although I expect they'll need to do another inspection first. He's hoping for Christmas, but Miss Bellamy and I told him it's more likely to be well into January – if then. The great thing is that we've set it in motion, and the jumble sales and whist drives can go back to whatever else it is they want to raise money for. There's always something.'

'There certainly is. But the village will be very grateful to you. And Hilary's going to be delighted. Did she know about this before she went off on honeymoon?'

Gilbert shook his head. 'I didn't even think of it until after the wedding. Don't know why I didn't before. We've all known the organ was in a bad way and it'd be difficult to get the money together. The church is one of my responsibilities, after all.'

'Not to the extent of providing a new organ.' Travis smiled. 'And you've had a lot of other things on your mind, as well as being ill. But now Hilary's married and you're fit and well again...' He gave his employer a speculative glance.

'I'll be wanting to take the reins in my own hands. That's what you're thinking, isn't it?' Gilbert shook his head 'It's all right, Travis, your job's safe! I'm as keen as ever to be involved in estate matters but I'm not fool enough to think I can do all you do. Not these days. And I don't imagine that Hilary's going to give up either, just because she's married. Got modern ideas in her head now, although she may have to change her ways a bit once the family starts to come along.'

'If she asks my wife,' Travis said with a grin, 'she may learn that looking after a husband and baby is a full-time job. Not that Jennifer complains –

not in my hearing, anyway.'

'Nothing to complain about,' Gilbert declared. 'Husband with a good job, fine house to live in, pretty little daughter. What else could a woman want?'

'I can't imagine,' Travis said, his mouth twitching. 'But plenty of women do seem to want more. A job of their own, for instance.'

Gilbert snorted. 'And that's absolute nonsense! A woman's job is in the home, looking after her family. There's plenty to keep them occupied there. I tell you, Travis, those who insist on going out to work will regret it when they find they've got to do all their housework in the evenings and weekends, not to mention putting a decent meal on the table every evening. They can't expect their husbands to help after a day's work.'

Travis knew that Jennifer would have found a flaw in this argument but he didn't say so. She was content now to be at home with Molly and the new baby, if one really was on its way, but would she be as content when the children were older and out at school all day, leaving her alone? Might she not then feel lonely in the isolated cottage, and at a loose end when the housework was done? Might she feel that she still had more to give, outside the home?

Still, that was in the future and needn't be worried about now. He returned his attention to his employer and the estate matters they had met to discuss. There was a busy day ahead.

'No,' Joe said positively. 'We're not calling off the wedding. Though there was a sticky hour or two

98

when it looked as if that was in Dottie's mind. But I hope I've talked her round.' He glanced at the little woman beside him, and she turned pink and nodded. 'The thing is, vicar, Dottie don't feel happy about being out of Burracombe for half of every year, and I've got to respect that. I don't want her miserable, hankering for the village and the folk she's lived amongst for so long. But at the same time, I can't feel easy about leaving my own family.'

'Yes, I understand that, Joe.' Basil looked thoughtful. 'So what do you want to do?'

'Well, just talk it through with someone we trust and respect. See here, we've talked it round and round ourselves until we're just going in circles. We need someone else to look at it, see if there ain't some way round that we've not thought of. Or take all the ways we *have* thought of and help us to see which is the right one.'

'But only if you've got time,' Dottie said. 'We don't want to interfere with whatever else you were going to do.'

Basil thought of the organ and his plan to telephone the repair company as soon as they were open for business.

'Of course I've got time,' he said. 'There's nothing more important at the moment than you two and your happiness. We can take all morning, if you like. All day, even.'

'Lord above us, I hope it won't take that long!' Dottie exclaimed. 'I've got some Cokers in the larder that want eating and I meant to fry them up for dinner today.'

Joe laughed. 'Those Cokers have been hanging

over our heads for the past two days. I tell you, vicar, it comes to something when our whole future depends on a pan of sausages!'

Basil smiled. 'It doesn't seem too serious a problem, if you can make jokes about it – and I'm not talking about the sausages. Now, Dottie, tell me why you suddenly began to have doubts, because you seemed sure enough the last time I spoke to you. And you must be absolutely honest. This is no time to spare anyone's feelings. The rest of your lives are at stake.' He glanced from one to the other and his eyes twinkled. 'I must say, this is quite a new experience for me. I've counselled plenty of couples about their wedding over the years, but they've usually been rather younger ones. Dottie?'

She hesitated, looking first at Joe. Then she took a deep breath and said, 'It's not that I've got any doubts about marrying Joe, none at all. I know how lucky I am to have a second chance. And I don't even have any worries about living in America – some of the time, anyway. It's just – well, if we do as we planned and spend half the year there and half the year here, there's things about Burracombe I'll never see again. It don't matter what time of year we go – Christmas, summer, bluebell time – I'll never be here at that time again, in my whole life. And that's almost like leaving for ever.'

There was a long pause. Then Joe looked at the vicar and shrugged slightly. 'You see? Half the year here, half the year there – it cuts both ways. And I don't see any way round it. Unless we stay a whole year at a time, which, I suppose, we could do... But neither of us is all that keen on that either. And making it shorter visits doesn't help – it's a lot of toing and froing, and at our age, and considering Dottie's health, that don't seem to be any solution at all.'

'Dear me,' Basil said. 'Yes, I can see you have got yourselves into a tangle. But–'

'And there's another thing,' Dottie broke in. 'We're not getting any younger. Another ten years down the line and we'll be looking at our seventies. What happens then? Will we really want to be traipsing backwards and forwards across the Atlantic? Not to mention the cost. It's not like going across the Torpoint ferry. And even if we're still fit and healthy enough then, what about in ten years after that, when we're getting on for eighty? I don't see–'

'Dottie, Dottie!' Basil exclaimed, lifting his hands in the air. 'None of us can look that far ahead. How do we know what conditions will be like in ten or twenty years' time? You'll probably be able to fly there, in just a few hours, for less than the cost of a passage on the *Queen Elizabeth*. And how can you know what you will want to do anyway? It seems to me that you've got yourselves into a knot over this. It's as if you're lost in a maze and can't see your way out.'

'That's just what it do feel like,' Dottie said. 'Proper mazed. That's what I be, all right.'

Joe looked helplessly at the vicar. 'So can you see a way out? Because she's got me as lost as she is.'

'I think you both need to draw breath and think about it,' Basil said firmly. 'And don't say you've been thinking about it all night – I can see you have. And all the worry about Jackie has made it worse. What news is there of her, by the way? No, tell me that later. Let's stick to the matter in hand.' He leaned forward a little. 'First, why do you feel you have to spend half the year in each place?'

Joe and Dottie looked at each other.

'Why, because it seemed fairest,' she said at last.

'Fairest to whom?'

'Our families, of course. Joe's got his three children over in Corning, and Ted and Alice here, and I know I've got no real family, but there's Maddy and Stella and Felix and – and, well, all of Burracombe really. I feel like the whole village is my family.'

Basil nodded. 'And none of them would ever move away from either of you, of course. Nobody would leave Burracombe, because it would mean leaving Dottie, and none of your family, Joe, would think of leaving Corning.'

'Well, as to that, my Elaine and her husband have been talking of moving to Buffalo for his work...'

'Quite. And would you expect them not to, for your sake?' He turned to Dottie. 'And have you ever told Maddy she can't leave Burracombe and perhaps go to Canada with Stephen, because you'd miss her?'

'Of course I haven't! I wouldn't dream of it! They got their own lives to live...' She caught his eye and fell silent. 'But that's different,' she added a little weakly. 'They're young people.'

'And that makes no difference at all,' Basil said firmly. 'Dottie, we *all* have our own lives to live and while we should certainly consider others, especially those close to us, and while it's good to look ahead and be as sure as possible that we're living them in the right way, we do have to live them *for ourselves,* and in the way that seems best at the time. None of us can live now in accordance with what we think might be happening in twenty years' time. If we do, we may find that when those twenty years have passed, we have nothing but regrets for what we might have done. We can only live for what seems right *now.* Don't you agree?'

'Well, yes, that do make sense,' Dottie said after another pause. 'But I still don't feel happy about being out of the village all that time.'

'Then don't be.' Basil turned to Joe. 'You have close family in Corning. Would you feel the same about missing them for half of each year?'

'I don't know as I would,' he said slowly. 'The girls are both settled with their families and, as I just said, Elaine's thinking of leaving the town anyway. And Russell's pretty well taken over the business now and doing well. He'll probably be getting married himself in a year or two. They don't need me on their heels all the time.'

'Then suppose you make your permanent home here, where you were born and also have family, and visit Corning once a year for a shorter time? For, say, three months – and a different three months each time? Could you do that, do you think?'

Joe and Dottie looked at each other.

'I reckon I could,' he said at last. 'What about you, sweetheart?'

'I could think about it,' she said cautiously. 'But I'm still a bit worried about what we do as we get really old. Suppose–'

'And I've told you,' Basil said, a little sternly, 'that you must leave the future to take care of itself. Leave it in God's hands. What did our Lord say? *"Take therefore no thought for the morrow; for the morrow shall take thought for the things of itself."* Time changes all things, and we can't look ahead and say what we will do in even a week's time, because everything may be different again by then.' He paused, and then his eyes twinkled and his smile returned. 'All the same, I hope you won't put off your wedding. God willing, we shall all be here for that!'

'I reckon we will,' Joe said, clearing his throat. He reached out, took Dottie's hand in his and looked into her eyes. 'I don't know about you, sweetheart,' he added, a little huskily, 'but as far as I'm concerned, the vicar's cleared it all up, just like we hoped he would. What do you say?'

'I say so too, Joe,' she whispered, and used her free hand to brush a tear from her cheek. 'And now I think we've taken up enough of the vicar's time. We'll go back to the cottage. I've still got a few stitches to put in my new costume – and I've got them dratted Cokers to cook as well!'

Chapter Nine

'So that's how things stand now,' Alice finished. 'Elaine and Earl have been to see Jackie in the hospital and arranged for her to be taken back to Corning, and that's where she'll have to stop until her leg's better. She's conscious, and apart from her broken leg, two broken ribs and a lot of bruises, she don't seem any worse hurt, thank the Lord – not in her body, anyway. It's her poor broken heart that will take most healing. But me and Ted will be sailing on the thirteenth of October so we'll be with her on the twentieth, or thereabouts.' She sighed. 'It do seem an awful long time to wait, though.'

The whole family was gathered in the Tozers' kitchen, where they had come to hear the latest news over a cup of tea. Tom was tucking into a slab of fruit cake before starting on the afternoon milking, Minnie was crocheting a blanket for Robin's bed, Joanna was darning a pile of socks and Robin, Heather and Christopher had been sent outside to feed the hens.

'It's the quickest it can be done,' Val said comfortingly. 'And now Jackie's conscious, she'll understand. She's got her cousins with her, after all.'

'It's not the same as having her mother,' Alice fretted. 'Or being in her own home. And it's not just her own injuries – she's lost her man too. It's all wrong, being so far away from home.'

'Well, it's what she wanted. Going to America, I mean. And at least she's not in danger, like Hilary and I were when we were in Egypt during the war. She's safe and well looked after, and you'll be there as soon as you possibly can. And in the meantime, the rest of us have got our own lives to lead.' Val stopped, aware that she was speaking more brusquely than she had intended. But it was too late – Alice, always rather prickly when Egypt was mentioned, took her up straight away.

'That's the trouble with you, Val – always got to try to belittle your sister, no matter what happens to her. She could have been killed in that accident, you know, like Bryce was.'

'I know that, Mum. But she wasn't, was she? And I'm not trying to belittle her. I was as upset about it as you. I was trying to make you feel better, that's all.'

'Well, you've got a funny way of doing it!' Alice snapped. 'You had a real nasty tone in your voice when you said that, about the rest of us having our own lives to lead. As if we didn't all know that! And what's so wrong with your life, anyway? A nice home, a lovely baby, a husband who's earning good money and making a name for himself … I'd have thought you'd be grateful.'

'I am. Of course I am. Look, Mum, I didn't mean anything by it. It just came out wrong, that's all. Anyway, I've got to go now. I've got things to do at home.' She stood up and collected her basket, which Alice had earlier filled with runner beans and tomatoes from the kitchen garden. 'Thanks for the veg, Mum. I'll pop up again tomorrow to see if there's any more news. 'Bye, Granny.'

She bent to kiss her grandmother's cheek and then, after a brief hesitation, her mother's. Joanna and Tom gave her a grin and she went out, calling a goodbye to her father, who was already in the milking parlour, and dragging a reluctant Christopher away from the hens.

'I really don't think she did mean anything by it, Mum,' Joanna said after a pause. 'You know what

106

it's like when your words come out wrong and it sounds different from what you meant. And it's easy to misunderstand when you're feeling upset anyway.'

'That may be,' Alice said, only half mollified. 'But it's struck me more than once that Val's a bit jealous of our Jackie. I sometimes think she feels a bit trapped, stuck here in Burracombe while Luke spends so much time in London. She never really wanted him to go, you know.'

'They seem to have come to an agreement over it, though. He only spends one week a month away. It could be a lot worse. If he was in the Navy he'd be away for months or even years at a time.'

'He's not in the Navy, though. He's an artist and he's given up a regular job teaching at Tavistock Grammar to do this. Val was used to him coming home at teatime every day, being there in the evenings and at weekends, and now he's away for a whole week, and sometimes it's more, and when he is home he spends half his time at that old charcoal burner's cottage in the woods that he uses as a studio, and she barely sees him. She never knows where she is with him.'

'Come on, Mum,' Tom said, scooping up the last few crumbs of fruit cake. 'You're starting to sound as if you're on her side now, and a few minutes ago you were accusing her of not being grateful for what she had! You can't have it all ways.'

'I don't want to have it all ways. I just want all my children to be happy in their lives, like any mother would.' Alice got up and started to clear the table. 'Anyway, I think it'd be a good thing if we stopped talking about it now. I can see whatever I say will be wrong, so I won't say anything at all!'

She carried the plates to the sink and then left them and went upstairs. They heard her footsteps as she went along the passage, and looked at each other.

'She's upset about Jackie,' Minnie said, coming to the end of a strand of red wool and picking out a blue one. 'Take no notice. She'll be all right when she's had a few minutes to herself and a bit of a cry.'

'None of us wants to upset her,' Joanna said uncomfortably. 'We all know how worried she must be. We're just as worried ourselves.'

'And she knows you are. She's just on edge, that's all. Carry on as you always do and let her be. She don't want arguments any more than any of us do.' Minnie glanced out of the window. 'You'd better go out and see what Heather means to do with that bucket of eggs, because she don't seem to be bringing them indoors.'

'Oh my goodness!' Joanna jumped up and ran to the door. 'She's got this idea that if she can get one of the cows to sit on them, they'll hatch into calves! I think we're going to have to talk to our daughter, Tom.'

Tom laughed. 'A bit young for the birds and the bees, but you may be right! Anyway, it's time I went out to get on with the milking. See you later, Gran.'

Alone in the kitchen, Minnie went back to her crochet. She had seen all this before, she thought – family joys and misfortunes, even tragedy such as when little Heather's twin sister Suzanne had died suddenly in her pram – but it all passed, one way or another, and somehow the family carried on. Nothing was ever bad enough to break it apart.

Still, you couldn't help worrying about each event as it came along, and she was more concerned now about Val than she was about Alice or even Jackie. Alice would be happier when she was with her younger daughter and able to comfort her, and Jackie was young and resilient and would recover from her own tragedy. But Minnie had the feeling that there was something deeper worrying Val, something that she had not told any of them, something that might be more serious than anything that had happened yet.

Val and Christopher strolled home slowly, picking blackberries from the hedges as they went. They had already picked several pounds during the past few weeks, eating them for breakfast with cornflakes, for dinner with apples as crumble, pies or just stewed, and (in Christopher's case) for supper with bread and milk. Val had also made ten pounds of jam and jelly, which stood on the top shelf of the larder along with ten more pounds of plum and some Kilner jars filled with bottled fruit.

'We shall look like blackberries, if we go on like this,' she said to her son. 'Still, they're better for you than sweets.'

'I like sweets,' Christopher said, cramming his mouth and staining his lips with black juice. 'Can we go to the shop?'

'Not today. Daddy's coming home and I want

to cook a nice dinner for him.'

'Daddy!' the toddler cried, jumping with both feet into a puddle. 'Daddy home!'

'That's right. And he'll be home for three whole weeks. Won't that be nice?'

'Daddy home,' he repeated, stamping along and leaving wet footprints on the road. 'Daddy *stay* home.'

'Just for three weeks,' Val said. 'Then he'll have to go away again. But that's a long way off, so we won't worry about it now, will we? Just for the time being he'll be here with us and, if you're very good, he'll take you to the cottage while he paints.' She glanced up as someone came round the corner, and smiled. 'Hello, Miss Kemp. I haven't seen you since just after the fair. Have the Crocker twins recovered from being a dragon?'

'Don't remind me,' the schoolteacher begged. 'It's not so much have *they* recovered as have the *rest* of us recovered! How they didn't set fire to themselves or get trampled by your father's bull, I shall never know. And to think we've got another five years of them in the school before they go up to secondary education...' She looked at Christopher, who gazed back at her with innocence all over his blackberry-stained face. 'You wouldn't behave like that, would you? Or maybe I shouldn't ask!'

Val laughed. 'At least he's not twins! I wonder if anyone will ever learn to tell those two apart.'

'If not, the young women of this village are going to have problems,' Frances Kemp prophesied grimly. 'But by then, I shall be long retired and have no more responsibility. And how is your

110

sister, Val? James and I were very sorry to hear about the accident.'

Val noted the 'James and I'. Most of the village had speculated on the growing friendship between the two schoolteachers and it seemed that they were now ready to be bracketed together, as close friends if nothing else. She said, 'Yes, it was a terrible thing to happen. But we've heard that Jackie is conscious now and doesn't seem to have anything worse than a broken leg and two broken ribs, thank goodness. We were afraid she might have spinal injuries like Stella. Mum and Dad are going over there the week after next – they've booked their passage now. They couldn't go sooner because of having to get passports.'

Frances nodded. 'It all takes time. I'm sure your mother wishes she could be there much sooner. But there must be so much to arrange anyway, with the farm to think of. It's nice that she'll be here for the wedding, anyway. We're all looking forward to that. Well, I must let you get on. This young man probably wants his tea.'

Val smiled. 'We've just come from the farm now. He's full of Granny's buns and fruit cake, aren't you, Kester?' She poked her son's tummy. 'Not to mention about half a pound of blackberries.' She said goodbye and went on her way.

There was just time to prepare the vegetables to go with the meat pie she had already made for Luke's welcome-home supper, and to get Christopher bathed and ready for bed. Then she and her husband would be able to spend their first evening together quietly, exchanging news and looking forward to three whole weeks before he

111

needed to go back to London.

It was strange how quickly those three weeks of each month would go, and how slowly the week would go when they were apart.

Chapter Ten

Frances Kemp let herself into the little house attached to the village school and began to unpack her shopping bag. She was cooking supper for James this evening and wanted it to be a special one, so she had bought two pork chops from Bert Foster and intended to cook them in cider, with vegetables from her own garden. An apple and blackberry pie with fresh clotted cream would complete the meal.

She had finished her preparations and set the small garden table with a bottle of sherry and two glasses by the time James arrived. He was carrying a sheaf of chrysanthemums and as he handed them over he bent to kiss her cheek. Frances took the flowers and thanked him.

'They're lovely, James, but they're from your own border – you shouldn't have picked them. They looked so beautiful where they were.'

'I wanted to share them with you. There are plenty left. Shall I pour a drink while you put them in a vase?'

Frances went indoors, returning to find him sitting at the table, his face lifted to catch the warmth of the early evening sun.

'We won't be able to do this much more. The evenings are beginning to draw in now and there's a definite touch of autumn in the air.'

'I know.' Frances took the other chair and lifted her glass. 'I thought we'd better make the most of every chance we get. Good health, James.'

'Good health,' he said, touching her glass with his. 'Good health and happiness. For both of us.'

There was a short pause. Then he said, 'Frances, I–'

Frances got up quickly. 'I must just go and make sure the chops are all right. I may have set the oven too high.' She hurried into the house and he sat back with a little sigh, then quirked an eyebrow at her as she came back and sat opposite him again.

'You won't escape that easily, my dear. I'm here for the whole evening and you can't keep finding excuses to run away.'

She smiled. 'I know. I'm being very silly – behaving like a young girl. But – well, the last time this kind of thing happened to me, I *was* a young girl! I'm afraid I'm very inexperienced, James.'

'Apart from having been married, so am I. Dorothy was my first and only girl and there's been nobody since she was killed. Nobody until you,' he added quietly. 'In fact, I didn't think there ever would be anyone else.'

Frances reached out her hand and he took it. She said, 'Are you really sure now, James?'

'I am. Quite, quite sure. And you?'

She looked down at their entwined fingers. It was, as she had said, many years since she had held a man's hand like this. She had been a young girl then, in love for the first – and until now, the only – time, and she had thought that her way was clear before her. But the First World War had snatched away her happiness and since then she had never had the desire, or perhaps the courage, to look for more. Now James had come into her life and although she had resisted her own feelings at first, she knew that she had the second chance that came to so few of her generation. There were thousands of women like her, their sweethearts or husbands torn away from them during that cruel war, who had remained single for the rest of their lives. Too many men had been killed during those terrible years, too many women had been left alone. And, like many of them, Frances had accepted her fate and made her own life, with a satisfying career as a village schoolmistress, and had never expected love to come again. But now...

'Yes,' she said. 'I'm quite, quite sure.'

The chops eaten, the pie demolished and the washing-up done, James put a match to the wood fire Frances had laid and they settled down on the small sofa in front of it. The flames crackled and sent out the sweet smell of apple wood, and he sniffed appreciatively.

'There's nothing like the smell of the first fire of autumn. I don't know what the difference is between that and every other fire, but there definitely is one.'

'Jacob gave me these logs from a tree he cut down in Miss Bellamy's garden. She says she's too old to need them all! Ridiculous, of course, she must have years in her yet, but you know what she's like. It's not really cold enough yet for a fire, but it's nice to have when it starts to get dark earlier.' Frances stopped and laughed. 'I'm chattering, aren't I!'

'A bit, but it's nice. I like hearing you chatter. I rather think you've not done enough of it over the years.'

'Well, I've not had anyone to chatter to. But I used to be a real chatterbox when I was young.' She smiled at him. 'You must be giving me back my youth, James,'

'If I am, it's because you're giving me mine. I didn't know it was possible to feel like this at my age.' He hesitated, then said, 'I really am very much in love with you, Frances.'

'Oh, James,' she whispered, and leaned her head on his shoulder. 'Can this be real? I'm not dreaming, am I?'

'If you are, I'm dreaming the same dream. And I want to go on dreaming it for the rest of my life.' He sat up straight. 'My love, we've got a lot of talking to do. About where we go from here. What we're going to do.' He paused again. 'You *are* going to marry me, aren't you?'

Frances raised her brows. 'Is this a proposal?'

He blinked. 'I suppose it must be. I was thinking of it more as a confirmation, but since I haven't asked you properly yet – maybe I should do it now. On one knee, is it? It might be a bit of a struggle, but I think I can manage it.'

Frances laughed. 'You don't have to. You don't even have to ask, if you don't want to.'

'Don't want to?' he exclaimed. 'Of course I want to!' Then his face grew serious and he took both her hands in his and looked gravely into her

115

eyes. 'Frances, I love you and I want you to be my wife. Will you marry me? Please?'

Frances caught her breath. Although hardly unexpected by now, the words still seemed to have the power to surprise. Her throat tightened and she felt the heat of tears in her eyes.

'Oh yes, James,' she whispered. 'Yes, please. I will.'

Luke finished his second helping of meat pie, pushed back a thick lock of dark hair and smiled across the table at his wife. 'That was better than anything I get in London. If I had no other reason to come home, your cooking would always bring me back!'

'Well, that's good to know,' Val replied. 'Does that mean you've got no room for stewed blackberry and apple?'

'It means nothing of the kind. I've got room for at least one helping, especially if there's good Devonshire cream to go with it.'

'I don't know how you stay so thin,' Val remarked, removing his plate and replacing it with a pudding bowl. She served them both stewed fruit and put the dish of crusty yellow cream on the table between them. 'Christopher helped pick the blackberries this afternoon, although I think more went into his mouth than into the basket.' They ate in silence for a few minutes, then she asked, 'And how are things in the big city now?'

'Much the same as usual. I told you about the new commission. It means I'll have to spend ten days there next time I go instead of a week, but it will be worth it. Oh, and I met an old friend – an artist I knew years ago, before the war. We studied together and ran across each other a couple of times in the army. He's talking of coming down to Devon some time and I wondered if we might put him up for two or three nights. He could doss down in the front room. You'll like him, Val. Ben, his name is – Ben Mallory. He paints landscapes.'

'Like yours?'

'More Impressionistic. They're rather fine. We've been exhibiting them in the gallery.'

Val looked thoughtful. 'I suppose if he doesn't mind a camp bed...'

'He won't mind that. And he'll be no trouble – out most of the day, like me. I can make room for him to keep his stuff and do a bit of work in the charcoal burner's cottage. So is it all right for him to come?'

'Well – yes, I suppose so. When were you thinking of?'

Luke glanced sideways. 'The end of the week?'

'The end of *this* week? But it's Wednesday already! How can I get ready for a visitor in two days?'

'Ben's not a *visitor*. Not in that sense, anyway. I'm sorry, Val, but I couldn't say no. It was so good to see him again and he helped me a lot in the old days. Look, I can put him off, if you really can't manage it, but there's not that much to do and I'll help. You won't have to lift a finger. Just a bit of breakfast in the mornings and we'll be out of your way until suppertime.'

'But I was hoping we could have some time together in the evenings. You're always so busy when you're at home, and if there's someone else in the house as well...'

'Just a few days,' Luke said persuasively. 'A long weekend, that's all. We'll still have two weeks before I go back to London.' He tilted his head to one side and looked at her through long dark lashes. 'And if you don't like him, he need never come again. But I'm sure you will.'

'Oh, all right.' Val finished her pudding and held up the tablespoon enquiringly. Luke nodded and she served him another helping. 'But you're not to go disappearing for hours on end and leaving me and Kester alone. He's been looking forward to having his daddy home again and he'll be wanting to go up to the cottage with you, just as he always does. I hope this Ben realises that.'

'He knows all about it,' Luke said cheerfully, piling clotted cream onto his stewed fruit. 'He's looking forward to meeting you both. I tell you, Val, we'll be just one big, happy family.'

'Perhaps now Luke's home again Val will be a bit more settled,' Alice said as she and Minnie sat darning socks and listening to *Life with the Lyons* on the wireless that evening. 'She always seems a bit on edge when he's away. Like I said this after-noon, she never really wanted him to go. I wonder sometimes if she really trusts him.'

Minnie put down one of Tom's socks and stared at her. 'Trust Luke? Of course she trusts him! If she doesn't, she's a silly girl.'

'I don't know, Mother. I wouldn't blame her if she had doubts. Away up there in London with nobody of his own to go back to of an evening – and you know what they say about artists.'

'No, I don't,' Minnie said tersely. 'What do they say? And who are "they", anyway?'

'You don't need to take me up so quick, Mother,' Alice said, taken aback. 'Just "they" – you know, ordinary people. Nobody in particular. And you got to admit it, artists are different from the rest of us. They don't think the same way.'

'Luke's always seemed to think perfectly well as far as I could see. He's a good man, Alice, and a good husband and father. He thinks the world of our Val and little Christopher and spending a few days a month in London's not going to make any difference to that. And Val's got her head screwed on the right way. She knows very well what a lucky young woman she is. I don't know why you've started on this tack, I don't really.'

'I'm beginning to wish I hadn't,' Alice said. 'All I said was that I hoped she'd feel a bit more settled now he's home. I don't know why people seem determined to take me up wrong on everything I say today.' She bit off a length of grey darning wool. 'I just think there's something troubling her, that's all, and as her mother I want to see her happy. I don't know what's so wrong about that.'

Minnie stretched out her wrinkled hand. 'There's nothing wrong about it, maid, and I'm sorry I spoke sharp. Maybe we're all a bit on edge just now, with Jackie in hospital all those miles away, and you going off halfway round the world to see her. It seems everything's upside down just at the moment and it's no wonder we're all a bit at sixes and sevens.'

Alice nodded and touched her hand briefly

before returning to her work. 'It's all right, Mother. The truth is, I'm not looking forward to going all that way. Suppose I'm seasick the whole time. I felt queasy enough that time we went on that boat trip round Plymouth Sound, and I've never been all that good in charabancs. And it's all going to be so different over there. I don't know how I'm going to manage.'

'Go on with you, you'll manage perfectly well. Hasn't Dottie been over? And she seemed to come back all in one piece. And Joe's girls will be there, and Russell too; they'll look after you. It's not as if people speak a foreign language either. You'll be all right.'

'I wish Dottie and Joe were coming,' Alice said. 'They meant to, you know, but Ted says he'll feel happier if Joe's here to help Tom around the place. And Dottie's not really up to the journey, not yet.'

'You'll be all right,' Minnie repeated. 'And so will we. You don't mean to be gone all that long anyway, do you? Three or four weeks, didn't you say? And you may even bring Jackie back with you. Now that's something to look forward to!'

'It would be, if she'll come, but you know what an independent little madam she is.' Alice rolled up the darned socks and put them into her basket. 'There, that's all I'm doing tonight. The men'll be in from the Bell in a few minutes and wanting a bite to eat before they go to bed. I'm making scrambled eggs. Do you want some?'

Minnie shook her head. 'I don't want anything now, maid. I'll go up to bed.' She rose stiffly and patted Alice's shoulder. 'And don't you go worrying any more about your Val. She has her moods,

120

as she always has had, and I know she don't like her man being away but she's got to learn to make the best of that. There's nothing really wrong, so don't go reading more into it all than there is to be read.'

She went upstairs and Alice began to prepare the snack the family always had last thing at night. She paused in the middle of slicing bread, thinking over what Minnie had said, and hoping she was right.

I do worry too much about them, she thought. I suppose it's what all mothers do. All the same, I'm really not happy about Val. There's something – something I can't put my finger on. I just hope whatever it is comes right before we go to America.

Chapter Eleven

Dottie and Joe got married on a fine morning at the beginning of October. The leaves of the tall elms around the church, and the great oak on the village green, were turning to bronze and gold, and the sky was the blue of Dottie's own costume. She had no child bridesmaids but she was attended by Stella and Maddy, each wearing sheath dresses of silk the colour of Devonshire cream with a short jacket to cover their shoulders, and they all carried late roses from Dottie's own garden.

The church was full and the doors were left open

so that the notes of Henry Warren's piano could be heard outside, where those who hadn't managed to get a seat could linger in the sunshine and hear Joe's strong voice make his vows to the girl he had loved as a young man. Dottie's responses were quieter but those inside had no doubt of the sincerity of her soft tones and could see the tears on her cheeks as she looked up into Joe's face and gave him her hand. There were tears on many more cheeks than hers as the wedding party, with Ted and Alice Tozer as witnesses, crowded into the tiny vestry, and if it had been seemly to cheer inside a church the entire congregation would have cheered – and even stamped its feet – as they came out again and proceeded, with radiant smiles, down the aisle to the door.

The bells, led today by Travis Kellaway, rang out above their heads as they came out and those in the churchyard gave them the cheer that the ones inside would have liked to have given. They stood for a few minutes, smiling and waving, and then Roy Pettifer, who had recently bought a new camera and fancied his ability with it, took photographs of the couple together, the couple surrounded by family members, the couple surrounded by the congregation, and would have gone on to take photographs of the couple surrounded by the entire village, together or individually, had not Ted Tozer intervened and told Roy he'd taken enough to fill several albums already. 'Dottie and Joe don't want every ugly mug in Burracombe staring out at them, and anyway, film's too expensive to go wasting any more rolls.'

'It won't cost all that much,' Roy protested. 'I'll

develop and print them myself. I use our kitchen as a darkroom, with old blackout curtains at the window.'

'You've took enough, just the same, and us wants to go on down to the hall for the reception and the speeches. They want to get to Perranporth before it's dark.'

'Don't you reckon they'll be able to find all they need to find, if it's dark, then?' Roy asked cheekily, and Ted scowled at him and aimed a swing at his head. Roy chuckled and dodged away but he folded up his camera and slipped it back into its case and the party set off down the church path and across the green to the village hall, where Alice and half the village women had set out a feast of ham and salad, with great bowls of trifle to follow and the wedding cake George Sweet had made taking pride of place on the top table.

'My, this brings back memories,' David Napier said to his wife. 'Remember our wedding, darling?'

'I ought to, since it was only three weeks ago! We've only been back from our honeymoon a few days. Mind you, it doesn't seem possible that that's all it was – I feel as if we've been married for ever!' Hilary shook her head. 'It's lovely to see Dottie looking so happy, isn't it? To think that not long ago she was in hospital, and Joe was over in America. You know, if she hadn't had that stroke, he might never have come back and made her agree to marry him. She told me she'd refused him more than once.'

'She was worried about living in two different countries,' Stella said, joining them. 'Not only that, but on two different continents! But they

123

seem to have sorted it out and they've decided to stay here until next spring and then go to Corning for the summer. It'll lend her time to recover completely, and Joe can give a hand on the farm while Ted's away.'

'Are they going to live on the farm?' Hilary enquired.

'I don't think so. They want to stay in Dottie's cottage but I think there's some idea of finding somewhere bigger as their permanent home here. I'm not sure where it will be, though – not many houses in Burracombe come up for sale as it is, and finding the right one will be quite difficult.'

'Perhaps they could build one,' Hilary said. 'People are beginning to do that now. Oh – they're calling you up to the top table, Stella. We'd better find our places and sit down.'

She and David found their seats and smiled at each other. It was the first wedding they had attended since their own and, when they raised their glasses in a toast to Dottie and Joe, they made a private toast of their own – to each other.

'Happy days, darling,' David said quietly. 'Happy, happy days.'

'It's a Ford Consul,' Henry Bennetts, Micky Coker's best friend, told Micky when the two boys had come out from ringing the bells in the church. They paused to admire it parked by the green. 'It's brand new. My dad says Mr Tozer told him he wasn't going to hire cars any more now he'd be living in Burracombe a lot of the time so he went and got this.'

'It's smashing,' Micky said, stroking the

124

gleaming new paintwork. 'But didn't it ought to have "Just Married" written on it and a few old boots and tin cans tied to the back? That's what our Betty had on the car she and Edward went off in after they got married.'

'I suppose nobody's thought of it,' Henry said reflectively. 'I don't know what you use to write on a car, anyway. Don't suppose they'd be very pleased if we used paint.'

'I think the best man did it at Betty's wedding, and he borrowed a lipstick.'

'Well, Mr Tozer – Ted – was best man, and he's not likely to go writing on cars, and us don't have no lipstick, so that's no good. I can't go pinching my mother's. Dad would have me fried for breakfast if I did that. And your mother doesn't wear it.'

They regarded the car, despondent about the chance that was passing them by, and jumped when a voice accosted them. It was Vic Nethercott, who had also been one of the ringers and had gone with the others to wet his whistle at the Bell Inn.

'I hope you two aren't planning any mischief.'

They turned innocent faces towards him.

'We're not planning nothing,' Micky said virtuously. 'We're just keeping an eye on Mr Tozer's new car, so that no one don't come writing on it with lipstick. I don't suppose you got any lipstick with you?' he added hopefully.

Vic grinned. 'Do I look as if I carry lipstick about? And what would you want to do with it if I did? You'd better not write anything on that car, with lipstick or anything else, or Mr Tozer will have your guts for garters.' He joined them and

125

the three stood gazing pensively at the car. 'Still, it ought to look more like a honeymoon car when the happy couple drive off, and Ted Tozer's not likely to see to it. Maybe an old boot or something – isn't that supposed to be lucky?'

'And some horseshoes,' Henry added excitedly. 'You must have millions of horseshoes lying about at home, Mick.'

'Dad usually gets rid of them but I bet I can find a few. We'll want some twine as well. I'll come with you.' He turned back to Vic. 'Don't you tell anyone, mind. And don't let anyone else do anything before us gets back.'

The two boys ran off and Vic leaned against the wall. He took a packet of Players cigarettes from his pocket and lit up. A few minutes later, Roy Pettifer strolled out of the pub and came across the green.

'You been detailed to keep an eye on Joe Tozer's new car, then? I bet he's scared stiff someone'll write rude messages on it.'

'I don't reckon it's occurred to him,' Vic said, blowing a smoke ring. 'Or he'd have put it somewhere out of sight. Leaving it here's just asking for trouble.'

'I'll say so.' Roy leaned against the wall beside him and Vie offered him a cigarette. 'No, thanks. I don't like smoking much.' He unwrapped a piece of chewing gum. 'You know they're saying tobacco might cause cancer?'

'I don't believe that. If it was true, the cigarette companies would do something about it, but they say it's all right, so I reckon it is. You don't happen to have a lipstick on you, do you?'

Roy stared at him. 'No, of course I don't. What on earth are you on about?'

Vic laughed. 'It doesn't matter. Look – here come those two boys. Now we'll see some fun.'

Micky and Henry arrived panting, their arms full of discarded horseshoes and a bundle of boots and shoes. Vic looked at them doubtfully.

'You sure it's all right to take all those?'

'Oh yes,' Micky said. 'The horseshoes ain't no good now, and Dad must be going to throw these old things away too. They were just lying in a corner. You can see they've all got holes in them.'

'I've got some binder twine too,' Henry said. 'We can tie 'em all over the car. It'll look grand. And here's an old cornflake packet; we can use that to make "Just Married" signs. I've got a bit of crayon in my pocket. It'll be just as good as lipstick. And here's a couple of baked bean tins to make it rattle.'

They set to work and soon the car was festooned with shoes of all styles, from ladies' high heels to men's working boots. They were tied on in bundles wherever it was possible – to door handles, wing mirrors, the exhaust pipe – and the signs, made from the back and front of the cornflake packet turned inside out, were stuck on with Roy's chewing gum. After a few moments they ran out of places to tie things on, and stood back to survey their accomplishment.

'Don't it look fine,' Micky said proudly. 'And those old tins are going to wake everyone up all the way to Perranporth. There won't be nobody thinks they're an old married couple.'

'I went to Perranporth once,' Henry said wistfully. 'It's a smashing place. People lays on boards in the sea and let the waves carry them in.'

Micky stared at him. 'Boards? What are you talking about?'

'That's right,' Roy said, making an adjustment to a bundle of boots. 'Surfing, it's called. You can hire them for a tanner an hour. You walk out into the sea and then turn round and lie on the board and if you get a big wave, it carries you right onto the beach. I had a go when I went there with the church outing.'

'Church outing? You?' Vic stared at him and grinned. 'I suppose that was when you were sweet on Jackie Tozer. I never knew you went into the church, once you left school and could make up your own mind. Nearly had to go again once, though, didn't you – I heard you and Jackie had a bit of a fright!'

Roy flushed and glanced quickly at the two boys who were listening with interest. 'Well, you heard wrong, and you can tell whoever told you that, as well. Anyway, it was years ago me and Jackie were going out – it was just a boy and girl thing anyway, nothing serious.'

Vic laughed. 'So you won't be going over to America to hold her hand?'

'Her mum and dad are doing that. Anyway, we'd better get out of sight before they all comes out to send the happy couple off on their honeymoon. We don't want to be found hanging about round the car.' He grinned. 'Wish I had some film left in my camera, but I've used it all up on wedding photos.'

The four of them retreated to the other side of

the green, where Bernie and Rose had put a few benches outside the pub for customers to enjoy the sunshine while they drank. Roy and Vic went in to buy a beer while they were waiting and came out with lemonade and a bag of crisps for the two boys.

'Can I have your salt, if you don't want it?' Micky asked Henry as they tore open their packets and found the little screw of blue paper inside.

'You can have a bit.' Henry sprinkled salt on his crisps and then handed the screw to Micky. 'It makes me too thirsty if I use it all.'

They sat in silence for a while, eyes fixed on the village hall. Roy stirred restlessly.

'What d'you reckon they're doing in there? Holding a parish meeting?'

'They got to have their dinner and a lot of speeches,' Vic pointed out. 'And Ted Tozer'll be making one of 'em, being best man and all. You know what he's like when he gets going, he drags everything out. Nobody can shut him up.'

'His mother will,' Roy said with a grin. 'Ah – look, summat's happening. People are coming out. Better get out of sight.'

They retreated to the churchyard and concealed themselves behind the hedge, peering out as the wedding guests emerged from the village hall and crowded round the car. Exclamations could be heard, of amusement and indignation, but before anyone could do anything Joe and Dottie themselves came out, smiling and waving. They stopped short as they caught sight of their brand new car in all its glory.

'Flipping heck!' Ted Tozer said, his voice carry-

ing clearly across to the watchers in the churchyard. 'Who in the name of thunder did this?'

'Oh, Joe!' Alice said, hurrying to get a better
view. 'They haven't damaged your car, have they?
Whoever could it have been?'

'Some of the village boys, of course, and looking at all the horseshoes, I can make a pretty
good guess which ones.' Ted looked up and down
the street as if expecting to see Micky Coker
strolling along to view his handiwork. 'I'll be
having words with young Micky over this.'

'I don't reckon you'll be the only one, Dad,' Tom
said, grinning. 'It's not just horseshoes they've tied
on – it's ordinary shoes and boots as well. Didn't
you tell me Alf was doing a bit of cobbling as well?
I reckon those belong to half the village and they'll
be expecting them back, mended and as good as
new! Micky's going to find himself very unpopular
around here when folk find out!' He raised his
voice as he spoke, knowing the miscreants would
be somewhere near.

Joe laughed and opened the front passenger
door. 'In you get, sweetheart,' he said quietly to
Dottie. 'We'll drive round the corner to give the
lads their fun and then stop and take it all off.
Tom'll come along and pick it all up, won't you,
lad?'

Tom nodded. Alice came forward, followed by
Maddy and Stella, to give the new Mrs Tozer a
last kiss, and she and Joe got into the car. He
started the engine, tooted the horn and the Ford
Consul, which had looked so smart and new an
hour ago, drove off with a clatter of horseshoes
and tin cans, bundles of boots and high heels

bumping behind it and the two 'Just Married' signs displayed prominently on the doors.

Micky and Henry, who had heard Tom's words but not Joe's, turned to each other in dismay.

'You never said your dad was doing cobbling,' Henry accused Micky.

'I forgot. He's only started it lately, with not so many people using horses on the farms now. Was that really people's shoes, waiting to be mended?' Micky had turned pale. Alf Coker's hands were not only as big as a pound of sausages each, they were hard as well, as Micky had discovered to his cost more than once. 'How far d'you reckon they'll go before they takes 'em off?'

'All the way to Perranporth, I should say,' Vic said cheerfully, and stubbed out his cigarette. 'Well, we'll leave you two to it. Roy and me are catching the bus to Plymouth. We're going to the pictures to see *The Dambusters*. Let us know how you get on.'

The two boys gazed at them in despair. 'Aren't you going to stay and stick up for us?'

'What for? You were the ones who got all the stuff.' The two young men grinned callously and sauntered away. Micky and Henry stared after them.

'I might as well run away to sea right now,' Micky said morosely. 'When my dad finds out what we've done, he'll skin me. Whose idea was it, anyway?'

Neither of them could remember. But as they stood there, making patterns in the dust with the toes of their plimsolls, they saw Tom Tozer come round the corner, laden with boots and shoes.

'They left the horseshoes on,' he called, spotting the two guilty faces. 'But I thought you might want these back. Come on – don't look so miserable. You can get them back to your dad's workshop before he even misses them, and no harm done.' He handed them a bundle of footwear each to carry. 'It was a good idea, but next time, make sure they're shoes nobody wants any more. And when you've finished, nip back here and I'll buy you a lemonade. It was worth it just to have seen the expressions on everyone's faces when they came out of the hall and saw that car!'

Chapter Twelve

Val disliked Ben Mallory from the moment she met him. She could not have said why – he was pleasant enough, shaking her hand warmly when Luke introduced them, bending to speak to Christopher and asking her first before producing a bag of sweets for the little boy, and dumping his old army rucksack behind the settee where it wasn't in the way – but there was something in his dark eyes that unsettled her, and a quirk to his lips that made her feel uncomfortable.

'I get the feeling he's laughing at me,' she said to Luke later, while Ben was looking at the garden. 'As if he knows something he shouldn't, or maybe something I should. What have you told him about us, Luke?'

'Nothing. Only that you're a wonderful wife

and Christopher's the most wonderful baby in the world. What else is there to tell?'

'Now you're laughing at me too,' she said irritably, and went to start preparing supper. 'You'd better take him up to the Bell for a drink while I do this. I don't want you under my feet.'

'I'll show him the charcoal burner's cottage. He'll be spending most of his time there, anyway, so we might as well take his painting gear with us.'

Ben had arrived about an hour after Dottie and Joe had driven away in their highly decorated car. The village hall had been cleared and tidied and most of the guests had gone back home, feeling a little flat after all the excitement. Alice had dropped in at Jed's Cottage earlier that day and invited Val and Luke back to the farm once it was all over, but Val had shaken her head and told her mother about their visitor.

'You can bring him as well,' Alice said, but Val shook her head again.

'I'll see what he's like before I make him feel too much at home. Anyway, Travis gave me a brace of pheasants the other day and it's time they were cooked. We'll have them for supper.'

'Well, you'll make him feel at home all right with food like that,' Alice observed. 'I don't suppose they get pheasants up in London, except in posh restaurants.'

Val had made a casserole, which could be put in the oven and left for the rest of the afternoon, giving her time to take Christopher down to the ford while Luke took Ben to the cottage. But when she told the men of this plan Luke immediately suggested that they should come with her.

'It's one of my favourite spots for painting,' he told Ben. 'You've seen some of my pictures. You'll want to start straight away.'

The artist shrugged his shoulders. He was an inch or two taller than Luke, and as lean as a string bean, with dark eyes and brown hair that looked as if it needed cutting. 'I'm rather veering away from the biscuit-tin style, myself. Some of those paintings don't look much different from coloured photographs.'

'Oh, they do!' Val exclaimed. 'The colour in photos is awful. Everything looks green. Luke paints scenes exactly as they are.'

'That's what I mean. I like to blur it a bit – give it a touch of atmosphere, of mystery, so that the person looking at it can make up their own mind what's there. Or so that the longer you look at it, the clearer it becomes, rather than being able to take it all in with one glance and then move on.' He smiled at her and she felt a twinge of discomfort. 'Rather like looking at life, in a way. Some people prefer it in black and white, or primary colours that can be understood with one look, and others know that there's a great deal more to it than that. Hidden depths, as it were.'

She turned away from his glance, annoyed that he was coming to the ford with them when she had looked forward to an hour or so on her own with Christopher and even more annoyed because what she had really wanted was an hour or so with Luke. He had only been home for a couple of days and with the flurry of preparations for Dottie's wedding they had had little time to themselves.

Now this intruder was here, taking up space in their home and accompanying them on their walks. Still, with any luck, he would decide to spend the rest of the weekend sitting somewhere on a folding chair with his easel, painting his Impressionistic pictures and leaving them alone.

'You ought to go up to the Standing Stones as well, then,' she remarked. 'There's plenty of atmosphere and mystery up there.'

'An excellent idea,' Ben said, smiling at her again. 'Perhaps you'll go with me and show me the way.'

'There's no need for that. You just carry on up the path that leads to the charcoal burner's cottage and you're there, at the top of the hill. You can see all over the village, too. You'll be able to sit there painting for hours.'

'It sounds wonderful,' Ben said, stretching his long arms above his head. 'You know, I think I've fallen in love with Burracombe. I may never want to go back to London at all!'

'What a lovely wedding,' Frances said as she and James relaxed in his cottage that evening. Darkness had fallen and a fire crackled in the grate. They had eaten a simple supper of poached eggs on toast and were enjoying a varied programme of radio entertainment on the Home Service – a Gilbert and Sullivan light opera, followed by a short play and then *Variety Playhouse,* with Vic Oliver presenting an array of stars which included the comedian Bill Maynard, the pianists Rawicz and Landauer, singer Anne Shelton and a sketch with Richard Murdoch and Kenneth

135

Horne, famous for their wartime series *Much Binding in the Marsh.*

'It was a very good day,' James agreed. 'I was flattered to be invited, though I suspect it was only because you were. People are beginning to think of us as a couple, you know.' He glanced sideways at her. 'It seems to me it's time we made it official. I want to buy you an engagement ring, Frances.'

'Oh, do you think that's necessary? I mean, at my age–'

'We're engaged,' he interrupted firmly. 'At least, I presume we are, since you've accepted my proposal. That means a ring. I'd have taken you into town to buy it today if it hadn't been for the wedding.'

'It would probably have been the best time to go,' she said wryly. 'With everyone busy in the village, we might have got away with it without being seen. You must have heard about the Kellaways, when they went to buy Jennifer's engagement ring. They arrived back in the village to find that not only did everyone know about it, but they'd also fixed the date for the wedding! To their chagrin, it was the date Travis and Jennifer had chosen themselves. Jacob Prout was most put out, thinking they hadn't bothered to tell him first.'

'Let's go on Monday, straight after school. And once we've done that, we can think about our own wedding.'

'James! Not so fast! Let's just enjoy being engaged for a while first. Besides, we don't want people gossiping.'

'You mean they might think it's a shotgun wedding?' he asked with a grin. 'I can't believe anyone will think I've "got you into trouble" – not at our age!'

'Of course not.' She smacked his arm. 'But we do have a certain standing in the village and an example to set. Rushing into a sudden marriage – well, it's not Burracombe's way.'

'So when do you suggest? I hope you aren't talking in years – we're not in our early twenties, with all our lives ahead of us.'

'We're not in our dotage, either. But I don't want to wait any longer than necessary, either. Maybe after Christmas – in the spring.'

'That's six months. It seems an awfully long time to me. Why not at Christmas itself? A winter wedding, with our honeymoon during the Christmas holidays. Could we be ready that quickly, do you think? There's not all that much to do, is there?'

Frances closed her eyes. 'Not all that much to do... Have you forgotten already the spin that Hilary Napier was in before she and David got married? And then Dottie and Joe Tozer? They're not in the first flush of youth, and Dottie didn't have a big white wedding, but there still seemed to be a lot of preparation.'

'But they're both different. Hilary's the squire's daughter and they had a lot of guests from outside the village, not to mention all the rebuilding and so on after the fire. And Dottie and Joe are very well known locally, so had pretty well all the village in the church and most of them at the reception, and Dottie's still recovering from her stroke, so a lot of people had to help. It'll be different for us – neither of us has much family and I don't suppose you'll want a long white dress. It can all be very simple.'

'However simple it is, I'll still have to wear something, and we may not have much family but we do have a school. And it's not just the children there now – I've been here a long time, James. I've taught practically everyone in Burracombe under the age of thirty.'

'We don't have to invite that lot, surely!' he exclaimed in a horrified tone, and she laughed.

'Not to the reception, no, but a good many will turn up to see us come out of the church, even if they don't come to the service. And they'll discuss it at length afterwards. Whether we like it or not, James, we do have a certain position in the village.'

'*You* do,' he said gloomily. 'I've only been here five minutes. But I still don't see why it can't be kept simple. Just us and a few friends, maybe a nice lunch at the Bedford Hotel or even out at Two Bridges, and then we can slip away for a honeymoon. What's so difficult about that?'

'The time of year, for a start. Christmas, if you haven't forgotten, comes at the end of December. I must invite Iris, and she's got to travel from Malvern. She's really not very mobile now, and we don't know what the weather is going to be like then. How can we invite her down here and then abandon her while we go off on honeymoon? And the Two Bridges Hotel is lovely but it's in the middle of Dartmoor – how are people going to get there if we have snow? It would be far nicer in spring. And it's not just the wedding, James – we have to decide where we're going to live. You've only just settled into your cottage but as school headmistress I ought to be in the schoolhouse.

There really is a lot to think about.'

'I suppose so.' He sighed heavily. 'But—'

'Please, James,' she said, 'let's just have a few months of being engaged first, and let everyone get used to the idea. We'll start serious thinking and planning after Christmas. We can set a date now if you like – it'll need to be around Easter, so that we can have the school holiday for our honeymoon – but apart from that, let's leave it alone.'

'Can't we even talk about it a little?' he asked plaintively. 'I won't be able to stop looking forward to it. We can make a *few* plans.'

'Of course we can,' she said with a laugh. 'I'm not saying it's to be a forbidden subject. But I just want to relax and flaunt my engagement ring for a while. And don't forget how busy the Christmas term is! You've got six new little infants in your class for a start, and then there's the Nativity play, the carol service, the Christmas party – we wouldn't have time to plan a wedding as well.'

'We would if I had my way. We'd just fix it up with Basil, ask a few friends along and slip off for lunch and then a honeymoon afterwards. I still think that would be best. Once we let the good folk of Burracombe get a hand in it, we'll have a circus on our hands!'

Nobody considered that Dottie's and Joe's wedding had been a circus. A good old-fashioned village celebration, that's what it had been, with everyone welcome to take part in some way. Even if you hadn't been invited to the reception – and everyone understood that this had to be just for family and close friends, especially as Dottie's close friends seemed to comprise half the population – you could go along to the church and either squeeze in at the back for the service or wait outside until the bridal couple came out. There was hardly a soul in Burracombe who wasn't part of it, one way or another.

George and Ivy Sweet had been invited because George had made the wedding cake. Ivy, who had a deft hand, had iced and decorated it, hindered rather than helped by her son Barry. There had been some disagreement over what form its decoration should be.

'Little cherubs look nice on a wedding cake,' Ivy had said. 'But somehow it don't seem to suit Dottie and Joe, not at their age.'

'Couldn't they have a stork on top?' Barry had suggested. 'I saw a cake in Ellis's window in Tavi, and that had a stork on top. And Miss Friend likes birds – she puts bread and stuff out for them in her garden.'

'No, they couldn't have a stork,' Ivy had said. 'That's for christening cakes. I think roses would be best. Dottie grows a lot of them and they're easy enough to make.'

The cake, when finished and embellished with roses, looked almost as good positioned on the top table as if Dottie had made and iced it herself, which of course, as she told Joe, she would have done if it hadn't been for that dratted stroke. It was soon cut and distributed amongst the guests, with more kept back to be cut up later and sent in small white boxes to those who could not be present. Alice was given a chunk to take to America for Joe's family.

'And now that's all over,' she said to Ted later

140

that evening, when they were all back in the farm-house, listening to the same wireless programmes as Frances and James, 'we can get on with our packing for America. I still think you ought to have got a new suit.'

'What do I need a new suit for? We're going to see Jackie in hospital, not to pay calls on the President. My Sunday suit will be good enough if I do need to be dressed up at all, and the rest of the time I'll just wear my ordinary clothes, same as Joe does. Anyway, he says I can borrow some of his things if I need to, so we don't need to take enough to fill a trunk.'

'We're not going to. We've only got that old suitcase we had before the war, and the one Val's lending us. Now, have you got everything sorted out with our Tom for the farm?'

'Stop fretting, Alice. Tom can run this farm on his own with one hand tied behind his back, and he'll have Joe to give a hand, not to mention Nor-man and the other men. They probably won't even notice I'm gone.' Ted spoke confidently but in reality he was no more happy about leaving the farm than Alice was. He had never been away for more than a few days at a time and could hardly bear to think of not being in daily contact with his cows and sheep, or the couple of pigs that lived across the yard and screamed like souls in torment for their food every afternoon, or to be unable to lean on a gate chewing a straw and watch his crops grow. He couldn't say that to Alice, though. She was already in a tizzy over the whole thing and he needed to stay calm and act as if everything was all right.

'You will watch out for Bluebell, won't you?' he had said to Tom a dozen times. 'She gets mastitis easy as anything. And I'm not happy about one or two of the others. Just don't let anything go. And what about the shearing? We done all ours, but didn't old Jim Thornbury ask you to go over and do his? How are you going to find the time? And then there's the winter wheat...'

'Stop fussing, Dad. It'll all get done, same as ever. You know we got plenty of help if we need it. Norman's happy to work extra hours and Travis Kellaway says he'll send over a few chaps if we should need 'em. He says I can borrow the new estate tractor, too. Get the work done in a tenth of the time it takes with Barley.'

Ted stared at him. 'I don't want to come home and find you've got rid of Barley and bought a fancy new tractor.'

'You won't. I won't do anything like that till you're back again. But then I think we should sit down and think about how we're going to go in the future. More and more farmers are getting rid of their horses–'

'Get rid of Barley? Val will never speak to us again. You know what she thinks of that old horse.'

'I know, and I didn't mean get rid of him in that sense. Just work him less, that's all.' Tom hesitated. 'I know neither of us liked the ideas our Brian had when he was here, but some of them do need thinking about. Farming's changing, Dad, and it's no good fighting against it. Tractors are going to take the place of horses, like it or not. In five or ten years' time it'll be a rare sight to see a horse drawing a plough.'

'And more's the pity,' Ted had retorted, but in his heart he knew Tom was right. Changes were coming and you might fight against them, you might even win the fight in some cases, but you couldn't stop them all. You just had to decide which ones would turn out right in the end, and learn to make the most of them.

'Joe says things are a lot different already over in America,' he said. 'Maybe I'll use the time while we're there to have a look round, see what's going on. And when I come home we'll put our heads together and think about the future for Burracombe.'

As he and Alice went to bed that night, exhausted after the wedding and their heads buzzing with preparations for their journey across the Atlantic, he thought of all this and sighed. Neither he nor Alice liked change, and both had hoped to see their days out in the way they had started, just after the First World War. But he had to admit that there had been many, many changes in that time – changes that perhaps they had scarcely noticed as they took place.

Why did thinking about it all seem so ominous now? Was it because of their worries over Jackie, hurt and bereaved in America? Or were the changes that were coming to them more vital than any that had gone before?

'I dunno,' he said to Alice as he took off his shirt. 'We've lived through two world wars, we've seen motor cars and aeroplanes and wireless and television and telephones come to be taken for granted, and still nothing seems settled. What more can happen, d'you reckon? Sometimes, I

143

think I've seen enough.'

'And sometimes I think you've drunk too much ale or cider,' she said from the bed. 'Come on, Ted. You're just tired. Turn out the light and get into bed. It'll be a new day tomorrow and everything will seem different. It always does.'

Chapter Thirteen

Frances and James announced their engagement in both the *Tavistock Times* and the *Tavistock Gazette* that week. The village was divided between those who were surprised and those who nodded their heads wisely and said they'd been expecting it. As always, there was much speculation and, as usual, a lot of it took place in the village shops.

For once, Bert Foster's butcher's shop seemed to be the centre of gossip. It was Saturday morning, the day for buying the Sunday joint, and there was already a gathering outside when he turned his notice round from Closed to Open and unlocked the door. The conversation was animated.

'Fancy, at her time of life!' Aggie Madge marvelled, coming in first. 'She's been here so long I thought she was a fixture. I'd like a piece of topside, please, Bert.'

'I wonder if she'll carry on as headmistress,' Mabel Purdy said, looking critically at the lamb chops Bert had laid out on an enamel tray. 'It could be a bit awkward, her being the boss, as it were.'

'They seem to have managed all right so far. And half a pound of pigs' fry for today, Bert, please. It's where they're going to live that could be a problem, with her having the schoolhouse and him just bought that cottage. I suppose he could move in with her and let it till they both retire.'

'Well, at least they won't be having a family!' Mabel said, and the little group laughed. 'I tell you what, there's been so many weddings in the village lately there'll be nobody left single soon. Why don't you and Edie tie the knot, Bert? You're round her place half the time as it is.'

'And that's how it's going to stay,' Bert said tersely, weighing up the pigs' liver and wrapping it in greaseproof paper. 'Me and Edie are just friends, as well you know, and 'tis none of your business how we arrange our lives.' He handed two parcels of meat over the counter. 'That'll be six and threepence-ha'penny, Aggie.'

Brenda Culliford came in, carrying her mother's shopping bag, and the other customers forgot the two schoolteachers and turned to her as a source of other interesting information.

'So how be things up at the Barton now?' Aggie enquired, pausing on her way out. 'I dare say it seems a bit different now, with the new doctor living there. Makes a bit more work for you and Mrs Curnow.'

'Not that much,' Brenda said, taking her place at the end of the queue. 'There's more washing, of course, but with Mr Stephen and Maddy away again it don't really make much difference. And Miss Hilary – Mrs Napier Hunter, I mean – and Mrs Curnow are teaching me to cook. I'm doing

Sunday dinner at home tomorrow,' she added proudly.

'Well, I bet your mum's pleased about that. Doing a proper roast, are you?'

Brenda nodded. 'A half shoulder of lamb, if Mr Foster's got one. Now Dad's got regular work and our Jimmy's doing his apprenticeship, Mother says we can stretch to that once in a while, and I'm going to make a shepherd's pie with the leftovers.'

Mabel, having bought her lamb chops, joined Aggie Madge outside and they made their way into Edie Pettifer's general store. Here, they found Jacob Prout stocking up on tobacco and Ivy Sweet buying the few staples, such as tea and cocoa, that she couldn't take from the stores George used for his baking.

'I'll have a couple of ounces of liquorice toffees for George too,' she said, putting her purchases into her basket. 'And a Mars bar for Barry, if you please.' She glanced round as Mabel and Aggie entered and added rather loudly, 'I don't know if I mentioned it, but we're getting a television set at the weekend. Bert's got one, hasn't he, Edie? How d'you like it?'

'Some of it's all right,' Edie said, weighing out the toffees and tipping them into a white paper bag. 'Jeanie and Jessie Friend got one for their Billy, to see the cowboy films. He likes Roy Rogers and Hopalong Cassidy. They put football on too, and boxing. And there's a serial about a family, called *The Groves*. It's about ordinary people.'

Jacob Prout stared at her. 'Ordinary people? People like us, you mean?'

'That's right. Just ordinary families, in a town.'

146

'But what's the story about? I mean, people like us don't have interesting things happen, not like in the Wild West of America, with cowboys and such. I can't see how they can make a television serial about ordinary people.'

'Well, they do and I quite like it. It's like *The Archers*, on the wireless. You get interested in the folk and want to know what's happening to them. And I don't know what you mean about not having interesting things happen to us, Jacob. Seems to me there's never a dull moment in Burracombe.'

'What, the church organ breaking down and two teachers in their fifties getting married?' he retorted scornfully, pocketing his tobacco and turning to leave. 'I wouldn't have thought that would make much of a television serial. I tell you what, if that's all they can find to entertain folk, it'll all fizzle out in a year or two. I always did say it wouldn't be worth a row of beans once the Coronation was over.'

'Jacob Prout's getting more and more cantankerous as he gets older,' Mabel observed. 'Don't you take no notice of him, Ivy. We're thinking of getting a television set too, as it happens. We thought we'd go into Beckerleg's on Saturday – might see you there.'

'Looks like everyone in the village will have one soon,' Aggie said. 'I suppose that means we'll see those ugly aerial things on all the roofs. I've seen them in Tavistock, sprouting up beside the chimneys. Spoil the outlook, they do.'

'Well, you can't have it without them. The picture won't come in.' Edie had finished serving

147

Ivy and stood behind her counter, her hands on her hips. 'And talking of coming in, I suppose you all came in here to buy something I do sell, not just for a discussion about televisions that I don't. Or do you want me to put out chairs and serve you all a nice cup of tea while you have a chat?'

Ivy smirked and the other two women laughed. Aggie dumped her basket on the counter and took out a scrap of paper. 'Well, since you mention it, there were one or two bits and pieces. I've got a list here – got holidaymakers coming in for a few nights.'

'And I'd better be going,' Ivy said. 'I've got a lot to do at home before I go to the Bell for twelve o'clock opening. Bernie and Rose seem satisfied with my work so they've took me on permanent now.' She went out, and the doorbell tinkled behind her.

'Well, fancy that!' Aggie said. 'I never thought she'd last more than five minutes, did you? Mind you, she do seem to have cheered up a bit lately. She didn't make one nasty remark all the time she was here just now.'

'She knows better than to try, in my shop,' Edie said, weighing out sugar and pouring it into a cone of blue paper. 'She knows I'll ban her if she starts anything. But Bert says she's different behind the bar, much more friendly. Maybe that's because it's mostly men who go in the pub.' She twisted the end of the cone to seal it. 'Anyway. I'd rather not have gossip in here, not even about Ivy Sweet, if you don't mind. Is that all you want, Aggie?'

'I'll take half a pound of tea as well,' Aggie said, a little tightly. 'All I was saying was she seemed a bit happier in herself just lately. I don't know how that can be taken as gossip, any more than your remark about her and men. Anyway, I don't have time to stand around – like I said, I've got visitors coming and they've asked for evening meals as well as breakfast, and there are the beds to make up as well.' She paid for her groceries, put them in her basket, and hurried out.

October was late in the year for holidaymakers but there were still a few about, mostly older people who preferred the quieter times and enjoyed the simple pleasures of walking on Dartmoor or exploring the towns and villages of the area. However, the couple who were arriving that day were quite young. They arrived in a small car and drew up outside Aggie's cottage just after four o'clock that afternoon. Aggie welcomed them in and sat them down in the parlour with a tray of tea and a plate of scones liberally spread with strawberry jam and cream.

''Tis my own jam, made back in the summer, and the cream's from Tozers' farm at the other end of the village. And how do you like your tea, my dears?'

'Strong, with sugar, please,' the woman said. She was small and dark, with short, curly hair, and looked somewhere between twenty-five and thirty. She spoke with an accent Aggie didn't recognise but thought might be American, although she didn't sound like Joe Tozer, who had acquired an American accent through having lived there for so long. Perhaps it was Cockney, or somewhere else in England – Norfolk, or maybe Northumberland. They did say if you put a Geordie and a Cornishman in a room together they'd each think the other was talking a foreign language, and Aggie didn't suppose it was so very much different for a Devonshire maid like herself.

The young man, who looked a year or two older, asked for his tea to be strong too. Aggie poured, wondering if they really were brother and sister, as they'd told her. Even though they'd asked for separate bedrooms, you never really knew, and you had to be so careful when you took in strangers. She didn't want anything untoward going on in her cottage.

'So what brought you to Burracombe for your holiday?' she enquired. 'It's not that we don't get a few visitors, mostly in the season, but we do be a bit off the beaten track.'

'We've come to find out about our family,' the girl said, stirring her tea. 'We think they lived here years ago. Maybe some of them still do. Our grandfather was born in Devon, you see. He left – oh, years and years ago, back in the 1880s. He never talked about the family much so we don't know a lot, but when he died, Mum found some old letters and a few really old photographs, and the name Burracombe was on some of them. And there was an old postcard, with a picture of the village street and a green just like the one here, and a church. Look – I'll show you.' She took an envelope out of her handbag and drew out a bundle of papers. Sorting through them, she extracted a worn postcard, spotted with brown freckles, with a faded sepia photograph on it. She handed it to Aggie, who peered at it and then turned to take her spectacles from the mantelpiece for a better look.

'Why yes,' she said. 'That do look like Burracombe might have been, back – when was this, do you reckon? Years ago, before even the First World War, I should think, looking at those cottages and the clothes those little tackers are wearing. And that do look like our church.' She handed the postcard back. 'So where did your grandad go when he left here? And what was his name?'

The girl smiled. 'Don't you recognise our accents? We're Australians! Grandfather went to Perth, in Western Australia, and made his life there. And his name was Bellamy.'

Chapter Fourteen

It was time at last for Ted and Alice to carry their suitcases out to Joe's car and leave for Southampton to start their journey to America. Joe and Dottie were to go with them as far as the dock and wave them on their way, and after that they would be on their own.

'I wish you were coming too,' Alice fretted as she stared up at the huge ship. 'I've never been on anything bigger than the Torpoint ferry! It must be like a maze in all those passageways. I'm sure we'll get lost.'

'You'll soon find your way about,' Dottie said comfortingly. 'There's plenty of signs and notices, and the stewards are ever so helpful. You'll enjoy it, Alice.'

'I don't know about that. I might be seasick all

the way over. And how will we know what to do when we get there?'

'You won't have any problems at all,' Joe said firmly. 'They'll make sure you know what to do and where to go, and Russ will meet you and take you to Corning. And don't forget why you're going – when you get to Corning, you'll see Jackie. Elaine says she'll be out of hospital and home by the time you get there.'

Alice nodded but looked unconvinced. They were being waved onto the gangplank now, and she burst into tears and threw herself into Dottie's arms. The two women hugged and Joe and Ted shook hands.

'You will keep an eye on things at the farm, won't you?' Ted asked. 'Tom's got his head pretty well screwed on, but 'tis a young head just the same and even though you've been away from the farm most of your life, you might still be able to keep him in check if he looks like getting ideas. He's been worrying me a bit lately with his talk of modern farming.'

Joe grinned. 'I'll do my best, Ted, but you ought to take advantage of your trip to see what's happening over there. There's plenty of farming country round Corning and Russ'll be glad to take you about to have a look.'

'Come on, Ted,' Alice begged. 'They want us aboard. We don't want to be left behind at this stage.' She dragged him away and they started up the gangplank, turning at the top to look down. Alice looked petrified and Ted's face was rigid. Joe and Dottie waved encouragingly and Joe laughed.

'They look as if they're going to the guillotine. Poor old Ted – he's trying so hard to look as if this is something he does every day, and Alice looks scared stiff.'

'You've forgotten what it's like to go so far from home to a place you don't know,' Dottie said, taking his arm. 'I felt much the same when I went, but at least I had you to show me what to do. They've got nobody. It's a pity we couldn't go as well.'

'I know.' He patted her hand. 'But Ted seemed to feel easier if I was here, though goodness knows why, and Dr Latimer thought it would be best for you to stay quietly in Burracombe for a bit longer before starting your travels. And I think he's right. We've all had a lot of excitement lately and I mean to take care of you.'

'Where have they gone?' Dottie asked, craning her neck to look up. 'I can't see them– Oh yes, there they are, standing at the railings. Wave, Joe!'

They both waved vigorously and the other couple waved back. They appeared to be shouting something but the sound of their voices was drowned by the noise of the gangways being removed, and all the other bustle of preparing the ship for casting off. And then, slowly, the gap between the ship and the jetty widened and she began to move out into the open water. Ted and Alice's faces blurred and grew smaller until it was impossible to make them out any more, and Dottie stood staring as they were borne away on their voyage to America.

'Oh, Joe,' she said tremulously, 'they've gone.' She turned to him with tears in her eyes.

'They'll be all right,' he said, putting an arm about her shoulders. 'In a few days they'll be ashore in New York and by this time next week they'll be with Jackie. Once they're there, Alice will feel a lot better.'

'I'm not so sure about that,' she said as they turned and began to walk back through the docks. 'You know what Alice is like. As soon as she's settled there and happy about Jackie, she'll start worrying about the rest of the family, at home in Burracombe!'

'Bellamy?' Minnie Tozer repeated. Aggie Madge had come up to the farm first thing next morning with the news. She moved the kettle over on the range and took the tea caddy down from its shelf. 'And you think they might be related to Miss Constance?' She looked uneasily at the village woman.

'I don't really know. Bellamy's quite a common name hereabouts after all, but I wondered if they might be. That's why I thought I'd talk to you about it, you having been Miss Constance's nursemaid, before I send 'em up to her house. I mean, I don't know nothing about them. I don't want strangers going worrying her if they're nothing to do with her family.'

'It would take more than a pair of Australians to worry Miss Constance,' Minnie said. 'Tough as old boots, she is. But all the same...' She frowned and drew in her upper lip. 'What did they tell you about what they know of the family?'

'I don't know as they do know a lot. But from what they say, their grandfather was their mother's father, so their name's not Bellamy, it's Kemble,

154

Gregory and Katherine Kemble. Want me to call them Greg and Katie, if you please.' Aggie sniffed. 'Only known me five minutes, too. Anyway, they say this grandfather of theirs left home as a young man right back before the turn of the century, sometime in the 1880s, but he don't seem to have kept up with the family in Devon at all.' She looked at Minnie. 'I didn't like to say, him being their grandad, but it struck me that maybe he went under a bit of a cloud. A lot of young men did that. Got into some sort of trouble and their families sent them out there to get rid of them. Or maybe he went to seek his fortune, as they say. Wasn't there some sort of gold rush in Australia?'

Minnie shrugged. 'I've got a vague sort of feeling there was. He was probably a miner, and nothing to do with our Bellamys at all.' She made the tea and brought it to the kitchen table. 'I'll just get the milk.' She disappeared into the outer kitchen, once used as a dairy with slate shelves to keep milk, butter and cheese cool, and returned to pour the tea. 'Have one of these ginger biscuits, Aggie. Our Joanna made them.'

'I will, if you don't mind me dipping them in my tea. My teeth aren't what they were.'

'Mine are the same.' They each took a biscuit and dunked it, silent for a few minutes. Then Aggie said slowly, 'Weren't there some kind of scandal in Miss Constance's family, backalong? It was before I was born but I remember my mother talking about it with my aunties. They used to talk about all sorts of things, thinking I wasn't listening, but you know what kiddies are like; they got long ears. Not that I understood

155

half of it then, mind. But you might remember it, Minnie.'

'Can't say as I do for sure,' Minnie said vaguely. 'There might have been something. An uncle, would it have been? I don't really know. There was nothing while I was working there, so if it was in the 1880s, it must have been late on. Miss Constance would have been – oh, ten or eleven – and I wasn't her nursemaid by then, I was back home, looking after my old dad.' She shrugged. 'I don't suppose it was this chap anyway. Like I said, he was probably a miner.'

Aggie took another biscuit. 'There must have been any amount went out there then, what with the mines closing down and the colonies crying out for people to go and help set up. There were sheep farmers too; they've got huge farms out there, I've heard. And the name Bellamy isn't all that uncommon. I expect you're right and it's someone quite different, not even from Burracombe...' She thought for a moment. 'Mind you, she do have those pictures. The postcard looks just like our village street as it might have been years ago. I can't help feeling there's some connection.'

They sat in silence for a minute or two. Then Aggie spoke again.

'Anyway, if I don't tell them about Miss Constance, someone else will, and then it'll look a bit funny me not having said anything. But I don't like the idea of them turning up on her doorstep without any warning. Why don't we go up and see her? Likely as not she'll remember this uncle, and know if the family ever did hear any more of him, and she'll probably be able to say straight off it couldn't have been him as was their grandad.' She finished her tea and stood up, moving over to the back door where she had hung her coat. 'What do you think, Minnie? D'you feel up to coming along with me?'

Minnie looked at her and sighed. 'I suppose we'd better. Like you say, some busybody will soon point them in her direction and it will look queer that you never mentioned her.' She got up and ferreted in the dresser drawer, taking out an old envelope and a pencil. 'I'll leave a note so no one wonders where I've gone. That's the trouble with being old, Aggie, folk think you're not fit to be let out on your own.'

The two women set off through the village, walking rather slowly, for spry as Minnie was for someone approaching ninety, she no longer strode everywhere as briskly as she had twenty years ago. As usual, they encountered a number of villagers along their way, all of whom were more than ready to stop for a chat, and it was over half an hour before finally they arrived at the Grey House, where Constance Bellamy had lived since she was born.

The gate leading through the high stone wall stood open and there was a wheelbarrow standing on the path, half full of leaves that had blown down from the oak tree that had been planted to celebrate Constance Bellamy's birth. She had obviously been doing some gardening but as there was no sign of her outside, the two women made their way round to the back door and Minnie rapped sharply with the horseshoe that served as a knocker.

Constance Bellamy flung open the door. Her weather-beaten face, always as crinkled as a walnut, was wreathed in smiles and her little black eyes glittered with excitement. Minnie, who knew her as well as she knew her own family, felt her heart sink.

'Just the people I wanted to see!' the little woman greeted them, bending to catch her dachshund as he tried to rush out into the garden. 'Come here, Rupert... I've had such a surprise this morning. Well, *you'd* know that, Mrs Madge – they're staying with you. Why ever didn't you tell them I was here? And Minnie – you'll remember all about it, won't you? You were in the village at the time. Come in, come in, both of you.'

Minnie gave her a reproving look. 'You're getting over-excited, Miss Constance,' she said in the tone she had used when she was a fourteen-year-old nursemaid and Constance her four-year-old charge. 'Calm down a bit, do, and tell us what all this is about.'

Constance laughed. 'You never forget I once had to do as you told me, Minnie! But I'm sure Mrs Madge has told you already, and that's why you've come. I've got visitors! They arrived half an hour ago.' She drew them into the house and through the kitchen to her cluttered sitting room. 'Long-lost cousins, all the way from Australia! What do you think of *that?*'

'...and so we thought we'd combine our trip to England with finding out about Grandfather,' Katie said. She had been sitting on Constance's elderly chesterfield, sipping coffee, when Minnie

158

and Aggie arrived, and she put the cup back in its saucer on the low table at once, jumping up to greet them. Once they were all settled, with tea for the new arrivals, and the dachshund snuggled against her side, she continued with her story. 'It's so strange that we know so little about him. We never even knew about Burracombe until Mum found these photos. If one of them hadn't had the name of the village on it, we might never have known where it was. And then there's the postcard, too. It really does look just how Burracombe would have been.'

'He could have just come here on holiday,' Minnie pointed out. 'Or someone could have sent it to him.'

'No, it's never been posted – see?' The Australian girl had brought the small packet of photographs with her and spread them out on the table. 'And there's no writing on it. I think he kept it because it was a picture of his village. They didn't have photographs much back then, did they – only studio ones like these others, of families. We thought some of them might jog someone's memory.' She picked one up and studied it, then looked at Constance with excitement. 'You know, this old lady here looks just like you!'

'That don't mean nothing,' Minnie said at once, as Constance took the photograph and examined it. 'Bellamys are all connected, one way or another, for miles around and there's cousins right over the other side of Tavistock who've got that look about them. It's the Bellamy nose and eyebrows – they go right through the family.'

'Still, it proves there's some local connection.

159

And his name was Bernard after all, just like Miss Bellamy's uncle, and with the postcard of the village *and* the letters...'

'What do the letters say?' Constance asked. 'They must give some clue, surely.'

'Well, not really.' The girl picked up the fragile sheets of paper with their faded handwriting. 'They're not very nice, actually. Just saying they hope he's settling down and living right, as the family would want him to, and not to think of coming home again but to make a new life – all that sort of thing. And there's no address on them. I suppose whoever wrote them didn't think it was necessary to put one on.'

'It do sound as if he left under a cloud,' Aggie observed. 'You can't help feeling sorry for him, in a way – whatever he'd done, he was out there all on his own with no family round him, and the ones back here didn't seem to want to keep in touch.'

'Yes,' Constance said thoughtfully. 'He must have been very lonely. But it doesn't sound as if he was a miner, does it? He could have been a mine captain or manager, perhaps. They must have gone as well. That's supposing he wasn't my uncle after all.'

Minnie nodded. 'Aggie was saying to me before we got here, there were any number of young men left these parts about that time. Why, I remember when I was a little maid, thousands of miners went from Devon and Cornwall, travelled all over the world, they did, looking for work. Skilled men too – started up mines in all sorts of places. "Cousin Jacks", the Cornish ones were called. And there'd have been Bellamys amongst them, for certain. Your uncle could have gone to America or South Africa, just as easy as Australia, Miss Constance.'

'Why did so many go?' Greg asked. 'It doesn't look like mining country round here.'

'My stars, the place is riddled with mines!' Aggie exclaimed. 'You can see the adits all over the moors and down in the valleys, wherever you look. There's one not far from here.' She turned to Minnie and Constance. 'Remember those boys – Alf Coker's Micky and young Henry Bennetts – taking that French tacker of the squire's down one a year or two back. Nearly killed, they were.'

'So what happened to it all? And what were they mining? Coal?'

Constance shook her head. 'Copper, mostly. In Cornwall it was tin as well. And then arsenic – they didn't think it was worth anything to start with so didn't bother with it, but when the copper started to fail they took that out as well.'

'Arsenic?' Katie exclaimed. 'But that's a poison!'

'It is, my dear, a deadly poison. But it had its value and there was plenty to be found.'

'I remember my father telling me there was enough arsenic stored on the quayside over at Morwellham Quay, on the river Tamar, at one time to kill every man, woman and child in the world,' Minnie said. 'Devon Great Consols it was, the company that used to mine there and all along the valley – you can still see the old quarries and the mine dumps, like great red scars on the hillsides above the Tamar. Nothing will ever grow there again, and nobody's allowed in now because of the arsenic still lying about everywhere. You can get it on your hands, you see, if you go digging about on the dumps.'

'It all just ran out in the end,' Constance went on. 'Devon Great Consols closed down and that was when the miners were forced to emigrate, though they'd been leaving for years before that as the copper failed. There was no life for them here, no work, nothing. Morwellham's a forgotten village now, not much more than a ruin.'

The two Australians were silent for a few moments. Then the girl said quietly, 'What a sad story. And that's why so many came to Australia and got involved in the gold rush.'

'Not that there was much gold in Western Australia,' Greg said. 'There was that huge nugget that was found, that started it off, but although there's probably plenty there if you know where to look, it's not easy to find and the bush is a terrible place to live. A lot of men died out there.'

'Still,' Katie said, it does look as if we've come to the right place. Don't you think so, Greg?'

The young man inclined his head. 'Maybe, Katie. But we shouldn't get carried away before we know a bit more.'

'That's right,' Minnie said. 'Like looking for a needle in a haystack, it would be, trying to find out who your grandad was amongst all those people.'

Katie looked disappointed. 'But all the same…'

'I think it's worth looking into,' Constance declared. 'What you say's true enough, Minnie, and Katie's grandfather might be no relation of mine at all, but the timing's about right and the name, and if there's a chance he could have been my

162

Uncle Bernard, we don't want to disregard it. What we need to do is find someone who knows how to go about finding out. And I know just who could help us.'

The Australian girl's dark eyes lit up and she turned to her brother in excitement. 'Greg, we're on the right track, I'm sure of it!'

'Who be you thinking of, Miss Constance?' Minnie asked. 'There's nobody much older than me in the village, not who's still got their memory anyway.'

'Why, Mr Warren, of course. Henry Warren. He knows all about local history – why, his wife was telling me only the other day he's writing a book about it when he's not busy in his office in Tavistock. And being a solicitor, he's bound to know how to find out something like this.'

Katie bounced up and down with excitement. 'We *are* on the right track – I know we are! Oh, Aunt Constance – do you mind if I call you that? I know that properly you're a second cousin, or something, but that's what you seem to be more like – our aunt. I hope you're as thrilled as I am. When can we go to see this man – Mr Warren, did you say? Does he live nearby? Will he really help us?'

'Nearby?' Constance said with a laugh. 'Why, bless you, he lives only a footstep away. And I'm sure he'll help you – and his wife Joyce, too. It's just the sort of thing they both enjoy.'

Minnie stood up. 'Well, it looks as if it's all going to work out very nicely for the three of you,' she said rather stiffly. 'I'll be interested to know how it turns out. And now I'd better be getting back to the farm. I'm supposed to be doing the vegetables for dinner and Dottie and Joe will be getting back from Southampton later on and wanting to tell us all about how Alice and Ted got on, setting off for America. Aggie, if you wouldn't mind walking back with me part of the way I'd be grateful. I'm feeling a bit tired all of a sudden.'

She and Aggie departed, and the girl looked after them with some concern.

'Is the old lady all right? She seemed a bit upset. Did she know your family well, Aunt Constance?'

'She knew us better than we knew ourselves. She was my nursemaid until I was eight years old. But I'm sure she's all right – she's old, you know, and gets tired easily. And there's been quite a to-do in her family lately, what with a wedding and then her son and his wife going off to America...' Constance frowned. 'All the same, I'm surprised she didn't have much to say about your grandfather. I'd have thought she'd remember him. Never mind, we'll ask her again another day. And now, my dears, let me have another look at these photos and letters and see if there isn't some other clue as to whether he could have been my uncle.' She smiled at them, her face crinkling again into a thousand tiny creases. 'And even if he wasn't, you'll have brought a bit of interest into my life. I was just thinking, with all the excitement of the weddings over, and winter coming on, it was going to seem rather dull in Burracombe.'

Chapter Fifteen

'And you mean to say these two are related to Miss Constance?' Dottie, sitting at the Tozers' kitchen table with a cup of tea and a plate of scones in front of her, shook her head in wonder. 'After all these years, they turn up out of the blue and say they're her cousins, or nephew and niece or something? What a surprise.'

'We don't know that they are,' Minnie said, pouring Joe a second cup of tea. They had spent the first half-hour after the newly-weds' arrival in talking about Ted and Alice's journey, what the ship had been like and how Alice had looked as she waved goodbye from the railings, and now Minnie had just finished telling them about the two strangers. 'It could be all pie in the sky. They might not be any relation at all. And how are we to know they're who they say they are anyway? They could have got those photos from anywhere.'

'What's the matter, Ma?' Joe asked, spreading strawberry jam on his third scone. 'You're not usually so suspicious. What do you think they're up to?'

'I'm not saying they're up to anything. I'm just saying we don't know.' Minnie moved her shoulders impatiently. 'I think we should take it with a pinch of salt, that's all.'

'Not that it's really anything to do with us,' said Joanna, who had been listening while giving the

165

children their tea. 'And Miss Bellamy's not one to have the wool pulled over her eyes. Sharp as a needle, she is. Robin, if you don't eat your fish paste sandwich, you can't have a scone.'

'Up until today, I'd have agreed with you,' Minnie said. 'But to see her this morning, as excited as a young maid because she thought these two might be related to her – well, you'd have thought Christmas had come. And why *have* they come? Why go to the trouble of coming all the way from Australia just to see an old lady? I tell you, I don't like it.'

'But from what you say, they didn't know they *were* coming to see her,' Joe pointed out. 'They were just looking in a general sort of way for anyone who might be related to this – what was his name? Bernard? They didn't know anything about Miss Bellamy until this morning.'

'That's what they *say*,' Minnie said darkly. 'But how do we know that's true? We don't know anything at all about them, who they really are, why they're here and what they want. We don't know whether to believe them or not. And until we do, I shan't feel easy about it. I shan't feel easy at all.'

There was a long silence. Robin finished his bread and fish paste at last, and Joanna allowed him to spread his own scone with jam and cream. She poured him some more milk and cut a slice of sponge cake into small cubes for Heather.

Tom came in from the yard, stamping his feet on the doormat and taking off his boots. He looked at the little group round the table.

'You all look very solemn. What's going on? Was Mother all right when she went aboard the ship?'

'Oh yes, they were both fine,' Joe said. 'It's your grandmother who's worrying now, over these visitors from Australia.'

'Oh yes, I heard about them.' Tom sat down beside Joanna and helped himself to a scone while she poured him a cup of tea. Robin stared indignantly at his father, obviously ready to complain that he hadn't had to have a fish paste sandwich first, but Joanna gave him such a stern look that he kept quiet. 'What's the problem?'

They explained and then Dottie said, 'Joanna's right, though. 'Tisn't really any of our business. I don't see what we can do about it.'

'And there's probably nothing to worry about anyway,' Joanna said, giving Heather her last cube of sponge cake. She got up to fetch a flannel to wipe the little girl's chin. 'They'll stay for a few days, find out what they can about the family, and then go back to Australia, and nothing more will be heard from them, except maybe a Christmas card. And if it makes Miss Bellamy happy to think she's got relatives she never knew about, where's the harm?'

'If that's all it comes to, nothing at all,' Minnie admitted. 'But suppose they just stir up a hornet's nest. Whatever the reason why this uncle left, it must have been one the family didn't want known in the village. Miss Constance might be upset over something she need never have found out about.' She stopped, looking down at her plate.

'Well, I can see that might happen,' Dottie agreed. 'But people left for all sorts of reasons, and it might just be that he didn't get on well with the rest of them. I don't suppose he did anything really bad, or it *would* have got known about.'

'All right, then,' Minnie said. 'Suppose it was nothing he did at all. Suppose they're not related. Suppose they're just crooks, found those photos somewhere and decided to come to Burracombe and see what they could get out of her? Suppose they're after her money?'

The others stared at her. Tom laughed.

'Grandma, you've been listening to that Paul Temple serial on the wireless! Things like that don't happen in real life. Not in Burracombe at any rate.'

'Anyway, I shouldn't think Miss Bellamy's actually rolling in money,' Joe said. 'If she is, she doesn't spend much on titivating herself up. She's still wearing the same hat and coat she had before I left Burracombe in my twenties.'

'Don't talk so ridiculous, Joe!' his mother said sharply. 'She might not throw her money about like young folk do today, but don't forget she's lived through two world wars, same as I have, and you yourself, come to that, and we know what it means to be careful. And that's a big house she lives in, and there's a lot of old silver and furniture and such come down through the family. That's probably worth a bit. I tell you one thing, if I were she, I wouldn't leave those two alone in the parlour, not for a minute I wouldn't.'

The family looked at her uneasily. Then Joe reached out and patted his mother's hand. 'I'm sorry, Mother. I didn't mean to make fun of her. She's a grand old lady, just like you are, and you're right – we ought to take care of her. She's got no one else to do it.'

Minnie's eyes misted. 'That's right, Joe. That's how I feel. Having been her nursemaid all those years ago, I feel a sort of responsibility for her. Maybe I am worrying too much – maybe these two are all they say they are and have come here out of kindness and family feeling but I still think we ought to keep an eye on things. I'd never forgive myself if they treated her wrong and we turned a blind eye and never lifted a finger to help.'

'Well, we'll do whatever we can,' Joe said. 'But didn't you say she was going to ask Mr Warren to look into the family history? He's a solicitor and he's pretty sharp – he won't let them get away with anything.'

'That's right,' Dottie agreed. 'He'll look after her. But we'll do our bit too. And there's another thing – Burracombe's always been known for being a friendly village. It seems to me we ought to give these two the benefit of the doubt until we know different. Give them a proper welcome. After all, if they do turn out to be Miss Constance's relatives and we've been acting stand-offish it won't look good and it won't please Miss Bellamy neither. And if they don't – well, we'll have nothing to reproach ourselves with anyway.'

The others thought this over and then nodded, although Minnie's agreement seemed a little less than wholehearted. 'Well, all right. But that don't mean we've got to ask them to tea or anything, mind. Just be polite if we happen to meet, that's all. And I shall be going up to see Miss Constance regular while they're here, to see for myself.'

Joe smiled. 'That's right, Mother. You do that. I

169

reckon she'll be pleased to see you and tell you all about it. You've always been good friends and it would look strange if you kept away now. Just tell me when you want to go and I'll run you up in the car. It's too far for you to keep walking there.'

'As to that,' Minnie said tartly, 'I'll do as I please. You'll have plenty to do, helping Tom on the farm. Now, how far d'you reckon Ted and Alice have got in that ship? Will they be past Land's End yet?'

Joe laughed outright. 'Good lord, I hope so! They've been at sea over twenty-four hours. They're probably out of sight of land now, out in the Atlantic.'

'Out of sight of land! Alice won't like that.'

'She must have known it would happen, Gran,' Tom said. 'And I bet she's having a whale of a time anyway. She'll be a real old salt by the time they come home and wanting to go again. Dad's going to have a hard time pinning her feet to dry land once she's seen a bit of the world.'

They all laughed and began to push back their chairs, ready to continue with their afternoon jobs. Tom went out to the yard to finish cleaning the milking parlour, Joanna took the children into their own sitting room to listen to *Children's Hour*, and Joe and Dottie set off back to Dottie's cottage. Minnie was left alone by the kitchen range.

'Don't look so worried, Granny,' Joanna said, coming back to do the washing-up. 'I'm sure they don't mean Miss Bellamy any harm, and even if they do, she's got plenty of people around to look after her. Burracombe won't let anything happen to her.'

'I hope you're right, Joanna my dear,' the old woman said fretfully. 'But I don't mind telling you, I wish they'd never come. It's going to cause trouble, mark my words, and I shall be glad when they've gone back where they came from.'

Henry Warren was in the church, practising hymns on his grand piano, when Constance arrived, flanked by the two Australians. He had left his office in Tavistock a little early so that he could practise before that evening's Rotary Club meeting and was trying to get to grips with some of the lesser-known Harvest Festival hymns for the following Wednesday. He looked up as the trio came through the south door.

'Hello, Miss Bellamy. Have you come to offer your services?'

Constance chuckled and held up her hands. 'With these knobbly old things? My piano-playing days are long over, I'm afraid. No, I came to ask your help, but I don't want to disturb you. I'll show my visitors around the church while you carry on.' She took a step, then paused and slapped her own wrist. 'Manners, Constance! I haven't even introduced you. These are Greg and Katie Kemble, from Australia, but their mother was a Bellamy before she married. Katie – Greg – this is Mr Warren.'

Henry stood up and leaned over the piano to shake hands. 'Bellamy, you say? Does that mean you're related?'

'We think we might be,' Katie said. 'All we've got are got some old photos and a few letters and a postcard, but it looks like Burracombe.'

171

'That's why we've come to ask your help,' Constance said. 'It's not much to go on but I do know I had an uncle who went to Australia about the right time. We just don't know how to go about finding out if he was Katie and Greg's grandfather.'

Henry took the music from the piano and closed the lid. 'This sounds most interesting. No, it's quite all right – I've done enough practice for this evening. Why don't you come back to the house with me, so that we can discuss it over a glass of sherry? Joyce would be delighted, I know.'

'That would be very kind, but we don't want to impose,' Constance began, but Katie, smiling up at the solicitor, broke in, 'We'd love to! We walked here, but Greg could easily run back and get the car, couldn't you, Greg?'

'There's no need for that. I live only a hundred yards or so up the lane. You can tell me about it on the way.' He shrugged his tall, thin figure into his overcoat and led the way out of the church, pausing to lock the door. 'I just have to drop the key in through Basil's front door. So which part of Australia are you from?'

'Western Australia,' Greg replied. 'We grew up in Perth.'

'It'll be lovely if we really are related to Auntie Constance,' Katie said, hugging the old woman's arm to her side. 'You see, I'm already sure I am! And I know that we'd really be second cousins, not aunt and niece, but to me she seems like an auntie. And I feel so at home in the house, it's as if I've lived there before!'

'Really?' Henry said a little bemusedly. 'But you

say you have photographs, and I expect you've heard your own relatives talk about it, so maybe–'

'Oh no! We don't know who the people are in the photos, and there are none of the house, and just the one old postcard of the village. Apart from that, we'd never seen any of it until we came here, and Mum didn't know anything at all. But you know how you get these feelings...' They were out in the lane by now and she stopped to gaze around the countryside. Dusk was falling and the moors were a distant purple shadow against a sky beginning to prickle with stars, while nearer at hand lights were glowing from cottage windows and the smell of wood smoke came from chimneys. 'I just know in my heart that this is where our grandfather lived. This is where we belong.'

There was a short silence. Then Henry cleared his throat.

'Yes. It may indeed be so, but we'll need to search the records first. You'll have to show me the documents you have and tell me all you know about your grandfather and why you think you're related to Miss Bellamy.' He turned to the little woman trotting along at his side. 'You say you had a relative who emigrated to Australia and might be the grandfather?'

'That's just the difficulty,' Constance said. 'The only one I can think of was Uncle Bernard, and Katie's grandfather's name was Bernard, so it does seem possible... But I was only a child when he left and he was never talked about after that. I'd almost forgotten him.'

'There must be family records, though. His birth certificate, obviously, and marriage certificates...

Was he single when he left, do you remember?'

Constance shrugged helplessly. 'I've no idea. I don't remember a wife – she would have been my aunt, of course – but I was very young and you know how children were brought up in those days. I was more or less confined to the nursery and looked after by Minnie Tozer. I only saw my parents and any other relatives or visitors for an hour or two each day. I wasn't all that interested in them, to tell the truth.' She paused, thinking. 'I do remember Uncle Bernard, though. He must have been quite young then – in his early twenties, I should think, although of course to me he was grown up, and therefore old. But I'm fairly sure he wasn't married.' She turned to smile at Katie. 'He was one of my favourite uncles. He used to play cricket with my older brothers and he always included me too. I was quite upset when he stopped coming to see us, I must have been nine or ten by then but nobody ever explained why.'

'Grandad always did like cricket!' Katie said, laughing. 'He talked about it all the time. He saw W. G. Grace play once, you know, at the Oval.'

'Really?' Henry asked in amazement. 'Goodness me! That was the first time he played in a Test match, against Australia. And your grandfather actually *saw* him?'

'Yes. He must have been about eighteen or twenty, I should think. It was one of the few things he told us about his life in England. But his real hero was Don Bradman. Grandad said he was even better.'

'He's the greatest batsman who ever lived,' Henry said reverentially. 'I saw him play in his last

174

Test, in 1948. That was at the Oval, too. Imagine, I might have sat in the very same seat as your grandfather!'

They had arrived at the Warrens' house now, and Henry paused to open the front door. He smiled at the little group.

'I think this is going to be a most interesting investigation. Come in and tell me all you know. I'm only sorry I never met your grandfather myself. We could have talked for hours!'

Chapter Sixteen

Ben Mallory's visit seemed to be passing off better than Val had expected. After that first afternoon when he had accompanied them to the ford, he had taken himself out on his own, up on the moors or through the woods to the charcoal burner's cottage where he sketched and painted, returning as dusk fell to eat at the kitchen table and stretch his long legs out afterwards by the fire, talking to Luke about painting and about London.

Val sat silently, sewing or mending, listening to their conversation, and looking forward to the time when she would have her husband to herself again. Occasionally, she glanced up to find Ben's dark eyes on her and looked away quickly. When she looked back, his mouth was curled with amusement and she bit her lip in annoyance.

On the last evening, as they finished their supper, Luke pushed away his plate, leaned back in his chair and said, 'I forgot to tell you, I saw Uncle Basil this morning. He asked me to drop in this evening. You two don't mind if I leave you alone for an hour or so, do you? Uncle Basil is the vicar here,' he added to Ben. 'He's my godfather – in fact, I'd never have come to Burracombe at all if it hadn't been for him, and then I'd never have found Val again. So I've a lot to thank him for.' He smiled at his wife. 'You can entertain Ben for a while, can't you?'

'Well ... yes, I suppose so.' She shot a quick look at their visitor. 'Not that Ben really needs entertaining. I expect you've got packing to do, haven't you, Ben?'

'Not much, no,' he answered, with a lazy smile. 'I only brought a few clothes and there are three or four canvases, nothing much. It won't take me more than ten minutes in the morning.'

Val looked at Luke. 'Wouldn't it be better to go tomorrow, after Ben's gone? Another day can't make any difference, surely.'

'It can, as it happens. He and Aunt Grace have got a visitor too – cousins of theirs. They want me to paint a portrait for them. They're leaving to-morrow as well, so it has to be tonight.' He gave her a small frown. 'What's the matter, Val? Anyone would think you were afraid of being left alone with Ben. He's quite civilised, you know. He's not going to attack you with a kitchen knife!'

'I know that. Don't be ridiculous, Luke. I just think it's a pity to leave him on his last evening.'

'Ben doesn't mind, do you, Ben? I'll only be gone an hour or so, anyway. Tell you what, I'll take the big jug with me and get some beer from the

Bell on the way back. You can put out some cheese and pickled onions and we'll have a party!'

'Some party,' Val commented, but she knew it was no use arguing, and she couldn't even have said what her objection was anyway. She just knew that she didn't want to be alone with Ben Mallory. He gave her an odd feeling deep in her stomach, and she would be thankful when he had gone back to London.

Luke went out just as darkness began to fall. Christopher was asleep and the cottage was quiet. Ben took Luke's chair at one side of the fire and cocked his eye at Val.

'It's all right if I sit here, isn't it? Just while the master of the house is out?'

'Don't be silly, of course it's all right.' Val sat opposite and picked up the *Radio Times*. 'Is there anything you want to listen to? *The Goon Show's* on, and there's a concert later.'

'Why don't we get your record player out? Luke says you've got some quite good country music.'

'We've got a few records,' Val said reluctantly. Getting the record player out meant records spread all over the floor and an atmosphere of intimacy she would rather avoid. 'I don't suppose there's anything there you'd like.'

'Let's have a look and see.' He grinned at her and she got up and went to the cupboard where the record player and records were kept. She lifted out the machine and Ben plugged it in and opened the lid. Val dragged out the box of records and he started to sort through them. In no time at all, just as Val had foreseen, they were spread out on the carpet and Ben was on his knees examining them.

177

'Hey, you've got some really good ones here. Look – Jim Reeves, Patsy Cline, Tennessee Ernie Ford. And some jazz – Dave Brubeck, Thelonious Monk – all the stuff I like. Why didn't we get these out before?' He sorted through the covers. 'And look at this! Bill Haley and the Comets with *Rock Around the Clock!* That's only been out a few months.'

'Well, we're not completely behind the times in Burracombe,' Val said drily. 'Luke and I went to see the film when it came to Tavistock.'

'Blackboard Jungle.' He nodded. 'I saw it too. Had people dancing in the aisles.' He sat back on his heels, beaming at her. 'We've got more in common than I thought, Val.'

'What do you mean, more than you thought?' She watched as he put on the first record and the voice of Jim Reeves filled the room.

'Well, you seemed a bit cool. I thought you probably didn't like me much.' He cocked an eye at her and grinned. 'I've heard there are people like that!'

Val felt her cheeks redden. 'That's silly. Why shouldn't I like you?'

'I have no idea. In fact, I've lain awake at night trying to puzzle it out.' His grin grew wider. 'Come on, Val, loosen up! There's nothing to be afraid of, you know.'

'I'm not afraid. I don't know what you're talking about.'

The song came to an end. Ben took the record off the turntable and slipped it back into its sleeve. He chose another one and set it spinning, lowering the needle to the grooves and then sitting back again.

'I think you're the one who's being silly,' he said quietly. 'You know perfectly well what I'm talking about.' His dark eyes met hers.

Val scrambled up from the floor. She said tightly, 'Don't talk like that.'

Ben shrugged and took another record from the pile. Val sat down in her armchair, trembling a little, and her heart gradually slowed down. She wondered how long it would be before Luke returned.

'I think it would be better if you went out for a while,' she said at last.

The record stopped and he replaced it with his next choice. The slow notes of Dave Brubeck's jazz piano sounded gently and she recognised *Stardust* – one of her and Luke's favourite songs. She looked at Ben.

'You're quite safe, you know,' he said quietly. 'Just because we're left alone for an hour or so doesn't mean I'll tear off all my clothes and attack you.'

Val felt her face burn again. 'I don't think that!'

'You're behaving like some prim little Victorian miss, terrified to be alone with a man. What I don't understand is, why? You haven't lived a sheltered life, home with Mummy and Daddy. You were in the Forces during the war – you served in Egypt. Luke told me that's where you first met. You're married to an artist, and we're not the most conventional bunch. You must be aware of that. So why the coyness? Why do you shrink away whenever I happen to touch you? What's the matter with you?'

'Nothing's the matter with me!' Val retorted furiously. 'I just don't want to be touched – not by someone I hardly know.'

'For heaven's sake, I'm not touching you on purpose! This is a small cottage, with small rooms – people can't help bumping into each other. You know something, Val? You need to grow up. I'm willing to bet you were never like this when you were in the Forces. If you were, you were the only one!'

'And what is that supposed to mean?'

'Come on, Val, you know what it was like. Men going off to the Front, girls left behind – especially out in Egypt – hot nights under the stars, parties … don't tell me you didn't get your share of it all.'

The music stopped and he lifted the needle from the record. He put it back into its sleeve and began to look through the pile again.

Val stared at him. Her face was flaming and she was breathing quickly. She clenched her hands tightly together in her lap, hardly trusting herself to speak, but at last she said in a taut, angry voice, 'Leave the records alone, Ben, please. And then I'd like you to go out. Go and meet Luke, have a drink with him in the pub, do whatever you like, but don't come back until he's here. I don't care what you think of me, I just don't want you here without him.'

Ben's eyebrows rose in amusement. He shrugged again, put back the record he had been taking out and uncoiled his long legs. Val hesitated as he stood up, uncertain of whether to rise and face him, or stay seated, looking up. Before she could make up her mind, he moved away and she found she had been holding her breath.

'OK,' he said lightly. 'Point taken. You really don't like me, do you?'

'No, not much.'

'Or maybe you're just telling yourself that. Well, I've never been one to stay where I'm not wanted. It's lucky I'm leaving tomorrow morning – that's if you can bear to have me under your roof for one more night, of course. I'll go and sleep in the other cottage if you'd rather.'

'Don't be silly. Luke would be upset if you did that.'

He nodded and gave her a slow smile. 'I expect he would. So this is to be just between the two of us, is it? You're not going to tell him I annoyed you?'

'There's no point. You won't be coming here again, after all. I don't suppose we'll ever even see each other again.'

He inclined his head. 'You may well be right. On the other hand' – he turned towards the door and picked up his jacket from the chair it had been hanging on – 'we never know what the future may bring, do we? See you later, Val.'

He went out, closing the door quietly behind him, and Val let out another long breath. She felt suddenly dizzy, as if she had been turned upside down and shaken. For a few minutes, she sat quite still, looking down at her hands, and then, slowly, she slipped out of the chair to her knees and began to pick up the scattered records.

Why do I dislike him so much? she wondered. He hasn't been unpleasant, he hasn't been rude, he's been good with Christopher, he's helped wash up ... and, anyway, he's been out a lot of the time. As a guest, he hasn't put a foot wrong.

And yet... There was something about him that seemed to scratch a nerve deep inside her. He made her feel uncomfortable, with his dark, unreadable eyes, his furrowed eyebrows, his wide mouth curling in that smile that made her shiver. When he was near, she felt as if she had been stripped of a layer of skin and the only way to ease her discomfort was to snap at him. And when she did, she knew that Luke's eyes were on her and she felt wrong-footed.

He'll be gone tomorrow, she thought with relief, putting the records and record player back in the cupboard. I'll have Luke to myself again and we can be a proper family for a couple of weeks, before Luke goes back to London. And I need never see Ben Mallory again. Never.

Ivy Sweet was behind the bar when Luke and Ben entered the Bell Inn. She served the two young men with a pint of bitter each and they took their drinks to a seat in the corner. The pub was half full and they could talk without being overheard.

'It's been good to have you here, Ben. Now you know where we are, you must come again.'

'I'm not sure Val would agree with that. She'd rather have you to herself.'

Luke laughed. 'Maybe you can persuade her to come to London with me sometimes, then. I try, but tearing her away from Burracombe is like unsticking a limpet from its rock.'

'I gathered that. Odd really, when she's been abroad during the war. You'd think a small place like Burracombe would bore her after that.'

Luke shook his head. 'Val's a home bird at heart. Her family ties are very strong. But she likes having visitors and we don't get nearly enough. You must come again, soon. I insist!'

Ivy looked at them across the bar, laughing over their drinks. She said to Rose, 'That's a good-looking young chap with Luke Ferris. I've seen him around the village a couple of times these past few days. Someone said he's staying with the Ferrises. Friend of theirs, is he?'

'Seems so.' Rose was busy polishing glasses. 'Another artist, Bernie says. They were in here the other dinner time when it was quiet and got talking. He's been down at the ford and up at the Stones quite a bit, painting. He showed Bernie one of his pictures, said it was the bridge, but Bernie couldn't make head or tail of it to start with. He said it was all a mish-mash, but that if you stared at it long enough, you could see it was water and trees, and just make out a bridge in amongst it all. He reckoned young Robin Tozer could have done a better job.'

Ivy nodded. 'Some of this modern art, as they call it, don't seem like art at all to me. Well, I don't suppose he'll come again. Once in Burracombe is enough for most London folk.'

'Are you and George thinking of going to London again?' Rose enquired. 'You had a good holiday up there a few weeks ago.'

'And once was enough. It's too busy and noisy for us. Our Barry enjoyed it, mind. We took him to the Tower, and to see Big Ben and Buckingham Palace, and we climbed all the way up to the top of St Paul's Cathedral. There's a gallery round the inside of the dome and if you stand one side and whisper something, people on the other side can hear you. My George didn't like it up there much. You look down and it's miles to the floor, and he's a not a good one for heights.'

'To hear Barry talk, you'd think he only went to the zoo,' Rose commented. 'My brother's youngest is in the same class as him at school and he says Barry never stops telling them about the elephants and the lions. Had a ride on a camel too, he says. All the tackers want to go there now.'

Ivy smiled and turned away to serve Luke with another two pints. 'Your friend seems to be enjoying himself in Burracombe.'

'I'm trying to persuade him to come again,' Luke said, handing over a florin. 'I know Val would like him to.'

Ivy took another look at Ben, noting his dark eyes, his slow smile and his long, lean body. So she might do, she thought, but you ought to be careful who you bring down from London to stay. It's easy for a young woman to be led astray by someone a bit different, and we all know what artists are like.

She let her thoughts drift back to the days of the war, when she had served in the pub in Horrabridge and many young airmen had come in from the nearby airfield. Far from their homes in Poland and Czechoslovakia, they had craved the companionship that an English inn could give them, and Ivy had spent many hours listening to their talk of home and families and the sweethearts left behind. Many of them would never see those homes, families or sweethearts again; even if they themselves survived, there would be nothing to return to once it was all over. Ivy, whose heart was more easily moved than some people supposed, had felt a deep sorrow for them and it was not surprising that she should find herself more deeply involved than she had ever intended. Only too late, when she had found her marriage and her whole way of life itself in jeopardy, had she seen the danger.

Val's position was nothing like this, of course. Yet Ivy could see parallels – the young woman, tied to her home by her baby, left alone for a week or more every month. One week – it wasn't much, yet on the few occasions Ivy had talked with Val, she had sensed her loneliness and understood the danger. And now Luke had brought Ben Mallory into the home, it was like bringing a slow-burning firework indoors and leaving it to smoulder.

Being Ivy, however, she could not put these thoughts into words and when she tried, what she said was, 'I dare say she would like it. But what we like isn't always what's good for us, nor good for other folk neither. You want to watch out, Mr Ferris. Friends like him are best left where they came from.'

Luke's eyebrows rose and he flushed with annoyance. He took the two tankards and turned away. 'I don't know what you mean by that,' he said tersely. 'But Ben happens to be a good friend of mine and I won't hear a word said against him. Especially by people who know nothing about either of us.'

He went back to the corner and Rose moved

over to stand beside Ivy. 'I heard that,' she said quietly. 'You'd better be careful, Ivy. You won't do yourself no good here by insulting our customers.'

Ivy felt her cheeks colour. 'I never insulted him! It was a friendly word, that's all, and if he chose to take it the wrong way, that's his lookout. I just feel sorry for his wife, that's all, left looking after the baby while he brings his fancy London friends down to enjoy theirselves.'

'You'd better keep your pity to yourself, then. Luke and Val Ferris are a happy young couple and don't need you putting poison in their ears. I don't want to hear no more talk like that, Ivy, or we'll be advertising for two new barmaids, not just one.'

Ivy turned away. She picked up the bowl of water they had been using to wash glasses, and carried it out to the small kitchen. As she tipped it down the sink and turned on the tap, she felt the tears burn her eyes.

It's always the same, she thought bitterly. Whatever I say comes out wrong, even when I only mean to be friendly. Sometimes I just wonder why I bother.

Chapter Seventeen

'I really called in to see if you had any news from Alice and Ted,' Hilary said, buttering one of Dottie's scones fresh from the oven. 'I didn't expect to be treated to a full Devonshire tea!'

'You should have known better than to come

up to the farm in the middle of the afternoon, then,' Joe Tozer remarked with a grin. 'Dottie thinks teatime is sacrosanct, like going to church on Christmas morning. She wouldn't feel right if we missed it.'

'Don't talk so daft,' his wife said, placing a seed cake in the middle of the kitchen table. 'It's the least I can do, to help out here while they're away. Joanna's got enough on her hands with the little ones as well as looking after the farmhouse and Alice's kitchen garden, and someone's got to keep Minnie in check and see she don't overdo it.'

'You shouldn't be overdoing it, either,' Minnie said to Dottie, passing Hilary the strawberry jam. 'It's not long since you had that stroke, and you're a married woman now and got other responsibilities.'

Joe choked over his scone and Dottie gave him a look before replying. 'I don't know what you're talking about, Minnie, unless it's darning those everlasting holes Joe keeps wearing in his socks. Anyway, when making a few scones and cakes starts to count as overdoing it, I reckon I'll be ready to go to my own Maker. Don't you take no notice, Miss Hilary. Us newly-weds have got to stick together.'

Hilary laughed. 'Quite right, Dottie! So, what news have you had? How is Jackie now, and how do Ted and Alice like America?'

'They seem to like it pretty well,' Minnie said, getting up to fetch a blue air mail letter from behind the clock on the mantelpiece. 'Alice gets on well with Joe's two girls and their husbands, and they already knew Russell, of course, from when he was over here. Mind you, reading between the lines, I get the idea she's a bit homesick. Seems to think Heather will have forgotten her already! I wrote straight back and told her not to be so daft, the little maid never stops asking when her granny will be home again.'

'And what about Jackie?'

'Well, she's home now and Alice is looking after her. Still in plaster, of course, but she's starting to get about a bit with crutches. They're hopeful she might agree to come home with them when the doctor says she can travel.'

'Do you think she will?' Hilary remembered the girl who had once been her housemaid but had always longed to stretch her wings. 'I'm not sure Jackie will ever settle in Burracombe again, or even in England.'

'I think you're right,' Joe agreed. 'If she does come back, it will only be for a visit. She's one of those who always wants to see what's round the next corner or over the brow of the hill.'

'Like you,' Dottie observed. 'Itchy feet must run in the family.'

They all laughed at that remark and the door opened to admit Joanna with the two children. Heather ran straight to Dottie and was lifted onto the little woman's lap, while Robin, who was tousled and grubby from the school playground, was marched to the kitchen sink to be washed before being allowed any tea.

'How's life at the Barton now?' Joanna asked, drying Robin's face and hands. 'Does your father like having a doctor on the premises?'

'He tries to forget that's what David is,' Hilary

said. 'You know what Dad is like about his health. He treats his heart attacks like personal affronts and any suggestion that he should take things easy as an insult. David hardly likes to say "How are you this morning?" in case Dad tells him he's there for breakfast, not a consultation!'

'He and Dottie should get together,' Joe said. 'They could have a good old moan about being wrapped in cotton wool all the time.'

'What the rest of you seem to forget,' Dottie told him, cutting the seed cake into slices, is that when folk get to a certain age, they've got a pretty good idea of what's good for them. Squire and me aren't the sort to want to spend our time sitting about watching life go by without us.' She turned to Hilary. 'And since you came here to get news, perhaps you can give us some of your own. Have you heard from Maddy this week? I had a letter last Wednesday but nothing since then.'

Hilary nodded. 'Yes, and I was going to tell you. She says Stephen is doing really well; his arm's healing more quickly than they expected, and since he's nearly at the end of his National Service he's going to be discharged as soon as he's properly fit. I'm surprised she hasn't written to tell you as well. But I only got the letter this morning, so maybe yours is on its way.'

'Oh, that is good news!' Dottie exclaimed. 'I expect mine's at the cottage now – Joe and me have been up here all day. So what are they going to do? Come back to the Barton?'

'To start with.' Hilary accepted a slice of seed cake. 'But I don't think they mean to stay. Stephen's another one who can't stay still. He'll find something to do with his life, but I don't think it will be in Burracombe.'

'And that's a pity, if you ask me,' Minnie stated as Joanna put Marmite sandwiches on the children's plates. 'Burracombe's where they belong, both of them. Where will they go, anyway? They're not still thinking of Canada, I hope.'

'I think they could be,' Hilary said. 'Steve doesn't seem to think having only one arm will change his plans about that. But we'll have to wait and see.' She bit off a piece of cake. 'And what about your news, Minnie? That's the most exciting of all!'

'My news? I don't have no other news.'

'Yes, you do, Granny,' Joanna said. 'The news about those two Australians who have come to see Miss Bellamy. Has Mr Warren found out yet if they're really related to her?'

Minnie sniffed and folded her lips together. 'Not as far as I know. He hasn't had much time yet, anyway. *They* seem to think they are. But I've told her, there's plenty of Australians would like to find a nice connection with their past, or what they think might be their past. It don't mean it's true. What I'd like to know is why they've really come and what they hope to gain from it.'

'Oh, Granny, you're not still suspicious of them, surely,' Joanna said at last. 'I must say, I thought they seemed quite nice when I met them in the post office the other day.'

'It don't matter whether they seem nice or not,' Minnie said. 'What matters is who they really are and why they're here. I've told Miss Constance she should be careful, and that's all I'm saying.'

190

She folded her lips again and sat back, looking determined.

Joanna glanced at Joe and Dottie. Joe gave her a small shrug and she turned her attention to the children again. There was a short pause and then Hilary said, 'I'd better be going. Brenda will have given Dad his tea but it's Mrs Ellis's day off and I'm cooking dinner tonight. I promised to do a lamb hotpot.'

'It's been nice to see you,' Dottie said, getting up to fetch her coat. 'And it's lovely news about Stephen. I hope they'll both be back soon and decide to stay here for a while before rushing off to the other side of the world. They'll find nothing there that's any better than what we have here.'

'I know,' Hilary agreed. 'But you know what Stephen is. Another of the wanderers. And there always have been that sort in Burracombe, after all – look at all the emigrants who went to America and Australia. Including your Joe and those two Australians here now. Or their grandfather, to be more accurate.'

'And like I've already said,' Minnie said abruptly, 'we don't know that Miss Constance's uncle had anything to do with them at all. If you ask me, it's just a tale they've made up to suit themselves and I shan't be happy all the time they're here. I hope they go back to Australia soon and never come back!'

'It was so odd,' Hilary said later to David as she took the hotpot from the oven. 'I don't think I've ever seen Minnie like that before. She's never been one to mince her words, but she doesn't usually speak out without good cause, and I really can't see what it could be.'

'If she honestly believes they're after Miss Bellamy's money, that would be a pretty good cause. It has been known, after all.'

'Yes, but it doesn't make sense. It's usually the other way about – "long-lost Australian uncle leaves fortune to family who had forgotten him" – that sort of thing. And from all that I've heard, they don't look hard up. Why would they come all the way to England on an off-chance that Constance *might* be related to them and *might* have some money to leave and *might not* have anyone else to leave it to?' She shook her head. 'It just doesn't add up. Could you get the plates out of the bottom oven while I strain the cabbage, please?'

'All right,' David said, doing as she asked. 'So that's not the reason. What's wrong with supposing that they're perfectly genuine? They've discovered their grandfather's roots and come to have a look. Why not?'

'Yes, but there's still a mystery there, isn't there? Even their own mother knew nothing about it until recently. Why didn't the grandfather ever tell his family in Australia about the family back home? Why doesn't Constance seem to know anything about her uncle, other than a vague memory? And why is Minnie so dead set against them? Don't forget, she's old enough to have remembered him – the uncle, I mean.'

Hilary loaded the dishes onto a tray and went through the kitchen door towards the dining room. David followed with the plates. Gilbert was already seated at the table and looked up as they came in.

'That smells good, Hilary. What have you been discussing so animatedly?'

'Constance Bellamy's mysterious Australian uncle,' Hilary replied, setting out the meal. 'You don't know anything about him, do you, Dad? He left some time around 1885.'

'Good lord, how ancient do you think I am? I wasn't even born then!'

'I know, but you might have heard talk. It seems as if he just vanished like a puff of smoke.' Hilary sighed. 'I suppose, if he was a black sheep, the family wouldn't talk about him much and the rest of the village would soon find other things to interest them. He'd soon be forgotten.'

'Except, perhaps, by Minnie Tozer,' David said thoughtfully. 'She may know more than she's saying. And she seems to be looking for reasons to suspect them.'

'*Looking* for reasons? Do you really think so?' Hilary paused in spooning out the hotpot and looked at him. 'But why would she do that?'

'I don't know. I don't know Minnie as well as you do. You say she's always open and not afraid to call a spade a spade, but she may know something she's not willing to talk about.' He took the plate she was holding and put it in front of Gilbert. 'Something that would upset Constance if it were known. Something that even Constance herself may not know. As you say, she was just a child at the time.'

'I suppose it's possible,' Hilary said, helping herself to cabbage. 'And Minnie wants to protect her, just as when she was Constance's nursemaid.'

'Well, she'll be disappointed in that, I'm afraid,' Gilbert remarked. 'Basil Harvey was here this afternoon and he says they've asked Henry Warren to look into it for them. So whatever this dark secret is, it's likely to come out.'

'And quite honestly,' David said, beginning to eat, 'I can't believe anyone will really think it matters, after all this time. Whatever happened, it was sixty-five years ago. Who, even in this hotbed of village gossip, is going to care tuppence about it now?'

Chapter Eighteen

Two people who were not likely to remember old scandals were Travis and Jennifer Kellaway. Neither was local to the area, Travis having come from Dorset only a few years ago and Jennifer from Plymouth. Although her parents had both lived in Burracombe she had known nothing of the village until quite recently, when she had come to try to find her father, and she still knew very little about its history.

'I just hope they're not going to be disappointed,' she said when Travis came home and told her about the two Australians. 'You can find out things you'd rather not know when you go poking about in the past.'

'Spoken with feeling!' Travis said with a smile, and put his arm round her shoulders. 'But it all turned out well for you in the end, didn't it? If you hadn't come to Burracombe you'd never have found Jacob. Or me, come to that!'

Jennifer turned her head towards him. 'I know. I was very lucky. But these two – from what you've said, they don't even know if they really are related to Miss Bellamy. And if they are, suppose they find out something that upsets her. There must be some reason why their grandfather never talked about his home.' She paused for a moment. 'Anyway, we've got more important things to discuss. I went to see Dr Latimer this afternoon.'

Travis looked at her. His eyes widened and he lifted his brows. 'And...?'

She nodded, her eyes dancing and a broad smile breaking out over her face. 'Yes! Next April, just as we thought. Oh, Travis!' She moved back into his arms. 'Another baby, when I thought we were lucky to have even one. It's like a miracle.'

'I hope you're not doubting my virility,' he said severely, and she laughed.

'Hardly! It's *my* ability I doubted. I am getting a bit old to start having babies, after all.'

'You're not old at all. Plenty of women older than you have had babies. My Aunt Ellen was forty-one when her youngest was born. Anyway, you've proved you can have them and you've proved you're a wonderful mother, as well as a wonderful wife.' He kissed her. 'And I am going to take the best care of you I can. I shall treat you like the finest porcelain!'

'I hope you won't! I just want to be treated as a perfectly normal human being doing a perfectly normal thing. You don't have to do anything special, Travis.'

'I'll be the judge of that,' he remarked. 'You do need to take care of yourself, however normal you are, and I shall make sure you do. That means a rest with your feet up every afternoon, and no clambering about in the trees sawing off branches like I caught you doing last week.'

'That branch was dangerous. It had got broken by the wind and could have fallen at any time. It could have fallen on Molly.'

'And I could have done any sawing off necessary. I mean it, Jenny. Ladders are no-go areas from now on. And so is anything else risky. I don't have to give you a list, do I?'

'No, darling,' she said meekly. 'And I promise I'll take care. I want this baby as much as you do. I won't do anything silly.'

'That's my girl.' He kissed her again. 'And I'm sorry – I haven't even said how pleased I am. I just started to lay down the law the minute you told me the news. Sweetheart, it's wonderful. You're a very, very clever wife, as well as being beautiful. What did I do to deserve you?'

'Who said you deserve me?' she asked mockingly, and then hugged him tightly, suddenly in tears. 'Oh, Travis – we're so lucky. *I'm* so lucky. I can't quite believe it.' She looked around the room, wiping the tears away with the back of her hand. 'If someone had told me a few years ago when I was living in that tiny little house in a back street in Keyham that I'd find a husband like you and a home like this in the middle of the woods near Burracombe – well, I'd have thought they were mad. And if they'd said I'd have a lovely little girl and another baby on the way –

well, I'd have *known* they were mad! But here I am. And here you are, and here's our little girl, and soon there'll be a new baby. A brother or sister for Molly.' She paused and looked at him, her eyes a little anxious. 'Do you mind which it is? I expect you'd like a boy this time, but–'

'I shan't mind at all. So long as it's healthy, what does it matter? It would be nice to have one of each but, other than that...' He steered her towards a chair. 'Now, you sit down and I'll get supper on the table. It's a casserole, isn't it? So all I have to do is get it out of the oven.'

Jennifer smiled and did as she was told. She watched as Travis laid the table, set out the plates and then fetched the casserole. Molly was in bed, fast asleep and they had the evening to themselves.

'A celebration,' he said, getting the best crystal glasses, a wedding present from the Napiers, out of the cabinet and filling them with water. 'I know you won't want a sherry or any other alcohol now, so what better than our own spring water.' He handed Jennifer a glass and raised his own, then put it to his lips. 'Here's to us ... and to our children.'

'A new baby?' Val exclaimed in delight. She jumped up from her chair and hugged her friend. 'That's marvellous. Congratulations, Jennifer.'

'It's very early days,' Jennifer said. 'I'm about ten weeks gone, Dr Latimer says, and that coincides with my dates too. We're not really telling people just yet but I had to tell someone so I thought it had better be you.'

'I won't breathe a word,' Val promised. 'Not that

that will make much difference. You know what Burracombe is – someone with sharp eyes will notice something and the next minute it'll be all over the village. But it won't be me who gives you away.'

Jennifer laughed. 'It's silly, really, to want to keep it a secret when everyone will know in a few weeks. It's not as if it's something to be ashamed of, after all. But – well, we just want to hug it to ourselves for a while. Until the first three months are well and truly over, anyway. You do hear of women losing their babies in the early weeks and it must be even worse if everyone knows about it.'

Val nodded. 'Now, you sit down here, Jen, and put your feet up while I make–'

'And that's the biggest giveaway of all!' Jennifer exclaimed. 'Suddenly treating me as if I might break. Travis is just as bad. Val, you're a nurse and you've had your own baby – you know it's not necessary. I feel as fit as a fiddle, honestly.'

Val grinned. 'You're right. It must be some sort of instinct. You do realise, of course, that it's not you we're concerned about – it's little Miss or Master Kellaway growing away inside you.'

'And just at the moment no bigger than an orange. She – or he – hasn't even started to kick yet.'

'All the same, Travis is right. It may be the most natural thing in the world but you do have to take care. A lot of important things are happening to that little orange. It's just about now it's turning into a little human being, with arms and legs. You don't want to take any risks. And I *am* going to make a cup of tea, whatever you say.'

'I won't stop you doing that,' Jennifer said. 'I seem to be thirsty all the time.' She lay back in the armchair, stretching out her legs and resting her feet on the stool Val slipped under them. 'Thanks. I've got to admit, it does feel nice. What are those other babies up to?'

Val peeped into the front room. Christopher and Molly were sitting in the middle of the carpet, earnestly and not very steadily balancing coloured plastic tumblers on top of each other. The tower fell and they screamed with delight and began to gather up the tumblers ready to start again.

'They're all right,' she said, going through to the tiny kitchen to fill the kettle. 'It's a real boon to have a room they can play in. My mother was very disapproving, of course – wanted us to have a proper parlour, like she has – a room nobody ever uses, just for show, with old, heavy furniture and speckled photographs of family members we never even knew. But we think it's a waste, especially in such a small house.'

'You are all right here, though, aren't you?' Jennifer asked a little anxiously. The cottage was really hers, left to her by the father she had only known in his last few months, and she'd been as glad to let it to Val and Luke as they had been to rent it. 'You're not thinking of moving? I know it's tiny, but–'

'Good heavens, no! We love it. Whatever made you think we might leave it? And where would we go? There are no other empty houses in Burracombe.'

'I don't know. I did wonder if you might decide to go to London after all. It can't be easy, being left on your own so much.'

'It's not that bad. It's not as if I'm left on my own for weeks or months at a time, like naval wives. And it's lovely when he comes back – except when he brings someone with him,' she added darkly.

Jennifer cocked an eye at her. 'I saw your visitor walking through the village a couple of times. He looked quite nice. Didn't you like him?'

Val shrugged. 'Not particularly. He was rather conceited, I thought. You know – God's gift to women. Not that he didn't behave like a perfect gentleman,' she added hastily, seeing Jennifer's eyebrows go up. 'I just didn't want visitors at all, to be honest. I see so little of Luke that when he is home I want him to myself.'

Jennifer frowned a little. 'But he's home for three weeks every month. You must see more of him than I do of Travis. Than most wives do of their husbands, in fact.'

'I don't. He's out nearly all the time, either sketching and painting or in the old cottage, making frames and things. He helps quite a bit with Chris, I'll give him that, but otherwise we're like ships that pass in the night.'

'Well, you mustn't be. You must make sure of time together. Keep Friday nights free, for instance. Or go out somewhere on Sundays, the three of you.' She looked rueful. 'I'm talking like the back page of a women's magazine!'

'You are, a bit. But it's sensible, I know. Just not very easy in practice. And when there's someone else hanging around the house – someone like Ben Mallory – well...'

'It's beginning to sound as if you liked him

200

better than you're prepared to admit,' Jennifer said teasingly, and Val coloured.

'Don't be ridiculous!' The kettle split the air with its sudden shriek, and she hurried to make the tea. After a moment or two she returned, still a little flushed. 'It's not that at all. He's just not my sort. And he says he'd like to come again.' She took cups and saucers from the cupboard by the fireplace. 'I really don't want him to, but what can I say? Luke thinks the world of him.'

'Well, perhaps Luke's right and you're wrong. Why not let him come? You might like him better as you get to know him more.'

Val didn't answer, and after a moment or two, Jennifer said, 'What's the latest about Jackie? And your mum and dad?'

'They seem to be getting on all right. We had a letter yesterday. Russ has been taking them about a bit. He's fixed up his car so that Jackie can go in it – she's still in plaster – and they've been going to look at the autumn colours. Mum says they're almost unbelievable. She says we think our autumn colours are lovely, but these almost make your eyes ache! Beautiful deep reds and golden browns. A lot of them are sugar maples and apparently they're the best of all. Luke's quite envious – says he'd like to go and paint them.'

'Goodness me,' Jennifer said. 'So do you think you'll all be off to America soon?'

'Not much chance of that. It costs far too much. I know Luke's doing quite well now, but we can't afford to go throwing money about. That's the trouble with painting, you never know when people will stop wanting your pictures. It's not like a permanent job.'

There was a scream from the next room and a howl that brought both women to their feet. Val hurried through the door and returned a minute later with a crying Molly in her arms. She was scolding Christopher at the same time.

'That was very naughty, Chris! You know you mustn't hit people and it's even worse when you hit them with a brick. Look at poor Molly's arm. She's going to have a bruise there.'

'Molly bit me!' he yelled back, his face red with temper. 'They're my bricks! Mine!'

'Six of one and half a dozen of the other by the look of it,' Jennifer said, taking Molly. 'Did you really bite him, you naughty girl? How would you like me to bite you, to show you what it feels like?' She pretended to bite and the little girl squealed and squirmed away. 'You see, you don't like it, do you?'

It took several minutes to pacify the two combatants and when they were quiet at last, their faces buried in mugs of orange squash, Val looked at Jennifer and grinned.

'Are you still sure you want two?' she asked. 'Now you've seen what little monsters they can be?'

'I'm beginning to wonder!' Jennifer said. 'But it's too late now. The deed's been done and there's no going back!'

Chapter Nineteen

The last Saturday in October was, by tradition, the day of the Deanery Ringing Festival, when all the churches with bells in the Tavistock Deanery were open for ringing at any time, without having to make a previous arrangement. The ringers treated it as a day out, travelling to as many as possible to ring the bells. They all came together at the 'host' tower to attend the service and enjoy a hearty tea – usually pasties and sandwiches, followed by an array of cakes, biscuits, cream and jam scones provided by the ringers' wives. Ringers' teas had a reputation for being the finest to be found and Burracombe, host tower for this year, had always taken pride in providing the best of all.

'I don't know why it always has to be the ringers' wives, mind you,' Joanna observed as she, Dottie and Minnie laboured over sandwiches and scones. 'And why can't the women be ringers too? Tom says there are some in Plymouth. There's even a Ladies' Guild.'

'It's probably different in towns,' Minnie said, buttering slices of bread. 'They do that scientific ringing there too, I don't doubt, like Travis Kellaway's teaching those boys.'

'I don't see what difference that would make. Method ringing doesn't make the bells any lighter. Anyway, if women can do it in other places I don't see why they can't here.'

Minnie stared at her. 'You're surely not thinking of taking it up yourself, maid?'

'Why not? We've already got three ringers in the family, now that Uncle Joe's started again, and Robin's going to want to learn when he's a bit older. Why shouldn't Heather too, if she wants to? And why shouldn't I?'

'I'd have thought you had enough to do already,' Minnie said with some asperity. 'And 'tis not fitting, to my mind, for a woman to be standing in a roomful of men, pulling on ropes and stretching up, showing off her body. And suppose the rope gets caught up in your skirt? And I can tell you this, there's places round here, not a million miles away, where they won't countenance women ringers, not even as visitors. Lamerton, for one. Our Ted will tell you that. There may be women ringers, he said once, but there're no ladies.'

Joanna dug her spoon into a pot of strawberry jam and splashed a dollop onto a scone. 'Well, this isn't Lamerton and Travis says he doesn't see anything against it. Where he comes from—'

'You mean you've asked him already? While Ted's away? He's still captain, don't you forget.'

'He doesn't have anything to do with the method practices. Travis does those and he can teach whoever he likes.'

'Not if Ted says he can't, and if he don't want women learning to ring in Burracombe, that's an end to it. And I'd have thought you'd have a bit more respect for your father-in-law than to go behind his back like that. I'm disappointed in you, Joanna. I really am.'

Joanna stared at the old lady. She felt her face

204

flush and her eyes redden with tears. Shakily, she put down her spoon and turned towards the door.

'I'd better go and see what the children are doing. Robin's supposed to be feeding the hens but you know what he's like.' She opened the door and blundered through, pulling it shut behind her.

There was a short silence in the kitchen as the two older women went on making sandwiches. At last Minnie said, 'It's not that I meant to upset her, Dottie. But with Ted away, she and Tom seem to be taking matters too much into their own hands. Taking up bell ringing, at her age! 'Tis just silly.'

Dottie stole a cautious look at her. 'Not all ringers learn when they're young. Over in Little Burracombe they've got a few who didn't start till they were older than Joanna. They lost three in the war, if you remember, and had to get a team going from scratch.'

'None of them's a woman, though.' Minnie finished her buttering and began to spread mustard on some of the slices before adding ham and building a pile of sandwich rounds. 'And I don't care what anyone says, it don't seem fitting to me.' She looked at Dottie and there was distress in her eyes. 'I tell you what it is, there's too many changes going on lately in Burracombe. Our Ted and Alice off to America, everyone chopping and changing in different ways, and now strangers coming in and upsetting us all. I don't like it. It's all going to lead to trouble, mark my words.' She picked up a bread knife and began to cut fiercely into her tower of sandwiches.

Dottie laid a hand on her arm. 'Minnie, stop doing that for a minute. We've got plenty of time.

Tell me what's really bothering you. All these changes you talk about – they're good ones. Hilary and David Hunter getting married. Me and your Joe – unless you don't think that's a good one after all! And, who knows, but Ted and Alice might bring Jackie back with them. So what's really upsetting you? It can't be Joanna wanting to learn bell ringing. Is it these two Australians?'

Minnie laid down her knife and sighed.

'I don't like it, Dottie. I don't know why they had to come here at all, digging up old stories that are best left buried. What are they after? It must be her money.'

'Well, would that be so bad? She don't have any other family to leave it to, and if finding some nice young relatives gives her a bit of happiness in her old age, why shouldn't she leave it to them? Blood's thicker than water, Minnie.'

'I know, but *are* they her relatives? That's what I want to know. And suppose one day she does leave them everything – the house and all. What will they do with it? They won't want to live in it.'

'Sell it, I suppose, same as whoever else she leaves it to. Minnie, you've got to stop worrying about it. Whoever Miss Bellamy leaves her money to – to a cats' home, for that matter – they can do what they like with it. And what's it got to do with us anyway?'

'Nothing, except that I've known Miss Constance ever since she was born. I used to look after her and I've always kept an eye on her in a way. I don't like to think of someone making her unhappy at this time of her life.'

Dottie looked at her carefully. There were tears

206

in Minnie's eyes and her mouth was working as if she were trying not to cry. Her wrinkled hands twisted together in her lap.

'There's more to it than that, isn't there?' she said gently. 'More than the money. And you've got no real reason to think they'd make her unhappy. Is it the man – the uncle who went away, the one who might be their grandfather? Is it something about him?'

Minnie's eyes met hers and for a moment or two, she thought the old woman might be about to tell her something. Then she turned away abruptly and picked up the knife.

'I don't want to talk about it no more,' she said. 'Whoever he was, he's in the past and should be left there. I don't hold with all this harking back. You lift up a stone and you don't know what's going to come crawling out. And that's all I'm going to say.'

Like all the other ringers who had taken part in the festival – more commonly known as Deanery Day – the Burracombe team had left as early as they could in the morning, straight after milking at the Tozer farm, and travelled a route round some of the other churches. This year, since they were the home team, they needed to be back in time to ring for the service at four, so they couldn't visit the more outlying towers like Thrushelton or Marystowe. Instead, they turned south and rang the light six bells at Bere Ferrers, where the church stood almost on the shores of the Tamar estuary, the heavier eight at Buckland Monachorum – where they also had a sandwich and a beer at the

Drake Manor Inn – and then Meavy and Sheep-stor before returning to their own village.

For Micky Coker and Henry Bennetts, now fully fledged members of the team, the day was even better than the village outing they'd been on to Ilfracombe in the summer. They had learned quickly and were both competent ringers, able to raise and lower the bells as well as ring a peal of call changes well enough for Ted Tozer to have promised them they could be part of the team for the next competition. But even better than that, in their eyes, was the style of ringing they were learning with Travis – the 'method' or 'scientific' style, which was common practice in most other parts of the country but looked on with disfavour in Devon and Cornwall where perfect striking was the aim, with the note of each bell spaced evenly, and no irregular gaps or jarring clashes.

'It's no more than a terrible jangle, that scientific ringing,' Jacob Prout had declared when Travis had first suggested that he might teach the boys. 'All over the place they be, banging and crashing into each other like a pile of saucepans being knocked to the ground. Burracombe ringers will never be able to hold up their heads again in decent ringing company if you allows that, Ted.'

But Ted had listened to Travis as he had explained method ringing, which involved the bells working to a complex pattern of sound with each ringer responsible for seeing that his own bell played its part. It could indeed sound to untrained ears like a meaningless jumble of sound – and it was certainly a lot more difficult to strike well than call changes – but once learned and struck well, it

could sound very musical, and it gave great satisfaction to the ringers.

'It'll keep the boys interested,' he had said.
'They can be learning new methods all the time.
They could easily achieve a quarter peal by this
time next year and they could go on to ring full
peals that take three hours or more, and demand
complete concentration all the way through. It
would be very good for them.' He hesitated, then
said, 'Boys like Micky and Henry are bright
youngsters but they're restless, always looking for
something to do, and you know what they say
about the Devil and idle hands. Method ringing's
not easy but they're keen to learn and it would
occupy them even between practices. They'd be a
credit to Burracombe.'

Ted had pushed out his lips. 'But you'd need a
few more to join in, surely. Three of you ain't
enough.'

'No, but some of the other younger ringers are
interested too – your own Tom, for a start.'

'Tom? He's never said nothing to me about it.'

'Well, he wouldn't, would he? Look, Ted, why
don't you let us tie the clappers so that we don't
make any noise, and practise silently? Then
nobody need be disturbed by it and by the time we
do ring out, the whole team will know what they're
doing and people will be able to hear what good
method ringing can be like. They'll enjoy it.'

'I can think of a few that won't. Jacob, for one.
He's dead set against it. And I don't want it to
spoil our call changes. Burracombe's always been
famous for its ringing round here. We don't want
to lose our reputation.'

'We won't. It won't spoil the call-change ringing at all. We'll make sure the boys understand the value of that too. And I'll talk to Jacob. He's a fair man, Ted, just like you – he won't condemn it out of hand.'

Ted wasn't so sure about Jacob but he liked to consider himself a fair man so after a bit more thought he agreed to Travis's proposal and it was arranged that every Monday evening Travis and the two boys would tie the clappers so that the bells could be swung silently, and the team would meet and practise the new style. Not that it was exactly new, Travis told them when he spent the first evening explaining the system – it had been first devised in the seventeenth century – but it had been developed since then until there were now hundreds of different methods, each with its own name, some quite simple and others too complex for any but the most advanced ringers to manage.

'We'll be starting with Grandsire,' he said. 'That's one of the oldest methods, and one of the most straightforward, so it's the one most people learn to begin with. Then we could go on to Plain Bob and Stedman. Once you've mastered all those, you should be able to learn anything you want to.'

'I'm going to ring peals,' Micky boasted. 'I'll ring the biggest bells too. I'm going to be a famous ringer.'

'I'll be even famouser,' Henry said immediately, and Travis laughed.

'It's not a competition! Don't forget, ringers are a team. They all need each other. Anyway, the first thing to do is learn Plain Hunt – it's like Grandsire but even easier – and once you've got the hang of it, we can go on to the rest. But it means a lot of hard work and you'll need to study these sheets of paper in between.' He handed out pages taken from an exercise book on which he had written out long columns of numbers. 'Take them home and we'll meet again next Monday and make a start.'

Since then, the team had practised in silence each Monday evening but by the day of the Deanery Festival they were eager to ring with the clappers untied and begged Travis to let them try.

'Us have never heard what it sounds like,' Micky said. 'We're ringing without any mistakes now. We can even do bobs and singles. It's not fair, if we're never going to hear it.'

'We could do it in one of the other towers,' Henry urged. 'Burracombe folk wouldn't hear it then so they couldn't moan about it.'

'No, but word would get back and Mr Tozer would be upset to think we'd risked Burracombe's reputation,' Travis said. 'If we're going to do it, it should be in our home tower. And I think Deanery Day would be a good opportunity to show ringers from all over the area just what Burracombe can do, and how good a touch of Grandsire Doubles can sound. We'll ring after the service, as everybody goes in to tea.'

The boys were satisfied with this and as soon as the service ended with the 'Ringers' Hymn' to the tune 'Tavistock' (composed only a few years earlier by George Grylls, himself a Tavistock ringer) and the blessing, the team scurried to the ringing chamber at the back of the church and took up their positions, their ropes in their hands.

'Look to,' Henry said. 'Treble's going. She's gone!'

The other ringers, who had heard what was about to happen, looked at each other with raised eyebrows and mistrustful expressions. They had all heard such ringing on the wireless, of course, and some admitted that it didn't sound too bad when you allowed for the ringers all being up-country folk, but they'd never expected to hear it in Burracombe. A good many of them, like Jacob, had hoped they never would.

'What the hang is that supposed to be?' Jacob himself demanded, stamping out of the church. 'You can't get your ears round it. There's no sort of music to it at all.'

'I don't know so much,' one of the Bridestowe ringers said reflectively. 'When you get used to that sort of catch, when they holds up on the handstroke, you can start to hear the rhythm. And you got to admit, they're not clashing with each other. The striking's pretty good.'

'Wouldn't win any competitions,' someone else grumbled. 'I just hope Ted Tozer don't get to hear about it. Travis Kellaway never ought to be doing it behind his back, I do know that.'

'It's not behind his back,' Norman Tozer broke in. 'Travis cleared it with Ted first. He's not the sort to go behind people's backs and you ought to know that, Alfie Doidge.'

'I just hope it don't spoil the bells,' Jacob said morosely, and Norman laughed.

'How could it do that, you daft great lummock?

Anyway, the boys have worked hard to learn it, so we could at least have the decency to listen. And to my mind, it sounds all right. Different, I'll grant you, and not up to good call-change standard, but all right. I reckon they should be allowed to ring out on their own on practice night and not have to tie those danged clappers up every Monday like they been doing.'

The ringing stopped as they all filed into the village hall for tea. The boys tied up their ropes and looked at each other.

'That sounded fine,' Henry said, and Micky nodded. 'I never thought it would sound so good.'

'You did well,' Travis told his team. 'Very well indeed. And now let's go and have our tea and see if the others think so too.'

'They're clapping!' Val said in surprise as the Burracombe team entered the hall last, looking self-conscious. 'What's all that for? Not that everyone seems pleased,' she added, seeing that some of the visiting ringers were looking down at their hands rather than putting them together, 'but a lot of them seem to have liked it. Oh well,' she went on, turning back to Joanna who was loading a tray with hot pasties for Val to carry to the long table in the village hall. 'Go on with what you were saying about Granny. Was she really upset?'

'I've never known her talk like that before,' Joanna said. 'She seemed really cross, yet all I'd done was say I wouldn't mind learning to ring. It was as if I'd said I wanted to – oh, I don't know – learn to fly an aeroplane or something. Yet women did that in the war. Women did all sorts of things then, and some still do. Why would learning to ring church bells be so terrible?'

'If you ask me,' Val said thoughtfully, 'there's something else upsetting Granny just lately. I think she's missing Mum and Dad more than she admits. It must seem very quiet at the farm without them.'

'Quiet? With Robin and Heather there? Not to mention me and Tom, and the farm hands in and out, and Dottie and Uncle Joe coming up every day to help. Honestly, Val, it's like Piccadilly Circus in that kitchen at times.'

'I know, but Mum and Dad have always been there too, and now they're thousands of miles away. We've got to remember she's ninety years old, Jo. She must wonder if she'll ever see them again.'

Joanna opened her mouth to protest, then nodded. 'You're right. I don't like to think of her not being here any more, but we have to face it – it's going to happen some time. And Granny must realise it more than we do. Perhaps that's what it is, and she's just fastening on these other worries to take her mind off the worst one.'

'I think it could be that,' Val said. 'It's like the way she's so set against the Australians. You'd think she'd be pleased that they'd come all this way to find their relations, and happy for Miss Bellamy. But, instead, she seems to have taken an instant dislike to them. It doesn't seem reasonable.' She hesitated, then said, 'I haven't liked to ask this before but – well, are there any other signs?'

'Signs of what?' Joanna asked, bewildered, and then saw the expression on Val's face and caught

214

her breath. 'You mean she could be going senile? Oh, Val, surely not! Her mind's as sharp as ever it was.'

'I know, but–' A shout from the men sitting at the table interrupted her and she said, 'I'd better take these pasties over before those men starve to death. They've only had one each so far, poor dears. I wouldn't like to see them fade away before our very eyes.'

She hurried across the hall to cheers from the ringers, and Joanna began to load another tray. Once these were gone they could start on the sandwiches and cakes. It was amazing how hungry a day's bell ringing could make a man, and how thirsty too. The big brown teapots had been filled time and time again and the other helpers were kept busy taking them round to refill the cups.

Val's question haunted her though, and she shuddered. Minnie Tozer, senile! It didn't bear thinking of. The old lady had been part of the village for almost a century and although she had come from humble beginnings, as the daughter of a farm labourer, she had married the son of the most important tenant farmer on the Burracombe estate. She and Ambrose Tozer had worked hard and their own son, Ted, had managed with the help of his wife Alice to buy the tenancy and he'd become a farmer in his own right. Not many could say that, and it was in part due to Minnie herself that he had been able to do so. Minnie had been a prominent figure in village life – one of the original members of the Women's Institute, a leading figure in the Mothers' Union, a Sunday School teacher and, even now, the only one who understood how to work out the harmonies used for the handbells that hung from the beams in the farmhouse kitchen. It was Minnie's harmonies that were rung at Christmas, when the carol singers went round the village, and at concerts and handbell festivals all over the area. It was Minnie who understood their music and knew just how it would strike most pleasantly and evocatively on the ear.

She could play the harmonium, too, the one that had been offered to the church as a temporary replacement for the organ before Henry Warren's grand piano had been brought in. Joanna, coming to the farm from Basingstoke as a wartime Land Girl, had been charmed by the Sunday evening and Christmas singing round the little instrument kept in the parlour, a miniature organ in itself. They were a common sight in Devonshire homes but she had never seen one before and loved to watch Minnie's hands move so surely over the keys while her small feet worked the pedals. It was still the essence of family life at the farm for her – the gathering of all ages, from little Heather to the old lady herself, and the simple music that they made together.

Minnie, senile? No. She couldn't be. It wasn't possible.

Val was back at her side with an empty tray and Joanna realised with a start that she was still holding the first pasty she had picked up. Hastily, she began to transfer the rest to the tray.

'Look, don't worry about what I said just now,' Val said, seeing the distress in her eyes. 'I'm sure it's nothing like that. You're right, she's as sharp as a needle and we hope she always will be. It's just – well, it can start with a change in behaviour just as much as forgetfulness. But I'm sure there's some other reason for that. It's just that she's missing Mum and Dad. That's all it is.'

'Yes, of course.' Joanna smiled at her and put the last pasty on the tray. 'That's all it is. Go on, Val – take these over and I'll start getting the cakes out. And I won't mention learning to ring again, not since it seems to upset her. We've got to look after Granny, Val. She's precious.'

'Yes,' Val said quietly, moving away. 'She is. She's very precious indeed.'

Chapter Twenty

After the Ringing Festival, the season seemed to change and wet weather set in, with heavy rain soaking the giant bonfire that had been built in the field behind the village hall and casting gloom over all the children who had been looking forward to their own firework displays on Guy Fawkes' Night. The talk amongst the adults, however, was the news that Princess Margaret had decided not to marry Group Captain Peter Townsend, and as usual opinions were divided.

'If you ask me, 'tis all the fault of the newspapers,' Dottie Tozer declared as she looked at the headlines in the village shop. 'Wouldn't leave the poor maid alone. All that prying and poking their noses into things that don't concern 'em –

enough to put anyone off, that is. I feel right sorry for her.' She had walked down to the village with Minnie, who wanted to visit Constance Bellamy, and they had called in for a bar of Constance's favourite chocolate.

'You got to remember who she is, though,' Edie Pettifer pointed out. 'She's the Queen's sister, when all's said and done, and got a position to keep up and an example to set. He's a divorced man so they wouldn't be able to get married in church. How could a royal princess get married in a registry office? I mean, can you see the Queen going to a wedding like that? It wouldn't be fitting.'

'Wouldn't be a proper wedding anyway,' Ivy Sweet chimed in, packing the last of her purchases into her shopping basket. 'The church wouldn't ever recognise it, so where would that leave any children they had?'

'I still think it's a shame,' Dottie said. 'I don't care about any of that; the poor maid's had to turn away the man she loves and nobody knows better than me what that's like.'

There was a short silence and then Ivy said, 'You're right, Dottie. She must be proper miserable now, but she's a princess and has got to put a brave face on it. I feel sorry for her too.'

She walked out and the other customers looked at each other.

'Well!' Dottie said. 'If that don't beat the band! Ivy Sweet, feeling sorry for someone other than herself. She spoke like she knew something about it too.'

'I always did say there was more in Ivy than met

the eye,' remarked Edie, who had never said anything of the sort that anyone could remember. 'Something happened to her during the war, we all guessed that, and it's not hard to figure out what it was. Soured her – not that she wasn't sour enough already, even as a girl she were always sharp tongued. But just lately she do seem to have softened up a bit.'

'Anyway,' Dottie said, returning her gaze to the front page of the *Daily Mirror*, 'whatever might have happened to Ivy Sweet, we can all see what's happened to this poor young maid. Such a pretty girl, too. Making her give up her sweetheart! Cruel, that's what I call it. I just hope it don't ruin her whole life.'

Minnie, who had been sitting silently on the chair Edie kept by the counter, spoke up. 'It'll only ruin her life if she lets it, and if folk lets it rest and don't keep harping on about it. That's what does the damage. If you've been hurt, the best thing to do is to let it heal natural without a lot of poking and prying from other folk, and that goes for broken hearts just as much as broken legs. Least said, soonest mended, that's what I've always found.'

'I dare say you're right there,' Dottie said. 'But 'tis hard for someone in the public eye like Princess Margaret. There's always someone watching and waiting for you to put a foot wrong.' She returned the newspaper to its pile. 'All I can say is, I'm glad I wasn't born a royal princess. They might have all the money a body could want and fine houses to live in, but they don't live a normal life. They don't even know what it is to walk down a village street to buy themselves a bar of chocolate. I wouldn't be one, not for all the tea in China.' She took out her purse to pay for the chocolate.

'You don't want that *Daily Mirror* then, now that you've read all the interesting bits for nothing?' Edie enquired. 'Not that it matters to me, of course. I'd give 'em away free to all my customers if I didn't have to pay for them and get up at half past five to take delivery and mark them up ready for the paper boy to take round. Why should anyone pay, after all, if they can just come in and pick one up and have a read–'

'Oh, stop it, Edie!' Dottie said, laughing, and handed over two more coppers. 'Here you are. I don't know what Joe will say when I go home with a *Daily Mirror* – he's an *Express* man, as well you know – but maybe I can give it to Alf Coker on our way past the forge, to light the fire with.'

She and Minnie left the shop and continued along the street to the Grey House. Minnie was frowning a little as they approached the high garden wall and Dottie looked at her with some concern.

'Are you feeling up to the mark, Minnie? We don't have to go if you don't feel like it.'

'Of course I'm up to the mark,' Minnie answered crossly. 'I don't know why everyone keeps asking me how I am just lately. Anyone would think I was in my dotage.'

Dottie laughed. 'You'll never be in your dotage, Minnie my dear. But you did look a bit serious just then. You're not still upset over Princess Margaret, are you?'

'Not much use me being upset over the poor maid. It won't make no difference to her, either way. In any case, I dare say she'll have more troubles than this one before she's finished. Not many people get through life without a few heartbreaks, and being royal won't alter that.'

'You're right,' Dottie said with a sigh. 'Look at what that whole family's been through just in the past few years. The dear King dying, only fifty-two years old, and Princess Elizabeth having to take over and be Queen so young, and her with two little children to look after. And she wouldn't ever have been Queen at all, if it hadn't been for her uncle abdicating because he couldn't manage without that American divorcée. At least the rest of us don't have to worry about those sorts of things in our lives.'

'It don't make our worries any easier, though,' Minnie commented. 'And what's happened to Princess Margaret's not much different from what could happen right here in Burracombe, in a way. Young women have had to give up their sweethearts all through history, whether they were lords and ladies, or just ordinary common folk like us, and it hurts just as much whoever you are.'

Dottie glanced at her, wondering if she was referring to Dottie's own history with Joe so many years ago, but she could tell nothing from the old woman's face and she decided it was best to let the matter drop. They were at the tall gates by now anyway, and she pushed one open to let Minnie go ahead into the garden.

'There!' Minnie said, stopping short with a snort of annoyance. 'They're here again, the two of them. I was hoping we might get a few minutes on our own with her.'

The French windows into the big drawing room were closed against the autumn chill of the morning, but through them could be seen the figures of Constance Bellamy and the two Australians. Dottie glanced at Minnie, whose frown had deepened.

'Would you rather come back another time? I don't think they've seen us.'

Minnie shook her head. 'I want to hear what they got to say for themselves. They've been here weeks now, Dottie, and we still don't know really what they're up to. She's all on her own, and needs her friends to look after her.'

'But Mr Warren's looking into it all. He won't let them do nothing they shouldn't.'

'That's different. He's a lawyer and has got a different way of looking at things. Anyway, they're waving, they've seen us now, so we'll have to go in.' She led the way round to the back door and pushed it open just as Katie came to let them in. To their surprise, she was wearing old clothes that she surely couldn't have brought with her and her curly hair seemed to be flecked with paint.

'It's all right,' Minnie told her. 'I've been letting myself in this door since before you were born. And I know my way to the drawing room, thank you very much, although Miss Constance don't use it all that much. She prefers to entertain her *friends* in the kitchen.'

Katie bit her lip and Dottie was afraid for a moment that she was going to cry. There's no need to be that acid, Minnie, she thought, but she knew that Minnie had taken an instant dislike to

222

these two and wasn't likely to change easily. It was a shame, because they did seem a nice, genuine pair, but as Tom had remarked when they'd discussed it at the farm, anyone could be nice when they wanted something. And it wasn't hard to figure out what these two might want.

She sighed. At least, whatever Minnie said, Mr Warren wasn't likely to let them get away with anything and Miss Bellamy was quite sharp enough to make up her own mind who she wanted to leave her money to, family or not. Not that it was anything to do with the rest of them anyway.

They came through to the drawing room and Constance looked up with a welcoming smile. 'Come in! We're just having coffee and some shortbread that Katie and Greg brought me. Katie, my dear, is there enough coffee for Minnie and Dottie? Or would you rather have tea?'

'I can make either,' the girl offered, hovering in the doorway. 'It's no trouble.'

Dottie glanced at Minnie and saw that she was about to refuse, so she said quickly, 'I think we'd like tea, if you don't mind, my dear. But we didn't really mean to stay,' she added, turning back to Miss Bellamy. 'We just looked in to see how you were.'

'As if I'd let Minnie walk all this way and not offer her a cup of tea!' Constance exclaimed. 'Now, sit down, both of you. Katie's quite at home in my kitchen now and knows her way round it better than I do. Some of those cupboards haven't been opened in months!'

Greg, who had been browsing the bookshelves when the two had entered, grinned and said,

'We've offered to do a bit of spring-cleaning while we're here, if Aunt Constance doesn't mind. May as well make ourselves useful.'

'Spring-cleaning?' Minnie said, raising her eyebrows. 'In October?'

'Well, it's spring now where we come from,' he answered with a laugh. 'Anyway, it doesn't matter what time of year it is. It's something we can do to help.'

Constance nodded. 'It's a big house and some of the rooms haven't been touched for years. The whole place needs a good clear-out.'

'So you're planning to stay in Burracombe for a bit longer then, are you?' Minnie asked as Katie came in with a tray of tea.

Constance beamed, her weathered face creasing into a mass of tiny wrinkles. 'That's what we were talking about when you arrived. Katie and Greg are going to stay here! It seems silly for them to be cramped up in Aggie Madge's cottage when I've got all this space. They're going to clear out two of the bedrooms and then move in. Just think – it's been just me and Rupert rattling about on our own for years and now the house will be properly lived in again. It's always felt rather empty.'

Minnie stared at her. 'Move in? Here, with you?' She turned to the Australians. 'But how long are you going to stay? I thought you'd just come over for a few weeks.'

Greg nodded. 'That was the original plan. You see, we never really thought we'd find any family – it was just luck that we had that picture of Burracombe and for all we knew it might have been no more than a holiday postcard. But now,

224

everything's different and we want to stay longer and really get to know Aunt Constance and Burracombe, and maybe even find out what really happened all those years ago when Grandad left.'

'Somebody must know,' Katie chimed in, placing a cup of tea on a small table beside Minnie. 'Do you take milk and sugar, Mrs Tozer?' She laughed. 'Of course, you're both Mrs Tozer, aren't you!'

'And we both take milk and sugar, thank you,' Dottie told her with a smile. She was feeling very uncomfortable about Minnie's reaction and wanted to make it up to them. 'But surely if Miss Bellamy herself doesn't know what happened, nobody will.'

'It seems it was all hushed up in the family,' Constance explained. 'As if it was something to be ashamed of. But whatever it was, I don't suppose people would take much account of it these days. There's been a lot of water under the bridge since then and people's attitudes have changed. It was probably nothing much at all.'

'It still don't mean it should all be dug up again now,' Minnie said. 'I've said it before and I'll say it again: old scandals are best left buried. You don't know what you might stir up. If your grandfather had wanted you to know, he'd have told you.'

'I can't believe it could be anything really bad,' Katie said. 'Grandad was a lovely old man. He wouldn't hurt a fly.'

'What I don't understand,' Constance said, 'is why you don't remember it yourself, Minnie. I was only a little girl, but you were a young woman at that time. There must have been some whiff of scandal, if that's what it was.'

'If there was, I don't remember it. I wasn't working for the family by then and was more interested in my own business than in worrying about other people's.'

'Perhaps Mr Warren will have something to tell us on Sunday,' Katie said. 'We're all going there for lunch. He's been looking into all sorts of family records – he even went to Somerset House when he was in London last week – so he may have found out something.' She pressed her hands together and her dark eyes flashed with excitement. 'It's all so thrilling!'

Minnie looked at her and then turned to Constance. 'But unless I'm mistaken, you still don't know for sure you're related, do you? Isn't all this a bit hasty?'

'Oh, Henry will probably confirm it,' the old lady said confidently, 'but we're all sure we are. Katie is the image of my cousin Geraldine – you remember her, Minnie, surely – and Greg uses his hands sometimes in a way that takes me right back to my Uncle Piers, the one who died in the Boer War. I don't have any doubt about it.'

Minnie was silent. Dottie saw that her hands were trembling. After a minute or so, the old woman said, 'I don't think I'll finish this tea, Miss Constance, if you don't mind. I feel a bit queer. I'd like to go home.'

There was immediate consternation. Constance Bellamy reached out in dismay and Katie came over to the old woman, who brushed her away impatiently.

'I'm all right. I just feel a bit tired, that's all, and it's stuffy in here, the room being one you don't use much in the general way.'

Greg jumped to his feet. 'I'll take you back in the car. It's just outside.'

'No, thank you. Ride through the village in a car when it's only a few steps? Dottie will see me back, won't you, Dottie?'

The Australian hovered uncertainly. 'I don't like to think of you walking all that way, not feeling very well.'

'I didn't say I didn't feel well,' Minnie retorted. 'Just a bit queer, that's all. The fresh air will do me good.'

'It's no good,' Constance told him. 'She's an obstinate old toad when the mood takes her. Dottie will look after her.'

The two women stood up and Katie rose as well. Minnie looked down at Constance.

'You just be careful,' she said, and her voice seemed to shake a little. 'Don't go stirring up no hornets' nests, and don't take everything you're told at face value.' She turned her eyes on the two young people. 'And you mind what you're doing, too. The whole of Burracombe's watching you, and don't you forget it!'

She turned and walked out of the room, her stride very purposeful for someone who had just said she was 'feeling queer', and Dottie, with an apologetic smile at the others, hurried to go with her. Katie came with them to the door.

'Are you quite sure you're all right to walk home? Greg would be very pleased to take you in the car.'

'I dare say he would,' Minnie replied tersely. 'But I'd rather walk. You get back to your spring-cleaning and your painting and decorating and never mind about me.' She marched away and when she and Dottie were outside the garden wall she turned and said bitterly, 'It seems like Miss Constance's got no time for her old friends now these two have arrived and wormed their way in. Proper got their feet under the table, if you ask me. And why this spring-cleaning, all of a sudden? What are they hoping to find – and what if they start taking stuff out? I don't suppose Miss Constance's got any idea what's in some of the rooms. I don't like it, Dottie. I don't like it one bit.'

Chapter Twenty-One

'What, again?' Val asked, staring at Luke in dismay. 'But it's not all that long since he was here before.'

'I know, but he enjoyed it so much and there were so many things he wanted to paint, and all the autumn colours will be gone soon. You know they're at their best the first couple of weeks of November. Come on, Val. He wasn't that much trouble surely. He was out a lot of the time.'

'The evenings were lighter then. It's dark by half past four now. And it's quite likely to be cold and wet most of the time. He's going to be indoors a lot more. I can't exactly lock the door against him.' I just wish I could, she thought. 'What is he going to be *doing* all that time?'

'Painting, of course. That's why he's coming. That, and because he likes being with us. Honestly, Val, he really felt part of the family. He's never had much family life, you know. He was a Barnado's boy and grew up in children's homes. Didn't he tell you that?'

'No, he didn't.' She felt guilty and resentful at the same time. 'But I'm not his mother, Luke.'

Luke laughed. 'Hardly! He's two or three years older than you. But you must know what I mean. He's lived in big houses with dormitories and common rooms and a lot of rules, like being at a boarding school but never going home for the holidays. Our rooms are small and cosy and home-like. Can't you see how different it must be?'

'Yes, I can,' she admitted. 'Stella's told me much the same thing about the way she grew up, after she and Maddy were separated during the war.' She sighed. 'All right, let him come, but I don't want it to become a regular thing. I like us to have our own family life, you and me and Kester, with nobody else here as a spare part.'

Luke looked serious. 'I wouldn't like Ben to feel he was that. I won't ask him if you don't feel you can make him welcome, Val.'

Val felt ashamed. 'Of course I'll make him welcome. Ask him to come. I'm sure it will be all right – he was very good with Kester when he was here before.'

But after Luke had returned to his painting she felt her doubts return. Ben Mallory had made her feel uncomfortable, especially when they were alone together. She thought of the last night of his previous visit and the remarks he had made –

innocent enough on the surface, perhaps, remarks that would have sounded ridiculous if she had repeated them to Luke as a reason for not wanting him to come again, yet with an undercurrent of meaning she didn't care to look into too deeply. Luke would have said she was reading too much into them, and perhaps she was. Perhaps she was too sensitive about what had happened in Egypt – look at the way she had reacted to Ivy Sweet's comments in the village shop not long ago. Perhaps I ought to be able to put it all behind me and forget it, she thought. But that would mean forgetting Johnny, too. My first baby, who died before he was born. And how could I ever forget him?

But Ben knew nothing about Johnny. Even Luke had known nothing until he had come to Burracombe, not realising that she was there. And he would never have told even his closest friend. Anything that Ben had said had been no more than a shot in the dark.

And yet he still made her feel uneasy, almost threatened. As if he were an intruder with his own plans – plans that were not to her liking.

I'm being stupid, she told herself. He's Luke's friend and he enjoys coming here. If he never had a proper family life as a child, he's bound to be a bit different, and he likes being part of our family, if only for a few days. And it *will* be only for a few days. If he comes at all after this, it will only be occasionally, and for very short visits.

I'll do my best to make him welcome, but I won't have him, or anyone else, intruding on Luke's and my life.

There was more for Val to think about than Ben's visit, however. When she walked up to the farm later that day, she discovered a buzz of excitement in the kitchen and Minnie, her old face wreathed in smiles, turned to her from the kitchen table where she was beating eggs for a sponge cake.

'You look pleased,' Val commented, dropping her bag on a chair. 'What's happened – has Tizzy had her kittens?'

'Not yet,' Joanna replied, putting Heather's coat on. 'That's it, sweetheart, second arm in. That's your left arm. The first one was your right arm. Now go out in the garden and play with Robin and Chris.' She opened the door and sent the toddler outside, then poured hot water from the kettle into the fat brown teapot to warm it and moved the kettle over to the hotplate to come to the boil. 'No, we've had a letter from your mother. They're coming home! They're sailing on Friday and they'll be in Southampton next Tuesday. And guess what – they're bringing Jackie with them!'

'My goodness.' Val sat down at the table. 'I never thought she'd agree to come. I bet she won't stay.'

'Mother didn't say, but I think she's hoping Jackie's had enough of travelling. Anyway, she'll have to stay put for a while, until her leg's properly healed. She's only just out of plaster.'

'It'll be good to have the maid home for a while anyway,' Minnie declared, folding flour and sugar gently into the beaten eggs. 'Maybe once she's here she'll decide home's best. 'Tis up to us to make her happy and comfortable so she won't want to go wandering again.'

Val doubted if that would work but she said

nothing. Jackie had had nineteen years of home life, but it hadn't stopped her wanting to see the world. A year or two in America, even with the tragedy she had just suffered, wasn't likely to change her mind.

'We're having a visitor too,' she said. 'Luke's friend Ben is coming down again next week.'

'Oh, that's nice,' Minnie said, turning the sponge mixture into two sandwich tins. 'I liked him. A very polite, pleasant young man.'

Joanna gave Val a quick look. 'You don't seem all that excited about it.'

'I'm not, to tell the truth. We don't really have room for visitors, and he was here only a few weeks ago. I don't want him to start thinking he can come any time.'

'Taking advantage, you mean,' Minnie said. 'Oh, I don't think he'll do that. He's not the sort.'

Val looked doubtful. 'How can you tell? You only saw him once, when he came up here.'

'You said he was good with Christopher, though,' Joanna reminded her. 'Well, take advantage of *him*. Use him as a babysitter and have a few evenings out on the town!'

Val laughed. 'That's an idea. A couple of nights trying to get Christopher to go to sleep should put him off. We'll have to arrange for him to come when Chris is teething.'

'And if that doesn't work, I'll bring Heather down as well,' Joanna said. 'That should do it!'

'You two, honestly!' Minnie said as they roared with laughter. 'He seemed a very nice young man to me. Devon folk are supposed to be friendly and welcoming.' She slid the two sandwich tins into the oven.

'And so we are,' Val said. 'But it doesn't mean we want to be friendly and welcoming *all* the time. Oh well, I suppose it'll be all right. He'll find himself a nice girlfriend soon and won't want to bother with us any more.'

'Anyway,' Joanna said, setting the teacups on the table, 'forget about him. I bumped into Hilary just now when I was meeting Robin from school and she told me Stephen and Maddy are coming home too. The village will be full of people!'

'Now that's *very* good news,' Minnie said. She stirred sugar into her tea and passed Val a plate of home-made ginger biscuits. 'So have they let him out permanent from the hospital or will he have to go back?'

'No, they've finished with him. He'll have to go to Plymouth hospital some time for a check-up but he's discharged from the RAF now, so really he can go wherever he likes. Hilary says she and her father want him to stay here for a while but then I expect he and Maddy will be off somewhere else. He still wants to go to Canada, apparently.'

'But that was for some sort of flying business, wasn't it?' Minnie asked. 'He won't be able to do that now.'

Val shrugged. 'I don't see why not, Gran. People do fly with only one arm. They're not like birds, who need both wings to flap!' She and Joanna began to giggle again and Minnie cast her eyes upwards.

'You're in a very funny mood today, the pair of you. Well, it seems like good news all round, and all coming at once. The squire must be happy to have his boy coming home again.'

'Stella will be pleased to have her sister back,' Joanna said. 'And Maddy will be able to get to know Stella's baby – he's Maddy's first nephew. Well, her only one, so far! I wonder if it will make her broody.'

'Oh, that reminds me,' Val said through a mouthful of ginger biscuit. 'You know Jennifer's expecting again, don't you? She and Travis kept it quiet for a while but she said they're telling people now. Some time next April, apparently.'

The other two exclaimed with pleasure at the news and by the time Val had gathered up Christopher and left to walk home through the gathering dusk, she was feeling better. As Minnie had said, Ben Mallory was a pleasant, polite young man and had really been no trouble as a visitor. Perhaps she had misread him on that last evening; perhaps she had been too sensitive and too ready to take offence. I'll be different this time, she decided as she let herself into the cottage. I'll be friendly and welcoming, like I'm supposed to be, and let him share in our family life since he's missed one of his own. Anyway, with Mum and Dad and Jackie coming home next week, I won't have much time to bother about him. He's Luke's friend, after all – so Luke can look after him!

As Joanna had foretold, Stella and Felix were delighted that Maddy and Stephen were coming home.

'It's just a shame they won't be staying here,' Stella said wistfully as they ate supper in the vicarage kitchen. 'But perhaps Colonel Napier

234

wouldn't mind if they came for a week or so. I'd love some late-night chats with Maddy, and time to do sisterly sorts of things together.'

'If you have Maddy, you'll have to have Stephen as well,' Felix observed, reaching for another potato. 'He won't let Maddy come without him, and he might want some late-night chats with her as well!'

Stella made a face at him. 'He won't want to do sisterly things, though.'

'No, that's true. You'll be safe there. What are "sisterly things", by the way?'

'Well, you should know – you've got sisters. Just – well, just being together, I suppose. Gossiping about things men aren't interested in. Taking Simon for walks and playing with him. Maddy needs to be here to get to know him properly. She's been away nearly all the time since he was born – she's pretty well a stranger to him.'

'That won't do. She's his only aunt, on your side. Yes, we must ask them to stay with us for a while at least. She needs to see him at his worst.'

'I beg your pardon?' Stella enquired haughtily. 'Simon doesn't *have* a worst.'

A howl from the nursery interrupted them before Felix could reply, and he raised his eyebrows and grinned. Stella shook her head at him and went to see what had disturbed their son. She came back carrying him in her arms.

'He's wet. It's your turn.'

Felix groaned and laid the baby on his knee while Stella went to fetch a bowl of warm water and a clean nappy. 'It always seems to be my turn.'

'That's because I have so many turns while

you're out. Here's his flannel. It's important to do things for him – it's the best way to get to know him.'

'Then Maddy must definitely come to stay, since she needs to get to know him too. She can have all my turns, if she likes. It's just a pity Stephen won't be able to take a turn as well, but I suppose we have to agree that having only one arm is a reasonable excuse.'

'I don't see why,' Stella said. 'If Stephen thinks he can fly a plane with only one hand, he can certainly learn to change nappies. And once he's seen our baby, he's going to want one of his own. He'd better learn what it's all about before he and Maddy take the plunge.'

'And that,' Felix said, swabbing the damp little bottom and pinning the fresh nappy expertly around Simon's middle, 'is something I was never taught at school. It would have been a lot more useful than some of the other things they rammed down our throats, I can tell you.' He buttoned the baby's romper suit together. 'There you are; a nice, clean, smart boy for an hour or two. By the way, darling, did I tell you I saw Patsy Pettifer this morning? She and Terry seem to have settled in very well at the farm.'

'I'm really pleased for them. Ann Shillabeer was finding it very difficult there by herself with the children since Percy was drowned. Patsy's a great help with all the paperwork and farm business, and with Arthur Culliford working there full-time with the other two men, Terry can still go on with his electrician's apprenticeship. They're nice youngsters, and ready to work hard – it's just a shame they started so badly. And Percy's accident was a tragedy.'

'I once heard a story about a Burracombe man who was crossing the river between the two villages,' Felix said thoughtfully. 'The river was in flood and he got stranded on a rock. A Little Burracombe man came by and the man called out for help, and the Little Burracombe man said, "Be you a Burracombe chap or a Little Burracombe chap?", and when the poor fellow told him he was from Burracombe, the other man walked on, saying, "Wait for a Burracombe chap to come by, then!" I don't suppose it's true,' he added hopefully.

Stella stared at him. 'What a nasty story. And I wouldn't be at all surprised if it was true. The two villages seem to have been at loggerheads since time immemorial. All the same, Burracombe people were ready enough to go and help Percy Shillabeer when he needed it, even though they were too late.'

'And even though he wasn't the nicest man in the world, he believed he lived by the Scriptures.' Felix nodded. 'He just got it all twisted up in his mind. It's a strange world we live in, but when it comes down to it, most people want to be good at heart. Even you, little man,' he addressed his son. 'Especially when you're fast asleep and not filling your nappy!'

'And you're quite sure you don't mind?' Luke asked that evening. 'Because if you really don't want him to come, I can put him off. You're right – our family life is what matters most to us.'

'But not to the exclusion of other people,' Val said. 'To be honest, Luke, I feel rather ashamed of myself. We've got so much – we always have had, with our own families and now each other and Kester – and he's had so little. You tell him he's welcome. We might even ask him for Christmas,' she added rashly, regretting the words as soon as they were out of her mouth.

Luke stared at her. 'Well, that's a turn around! And what would the family say? We always go to the farm at Christmas.'

'Well, perhaps not Christmas,' she amended. 'I wasn't thinking. New Year might be better. But we probably ought to see how this visit goes before we say anything.' She remembered the uneasiness she had felt before and wondered what she was doing. 'It's just that everyone else seemed to like him so much – Granny was saying this afternoon what a nice, polite young man he was. I thought perhaps I was just a bit out of sorts when he was here before.' She smiled at her husband. 'I'm willing to give him another chance, anyway.'

'We'll leave it at that, then, and not say anything about Christmas or New Year until after he's been here again. And it will be entirely up to you. I won't try to persuade you if you don't want him.'

Val nodded and the conversation turned to other matters. The most important topic was Alice and Ted's return with Jackie.

'There'll have to be a welcome home party, of course. We spent a good hour making plans for that and we need to consult Dottie as well.' She smiled ruefully. 'I expect half the village will get involved before we've finished.'

'They'll want all the bunting draped round, just like for the summer fair,' Luke said with a grin. 'And a brass band playing too, I wouldn't wonder. Well, the village skiffle group, anyway. Your parents have never been out of the village for more than a long weekend in the whole of their lives, and everyone's going to want to have a look at Jackie.'

'Of course they've been away for longer than that! Why, it's only a few months since they had that holiday in Perranporth. But you're right, they've never gone away all that much – farmers don't, do they – and everyone's missed them. It will be nice to give them a real welcome.'

'The village is full of homecomings at present,' Luke said. 'Your parents, Jackie, Maddy and Stephen. And those two Australians, of course – they're not coming home, exactly, but it's nearly a homecoming if it's true that their grandfather was Miss Bellamy's uncle.'

'We were talking about that this afternoon,' Val said thoughtfully. 'Granny seems really upset about them. I don't think she believes they're any relation at all. She thinks they've got some ulterior motive in coming here.'

'Like what? Fleecing the old girl of all her money? Getting her to leave them everything in her will? That's a bit far-fetched, isn't it?'

'I know it sounds it, but things like that do happen. Yet they don't seem at all hard up, so why come all this way on the off-chance? And Miss Bellamy's not that easy to persuade anyway. She's a strong-minded old lady.'

'She seems to have taken to them, though, from what I've heard.'

'Well, they do seem quite nice. I met them briefly the other day and I liked them. And there definitely was an uncle who went away in mysterious circumstances, but nobody seems to have any idea why. Granny's the one who would know but all she will say is that she wasn't working for the Bellamys at that time.'

'Perhaps she knows more than she wants to say,' Luke suggested, adding in portentous tones, 'a dark secret, entrusted to her by the family, which must never be revealed under pain of death.'

Val laughed. 'Don't be ridiculous! Whatever sort of secret would that be? No, I think she's just genuinely worried for Miss Bellamy. She thinks it's suspicious that they're making so much of her. They're moving in with her, you know.'

'What, into the Grey House?'

'Well, where else? That is where she lives. Apparently, they're planning to do a big clear-out and spring-clean, and that's another thing Granny doesn't like. She thinks they'll steal all the silver.'

'I suppose they could, at that,' Luke said thoughtfully. 'It does seem a bit reckless to give them the run of the house and permission to remove pretty well whatever they like under the guise of being "rubbish". Maybe your granny's right, Val, and we should all keep an eye on these interlopers.'

'Mr Warren will do that. He's been looking into all kinds of records and Granny said they're all going to Sunday lunch at the Warrens' house so that he can tell them what he's found out. He won't let them pull the wool over Miss Bellamy's eyes.'

'We'll leave it to him, then.' Luke stood up and gathered the supper plates together. 'And you're happy for me to invite Ben to come again at the beginning of next month?'

'Ben? Oh, yes,' Val said lightly. 'Tell him he's welcome.'

Yet even as she spoke, she was aware again of that strange feeling in the pit of her stomach at the thought of the dark-eyed artist coming into her home again. I'm being silly, she thought, turning away from her husband's glance. He's Luke's friend and I've got to make him welcome. I've got to get over this feeling I have about him. Especially as I don't really understand what it is...

Chapter Twenty-Two

Stephen and Maddy arrived in time for Sunday lunch at the Barton. Maddy was driving the little sports car that had been Stephen's pride and joy, and it was packed with luggage. Hilary, running down the Barton steps to greet them, shook her head at the mountain of suitcases Stephen was already dragging out with his right arm.

'I have never seen Maddy go anywhere without enough luggage to kit out an army. Is that all, or do you have to go back to the RAF station for another load?'

The question had been a joke but Maddy answered seriously. 'No, it's coming by carrier.' She hugged Hilary. 'Hello, darling. It's lovely to be here. Oh, David – thank you so much. Stephen shouldn't carry anything too heavy just yet. And how's Uncle Gil?' Gilbert Napier wasn't really her uncle, but she had called him that as a child when she had been adopted by Isabel Napier's best friend Fenella Forsyth, and had decided to revert to that title rather than use the term 'Father'.

'He's very well and looking forward to seeing you.' Hilary glanced back at the house. 'He'll be out any minute. Let's get all this stuff inside before it starts raining again. Did you have a good journey down?'

'Yes, not bad. I'll be pleased when Stephen can drive again, though. The doctor says there's a bit more healing to be done before he does too much. Even though he's not using the stump itself, he can pull the muscles if he's not careful.' Maddy hoisted up one of the cases and followed David, who was loaded like a pack mule, up the steps. Stephen picked up a bag too and grinned at his sister.

'It's a bore, but they say I'll be able to do almost anything eventually. I was lucky it was the left arm I lost.'

'And will you really be able to fly again?' she asked, as they went through the big front door to where Maddy was being enveloped in a giant hug by her father-in-law.

'You bet I will! I'm not giving up flying. Going into the RAF and becoming a pilot was the best thing that could happen to me. Hello, Dad. Good to see you again.'

Gilbert relinquished his daughter-in-law and

held out his hand to his son. 'Good to have you back, boy. Hope you'll stay a bit longer this time.'

'Oh, you'll soon get tired of having us cluttering up the place,' Stephen said lightly, and turned to Hilary. 'Usual room?'

She nodded. 'Brenda and Patsy spent hours in there cleaning and polishing it for you. And we've made space in the room next to it for you to put some of your stuff. Maddy will need at least four wardrobes.'

'Don't be silly,' the younger girl retorted. 'We've been living in RAF quarters, don't forget. The storage there is very sparse. Anyway, I'm sure we'll manage. Shall we take it all up now or leave some for later? It's nearly one o'clock – we don't want lunch to spoil.'

'Let's just take what we need to wash and brush up,' Stephen suggested, and Hilary nodded.

'David will do that and I'll just see to the last-minute things in the kitchen. Sherry in the drawing room in ten minutes. See you all there.'

Stephen gave her a wicked grin. 'That sounds a good idea. Just don't set fire to the kitchen in the meantime!'

'Oh, you!' said his sister, and aimed a punch at his head.

'In some ways,' Henry Warren said as the visitors sat in his drawing room gazing at the papers he had spread out on a low round table, 'I can't tell you much more than you already know.' He glanced apologetically at the two Australians. 'A lot of it is no more than confirmation of what you've already told us, but you will understand that I had to do that.'

'Oh, for sure,' the young man said. He glanced at his sister. 'We didn't expect to be taken at face value, did, we, Katie?'

She shook her dark curls. 'No, that's why we brought our birth certificates and Grandad's marriage certificate. The only thing we didn't have was his birth certificate, so we couldn't really prove he was your uncle, Aunt Constance.'

'Well, I've been to Somerset House and found a birth certificate for Constance's Uncle Bernard, which is the right date. That still doesn't prove that he was your grandfather, but all the details seem correct and, of course, his marriage certificate states his parents' names and occupations so I don't think there can be any doubt. A court of law would want to ensure that it wasn't a forgery, but I think we can discount that.'

'We certainly can!' Constance exclaimed. 'Why would anyone go to all that trouble and expense to come here on a chance that I might accept them? Why, I might have been a nasty old witch who wouldn't even let them through the door!'

Henry smiled. 'We also have the dates when your grandfather arrived in Australia, which tally with what Constance remembers of her uncle's departure. What we still don't know is why he left and what caused the apparent rift in the family.'

'There's no documentary evidence for that?' Greg asked.

'None. Nor would there be, unless a crime had been committed, and I've found no evidence for that.' He smiled at Constance. 'So I think you can rest assured that your Uncle Bernard wasn't sent away to the penal colonies as a convicted criminal!'

'He wouldn't have been, anyway,' Greg said. 'Western Australia was never a penal colony. It was settled after they stopped doing that. So we're no nearer to solving the mystery?'

'We don't seem to be. Our only hope is that there is documentary evidence of a less formal sort – letters, perhaps, or diaries. I understand you've moved into the Grey House for a while.'

'Yes,' Katie said, smiling. 'We want to help Aunt Constance clear out some of the things that have accumulated over the years, and perhaps do a bit of redecoration. Greg and I are good at that.'

'Well, you may come across something while you do that. It will be interesting to see what shows up.' He turned to Miss Bellamy. 'And you feel happy about this, Constance? You do need to be quite sure.'

'I'm perfectly sure,' the old lady declared. 'I don't need documents to know that these young people are my own flesh and blood. I'm pleased to see them and delighted to have them stay in the house. It's given me a new lease of life to have them around me.'

Katie leaned across and laid her hand on Constance's arm. 'That's a lovely thing to say,' she said quietly. 'And we're just as delighted to be here. And whatever we find – or even if we find nothing at all – we promise we won't let you down. Don't we, Greg?'

'Of course we do,' her brother said, moving closer to Constance's other side and putting his hand on her other arm so that for a moment she seemed almost captured between them. 'As you say, we're your own flesh and blood and we'll never let you down.'

'And this time next week,' Minnie said as Joanna ladled out roast potatoes, 'Ted and Alice will be here in their rightful place amongst us. I must say, I'll be glad to see them back.'

'We all will,' Dottie said. 'And me and Joe will move back properly to the cottage. I know we've been sleeping there but we've been up here and around the farm most days. It's time to get our own affairs in order.'

'I thought people only said that when they were going to die,' Tom remarked, passing Joe the carrots. 'You're not planning to pop off just yet, I hope.'

'Tom!' Joanna remonstrated. 'That's a horrible thing to say. You know very well she didn't mean that. They've got their own lives to lead, that's all. You won't have Joe to boss about on the farm once your father's back.'

'One thing we've got to do,' Joe said, ignoring Tom's grin, 'is look for somewhere bigger to live. Dottie's cottage is a cosy place but we do need a bit more space if we're to be here most of the year.'

'I don't know where you'll find it in Burracombe,' Joanna said doubtfully. 'There aren't that many bigger houses close to the middle of the village, and those that are don't often come up for sale. Nobody ever wants to move away.'

'As to that—' Minnie said, helping Robin to some more cabbage and ignoring the face he made. 'You eat that up for your great-granny, my handsome. It'll make your teeth strong.' She turned back to the others. 'I did hear as the Berrymans were looking to go over Exeter way, to be nearer their daughter.'

'The people who live in Moor View, next to the Warrens?' Tom asked. 'I hardly even know what they look like. You don't see them about the village much.'

'They only came here during the war,' Minnie said. 'Wanted to get away from Plymouth in the bombing. In fact, now I come to think about it, I got an idea their house was bombed. Anyway, I don't reckon they ever meant to stay this long and now their daughter's settled with her husband over there, they've decided to move. That's what I heard, anyway. It was only in passing.'

The family gazed at her in fascination. At last Tom said, 'If you managed to hear all that in passing, Granny, heaven knows what you'd have found out if you'd stood still a few minutes! So when is the house going up for sale?'

'I don't know that it is,' Minnie said, frowning at him. 'It's only a rumour. There might be nothing in it at all.'

Joe turned to Dottie. 'It might be worth enquiring, though. D'you reckon we could go and knock on their door and ask if they're thinking of selling up?'

'Joe! What an idea! Of course we can't do that.' She was silent for a moment or two, cutting up her meat. Then she said thoughtfully, 'Mind you, 'tis a nice enough house. Not as big as the Warrens' – we wouldn't want a place that size – but comfortable.

I used to go and see old Josiah Endacott when he lived there, before the Berrymans came. He couldn't do much for himself towards the last, poor old soul, so I used to give him a bit of a hand. It was dark and dingy then but the rooms are a good size and I dare say the Berrymans have done it up a bit.'

'We'd probably want to do more than that,' Joe said. 'Put in a couple of new bathrooms, improve the kitchen and so on. What do you think, Dot? Could you live there?'

Again, she was silent, thinking about it. Then she turned to him and said, 'I reckon I could, Joe. It would be a wrench to leave my little cottage, but I can see it's not big enough for us, not if we're to spend a good bit of time in Burracombe. I'd like to have a proper look at it first, mind. Even when I was going in to help old Josiah, I never saw it all.'

'That's fair enough,' he said. He looked around the table at the others. 'So we'd all better keep our eyes skinned and our ears open for any hint that it's going up for sale. Especially you, Mother. And I still think it'd be a good idea to approach them direct. They'd thank us for it, if it saved them an estate agent's fee.'

'Going back to next week,' Minnie said, 'we've got a party to get ready. Which day did you say you'll be fetching them back, Joe?'

'Next Wednesday. The ship docks in Southampton late Tuesday evening and they could stop aboard the ship if they want to, but they'll have to go through Customs and that, and I reckon they'll be better off staying in a hotel overnight

248

with me and Dottie. Then we can set off straight after breakfast, have a bite of lunch on the way and be here in time for tea.'

'That's perfect,' Joanna said. 'Half the village is going to be out to see them come back and they'll be more than ready for a proper Devonshire tea when they get indoors.'

'Dottie says she'll make tuffs and I'll see that there's a good bowl of clotted cream,' Minnie said. 'If you could do one of your nice Victoria sponges, Joanna, and a few sandwiches, that'll set them right till supper time, and we'll make a good hearty casserole to be ready whenever they feel like it.'

'Val and Luke will come up too,' Joanna said, 'Won't it be good to see Jackie again! I hope she'll be feeling all right after the journey. She won't be too cramped in the car, will she, Uncle Joe?'

He shook his head. 'She's out of plaster now and there's plenty of room in the front to stretch out, if we put the seat back a bit. We're going to send all the luggage separately. And I'll make sure we have two or three stops along the way, so that she's not in one position for too long.'

'Poor kid,' Tom said. 'She's had a rough time lately. We'll have to make a fuss of her, then maybe she won't be in such a hurry to leave us again.'

'And if she does,' Minnie said with a severe look at Joe, 'I hope you'll take better care of her. Letting her go jaunting off all over America with a man she hardly knew!'

'She knew him well enough to be engaged to him,' Joe protested. 'And I'd known him for years. Bryce was a decent young fellow and he thought

249

the world of Jackie. It was a tragedy for the whole of Corning when he was killed – and don't forget he'd already lost his first wife after only a couple of years' marriage. Seemed to me he and Jackie were well suited, and the motor accident wasn't his fault – that truck was coming round the bend on the wrong side of the road and too fast to stop.' He paused and looked at his mother. 'Sorry if I sound a bit sharp, Mum, but I don't like anyone saying I didn't take care of her. I'd have been happy for either of my own daughters to have married a chap like Bryce, and I can't say more than that.'

There was a short silence. Tom and Joanna glanced quickly at each other and then down at their plates. Robin, who had taken advantage of the discussion to push all his cabbage into a mound and pat it down as small as possible, placed his knife and fork on top of the heap and sat quietly, hoping that his mother would pick up the plate without noticing. Dottie looked uncomfortable, and Minnie crimped up her lips like a Cornish pasty and drew in a deep breath.

Joanna spoke quickly. 'Tom's right. We'll need to make a bit of a fuss of her after all she's been through, whatever the rights and wrongs of it all. It must have been a terrible time and she'll need her family round her.'

'And no hard feelings,' Minnie agreed, letting her breath out. 'Least said, soonest mended, as my own mother would have said. Not that you'll get away with speaking to me in that tone again, Joe Tozer. You're not too old for me to give your behind a good smack, so just watch your tongue!'

The others laughed and the awkward moment

passed. Joe reached over and patted his mother's hand.

'Sorry, Ma. I didn't mean to be cheeky. Won't do it again.'

They grinned at each other and Joanna got up and began to clear the table. She looked askance at Robin's plate and gave him a stern glance but said nothing and scraped the uneaten cabbage into the pig bin by the back door. Dottie fetched the pudding from the larder.

'Apple pie and custard. Who wants some?'

There was a chorus of yeses from the family and she began to slice the pie and put it into bowls. Minnie received hers and nodded with satisfaction.

'This is something our Jackie will have missed anyway. I doubt if they have apple pie like this in America.'

Joe let out a roar of laughter. 'No apple pie in America? Why, it's on every menu you come across. The Americans think they *invented* apple pie!'

Chapter Twenty-Three

'Well, I'll go to sea!' Ted Tozer exclaimed in astonishment as Joe drove the car into the village. 'Look at all they flags draped about all over the place. What's it all for? Is there some festival we've forgotten about?'

'Looks like a celebration of some sort,' Alice

remarked, leaning forward to peer through the window. 'What can it be, Ted? The only thing I can think of is St Andrew's Day and that's not till the end of the month.'

Joe and Dottie said nothing. Dottie, who was sitting in the back, with Ted and Alice, caught his eye in the mirror and turned quickly to look out of the window, afraid that she would laugh. Joe, straight-faced, drove past their own turning and into the middle of the village before pulling up by the great oak tree which grew on the green.

'Here, what's all this about?' Ted demanded. 'Forgotten the way home, have you?'

'And why is everyone standing around out here on a cold November afternoon?' Alice asked. 'For pity's sake, Joe, tell us what's going on. Is the Queen coming?'

'Better than that,' Joe said, chuckling. He got out of the car and pulled open the back door, then went to the front where Jackie was sitting and offered her his arm. 'Come on, everyone, out you get. This is what's known as a welcoming committee!'

'A welcoming–?' Alice began as she scrambled out, and then she stared at him. 'Joe, you don't mean to say this is all for us! Well, I never heard of anything so daft!'

Joe's roar of laughter was lost in the clamour that broke out as the villagers, some of whom were actually carrying small flags, burst into cheers. The Tozers stared in astonishment as their friends and neighbours surged towards them, beaming and chattering.

'Here you be at last! 'Tis master good to have

you back where you belong to be. We was afraid you'd decide to stop in America and turn into film stars.'

'Someone said you weren't coming back till after Christmas, and Christmas wouldn't be the same without the Tozers.'

'No, maid, you got that wrong, Ted Tozer wouldn't ever miss his Christmas bell ringing. I said to the old girl, I said, he won't ever miss that.'

'Anyway, you're here now and that's all that matters, and with young Jackie too. How be you, maid? Nearly over that nasty accident?'

'I'm getting on all right, thanks, Mrs Purdy,' Jackie said, leaning on her crutches and gazing at the throng of friendly faces and the cottages along the village street. A wave of emotion swept over her – a wild mixture of relief to be here amongst so many familiar, friendly faces, fresh grief at the thought of what she had lost and bewilderment at how quickly it all seemed to have happened. Was it really nearly two years since she had last stood here on the village green, beneath the spreading branches of the great oak, laughing and talking with Roy Pettifer and Vic Nethercott, with no idea of what lay before her? Had she really left home to go to America, stay in the little town of Corning with her Uncle Joe and her cousins, work at the glass factory and fall in love with Bryce? Or had it been all a dream and she had never left Burracombe at all? For a moment or two she felt dizzy with the strangeness of it all and then Roy himself, her first sweetheart, stepped forward and took her in his arms.

'Welcome home, Jackie,' he said quietly. 'It's

good to see you again and I'm sorry for what's happened to you.'

She looked up into his face, remembering how they had met and flirted on the little bridge with all the other young people of the village; how they had gradually drifted away, hand in hand, to walk alone along the riverbank. How they had climbed the hill to the Standing Stones and sworn always to love each other, and how frightened she had been when she had thought herself pregnant.

It had been a false alarm, but enough to scare Jackie from taking any more such risks, and she and Roy had parted. But she'd written to him when he had been sent to Korea on his National Service and for a while it had seemed that when he came home, they might draw together again. They'd both changed by the time he came back, she thought, and although they were friends now they would never be sweethearts again. All the same, she was glad to be in his arms and to know that he and Vic and the others she had grown up with were all around her, ready to be friends again.

Ted and Alice were also besieged by friends and neighbours, answering questions about America and saying that no, they hadn't seen any film stars, they'd been nowhere near Hollywood, and yes, Corning was a really nice little place, a bit like Tavistock in a way, quiet and peaceful, and folk were really friendly, but there was nowhere like Burracombe when all was said and done. 'East, west, home's best,' Alice declared, and Ted nodded.

'And now 'tis time we went home,' he said. 'It's been a long drive, Jackie, you look tired out.

Come on, my bird.' He helped her gently back into the car. 'Get the maid up to the farmhouse, Joe. She needs a cup of tea and some time to come to herself. It's all been a bit of a shock.'

Alice looked at the 'welcoming committee' that consisted of half the village and smiled rather shakily. 'It's real good of you all to take so much trouble to welcome us back, specially as we haven't been gone more than a few weeks, and we'll see you all again soon, but you can see the poor maid's worn out and needs to be home. So we'll say good afternoon to you all, and thank you for coming.'

'And that goes for me too,' Ted declared. 'When we saw all the flags we thought there was some big event we'd forgotten all about. To think you'd go to all this trouble just because the Tozers were back – well, it proper chokes me up. It does really.'

He got into the car beside Alice and Dottie. Jackie was already settled in the front seat, and Joe closed his door and started up the engine again. There was another huge cheer from the bystanders, and they moved slowly off along a path cleared for them through the small crowd.

'Well, whatever do you think of that?' Alice asked as they drove the last few hundred yards back to the farm drive. 'All those folk taking all that trouble just for us ... and I dare say you two knew about it all along,' she added, turning accusingly to her sister-in-law. 'That's why Joe passed our turning in the first place!'

'Well, of course it was,' he said smugly, grinning at Ted in the mirror. 'Been planning it all week, they have. And if you think *that* was a welcome, you just wait until you get indoors!' He drove through the gates Tom had come out to open and stopped the car in the farmyard. 'We're all as pleased as Punch to have you back, the three of you. The place hasn't been right without you.'

Alice got out and stood for a moment gazing at the farmhouse. The November sun was beginning to set now, its glow lighting the old walls with deep amber flecked with scarlet and gold. Smoke wreathed from the chimney with the scent of burning apple wood, and inside someone was lighting the lamps so that the windows sprang to life with a tawny light, each one a picture of the familiar life going on in the big kitchen. She could see Joanna, settling Heather at the table in her high chair, Robin putting away his toys, Minnie in her rocking chair by the range and Tom washing his hands at the sink.

Suddenly, there was nowhere in the world that Alice wanted to be rather than in that kitchen with her family around her. She pushed open the door and walked inside.

'I see the Tozers are back,' Gilbert Napier remarked as Basil led him through to his study. 'Saw the car turning in at the drive as I came past. Brought young Jackie with them too, I gather.'

'I don't think Alice would have come without her,' Basil said, showing him to a leather armchair. 'She's hoping that Jackie will stay this time, but I have my doubts. That young lady spread her wings when she left your employment and a little thing like a broken leg isn't going to stop her flying.'

Gilbert nodded. 'She's a bright young woman but I can't say I approve of her jaunting off to America. I know she's been staying with Joe Tozer, but he's not there now, is he – and not likely to be for some months, I gather. Didn't I hear that he and Dottie are looking to settle in Burracombe after all?'

'Not for the whole time,' Basil said, uncomfortably aware that this conversation was becoming decidedly gossipy. 'But it's true they're looking for a bigger house. Joe told me himself they're interested in Moor View – the Berrymans have decided to move nearer to their daughter. But you didn't come here to talk about the Tozers, I'm sure.'

'Indeed I didn't, though I like to take an interest in village doings. The Tozers haven't been tenant farmers for years, but their land marches with mine and they've been good neighbours. I won't forget how they took me and Constance in when we had that fire. Sat us down in their kitchen and gave us as good a Sunday dinner as I've ever had. And Ted and Alice are the backbone of the village. Salt of the earth, the whole family.'

He paused and Basil went to the cupboard and took out a bottle of whisky. He poured a measure each into two glasses, added water from the jug standing on his desk, and sat down opposite the squire, who took a sip.

'Good whisky,' he said appreciatively, apparently forgetting that he had given the bottle to Basil himself last Christmas. 'No, what I've come to talk about is the organ. How's the restoration getting on?'

'It's proceeding very well, as far as I can see. As you know, the whole thing has been taken to pieces – there are pipes everywhere in the church – but the restorer seems to know his job and he's been most industrious, working in there every day. Not the best time of year for it, I'm afraid, but we've managed to keep the church warm and dry, although I fear our heating bill is going to sky-rocket.'

'Call it part of the final cost. It's got to be done properly and a cold, damp atmosphere isn't going to help. And when does he expect to complete the work? Will we have our organ working in time for Christmas?'

Basil pursed his lips doubtfully. 'I'd like to think so, but it seems unlikely. He's a very meticulous worker and won't be hurried. It ought to have been done long ago, but what with the war and all the difficulties afterwards...' He shook his head. 'Finding a restorer at all was like looking for a needle in a haystack. The firm who used to do it lost two of their best men in Japan and it takes time to train new ones, and there have been so many churches needing their services. Now he's here, I want to be sure he has all the time he needs. We can't have the work scamped.'

'True. A few more weeks won't make much difference in the grand scheme of things.' Gilbert took another sip of his drink. 'But when it's back in action, I think we ought to have some kind of celebration. That's what I really want to discuss with you. It's been a fine organ in its day and it should be a fine one again. We want to give it a special welcome back.'

'There'll have to be a rededication service–' Basil began, but the colonel cut him short with a flap of his hand.

'As well as that, I mean. Something like – oh, like a party, but not a party as such, something more appropriate. Something that everyone in the village can enjoy.'

'That's a wonderful idea,' Basil said enthusiastically. 'What do you have in mind?'

'Well, nothing particular at the moment. That's why I want to talk to you. For us to put our heads together ... consult one or two other people. Constance, perhaps, if she's not too wrapped up in those two young Australians she's got staying with her. Frances Kemp and Major Raynor.' Gilbert strongly disapproved of James Raynor's decision to dispense with his army title, and persisted in using it. 'Charles Latimer ... Dorothy Doidge, I suppose, since she plays the thing, although I wonder if she's not getting a bit past it now.'

'Oh, I think we must include Miss Doidge,' Basil said swiftly. 'She's been our organist for years and has really struggled with it just lately. I'm sure that once it's in proper working order again you'll find her as proficient as ever. It would be most unkind to leave her out of any celebration. We ought to ask Henry Warren too, since he's been kind enough to loan us his grand piano, and also to play it at a lot of the services.'

'I suppose that means asking Mrs Warren too,' the colonel said without much enthusiasm.

'She is a very good organiser,' Basil pointed out. 'I know some people think her a trifle domineering–'

'A *trifle?* Quite honestly, Basil, if I believed in reincarnation I'd say she must have been a sergeant major in a previous life! But you're right, she does get things organised. Very well, we'll ask them both.' He counted on his fingers. 'That's nine of us. Plenty for a committee.'

'I could ask the congregation for ideas too,' Basil offered. 'Since it's basically their organ – thanks to your generosity,' he added hastily.

Gilbert's heavy brows came together. 'Quite right. They did raise half the money themselves, after all. I mustn't try to take over.' He finished his whisky and began to get to his feet. 'Well, I'll leave the idea with you, Basil. Chew it over and talk to your congregation on Sunday, and perhaps we could meet again some time next week. Perhaps you'll ask the others along one evening.'

'I will.' Basil saw him out and then went back to the sitting room where Grace was sewing up the hem of his cassock. He told her what the colonel had suggested. 'What do you think of that, my dear? Do you have any ideas?'

Grace laid down the folds of heavy black fabric and gazed at him. 'A celebration for the organ? Well, I would have thought it was obvious. It will have to be a concert, surely – a concert of organ music. In fact' – her eyes brightened and her voice quickened – 'it could be more than just an evening concert. It could be a whole day of organ music – not just church music – for everyone to enjoy, and with other organists invited to take part. They love playing other churches' organs. It could be a real festival!'

'An organ festival,' Basil said thoughtfully. 'Do

you know, Grace, I think you've hit the nail right on the head. An organ festival, in Burracombe. What a wonderful thing that would be!'

Chapter Twenty-Four

''Tis real good to have you back in the bosom of the family,' Minnie said, beaming fondly at her granddaughter. 'I don't mind telling you, maid, there were times when I thought I might never see you again.'

'Don't talk like that, Granny,' Jackie exclaimed. 'Of course you were going to see me again. I was planning – Bryce and I were planning–' Her voice quivered but she went on bravely: 'We were going to come over some time next year, after we were married. In fact, we were thinking of getting married here.'

'Oh, you poor dear,' Minnie said, reaching out both hands. 'That would have been just lovely. But there, I didn't mean to remind you of your pain.'

'Everything reminds me,' Jackie said sadly. 'All the things we did and saw together, and now I'm home all the things we'll never see or do together. I just can't get away from it, somehow. Mother thought coming back to Burracombe would help, but it doesn't – apart from being home with the family, of course. You just can't leave that sort of thing behind in one country. You take it with you wherever you go.'

'Of course you do, my pretty. You learn that as

you grow older, but 'tis cruel for you to have to learn it at your age. But there, we can't choose when bad times come upon us.' She sighed, then went on more briskly, 'And if being at home with your family helps, why, that's just as it should be and maybe you'll heal quicker than you think. From what I've seen myself, it's like waking up one morning and finding a headache gone that's been plaguing you for days. It just happens, slowly at first, and then suddenly you find you're looking out of the dark tunnel you've been in for so long and can see daylight ahead.'

Jackie smiled a little. 'I just wish I knew how far through the tunnel I've gone and how far there is to go. It feels like a very long one.' She looked up and met her grandmother's eyes. 'I know a lot of people think I'm too young to know what love really is, and that I'll soon get over it and find someone else. But that's not true, Granny. I'm almost twenty-one. A lot of girls have got married and started a family by now. And to tell you the truth, I don't think I'll ever find anyone else.' Her voice dropped. 'I don't even want to. Bryce was really special.'

Tears trickled down her cheeks and Minnie patted her hand. ''Tis natural you should feel like that, maid, and don't let anyone tell you otherwise. But my own mother used to tell me that time is a great healer, and 'tis true. Now, I'm going to fill the kettle and make a pot of tea, I dare say someone will be coming in from outdoors pretty soon and be glad of a cup. It's a wet, miserable old day out there and a hot drink makes everyone feel a mite better, no matter what their troubles may be.'

'I can do that,' Jackie said, levering herself out of her chair with her crutch. 'I want to be able to walk properly again as soon as possible and Dr Latimer says it's good for me to move about, so long as I don't put too much weight on my leg. It'll help the muscles to get back their strength and it might even help the bones as well.'

'So long as you're careful and don't do too much,' Minnie said, watching anxiously as the girl swung herself across to the sink and stood the kettle under the tap. 'You stop at once if it gives you any pain, mind.'

'Oh, I will, Granny, don't you worry!' Jackie laughed. 'I won't hurt myself if I can help it. I'm not that brave.' She hesitated for a moment, watching the water fill the kettle, then said, 'Did anything bad happen to you when you were young, Granny? You seem to understand so much better than anyone else what it's like.'

'Me? Bless you, I've always been lucky. There's been upsets and sadness, nobody can get through life without that. People in the family dying – my own mother and father, of course, and a brother when I was young. But that's the way of things, though I must say poor Joanna losing little Suzanne like that was a terrible blow to us all. But apart from that – no, nothing really bad. Not a thing...'

Jackie glanced at her. Her voice seemed to fade over the last words and she was looking away, towards the fire. After she had spoken she fell silent, her expression far away, as if revisiting the past. There was a moment of quiet in the kitchen.

Jackie leaned against the sink and heaved the

kettle over to the range, pushing it onto the hottest part of the top, then took cups and saucers down from the dresser and placed them on the table.

'It's a good job everything's within easy reach just here. I might have to ask you to pour the water into the teapot, though. I don't think I can manage to lift it with two hands and stay steady on one foot!'

'I expect someone else will be here by the time it comes to the boil,' Minnie said. 'I can hear footsteps on the path now. It might be our Val; she said she'd look up some time during the morning.'

The door opened as she spoke and Val appeared, towing Christopher by the hand. They were both swathed in mackintoshes, their feet encased in wellingtons which they pulled off at the step and left in the big stone porch before coming inside. Val took off her coat and shook the rain from it, then unbuttoned Christopher's blue mac.

'It's cats and dogs out there,' she said, shutting the door and drying her face on the towel that hung near the back door. 'And the wind nearly blew poor Kester off his feet. Everyone's going to come in soaked to the skin. Where are they all, anyway?'

'Your mother's gone to Tavistock to have her eyes tested for new glasses and Joanna's taken Heather to see Jennifer Kellaway,' Minnie said, lifting her face for a kiss. 'We were just making a pot of tea, only Jackie can't manage to lift the kettle so you've come just in time.'

'Did you actually fill it, then?' Val asked her sister. 'You must be doing really well. Don't try to do too much, though.' She tipped some hot water into the teapot and swilled it round. 'You don't want those bones breaking again.'

'I shan't risk that, don't worry.' Jackie sat down opposite her grandmother and held out her hand to her nephew. 'Come and say hello, Chris. Have you managed to do that puzzle I brought you yet?'

'He's done it half a dozen times.' Val laughed. 'He almost knows it off by heart. He likes the cowboy's horse best, don't you, sweetheart? I think he's already decided to be a cowboy when he grows up.'

'I hope not,' Minnie said. 'We don't want another one disappearing off to America.'

There was a short silence. Val glanced at Jackie and saw the colour in her cheeks. She knew that there had already been some discussion in the family about a possible return to America and that Ted and Alice were, predictably, against the idea. She was pretty sure, however, that Jackie had already made up her mind. She decided to change the subject.

'Did I tell you we've got a visitor this week? Luke's friend, Ben Mallory. He came with Luke in October and liked it so much he wanted to come again, to do some painting. Not that there'll be much to paint in this weather,' she added, looking out of the window. 'He wanted the autumn colours but this wind is blowing the leaves off the trees like coloured snow.'

'Snow's white, Mummy,' Christopher corrected her. He went to the window and looked out in his turn. 'Is it going to snow?'

'I shouldn't think so,' Val said, 'Not if it carries

on like this. It's far too mild.' The kettle had boiled and she made the tea.

'He ought to go over to the States if he wants autumn colour,' Jackie said. 'They call it "fall" there, you know. The trees were looking lovely when we left. They're about ten times as bright as yours are.'

Val noticed the 'yours' and gave her grandmother a quick look, then frowned at Jackie, who bit her lip in apology.

'I'll tell him he should go over as soon as possible,' she said lightly. 'To be quite honest, I'd be pleased if he did. He's just getting under my feet in the cottage.'

'Don't he go to the charcoal burner's cottage?' Minnie asked. 'I thought you said he was going to be there a lot of the time.'

'Well, he does use it, but he can't be there all the time, the lighting's not good enough, and he can't be outside much in this weather. And Luke's up at the vicarage a lot doing that portrait for Mr Harvey's cousins. They've come back specially for the wife to sit for him, so he has to be there. And that means Ben's got no other company but me.'

'You don't sound as if you like him much,' Jackie observed. 'Isn't he nice? I'd have thought Luke's friends would be just like him.'

'He's all right,' Val said offhandedly. 'I don't actually *dis*like him, I suppose. I just don't like having a man around who isn't Luke.'

Jackie burst out laughing. 'Not everyone can be Luke! You ought to have brought him up here to let us have a look at him.'

'I wanted to get away from him, not drag him

266

round the village like another child! You can come down to the cottage, if you want to see him. Get Tom to run you down in the truck.' She began to pour the tea.

'All right, I will.' Jackie accepted her cup. 'Thanks, Val. Would this afternoon be all right? Granny has a sleep then, don't you, Granny, and Mum'll be back from Tavi.'

'This afternoon will be perfect. It gets dark so early now, especially with all this rain and cloud, so he's bound to be in then. You come down and tell him all about America. You might even per-suade him to go – preferably on the next available ship!'

As Val had predicted, Ben was in the cottage by three o'clock that afternoon. The clouds were so low that the light was already beginning to fade and although he'd spent some time in the charcoal burner's cottage which Luke used as a studio, he had given up soon after eating the sandwiches Val had given him that morning and loped back through the village wearing a black waterproof cape that made him look like a giant bat.

Val made him a cup of tea and he sank into Luke's armchair by the fire.

'Does it always rain like this around here? I thought Devon was supposed to be sunny.'

'Not all the time,' Val said, sitting down opposite him. 'Where do you think all that cream comes from? It's the rain that makes the lush grass that makes the milk so rich and creamy and–'

'You sound as though you're going to end up with the words "and this is the house that Jack built"!' he said, grinning. 'I suppose it makes sense when you think about it, but people do always talk about sunny Devon, don't they?'

'Yes, but this is Dartmoor. It's not like Torquay or all those other seaside places. They're probably basking in scorching sunshine there!'

'Maybe that's where I should have gone, then,' he remarked. Val said nothing and he glanced at her. 'You don't really want me here, do you, Val?'

Val felt her colour rise. She looked down into her cup. 'Don't be silly. You're Luke's friend.'

'But not yours.' He waited a moment or two. 'Look, if you really don't want me around, I'll go back to London.'

'No!' The word came out quicker and sharper than she had intended and she felt herself blush again. More quietly, she added, 'No, you don't have to do that. Luke would be upset if he thought you felt unwelcome. I'm sorry if I've given you that impression.'

'You haven't, not really.' She looked up and found his dark eyes on her. 'I just think I know what you're feeling. And I think I make you feel uncomfortable.'

'I didn't say that–'

'You don't have to.' He hesitated, then added quietly, 'You don't have to tell me anything, Val, because I know it already. I know *you*. Just as you know me.' He waited for the length of a heartbeat. 'It's true, isn't it?'

'I don't know what you mean,' she said breathlessly.

'I think you do.' Their eyes met again and she found she couldn't turn away. 'Do you know why

I came back?'

'To paint. To see the autumn colours. To–'

'To see you.' The pause this time was of several heartbeats. 'You can't escape it, Val. You feel it too, don't you?' It was a statement rather than a question and although she tried to deny it she found herself faltering and looking down, unable to meet his gaze any longer.

'I don't know what I feel,' she said at last. 'And I don't know why you want to see me. What's so special–?' She looked up and caught her breath at the expression in his eyes, and suddenly she did know. She knew what that strange sensation was that she felt at the pit of her stomach when she thought of him, she knew why she had fought so hard against acknowledging it, and she knew exactly why he wanted to see her.

She knew that she had been denying her own feelings.

'You shouldn't have come,' she said at last in a low, trembling voice. 'You should have kept away.'

Ben sighed. 'I tried. I honestly tried. But you're there all the time. Your face is in my mind. I see you when I wake in the morning and you're my last thought as I go to sleep. You're in my dreams at night. You're in my sight during the day. I see you wherever I go, in the streets, on the Underground, in cafés and in the parks. I see a young woman ahead of me in the park and her hair swings just as yours does. I see a young mother with a little boy and I think it's you and Christopher. I see you in the turn of a head, the walk, the flash of a smile, and it's you, you, you...' His

269

voice grew more intense as he spoke, but then he stopped and went on more quietly, 'Only it never is and I had to come back to Burracombe to make sure that you're real, that you really do exist. I *had* to come back. And you know it.'

Val lifted her head and stared at him. She shook her head. 'You can't say those things to me, Ben. I'm married – married to your friend. How can you come here and stay in our house, *his* house, and sit in his chair and talk to me like that? What sort of a friend are you? You should be ashamed of yourself.'

'Oh, I am,' he said quietly. 'Don't think I haven't tortured myself with all those questions. But I can't help myself. I had to see you again – to see if my feelings were true or just an illusion. I hoped that's what they were, Val. I really hoped that when I saw you again the dreams would fall away and you'd be just an ordinary young woman.'

'That's what I am. Ordinary. There's nothing special about me.'

'There is. There's something very special – to me.'

'And to Luke,' she reminded him.

'Yes,' he said with a sigh. 'And don't think that doesn't make me feel bad. I hate myself for what I'm doing to Luke.'

'Then *don't* do it. Go away – back to London, where you belong. There's nothing here for you, Ben.' She looked at the darkened window. 'Even the weather is against you.'

'Is that what you want? Val, if I go now I shall never come back. We'll never see each other again. Is that really what you want?'

Val looked at him and opened her mouth to say yes. But the word would not come. Instead, as she sat staring at him, he came out of his chair and dropped to his knees beside her. He pulled her roughly into his arms and covered her mouth with his. For a moment she tried to draw away and then she gave in, taken completely aback by the surge of emotion and desire that welled up within her.

'Ben...'

'You do feel it too,' he whispered against her hair. 'I knew it. Val, we're meant to be together. We *need* to be together.'

'No!' She recovered herself and pulled back, trying to push him away. 'No, we *don't!* I'm married to *Luke.* I love *Luke.*'

'You may love Luke, but you want me. And I want you.'

'No! Ben – stop.' She put both hands on his shoulders and pushed but he did not move. 'Stop it *now.*'

'Val–' But what he was about to say she would never know, for at that moment there was a sharp rap on the door and Tom's voice called cheerily outside.

'Anyone in? Val? Are you sitting there in the dark?'

Val cast a desperate look at Ben. The room was indeed quite dark now, lit only by the flickering flames of the fire. She jumped up and switched on the light, then ran to the door, pulling it open. 'Tom! Oh, you've brought Jackie down. Come in, both of you. I must have fallen asleep. I do sometimes, when Chris is having his afternoon nap.

Jackie, let's get you inside and out of that wet coat. It's still streaming down. Ben's just come in too, haven't you, Ben.' She drew them into the little living room where Ben was standing by the foot of the stairs as if he had just come down from his bedroom. 'Jackie, this is Luke's friend, Ben. Ben, this is my sister Jackie and this is my brother Tom.'

Aware that she was chattering, she stopped abruptly. The others shook hands and she knew that Tom was eyeing the newcomer speculatively. He won't suspect, she thought. He'd never suspect. But her heart gave a little twist of fear.

There was a tiny silence and then Tom guided Jackie to the chair Ben had been sitting in.

'I'll come back for you in a couple of hours, if that's OK,' Tom said to Jackie.

'Oh, leave her here longer than that,' Val said quickly. 'You can stay for supper, can't you, Jackie? For the whole evening? We've hardly seen you since you got back. We want to hear all about America.'

'About nine, then,' Tom said. 'I'd better go now. I've got the milking to do.' He gave them all a cheerful grin, let his eyes rest a moment longer on Ben's face, then left.

Val, too, looked at Ben. Her head was still whirling with the memory of what had just happened between them. She needed time – time to herself – to examine her feelings and to discover what they were, even though she half feared the discovery. And she knew that she both longed for and dreaded the moment when she would be alone with him again.

It seemed that she had been granted a respite. But as she met his eyes she knew that respite was all it was. It was not an escape.

Chapter Twenty-Five

'A festival of organ music,' Joyce Warren said thoughtfully. Basil Harvey had called a meeting of the committee Gilbert Napier had suggested. As churchwarden, Ted Tozer had been included and now they were all ensconced in the Harveys' drawing room, Basil's study being too small for such a large gathering. 'That sounds a most interesting idea.'

'It was Grace's suggestion,' Basil said, smiling at his wife who sat quietly in a corner embroidering a tablecloth for a Christmas present for one of her nieces, ready to serve tea and biscuits when required, or even give an opinion, if asked. 'And an inspired one, if I may say so. It could bring people from all over the area to the village.'

'We must make it worth their while, then,' Gilbert declared. 'I'm not sure that just sitting listening to half an hour of organ music that they can hear in their own church will be quite enough.'

'It won't be just half an hour, though,' Basil said eagerly. 'Grace's idea is that we ask organists from the whole Deanery – just like at the Ringing Festival – to come and play. They're sure to bring a few of their own congregation, just to support them. And they needn't play only church music.

273

There's plenty of other music written or adapted for organs. Why, there's Saint-Saëns' *Organ Symphony*, Bach's *Organ Concerto*, Poulenc – all wonderful music.'

'Wonderful if we can find the organists capable of playing them,' Joyce remarked. She glanced at Dorothy Doidge, who shook her head.

'I'm afraid I've never attempted any of those. But I'm sure the Tavistock organist could do it.'

'They're a bit heavy for some folk, though,' Ted objected. 'We'd want something a bit more jolly to lighten it up a bit.'

'Like Reginald Dixon in *The Organist Entertains* from Blackpool Tower, on the wireless?' Basil enquired. 'I think that's an excellent idea. I'm sure every village organist would love to try more popular tunes as a change from hymns and solemn music.'

'Blackpool Tower?' Joyce queried a little disdainfully. 'Are you sure that would be suitable, Basil?'

'Oh yes. It's not all "Kiss Me Quick" and candyfloss, you know – the Wurlitzer they have there is a fine instrument and the organists who play it are accomplished musicians. Haven't you ever heard it on a Sunday evening, Mrs Warren?'

Joyce shook her head. 'We don't listen to the radio so much now we have a television set. But I'm sure, if you approve, Basil, it would be perfectly acceptable. What do you think, Miss Doidge?'

Dorothy Doidge curved her long, thin body towards the other woman. 'I think it sounds delightful. I'd like to try a selection of music from the

Gilbert and Sullivan operettas. I'm particularly fond of *The Gondoliers.*' She looked apologetic. 'I'm afraid I'd need time to learn and rehearse them, though.'

'Yes, and so would the others,' Henry Warren said. 'In fact, the more one thinks about it, the more one realises how much *organ*isation' – he smiled apologetically at his inadvertent pun – 'will be needed. First of all, we have to decide on a date for the festival, and then we have to decide whom to invite to play – I think Grace's idea that it should be every organist in the Deanery is a good one, but we need to consider how many that would be and how much time can be allotted to each one. We'll need to know what programme they would each like to play and make sure nobody clashes with anyone else. And–'

'My goodness,' Basil said in alarm, 'it's beginning to sound very complicated.'

'How many churches are there in the Deanery?' James Raynor asked.

'There's about twenty-four we has for the Ringing Festival,' Ted answered. 'But there's a few others that don't have bells. I dare say they got organs, though.'

'They might not all be able to take part,' Basil said. 'And a few of the more remote ones share an organist. But I think we should count on a couple of dozen. Even allowing each one only half an hour, that makes a good twelve hours.' He looked doleful. 'That does seem rather a lot. I'm not sure it's practical...'

'Of course it is!' Constance said robustly. 'Start at nine and finish at nine! Perfectly possible.'

'Yes, but who is going to sit in the church for twelve hours?' Basil asked. 'I sometimes think an hour on a Sunday morning is too much for some of my parishioners!'

'They're not listening to music, though,' Joyce pointed out, and then caught his expression. 'Well, you know what I mean.'

'He does have a point, though,' Frances Kemp said. 'Twelve hours is a long time. But nobody need sit and listen for all that time. I'm sure people would come and go all day, especially to hear their own organist. Suppose we offered other attractions too, so that they stayed longer in the village?'

'There could be refreshments in the village hall,' Grace put in from her corner. 'Morning coffee – light lunches – cream teas. People always love village hall refreshments.'

'What about some entertainment on the village green?' James suggested. 'Like we have at the summer fair? We needn't do quite as much as we do then – just have a few stalls and games – maybe the Morris dancers too, and the skiffle group, if Bob Pettifer's not too busy with that new girlfriend of his.'

'New girlfriend?' Basil asked, diverted. 'I hadn't heard about that.'

'Oh yes,' Frances assured him. 'She's a girl called Kitty Pengelly, from Lydford. You may know her parents – her father's a sidesman at the church. They met at a folk dance where the group was playing, so I heard. It seems quite serious, too. Her aunt lives in Little Burracombe and told Stella about it, that's how I heard.'

'Well, isn't that good news,' Basil said, his face rosy with pleasure. 'I hope it goes well for them. Bob's a very decent, hard-working young man.'

'Indeed,' James said. 'But to get back to the Organ Festival... People could go in and out of the church to hear the music, and enjoy the fun outside before having lunch or tea in the village hall. And the proceeds could go to the organ fund – there are bound to be a few extras to pay for, or it could just be put away for maintenance later on.'

The rest of the committee gazed at him.

'Have you any idea how much organisation all this takes?' Joyce Warren enquired at last.

'Well, not really,' James admitted. 'I thought we'd ask the people who run those things at the summer fair and it would all just happen!'

The others raised their eyes to heaven. Frances shook her head at him.

'You still have a lot to learn about village politics, James. Just have "a few stalls and games"! The whole thing could be a minefield if we don't tread very carefully. You've no idea how easy it is to offend people by not inviting them to take part. All the same,' she went on, 'it *is* a good idea, and would make a lovely festival.'

'Pity we couldn't have the bells as well,' Ted Tozer observed. 'But bells and organs don't mix, specially when 'tis a ground-floor ringing chamber like ours. You can't hear the calls.'

'We could have the handbells, though,' Basil said. 'Minnie does some lovely harmonies and they could be ringing outside in the churchyard, or on the green under the big oak. Or in the village hall if the weather's bad.' He frowned. 'I'm not sure how we'd manage if that was the case.'

'Let's have a marquee,' Joyce proposed. 'I'm sure we'd make enough money to hire one. We're not setting out to make a lot, anyway – it's a celebration, not a money-raising exercise. As Henry says, anything left over will go into the organ fund but thanks to Gilbert's generosity and the amount we've already raised, we don't really need it at present. And a marquee always looks so *festive*.'

'This is turning into a major village event,' Gilbert said, looking pleased. 'And if we're all happy with the idea, I think we should make a few definite decisions. Allocate some tasks between us – get other people involved – oh, and decide on a date!'

'Goodness me,' Basil said. 'It all seems to have developed so quickly, I hadn't even thought about a date.'

'When will the repairs be finished and the organ working again?' Frances asked.

'Not before Christmas, I'm afraid. There have been several hitches and Mr Mitchell, who is doing the work – and very efficiently, too – tells me he doesn't have much hope of finishing until well into January or even February.'

Gilbert frowned. 'Not a good time for the kind of festival we've been talking about.'

'Indeed, and we're also getting into Lent. We can't have anything like that in the church then.'

'So it looks like Easter,' Constance said, and Basil nodded.

'That would be a wonderful time!' Joyce Warren exclaimed. 'The church full of flowers for the Easter Day service – what date will that be, Basil?'

'The first of April,' he said and they all laughed.

'But I don't think we could have the festival that day – not on the Sunday.'

'No, but we could have it on Easter Monday,' Ted declared. 'That would be a fine and fitting day for it, to my mind. Everyone in holiday mood and ready for a day out – why, it couldn't be better!' He looked around the group of faces. 'Can anyone see any objection?'

Frances and James glanced at each other and then at Basil. Then Frances said a little diffidently, 'Well, there is just one thing. James and I were thinking of getting married that day!'

There was a moment of silence, then a flurry of excitement. They all knew, of course, that the two schoolteachers were engaged, but there had been no mention yet of a wedding. Gilbert shook both their hands and the other men followed suit. Joyce Warren, Grace and Constance Bellamy each gave Frances a kiss on the cheek and Dorothy Doidge clasped both her hands and whispered her good wishes.

'I'm sorry,' Frances said to Basil when the commotion had died down. 'We should have mentioned it to you before and made sure the date was convenient for you. But we've been so busy with school matters – the Christmas term is always so full – that we rather put it aside.'

'The date would have been absolutely convenient, and a very good choice,' Basil said, beaming under his halo of white hair. 'And of course we can fit a wedding in with the festival. It will make a delightful addition to the day.'

'Are you sure, Basil?' Grace asked, putting away

her embroidery. 'You've already got a twelve-hour programme, if all the organists accept. You can't rush Frances and James's wedding into a half-hour slot in the middle of it all!'

'Indeed not,' Joyce Warren agreed. 'Half the village will want to be there, including the stall-holders and other entertainers. We'll have to hold the festival on a different day.'

'Oh, no!' Frances protested, but Gilbert agreed with Joyce.

'The following Saturday would do just as well. Unless you'd like to have your wedding then, in-stead?'

'The only problem with that,' James said, 'is that we won't have so much time for a honey-moon. And I would rather like to take my bride away and have her to myself for a week or so. I sometimes feel I share her with the whole village.' He turned to Basil. 'Could we be married on the Sunday? There's nothing against that, is there?'

Basil looked surprised. 'No, nothing at all in principle. It's not very usual, but an Easter Day wedding...' He considered it for a moment. 'I think that would be rather nice, and very special. Perhaps at midday, following the morning service. And everyone will already be dressed in their best for Easter. Yes, I think that would be excellent.'

James turned to Frances. 'What do you think, darling? I ought to have asked you first!'

She laughed. 'I think it's a lovely idea. But we must wait until after the festival to go on our honeymoon. No whisking me off before I've heard all this wonderful organ music.' She looked at Basil. 'We will be able to have the organ for the wedding, won't we?'

'Oh yes. We'll be using it for the Easter Day service anyway – I don't think we need wait for the festival itself. And Miss Doidge will need time for rehearsing and getting used to it, won't you, Miss Doidge?'

The organist blushed and twisted her long fingers together. 'If you think I'm good enough...'

'Of course you're good enough!' they all cried, and then Grace, who had slipped out of the room a few minutes earlier, returned bearing a tray of savouries and small cakes. Basil took the hint and went to the sherry decanter and began to pour glasses for the ladies. He offered the men whisky.

'A celebration,' he declared, holding up his glass. 'First, a toast to our two schoolteachers and their forthcoming marriage. And then to the Organ Festival. We wish Frances and James happiness, and the organ success. And may both last for many years to come!'

The committee laughed and raised their own glasses. 'To Frances and James.' They drank, then raised their glasses again. 'And to the festival in Burracombe!'

Chapter Twenty-Six

'Your young sister's a bright spark,' Ben Mallory commented as he and Val walked along the lane out of the village, with Christopher in his new pushchair. 'She hasn't let that accident in America

281

get her down at all.'

Val considered. Then she said, 'You don't really know Jackie. She always does cover up her feelings with a lot of chatter – until she suddenly blows up. She's a lot more upset than you think. It wasn't only that she was badly hurt herself, she lost her fiancé as well. That's something she's going to take a long time to get over.'

'Really? I thought she was flirting with me, the other afternoon.'

'That's just Jackie's way. It's how she hides her feelings. You don't want to take it seriously.'

'You mean she doesn't find me attractive?' Ben put his hand on his heart. 'I'm devastated!'

Val eyed him coldly. 'Don't mess about with Jackie, Ben. She's a lot more fragile than she looks.'

'I have no intention of "messing about" with her,' he said haughtily, and then added with a wicked sideways look, 'I'd far rather be messing about with you.'

Val stopped dead. 'If you're going to start that again, I'm going straight home.'

'Oh, come on, Val. You didn't exactly object when I kissed you the other afternoon. In fact, if your sister hadn't arrived just then, I think we might have–'

'We wouldn't!' Val's cheeks were flaming. 'Whatever you were going to say, we wouldn't have! I've told you before, Ben, I love Luke and I'm married to him and that's all there is to it. I should never have let you kiss me. I didn't want it to happen and I don't know why it did.'

'Well, I do.' He faced her. 'It's because you *did*

want it – you wanted it as much as I did. And you still do.' He touched her cheek with the tip of one finger and Val felt a shiver go through her. *'Don't you?'*

It was not really a question. Val tried to deny it but she couldn't meet his eyes. Instead, she turned her head away and stepped back.

'Leave me alone, Ben,' she said huskily. 'And don't talk like this in front of Christopher.'

He grinned. 'It's all right when he's not here, then, is it?'

'No! It's not all right at *any* time.' This time she did meet his eyes. 'I mean it, Ben. It mustn't happen again – ever.'

He regarded her for a long moment, then said slowly, 'Are you telling me you don't feel this – this attraction between us?' He took a step nearer and she backed away. 'Are you telling me you haven't thought, over and over again, of that kiss? Wanted it to lead on to other kisses? Are you telling me, Val, that you haven't dreamed of making love with me?'

Val twisted the handle of the pushchair and began to walk rapidly back towards the village. Ben loped easily beside her. He put his hand on her arm and she shook it off angrily. He touched her again and she stopped and faced him. She was breathing quickly and her eyes blazed.

'Ben, you *must not* talk to me like that. It isn't fair. You're supposed to be Luke's *friend.'*

He waved his hand airily. 'Oh, Luke would understand. He's an artist, like me. We think the same way.'

'And what's that supposed to mean?'

Ben shrugged. 'A fling now and then – what does it matter? It helps us, creatively. Makes us better painters. Didn't you know that?'

'No,' she said tautly, 'I didn't. And I don't believe it. Luke doesn't think that way, I know he doesn't. And I'm a "fling" now, am I? Not so long ago you were talking about *love*.'

Ben laughed. 'Words, words! They're just ways of getting what we want.' He put his hand on her arm again and looked into her eyes. 'And you want it too, Val. Don't tell me you don't. I've kissed those sweet lips of yours and I know. So how about this as a solution? Neither of us will get any rest until we've taken what's between us to its natural conclusion, so why not just relax and go along with it? Yes, a fling, if you like – which we'll both enjoy, which will never affect anyone else because nobody else will ever know about it, and then say goodbye. A pleasurable episode and no more than that – all over and done with, with no hard feelings. What do you say?'

Val stared at him. Her heart was beating madly and she wanted to shake off his hand, but she could not move. At last she dragged her gaze away and looked down at Christopher who had, to her heartfelt gratitude, fallen asleep.

'I say I am going home now,' she said at last in a low voice. 'I should never have come out with you. I wouldn't have done, if Luke hadn't suggested you come with me and I didn't know how to say no – I thought you would be going to the hut to do some work. And that's where I think you should go now because I don't want to be alone with you ever again, Ben, either indoors or out. I don't trust you an inch.'

She turned away, but not before she had caught Ben's slow smile. And as she walked rapidly along the lane she heard his voice follow her.

'Is it just me you don't trust, Val, or is it yourself as well? Think about it...'

Ivy Sweet had been to Tavistock that afternoon to attend the carol service at Barry's school. It was his first term at the secondary modern and, to her relief, he seemed to have settled in well, although Miss Kemp had told her he was quite clever enough to go to the grammar school and would have passed the examination last year if he'd put his mind to it. Ivy had been upset about that, and angry with Barry for spoiling his chances, until George had pointed out to her that plenty of people who had been to St Rumon's – himself included – had gone on to make a good life for themselves.

'You don't have to be clever with your books to get on in the world,' he'd said. 'To my mind, there's always a place for a man who can do a bit of plumbing or electrical work, like the Pettifer boys, or carpentry like Henry Carr, or build a house like Ted Greening – or even bake a few loaves of bread like me. The world can't get on without them, and it's schools like St Rumon's that sends its boys to technical colleges and apprenticeships that brings those lads on.'

'Barry's still on about being an actor,' Ivy said ruefully. 'I don't know as any school can help him there, unless it's to make him see sense.'

'Well, he'll still need a trade at his fingertips,'

George said. 'From what I've heard about actors, they spend half their time what they call "resting" and not earning any money at all. I reckon he's best off where he is, Ivy, learning useful things like woodwork or metalwork, and then, if he still wants to go into acting, he'll have something to fall back on.'

Ivy had seen the sense of this and when she had been to the carol service and seen the boys and girls, all looking smart and tidy in their grey pullovers and flannel shorts or skirts, she'd felt a lot happier about Barry's education. Her only problem now, she thought, was the one of his grandmother in Poland and her son Konrad – Barry's uncle – who had recently discovered them and had wanted to take Barry to meet her.

Ivy and George had averted that danger for the time being, but she had an uneasy feeling that Konrad was not going to give up. And with Christmas approaching, she was afraid that he would be appearing in the village again.

As she rounded the corner of the lane, hugging her coat around her, she caught sight of Ben Mallory just ahead of her. He was turning into the gate that gave on to the path leading through the wood to the charcoal burner's cottage and as she came nearer he looked at her with an odd little half-smile. Ivy didn't much care for that smile – she hadn't much cared for Ben Mallory at all, on the occasions when he had come into the Bell Inn with Luke Ferris – and she just gave him a brief nod as she passed, before catching sight of Val walking briskly towards the village, her back stiff as if she had just 'had words'. Outstaying his welcome, I dare say, she thought, before turning her mind back to her own affairs.

She came into the bakery to find George sitting at the table, staring at a letter.

'Came by second post,' he said as she closed the door. 'You'd better read it, Ive.'

Ivy took off her winter coat and hung it in the cupboard. She felt a twinge of alarm.

'What is it, George?' As he pushed the letter across the table, she added, 'Make us a cup of tea, will you? It's bitter out there.'

George got up and went to the sink to fill the kettle. Ivy sat down at the table and drew the letter towards her, unwilling to see what it said. Whatever it was, she knew from his face that it wasn't good news and for a moment she felt that it was somehow going to change everything; if she didn't read what it said, everything would be all right. She stared at the words without properly seeing them, then took in a breath, found her reading glasses, and focused her eyes.

'It's from Konrad,' she said, and realised that she had known as soon as she'd come in that this was what it must be. 'What's he want now?'

'Read it and you'll find out.' George rinsed the teapot with hot water and got cups and saucers from the cupboard. His voice was terse.

Reluctantly, Ivy began to take in the sense of the words. She read to the end, saw the signature, turned back to the beginning, and read again. Then she looked up at her husband.

'He's brought his mother over to England. I thought he said she was too ill to travel.'

George placed two cups of tea on the table and

sat down opposite her.

'Obviously she's not. But it don't sound as if she's got long to live.'

'Poor old thing,' Ivy said, staring down at the letter again. 'I can't help feeling sorry for her, George. Lost all her family apart from Konrad in the war, some of them in those awful concentration camps, and never even knew she had a grandson in England till a few months ago. It's no wonder she wants to see him. But we couldn't let him go to Poland, could we – not at his age. I still don't think he properly understands it all.'

'And now she's in England,' George said. 'Up in Nottingham with her son. And you can bet your life the next thing is he'll want to bring her down here.'

Ivy raised her head in shock. 'You can't mean that! How could he do that, in her state of health? And it couldn't be kept secret, not a chap like that who'd stand out like a sore thumb round here anyway, with an old lady almost on her deathbed. The whole village would know – and if they didn't, they'd make something up. You know what Burracombe's like for gossip.'

'So what's the alternative?' George asked. 'Would you rather take Barry up there?'

'Oh, I don't know.' She put her hands over her face. 'I never wanted any of this at all. I thought all these years, with you never asking and nobody knowing a thing, it was all in the past. Barry was *our* son, yours and mine–'

'He *is* our son,' George broke in quickly. 'I've always thought of him that way and I always will. Nothing will change that, Ive.' He put out his hands and lifted hers gently away from her face so that he could look into her eyes. 'It's the man that brought him up who's his real father, and that man happens to be me.'

Ivy stared at him. Tears came to her eyes and rolled down her cheeks and she brushed them away impatiently.

'You're a good man, George,' she said huskily. 'I don't deserve you, and that's the truth.'

'Well, you got me, for better or worse, and what I reckon is that this isn't the worst that could happen to us, not when you takes into consideration all the other problems that could come along. You, me and Barry, we got our health and our strength and a good life, and we can face anything as long as we remembers that.'

'Yes,' she said slowly. 'And we've got a lot more than that poor old lady in Nottingham. All she wants, George, is to see her grandson before she dies. It's not really too much to ask, is it?'

'I don't reckon it is,' he said quietly. 'The real question is: is it too much for us to give?'

Chapter Twenty-Seven

Katie and Greg were busy with their 'spring-cleaning'. They had decided to tackle the house room by room, starting at the top. That meant the attics, which Constance told them had never been cleared out in all the years she could remember.

'Goodness only knows what you'll find up there,'

she said, her little black eyes twinkling. 'But if there are any skeletons in the family closet, that's where they'll be!'

'Oh, we're not expecting to find skeletons,' Katie said, laughing. 'Maybe a ghost or two, perhaps. Is the house haunted, Aunt Connie?'

'Not that I've ever heard of. It isn't that old – maybe two or three hundred years. It was probably a mine captain's house to begin with and got enlarged as time went on. You'll have noticed how the middle rooms and that inner hallway are the oldest of all. That's because they're the original building and as the years went by bits were added on, so it spread out from there.' She took them through to the passageway that led from the inner hallway to the back door. 'And that's where the men would have come in for their wages of a Friday night, so that they didn't have to enter the main house. There would probably have been a round table here with drawers all round it, holding wages and rent books. They'd be paid their wage and then have to pay their rent – I expect most of the money was out of their hands almost before they had a chance to see it.'

'But they must have had enough to feed and look after their families, surely?' Katie asked.

Constance shrugged. 'Barely. Wages weren't much more than enough to ward off starvation in those days, and I suppose the mine owners would have taken the view that it was up to the men how big their families were. And don't forget, a lot of the children would have been in the mines or working on the farms as well, by the time they were seven years old.'

'Seven?' Katie echoed in horror. 'But that's dreadful! Didn't they have to go to school?'

'When the Education Act came in, yes, but not for the hours children do now, and it would finish for most of them by the time they were twelve. Life wasn't easy for anyone then – except those who had the money. Even the Duke of Bedford, who built all those little cottages in Tavistock for his workers and made the square and everything look so nice, took a good deal of persuading before he saw reason. Anyway, that's all changed now and we understand that we're all human beings and deserve the same consideration. I expect it's the same in Australia, being a new country.'

Katie glanced at her brother and he said, 'I'm not sure it is, to tell you the truth. We really only allow people in who can be useful. And we have a colour bar – we don't let anyone in who isn't white. The Aborigines have a pretty thin time of it, even though it was their country to begin with. I'm not sure that's much to be proud of.'

Constance stared at him. 'No,' she said slowly, 'I don't know that it is. But at least young folk like you can see that, so maybe it will change as time goes on. Anyway, that's out of our hands now and you want to get on with your clearing out. I must say,' she went on as they returned to the big, warm kitchen, 'it's a tonic for me, having you two to stay. You really don't have to do all this hard work, you know. You could just have a holiday here.'

'Don't be silly, Aunt Connie,' Katie said, and gave her a hug. 'We love being here but we wouldn't be happy if we weren't doing something to help. And who knows what we might find up there in those attics? There might be all sorts of treasures.'

Constance laughed. 'Treasures? I don't think so. But I'll tell you what you will find – a lot of old papers, put up there years ago. They might be interesting, if they haven't fallen to pieces by now.'

'Papers?' Greg said, glancing at his sister. 'Yes – I should think they would be. Very interesting indeed...'

'Why ever didn't she tell us about these before?' Katie wondered, gazing at the trunkful of yellowing documents. 'She knew we were interested in family history.'

'I suppose she didn't think they were relevant.' Greg peered over her shoulder. 'She probably doesn't even know for sure what it all is. They're mostly newspapers, after all. I don't suppose there's anything in them about the family, apart from birth, death and wedding announcements.'

'All the same,' Katie said, closing the lid, 'I'd like to have a browse through them some time. Old newspapers are always fascinating, and these are local ones.'

'We'll take them downstairs,' he said. 'It will be something to do during the long winter evenings.'

Katie shivered. 'Yes, it will be much better to be sitting in front of a nice warm fire. I had no idea England was this cold, did you? And it's so dark! Even during the day, it doesn't seem to get properly light. I'm not sure I can survive till spring.'

'You'll struggle through,' her brother told her heartlessly. 'A couple of warm pullovers and a pair of wellington boots big enough for four pairs of socks, and you'll be fine. Now, what are we going to do first?'

'I hardly know where to start,' Katie admitted, gazing at the jumble of boxes, old suitcases and decrepit trunks. 'What a lot of hoarders our family must have been.'

'And still are! Think of that pile of stuff we found in Grandad's spare bedroom back home – years old, a lot of it. But you know what still strikes me as odd?'

'That we still don't know for sure he was Aunt Connie's uncle.' Katie nodded. 'I know Mr Warren said it seems fairly conclusive, but we don't have that one piece of proof that would settle it once and for all. And we don't know why he – or either of them, if Grandad wasn't her uncle – went to Australia and cut all contact with the family back home.'

'I'm beginning to think we never will. Nobody here seems to have any idea. The one person Aunt Connie thought might know is the old lady – Minnie Tozer – and she says she doesn't remember anything about it.'

'I'm not sure she'd tell us if she did,' Katie said thoughtfully. 'She seems to have taken a real dislike to us. She still doesn't trust us, you know. She doesn't believe we're really related to the Burracombe Bellamys and she thinks we're after the family silver. Not to mention the money!'

Greg laughed. 'Let's make a start. We'll open the nearest box and go on from there. And be prepared to get very, very dusty!'

'So how are you enjoying being back at home,

Jackie?' Felix Copley asked. He had called in at the farm on his way back from taking Stella and baby Simon to visit Dottie. 'It must seem rather quiet after the hustle and bustle of New York.'

'Corning's in New York *State,* not the city,' she informed him. 'And it's a very quiet town, not all that much bigger than Tavistock. Most of the people there work at the glassmaking factory.'

'Well, it's still America. It must be different from England.'

'In a way, I suppose. But it's more like England than you think. Everyone knows each other and says hello in the street, and they have just the same kind of things going on as we do. I suppose people are people everywhere, especially in small towns.'

'That's very true,' Felix agreed, thinking that Jackie had grown up a lot since she had been in America. But then, she'd been through the kind of experiences that made most people grow up quickly. He thought of Maddy and how desperate she had been after the death of her fiancé Sammy, and it occurred to him that Maddy might be able to help Jackie with her own grief. 'So how are you spending your time?' he asked. 'You must be quite restricted still by your leg.'

'It's getting stronger. I'm a bit bored, though.' She lowered her voice, for although they were alone in the big farmhouse kitchen, Minnie was upstairs having her rest and sound travelled through the old wooden ceilings. 'I can't do all that much outside and the weather's awful anyway – and I'm not much of a cook. They keep giving me *vegetables* to peel!' She rolled her eyes and Felix laughed. 'Val's been bringing me library books but you can only have two a week and when you can't choose them for yourself, you don't always get what you'd really like.' She sighed and looked away. 'I'm sorry, Mr Copley. I shouldn't feel sorry for myself, I know. I'm really very lucky.'

She didn't sound as if she felt lucky, Felix thought. And there didn't seem to be anyone here of her own age, which might have helped. He said, 'You can come over to us one day, if you like. Stella would love to see you.'

Jackie brightened a little. 'That would be nice. I could play with the baby too.'

Felix looked at her. Her energy seemed to have deserted her. She needs to get out and see other people, he thought. Being at home is good, but being stuck in this kitchen with only her family for company, when they came in from their various jobs, wasn't enough to help her get better.

'Why don't you come with me now? I'm going to see Miss Bellamy first, and then I'll collect Stella and Simon and we can all go back to Little Burracombe together. I'll bring you back after tea.'

'Oh, yes please! I'll just fetch my coat and tell Granny where I'm going.' She moved awkwardly towards the staircase door and called up to her grandmother. Minnie's voice could be heard replying and then Jackie unhooked her winter coat from the back of the door and picked up the walking stick Ted had cut from a hedge for her.

Felix helped her into the little Baby Austin standing in the yard and they made their way down the track and through the village to the Grey House. Jackie had been there before, of course, but not often and not for several years. Miss Bellamy had at one time made toffee apples every year, inviting the village children in to receive one each, and Jackie could remember sitting in the garden, under the apple trees from which the fruit had come, licking and chewing with other children from the school. She had come carol singing too, and had been invited into the big, warm kitchen for mince pies and hot blackcurrant juice. And of course Miss Bellamy herself had been a familiar sight, bustling about the village like a wind-up toy, her black eyes snapping with energy in the thousand tiny creases of her walnut-brown face.

Felix turned in at the big double gates and stopped by the back door. Everyone who knew Miss Bellamy entered by that way; indeed, some people doubted if she herself even knew the way through the house to the front door. He rapped the horseshoe-shaped knocker and pushed open the door.

As Jackie followed him in, he called out to let the old lady know who was walking in. 'And I've brought Jackie Tozer to see you. She's coming back to spend the day with me and Stella.'

'Jackie Tozer! Well, how good to see you, my dear.' Miss Bellamy was on her feet and already filling the kettle as they entered the kitchen. 'I heard you were back. And looking like a film star, too! Those clothes must be American – you'd never get slacks like that in Tavistock and I don't expect your mother would wear them if you could! Now, sit here – this chair will be better for you with that leg.' She bustled about, bringing out milk, sugar and a large biscuit tin from the larder.

'I'll call my young people down. You haven't met them, have you? They're up in the attics, sorting out a hundred years' worth of rubbish. They'll be pleased to meet another young person after spending so much time with an ancient relic like me!'

She stopped talking and took in a breath, while Felix and Jackie looked at each other and laughed. Constance gave them a reproving frown and went out of the kitchen. A moment later they heard her gruff voice raised to call the two far above her in the attics.

'I don't know if they heard me,' she said, returning. 'They're three floors up! I'll have to bang the gong.'

She disappeared again and the sound of the dinner gong reverberated through the house. Under cover of the noise, Jackie said, 'Shouldn't you tell her you've already had tea and biscuits at the farm?'

Felix shook his head. 'Drinking gallons of tea is part of a vicar's duty, and one which my wife will tell you I take very seriously! Hello, it sounds as if the rubbish-sorters have heard the summons.'

Footsteps sounded on the stairs and a minute or two later Constance reappeared, followed by two rather dusty apparitions in old dungarees with yellow dusters swathed about their heads. Felix took one look and snorted with laughter and Jackie found herself joining in, with the first real amusement she had felt for weeks.

'You may well laugh,' Katie said, unwrapping the duster from her head. 'It's like a dust storm up there. I don't think anyone's been near those attics since before the war, unless it was to dump yet more rubbish.'

'And we're talking about the *First* World War,' her brother added. He pulled off his duster too and grinned at Jackie. 'You're old Mrs Tozer's granddaughter, from America. Aunt Connie's told us about you.'

'Really?' Jackie said in surprise, and looked at Miss Bellamy.

'Certainly I have,' the old lady said briskly. 'I knew they'd be interested in you. A most enterprising young woman, going off to America. And going back again, I dare say, as soon as that leg's properly mended.'

'Well – yes, I hope so,' Jackie said, startled. 'But I haven't said so to anyone at home. Not definitely, anyway. Mother and Father are hoping I'll stay here so I don't think they'll be very pleased.'

'Probably not,' Constance Bellamy agreed. 'But it's your life, my dear, and you're the one who has to live it.' She began to pour tea and Katie went hastily to help her.

Greg brought a cup over to Jackie and sat beside her. 'You ought to try Australia next. You'd really like it.'

'I might.' She stirred restlessly. 'I wanted to see so much of the world, but it doesn't seem so important now. Apart from going back to America, I don't really know what I want to do.'

Felix glanced at her. He remembered again how depressed Maddy had become for a while and thought he saw the same signs in Jackie. These young people could be good for her, he reflected, and said casually, 'Maybe you could spend some time helping Katie and Greg here. That's if Miss Bellamy doesn't mind.'

'Mind!' Constance exclaimed. 'Of course I don't mind. It's been a treat to have these two around me and one more would be a delight. And you remind me of your grandmother when she was a young girl,' she added to Jackie. 'Full of fire and spirit she was, just like you – and just like she is now, come to that – and you look the image of her then. It would take me right back to my own young days to have you about the house.'

Jackie looked surprised. 'Nobody else has ever said I'm like Granny but I suppose nobody else remembers her at the age I am now. Well, if you're sure it would be all right, and if you think I could be useful' – she looked at Greg and Katie – 'I'd really like to help. Only, I couldn't climb all those stairs, not just yet.'

'We'll bring stuff downstairs,' Greg said, smiling at her. 'We were going to do that anyway. There are suitcases and trunks and boxes full of newspapers and things we want to look at. We can go through them together.'

Felix drank his tea. 'I'll have to be going soon, I'm afraid. I promised to collect Stella from Dottie's cottage at twelve and it's almost that now. Are you coming with me, Jackie, or staying here?'

Jackie hesitated. 'I'll come with you,' she decided. 'I told Granny I was doing that, so I better had. But I'll come back here tomorrow, if that's all right. It'll be fun to look through old papers. I bet we'll find all sorts of interesting stories.'

Greg helped her up and saw her to the back door with Felix, going out to help tuck her into the little car. 'It's been good to meet you, Jackie. I hope we'll see a lot more of each other.'

'I expect we will,' Jackie said. 'I'll get my brother to bring me tomorrow morning. I don't think I can walk quite so far yet.'

Felix started the engine and the little car disappeared down the drive and through the gates. Greg looked after it for a moment, then went indoors to continue the work of looking through Constance Bellamy's old papers.

Chapter Twenty-Eight

The Organ Festival occupied most of Gilbert Napier's waking thoughts these days but, grateful though Hilary was that he had found such an absorbing interest, she couldn't help feeling a little tired of the subject.

'We've got Christmas and all of winter to get through before then,' she pointed out at supper one evening. 'There are any amount of things to be thinking of. Joyce Warren is already making noises about a winter production and she wants both me and David to be in it.'

'You two?' Gilbert was diverted from his speculation about the music that the organists from all the different villages might choose to play at the festival. He frowned. 'I hope it will be something suitable.'

'Oh, absolutely,' Hilary said, keeping her face straight. 'We're going to be doing a pantomime.

David will be the dame and I'm going to be one of the two comic men in baggy trousers – you know, bailiffs or country yokels or whatever they happen to be. Or we might do that together and Stephen could be the dame,' she added thoughtfully.

Her brother choked over his potatoes. 'With only one arm? Well, at least it would be different. And there would be plenty of jokes about being "armless". Have you got any more bright ideas, Hil?'

'Let me see ... if we did Old King Cole, Dad could be the king. And Maddy could be a princess and we could all rehearse at home in the evenings. Or we could do Humpty Dumpty and–'

'Stop it at once!' her father commanded. 'I can see you're making fun of me. Maddy looks as if she'll burst and Stephen never could keep a joke to himself. So what is Mrs Warren planning?'

'Something along the lines of last year's Variety Extravaganza, I think,' Hilary replied, grinning. 'She's found out that David has a lovely tenor voice, which he's been trying to keep hidden, and with James Raynor being a baritone she wants them to do a duet together. The one from *The Pearl Fishers* or something like that.'

'That sounds more appropriate,' Gilbert commented. He looked at his son-in-law. 'More up your street than a pantomime dame, I imagine.'

'Probably,' David agreed, spearing a carrot. 'I wouldn't have time to rehearse for a pantomime anyway, with all the colds and flu going round Burracombe at the moment. The latest to go down with it is Billy Friend. I'm a bit worried about him.'

'Billy?' Maddy exclaimed. 'Oh, that's a shame. He's a dear soul. I remember him when I was little. He used to play with us then, even though he was a lot older, but he was never more than a child really. I always thought it was kind of Mr Foster to let him work at the butcher's shop.'

'Oh yes,' Hilary replied. 'He's very proud of his job, helping to carry the meat carcases about, and it gives him some pocket money to spend on sweets and going to the pictures. He and his sisters go to the cinema in Tavistock every Saturday after-noon. He's very fond of cowboy films.'

'Well, they won't be going this Saturday, or the next, if I'm any judge,' David said. 'He's quite poorly and I want them to keep him in bed for at least a week. In fact, I'd like him to stay indoors for a good three weeks. His chest doesn't sound at all good and you know people with his dis-advantages rarely live long into middle age. He's done very well to go on as long as he has.'

Hilary and Maddy stared at him in dismay.

'You don't mean he's going to *die?*' Maddy asked, horrified.

'I hope not. I'll do all I can to make sure we pull him through.' He looked at their shocked faces. 'Don't look so upset. I don't think it will come to that – not this time. But we have to face facts. Billy's had a very good life for one born as he was, and none of us can go on for ever.'

There was a silence as they ate the rest of their meal. Hilary served jam roly-poly for pudding, but nobody asked for a second helping. After a few minutes, David said apologetically, 'I'm sorry. I've put a damper on things and I didn't mean to. I'm

302

used to being part of a family of doctors, where we take such things as part of everyday life. And in Derby we didn't know our patients in the same way as we do here. I'm afraid I forget sometimes that you've known the people I see in my surgery all your lives.'

'It's all right,' Maddy said. 'It's not as if we're not accustomed to people being ill and dying.' But her voice was subdued and as soon as the meal was finished she said she was going to bed early, and escaped from the room.

Hilary glanced at Stephen, who shook his head slightly. 'I'll go up in a minute. She'll be all right.' He looked at David. 'It's just that she's lost rather a lot of people in her life – her parents and baby brother during the war, her sister Stella for years and years, thinking she might be dead as well, and then her first fiancé Sammy Hodges. And she thought for a while after my crash that she was going to lose me as well, so you see, anything like this rather brings it all back.'

David groaned. 'I'm a complete idiot. I ought to know better now than to talk like that. I really am sorry, Stephen. Is there anything I can do to make amends?'

Stephen shook his head again. 'No, no. She knows you didn't mean it. Just don't mention it again and it will all be forgotten by morning.' He got up from the table. 'I'll go up as well now, though. Goodnight, all. See you in the morning.'

He went out and David looked at Gilbert.

'I really am–'

'Don't say it again,' Gilbert broke in. 'We all know you're sorry, and we all know you didn't mean to upset any of us. It's just that the whole village is rather fond of poor Billy Friend and his sisters. I'm afraid it's an example of how carefully you have to tread in a place like Burracombe. There's bound to be someone ready to be affected, however hard you try. You just have to learn to hold your tongue and be tactful. Like me.'

Hilary gave a hoot of laughter.

'Hold your tongue and be tactful like *you*, Father? That's the best joke yet!' She turned to David and laid her hand on his arm. 'You just go on being your own sweet self, my love. Everyone in Burracombe likes you and is pleased to have you here as their doctor. And if anyone can help Billy pull through this, it's you. We all know that.'

Billy Friend was not the only one to go down with flu or a heavy cold in the weeks before Christmas. Half the school seemed to be laid up and the classes were small as the children made their Christmas cards and glued together strips of coloured paper for paper chains to festoon across the classrooms. One of the Crocker twins appeared alone one morning, wearing the 'George' jersey and said that his brother was poorly and he thought he ought to be at home too.

'Only if you're unwell yourself, George,' James Raynor said firmly, wondering if it really was George and not Edward he was talking to. Nobody had ever yet found a way of telling the two apart except for the jerseys which bore their names, and he would not have put it past either of them to come to school alone, wearing his brother's jersey and pretending to be the other.

'As long as you're fit and well, you must come to school.'

'But then I'll learn things he don't know,' George said, cleverly avoiding the use of his twin's name. 'And that's not fair. Us ought to know the same things.'

'*We* ought to know the same things,' James corrected him, but George's baffled stare reminded him yet again that none of the younger children had any idea when they were using the wrong pronoun. 'In any case, that's easy to put right – you can just tell Edward what you've learned each day and he'll know just as much as you when he comes back.'

'But what if I catches it too?'

James sighed. 'Then he'll have to teach you. And if he's not back by then, I'll give both of you extra lessons during playtime so that you don't fall behind.'

'I don't expect we'll need that,' George observed, and walked away, defeated in his bid to stay at home but determined not to lose any playtime. James smiled and turned to find Frances beside him.

'Those two!' she said, amused. 'They never miss a trick, do they? Are you sure that's George and not Edward?'

'I'm not in the least sure. I suppose you need to know, for the register and school log.'

'We'd better ask his mother when she comes to collect him. You do realise we are never going to have a full school this side of Christmas, don't you? It will play havoc with the Christmas party and Nativity play. We shall have to have understudies for the understudies, and it's hard enough finding even one child who can take each major part and say the words in anything but a mumbled undertone. And we'll no sooner have got through all these colds when the chickenpox will start. And the measles! Really, it's a wonder the children have time to learn anything at all.'

'We're going to be very ready for our honeymoon when Easter rolls around,' James said. 'A holiday in the sun, somewhere, so that we can just relax. We'll have to start making plans soon.'

'After Christmas,' she said firmly. 'I can't cope with anything else until that's over. Just let's hope we can get through the term without going down with colds or flu ourselves. That really would be a disaster.'

Joe was thinking about the flu epidemic too. He fussed over Dottie like a mother hen until at last she flapped her hands at him in exasperation and told him to leave her alone.

'I've looked after myself perfectly well all my life, thank you very much. I don't need telling to go to bed early and being brought cups of hot milk with brandy in, or breakfast in bed. Though to be honest,' she added, 'the hot milk and brandy is quite welcome. You can go on doing that if you like.'

Joe laughed. 'I'll go on doing all of it. You hadn't had a stroke before, remember. And if you need looking after, I'm the man to do it. You're my wife now, Dottie, and promised in church to obey me, if I remember right.'

'And beginning to regret it already!' she retorted, and smacked the hand he had laid on her arm. She smiled affectionately. 'You're a good man, Joe, and a good husband. I'll do everything you say, as long as you don't keep fussing. I'm not used to it. It's not even as if I've *got* this blessed cold that's going round.'

'No, and I mean to make sure you don't catch it. That's why I'm not keen on you coming up to look at Moor View with me this afternoon.'

'Well, you're not going by yourself, not if we're thinking of living there. I want to have a look at it too.' She gazed out of the window. 'The rain seems to be easing off now and that cold wind's dropped. If I wrap up warm I shall be all right. What time did you say we'd be there?'

'About two-thirty. Time for us to have our dinner and then stroll up and have a good look around before it starts to get dark. All right, Dottie, we'll go together. I didn't really want to go on my own anyway.'

There was time for Dottie to have a rest while Joe washed up the dinner dishes before they set out for their viewing. The Berrymans had finally decided to make their move away from the village and had told Joyce Warren, who had heard that Joe and Dottie were looking for a bigger house and had mentioned it to them, so that the Berrymans found themselves with a potential buyer before they even had time to decide on an estate agent. They welcomed Joe and Dottie in and took them straight to the living room, where a fire burned invitingly in the hearth.

'Oh, this do look cosy,' Dottie exclaimed. 'Much nicer than when old Josiah lived here. I used to come in to do a bit of cooking and cleaning when he couldn't manage for himself, and it was proper dingy then. You've made it look much lighter.'

'We couldn't live in it as it was,' Sonia Berryman said. 'We decorated right through as soon as we could – just plain cream walls, mostly, you couldn't get much coloured paint then, but at least it made it look brighter and cleaner. Then we did a bit more when we started to be able to get better paint and wallpapers but you'd probably want to change it now. It's two or three years since we decorated in here.'

'It still looks a lot better,' Dottie said, gazing round. 'And what a lovely view you got from the window. You can see right up the moor. I don't remember being able to see so far when Josiah was here.'

'That's because the garden was all overgrown, with shrubs and bushes pressing right up against the windows. Geoffrey cleared it all away and opened up the whole place.'

'With help from Jacob Prout, of course,' her husband said with a smile. 'What a jewel that man is! I should think everyone in Burracombe has had his help one way or another.'

'Well, it all looks lovely,' Dottie said, crossing to look out at the garden. 'The only thing is, we're going to be away quite a bit. I wouldn't like to see it neglected.'

'We can always get Jacob or someone else to take care of things while we're away,' Joe said. 'But before we make any decisions, don't you think we'd better look at the rest of the house?'

Dottie turned with a start. 'Oh – yes, I suppose

we'd better. What about the kitchen? That's what's going to be important for me.'

Sonia Berryman led them through to the back of the house and Joe saw at once that Dottie was won over. Fond though she was of her own cottage kitchen, even she had to admit that it was very small, but here was the kitchen of her dreams – even more so than his own modern kitchen in Corning. The room was big, with a large table in the middle and a dresser that took up a whole wall, with shelves for enough china to provide cups of tea for half the village, and a shining new Aga on the other side, with plenty of space for cupboards and worktops. Double doors with glass panels led out to the garden and he could see herbs growing in the plot nearest the kitchen door, just as Dottie had in her own cottage garden. He looked at her rapt face and smiled to himself.

'And the bathroom!' Dottie said later to the family as they sat round the Tozers' own kitchen table. 'You've never seen anything like it! Well, they have beautiful bathrooms in America, I admit that, and maybe this one's not so modern as those, but it's got a lovely big bath and a geyser that Mrs Berryman says gives gallons of hot water with no trouble at all, and a nice sink for washing, and tiles all round the walls. And there's even a little fireplace so you can heat it up and hang your towel in front to be warm when you gets out of the bath.'

'It sounds lovely,' Alice said. 'You'll like that, Dottie, after all these years filling up a zinc bath in front of the fire on Saturday nights. So are you going to buy it?'

'We haven't decided yet,' Joe said. 'No, don't look so disappointed, Dottie. There's other things to be looked at first – their septic tank, for a start, I'm not too happy about that, and it struck me the electrical system might want some attention. I'll ask young Bob Pettifer to have a look at that. But all things being equal – yes, I think it would be just the place for us. In fact, I'm surprised Dottie's taken to it so well. I thought I'd have the devil's own job winkling her out of that cottage of hers.' He smiled at her and added, 'There's only one thing bothering me about it.'

'What's that?' they asked, and Alice said, 'It's the idea of living next door to Mrs Warren! But you needn't worry too much about that, Joe. There's a big hedge between the gardens and you'll probably hardly know she's there.'

Joe laughed. 'No, it's not that! It's the fact that Dottie might have taken to it *too* well. How am I ever going to get her to leave it for a few months every year to come back to America with me?'

Chapter Twenty-Nine

'I don't understand,' Barry Sweet said. 'Why have we got to go to Nottingham to see my granny? I've got two grannies already. Nobody's got more than two grannies.'

'It's hard for you to understand, I know,' George said patiently. They had very nearly come to this point once before, when Barry had overheard him and Ivy talking about the Polish airman's visit to Burracombe, but then the excitement of their holiday in London seemed to have diverted Barry's attention. Now, he knew he would have to reveal at least part of the truth. 'And it's true that most boys do only have two grannies. But some have more. Look at Freddy Furseman, that you've made friends with at school. I know his dad, and I know for a fact he's got three grannies.'

'Has he?' Barry asked in surprise. 'He's never told me that.'

'Well, I don't suppose you boys talk much about grannies. Anyway, he has. His first dad died in the war and his mother got married again so he's got three grannies that way.'

Barry thought about this, then said, 'But you never died in the war, and Mum never got married again, so that's not the same, is it? I still don't see—'

Ivy broke in. 'You'll just have to take it from us, Barry, that you got three, never mind how for the time being. You'll understand later on, when you're a few years older.' She felt a dread at the thought of the sudden realisation that would come to him and hoped fervently that he would be able to understand also how it had been for her and his true father. 'The main thing is, the one in Nottingham used to live in Poland but she's in England now and wants to see you. She's old and very ill and she's got no other grandchildren, so we've decided, your dad and me, that it's only right to take you up there. It'll only be the once and you don't need to do nothing except be nice and polite, like you've been brought up. And then we'll come home and you can forget about it. And you don't need to go talking about it at school or round the village,' she added, hoping that George was right and boys didn't discuss their grand-mothers much.

Barry was silent again. Then he asked, 'Where is Nottingham, anyway? Is it further than London? And when are we going? Will we go on a bus?'

'Get that school atlas of yours,' George said. 'We'll find it on there. We'll go before Christmas, as soon as the holidays start.' Konrad's latest letter had indicated that his mother did not have much time left and they should go as soon as possible. It was a nuisance for George; it was his busiest time, apart from Easter, but it couldn't be helped. 'We'll have to go by train and stop some-where overnight. Maybe two nights.'

'It'll be like a holiday,' Barry said, looking more enthusiastic. 'And I'll be able to get a lot more train numbers too. I bet none of the other boys have been to Nottingham.'

'It's no use asking him to keep it secret,' Ivy said later to George. 'He's already looking forward to telling his friends all about Nottingham and the trains. People are bound to put two and two to-gether and it'll be all round the village, and good-ness knows what they'll make of it.'

'If you ask me,' George told her, 'it'd be better to let it all come out in the open. Then they won't have to wonder, and they won't have to make up their own stories. Didn't we say when all this started that there'd be no more secrets?'

'That was between us. Not for every gossip in Burracombe to know our business.'

'Well, it seems to me they do know – or think they know – most of it anyway, and what they don't know they've made up. It's time they were put straight. And quite honestly, Ivy, how much do you think they'll care? There's been enough talk about you and your red hair over the years but folk haven't turned their backs. Knowing the truth isn't going to make matters worse now, either for you or our Barry. It's all water under the bridge.'

Ivy was silent. She wasn't sure if he was right or wrong, but she knew in her heart that it didn't make much difference either way. The village had made up its mind about her years ago, and if they didn't like her much it wasn't because of what might have happened between her and a Polish pilot stationed at Harrowbeer airfield during the war. It was because of her own sharp tongue.

'I dare say you're right, George,' she said at last. 'There's not much we can do anyway, now that Barry knows about his granny. And I know I'm going to have to tell him about his father too, some time or other. It's up to him what he tells his friends. I can't make him keep secrets as well.'

George smiled at her and put his hands on her shoulders.

'You're a good woman really, Ive,' he said. 'And I reckon you've learned a lot, these past few months. I wouldn't be surprised if you won't feel quite a bit happier now, having it all out in the open. I reckon this is going to be a turning point for us all.'

Secrets seemed to have become a part of Val

Ferris's life too. Ben had gone back to London at the end of his previous visit with no more said between them, though his dark eyes had held hers intently as he said goodbye. Val had scowled fiercely back at him, but he'd just grinned, which annoyed her even more. It was as if he didn't believe her rejection and was confident that she would eventually give in. As if he knew her better than she knew herself.

She was also haunted by his words about Luke. *An artist, like himself who understood that 'flings' didn't matter.* Did that mean that he thought Luke himself was likely to indulge in the occasional affair while away from her in London? Did it mean that he *knew?*

Val shook herself, furious that she could ever allow such thoughts to enter her head. But she knew that, deep down, this was what she had always feared might happen when Luke spent one week in four in London, painting portraits or working at the gallery. She'd told herself she trusted him, that it was wrong of her even to entertain such suspicions, but there were moments when, feeling lonely at home with only Christopher for company, she had wondered what Luke might be doing at that moment. She had always pushed such vague, disquieting thoughts to the back of her mind. But now Ben had brought them to the surface and she couldn't shake them away.

Even if it were true, she thought, it didn't mean that she should behave the same way. She loved Luke and she intended to be faithful to him, and she believed – yes, she insisted to herself, she really did believe – that he felt the same about her. Ben was injecting poison into her mind, that was what it was, and she wasn't going to allow it to affect her.

She watched him stride off along the lane with Luke, relieved that he was leaving and determined that he was not going to come again. If Luke wanted to invite him for New Year, she would put her foot down and say no. Christmas and New Year were family times and Ben was not part of her family, and that was that.

She turned away from the gate. A group of women were coming along the road on their way back from the village shops and stopped to chat. Val, who had been hoping to get inside before they saw her, paused reluctantly.

'Was that Luke's artist friend?' Dottie Tozer enquired, shifting her shopping bag to her other arm. 'I saw him about the village once or twice. Nice-looking young man.'

'Yes, that was Ben Mallory. He came down to do some painting with Luke and stayed a bit longer than I expected. They've both gone back to London now.'

'Catching the train from Tavi?' Aggie Madge asked, and Val nodded. 'Well, if ever you don't find it convenient to have him to stay, you tell him I've got a room he can have. Stop all winter, if he wants, since I've got no lodger just now and no holidaymakers likely till next spring.'

'Thanks, Mrs Madge, I'll tell him,' Val said, without the least intention of doing any such thing. Have Ben stay in the village all winter, even if it were in Aggie Madge's cottage? She shivered at the thought and turned her head to find Ivy

Sweet's gaze on her face. She turned away again quickly.

'I'd better go in. I left Christopher in his high chair, eating his cereal. He'll be throwing it all over the room.' She hurried round the side of the cottage to the back door, thankful to escape their curious glances.

As she stood at the kitchen sink, however, washing the breakfast dishes, she found her mind straying to the image of Ben, lodging in Aggie Madge's cottage, free to call in whenever he liked. Free to call in when Luke was away...

'I thought Val Ferris looked a bit peaky this morning,' Aggie commented as the women went on their way. 'I hope she's not going down with that nasty old flu as well. There's been too much of it round the village.'

'Especially when she's going to be by herself for the next week,' Dottie agreed. 'She don't want to be on her own and poorly with a little tacker to look after, and it would be even worse if he caught it too.'

'I don't reckon it'll be finished with us until all Burracombe's had it,' Ivy Sweet observed. She didn't often walk along with the other women but they'd all come out of the village shop together and it would have been rude not to have fallen into step with them. And she really was trying to be more friendly, even though her efforts weren't always recognised. 'It seems as if Billy's got it proper bad.'

'It does.' Dottie nodded, her face solemn. 'Jessie told me the doctor's going in every morn-

316

ing now, and he's been in a couple of times in the evening, too. He must think it's serious. They think he's afraid of pneumonia.'

'I dare say that's what it'll turn to in the end,' Ivy said. 'Might even be a blessing in disguise and carry him off quick and easy. Folk like Billy don't make old bones after all.'

Dottie drew in a quick breath and Aggie said sharply, 'Well, there's no need to talk so callous, Ivy Sweet, as if he's no more than an animal. The whole village is fond of Billy, as well you know, and, what's more, he's a sort of cousin to Dottie here. We'll all be upset when the good Lord takes him for his own.'

Ivy turned on her. 'And *you* needn't be so quick to take offence where there's none meant, Aggie Madge. All I was saying was that if it came to it, it could be an easier way for him. Don't they say pneumonia's the old man's friend for just that reason? And we all knows Billy's lived years more than he was ever expected to.' She hesitated and the other two women were surprised to see tears in her eyes. 'I think as much of Billy Friend as anyone here, and I'll tell you why. It's because he's about the only person in the whole of Burracombe who's never said a nasty word to me. The *only one!* And I'll be as sorry as anyone else when he goes, and I won't have no one saying no different!'

She gathered up her basket and stalked away, her back rigid with offence. Dottie and Aggie stared after her, then turned to each other, looking a little abashed.

'Maybe I was a bit sharp with her after all,' Aggie mumbled. 'I never meant to make her cry.'

317

'I don't think I've ever seen Ivy in tears,' Dottie said uncomfortably. 'Not since we were girls together, anyway. I did see her piping her eye after Ted Tozer took up with Alice when her came to work as a maid at the farm, when we were all young together, but that's all.' She put her hand on the other woman's arm. 'But don't you upset yourself, Aggie. Ivy's offended enough people in Burracombe to have to take it on the chin when 'tis the other way about for a change. All the same, she do seem to be trying to be a bit more pleasant just lately, so maybe we ought to try to meet her halfway.'

Aggie nodded and the two women continued on their way. A few yards further on they encountered Joe, on his way to meet his wife. He took her basket from her.

'Whatever have you got in here, Dottie? Lumps of lead? How many times have I told you I won't let you go shopping if you keep trying to carry too much home?'

Dottie shook her head at him and turned to the other woman. 'See what's happened to me, Aggie? Only a few weeks married and I'm no longer my own woman. Take my advice and don't let yourself get caught again.'

Aggie laughed and Joe put his arm around Dottie's shoulders. 'Your own woman? Whatever gave you that idea? You're *my* woman, Dottie Tozer, and don't you ever forget it!'

Chapter Thirty

Billy Friend died two days before Christmas. His chest, always his weakest point, finally gave up the struggle and succumbed to pneumonia, and his heart gave out. His sisters were with him at the end, sitting on either side of the bed, each holding one of his hands as his heart stopped beating and the thin chest ceased its weary and uneven rise and fall. Their tears dropped simultaneously onto his cooling skin and they turned their eyes towards David Hunter, who stood at the foot of the bed.

He stepped forwards and took hold of Billy's wrist. Billy's eyes were already closed, for he had passed into a deep sleep a few hours before and it had been clear that the end was coming. David shook his head.

'He's gone, I'm afraid. I'm very sorry.'

'Oh, Billy,' Jessie whispered and she bent to lay her head on his chest. 'Poor, poor Billy.'

Jeanie wiped her eyes with her free hand. 'He was a lovely brother,' she said in a broken voice. 'I know he wasn't quite the ticket, but he was a dear boy in his own way. So loving and happy. And he was a real help to Mr Foster.'

'You looked after him very well,' David said. 'You gave him a good life. A lot of people like Billy were put into institutions as babies and have never known the joys of a real family life.'

'Our mother and father would never do that,' Jessie said, lifting her head. 'They used to say that "for better or worse" meant the children as well. Not that any of us ever thought of Billy as "worse". He was just one of us and it was only right to look after him as best we could.' She stroked Billy's pale cheek. 'The roses have gone for ever now, my dear,' she said softly. 'But we must thank the Lord that you'll never suffer no more.' She stayed quiet for a moment, then looked up again at David. 'It's going to seem proper empty round here now without our Billy. To tell you the truth, Dr Hunter, I don't know how Jeanie and me are going to manage without him.'

David carried out his necessary tasks and then left, promising to call Lucy Dodd, who attended deaths as well as births, to come and lay Billy out. The sisters would have to arrange for an under-taker to come quickly to collect the body, since it was now Friday afternoon and with Christmas intervening there would be no other opportunity until the following Tuesday and Billy could not be left in his bedroom above the post office until then.

'I'll do that,' Jessie said, getting up stiffly. 'You stop here for a few minutes on your own, dear. You were always specially close. It's a good job we let Morris's know the end was coming, so they'll be ready to send someone out.'

'Ask if we can keep him till tomorrow,' Jeanie begged, cradling one of Billy's limp hands in both of hers. 'I don't like to think of him rushed out as if we didn't want him no more. I'd like to sit up with him tonight, if I can.'

'We could take turns,' Jessie agreed. 'It won't do neither of us any good to wear ourselves out. We've had enough to do these past few days as it is, and there's still the last-minute Christmas post. Folk'll still be wanting their Christmas cards and parcels.'

The Tavistock funeral director agreed to come out the next morning and as Jessie replaced the telephone receiver, Lucy Dodd arrived, her face grave.

'I'm sorry to hear this news, and just on Christmas too. It'll be a sad one in Burracombe when this gets about.'

'The vicar said prayers for him in church last Sunday,' Jessie said, taking her upstairs. 'We'd better let him know. Come downstairs now and have a cup of tea, Jeanie, and then we'll walk over to the vicarage together if Lucy don't mind stopping for half an hour. We can't leave the poor dear on his own.'

'You could telephone him,' Lucy suggested, but Jessie shook her head.

"Tis not the sort of news I like to break over the telephone. We uses that mostly for business. We won't be long.'

'You take as long as you like,' the nurse said. 'Have your cup of tea and then go and see the vicar. I'll stay here till you come back.'

'That's good of Lucy,' Jeanie said as they walked through the village twenty minutes later. She had stopped crying for the time being, though both knew that fresh tears were on the way for both of them over the next week or so, until the funeral was over and they slowly became accustomed to life without their brother. But that was right and natural and neither would be ashamed to weep for him. Nor, they knew, would they be the only ones. Billy's round, flat face and the slanting eyes that gave his smile such a special charm were a familiar and beloved sight around the village and everyone would be saddened by his death.

Basil Harvey knew, the moment he opened the door to them, that one of his most innocent and vulnerable parishioners had died. He drew them from the darkening afternoon into his study, switched on the standard lamp to cast a comforting glow over the room, and sat them in two armchairs by the fire. He then called to Grace, who came hurrying from the kitchen and gave a little cry of sorrow before kissing both the sisters on the cheek.

'I'm so very sorry,' she said. 'Billy was such a dear boy.' Even though he was nearly forty, everyone in the village still thought of him as a boy and understandably so, since he had never really grown up. 'You must both be very sad.' She stroked Jeanie's hair for a moment, then said quietly, 'I'll make some tea.'

'Don't trouble yourself,' Jessie said quickly. 'We had a cup before coming out.'

'I'll make some just the same,' said Grace, who knew that it always helped to have a cup of tea in front of you at times like this, to fiddle with and hold, even if you took no more than a sip or two. 'You don't have to drink it if you don't want to.'

She knew they would, though. Tears – those already shed and those to come – needed replenishing. She went to the kitchen to put the kettle on and then slipped back into the drawing room where she and Basil had been taking advantage of a rare quiet hour or so to watch a comedy film on television. The laughter coming from the set was no longer appropriate to the afternoon and she switched it off.

As she took cups and saucers from the dresser and set them on a tray, she sighed. There was little enough respite for Basil at Christmas and now he would have a funeral to prepare for before the New Year, and one that would be attended by almost everyone in the village. There would be hymns to choose, tributes to be made, and his own eulogy to write. Basil always took his duties very seriously and this was one he would treat with the utmost care and respect.

What a shame it should be so close to Christmas, she thought. On the other hand, Billy had been very ill and it would have been far worse for his sisters to spend the season at his bedside, watching him suffer. He might even have been taken into hospital, which they had all dreaded. Perhaps it was better this way.

She was sure Basil would find the right words of comfort, both now and at the funeral. For all his apparently flustered manner, he was always ready with the sympathy and concern that his parishioners needed at such times, and he had an innate wisdom that they could always rely on. By the time she took in the tea, she knew he would have consoled and comforted both the sisters, and reassured them that their grief was right and natural. Over the next few weeks, he would be a rock in the troubled sea on which they had found themselves setting sail.

The news spread like wildfire around the village.

'Billy Friend gone!' The first intimation was the sign on the post office door, telling villagers it would be closed until the following morning. Jessie and Jeanie weren't really allowed to close it at all, but nobody was going to complain about it today. Those who still needed to post Christmas parcels – leaving it a bit late anyway, Jacob Prout commented – were advised in a second notice, put up by Joe Tozer, that they could take them to Dottie's cottage where Joe would pop them into Tavistock in his car and catch the last afternoon post. Those who had walked down to the post office carrying packages and envelopes and read both notices stood gazing at each other in dismay.

'Just before Christmas, too. That's cruel, that is.'

'Poor Jeanie and Jessie. They'll be beside theirselves. They thought the world of Billy.'

'We all did. He were a dear soul and never did harm to nobody.'

'When will the funeral be? It can't be till after Christmas.'

'I wonder if the vicar will mention Billy in his sermon. I'm going to make sure and go to church.'

'Me too. I reckon we all want to say a word in our prayers for Billy and his sisters.'

Dottie's eyes were full of tears as she came to the door to take in the parcels her friends had brought for Joe to post. They remembered too that Billy was her cousin and gave her their condolences.

'I remember when he was born,' Aggie Madge reminisced. 'Such a round little face, he had; he looked a bit Chinese with those slanty eyes, but the doctor – it was old Dr Brown then, Dr Latimer had only just come to the village as his assistant – he said it was the way he was born.'

'He wasn't expected to live long,' Dottie said. 'He could have gone any time but Auntie Maud said she wasn't going to lose him, and she made sure he fed proper and she looked after him day and night. The whole family took care of our Billy. I thought he'd go on into old age but the winters we've had in the last year or two have been hard on him.'

'And now it'll be hard on Jeanie and Jessie,' Aggie said, shaking her head. 'Well, in the midst of life we are in death, as the vicar often reminds us, and we've still got to celebrate Christmas in the proper manner. It's good of your Joe to take the parcels in, Dottie.'

'It's the Burracombe way, to help each other when the need arises,' Dottie said. 'And my Joe's a Burracombe man, when all's said and done. He might have lived most of his life in America but he was born and brought up here and knows what it is to be part of a village. And that will never change.'

Chapter Thirty-One

Ivy and George Sweet were in Nottingham on the day of Billy Friend's death. School had broken up on Tuesday, with the usual Christmas party, so they had not been able to leave Burracombe until the Wednesday morning. The train journey had taken over six hours in a cold, sooty train, and even Barry, who was eager to collect as many train numbers as he could, grew weary of it before they finally arrived. They were met on the platform by Konrad, who looked grave, and for a moment Ivy feared that they were too late and their journey had been wasted.

'She's not...'

He returned her anxious glance. 'No, fortunately, but she is very poorly. This wretched influenza – she is not strong enough to withstand it, I fear.' He looked down at Barry and held out his hand for the boy to shake. 'So. You are Barry.'

Barry stared up at him and Ivy, seeing them together for the first time, was struck by their resemblance. Konrad's hair was dark and Barry's red, it was true, but apart from that they both bore similar facial characteristics – the straight nose now beginning to develop on Barry's young face, the wide-set eyes and that funny little point to the ears which she'd always thought made Barry look like a little elf when he was very young. They were Igor's ears, she thought with a

326

pang, and they're Konrad's as well. And there were other things, too. Nobody looking at these two could doubt that they were related.

She hardly dared look at George for fear that he saw it too, but the comforting feel of his hand on her arm told her that George had accepted the truth long ago and had filed it away in some box where it could never damage his relationship with his son, for he had always, right from the start, looked on Barry as his and he'd made it clear that nothing was going to change that.

'Well,' she heard him say now as Konrad released Barry's hand, 'it's too cold to stand about here. Where have you found for us to stay?'

Konrad picked up Ivy's suitcase. 'There is a small hotel near my home. I could not put you up myself, you understand, for I have only one spare bedroom and my mother is occupying that. I thought I would take you there now and then come to collect you later, for supper with me. You can meet my mother then, if she is well enough. Sometimes she sleeps early.'

'Is she able to get up?' Ivy asked, and he shook his head. She felt her heart sink. This was going to be a difficult visit and she still wasn't sure that Barry understood what it was all about. Once again she wished that Konrad had never found those diaries that had enabled him to track her down. Her affair with his brother had happened twelve years ago. It was in the past and should have stayed in the past.

But Barry was very much in the present and in the future too, and he was the reason for her being here. *Be sure your sins will find you out,* she thought suddenly. *No matter how much time has gone by...*

The hotel Konrad took them to was small and plain but clean enough and promised them an evening meal if they required it and breakfast next morning. Barry had a small room of his own next to Ivy and George's and was obviously impressed by staying in a hotel at all. He unpacked his small case, arranged the two or three books he had brought on a shelf, and settled down cross-legged on his bed to fill in the train numbers he had collected in his spotter's guide.

'Some of them were really rare namers,' he told his parents excitedly. 'Billy Madge and Freddy Furseman are going to be proper jealous.'

'So they might be,' Ivy said, 'but what you got to do now is have a good wash – there's a bathroom just along the corridor – and get yourself ready for tonight. You heard what your Uncle Konrad said – we're going to have our dinner with him tonight and I want you looking smart and on your best behaviour.'

She waited for more questions, but Barry appeared to be looking on the situation as one of those mysterious things that you were told you would understand when you were grown up. There had been a few of those already just lately – odd things happening to himself and other boys that they sniggered over half fearfully in the school lavatories, and peculiar feelings in his stomach when he looked at some of the bigger girls in his new school. He didn't much like these sensations and tried to ignore them. It was harder to ignore this sudden arrival in his life of an uncle and grandmother he had never heard of before, but there were plenty of other things more interesting to think about, and they had at least got him this train journey and two nights in a real hotel. Freddy Furseman and Billy Madge were going to be mad with jealousy.

There were Christmas lights on in the streets of Nottingham when the Sweets rode to Konrad's house in the taxi he had sent for them. Barry pressed his face to the window as they went along, wishing that he could live in a big city where they had Christmas lights in the streets as well as in the big shops they were passing. They didn't even have street lights in Burracombe. He made up his mind that when he was grown up and an actor he would live somewhere like this. Well, he would probably live in London, which would be even better. He hadn't forgotten the trip to London they'd made at the end of the summer, and the lights they'd seen in Piccadilly one night. What must it be like to see those lights every night of your life!

He wondered what the old woman, who was so mysteriously his third granny, would be like. They might not be seeing her tonight, because she was ill and in bed, but his mother had told him that if she was too tired tonight they would come to the house again tomorrow and visit her then. Barry, who didn't much like old ladies, especially if they were ill and in bed, wasn't looking forward to this but he didn't think they'd be staying long. All he would have to do was be quiet and polite, as his mother had told him, and answer whatever questions she asked. They'd be about school, probably.

Grown-ups always asked about school, as if that was the most interesting thing in your life, whereas really it was the most boring.

He wished he could tell her about the train numbers and names he'd collected on the journey. But that wasn't likely to happen, and as the taxi arrived at the house where his Uncle Konrad lived, he shrugged and prepared himself for a tedious evening.

'He seems to be taking it all right so far,' George said later that night as he and Ivy went to bed in the small hotel room. Barry was next door so they kept their voices down in case the walls were thin enough for him to be able to hear. 'And I got to say, Konrad's put himself out to make us welcome. That pork stew he made us was proper tasty and I liked the dumplings.'

'Bit heavy for me,' Ivy said. 'It'll be lying on my stomach all night. And I thought Barry was going to turn up his nose at the cabbage, but he remembered what we told him and ate whatever he was given. You know what?' she added as she got into the rather lumpy bed beside George. 'I reckon us ought to get him that bike he's been wanting for Christmas, to make up for all this.'

'It's a bit late to get it before Christmas now, Ive. We won't be going home till Friday and it's Christmas Eve on Saturday. We could go into Tavi then, I suppose, and see what they got in the bike shop but they might not have much in Barry's size, that's if they got anything at all.'

'We wouldn't want a kiddy's bike, the way he's growing. Get him a proper one and put blocks on the pedals like Herbert Madge did for his Billy. He deserves it, George. It's not every boy who has to travel half across England just before Christmas to see an old lady he's never met before and didn't even know existed.'

George grunted and reached out to switch off the light. 'We'll talk about it in the morning, Ive. Let's go to sleep now. I'm tired out by all this travelling. And we've got a tricky day ahead of us tomorrow.'

The front bedroom in Konrad's house was darkened by thick curtains, half drawn to keep out even the gloom of the winter light. The Sweets entered cautiously, following the Polish man as he held open the door. Ivy found her heart suddenly beating hard as she stared down at the old woman lying in the high bed, and was swept by a wild mixture of emotions.

This was Igor's mother. The mother he had not been able to contact all through the war, from when he left Poland to come to England and train as a pilot, to the day he was shot down and killed. This was the woman who had carried him in her body, given birth to him, fed him at her own breast; who had known him as a child, as a young man; who had taught him right from wrong and felt pride in him as he went out into the world; who had expected to see him marry and have children of his own; who had looked forward to holding her first grandchild in her arms; who had had all of that snatched away by one of the cruellest wars the world had ever known.

If Ivy had married Igor, as once she had

dreamed of doing, this would have been her mother-in-law.

All that had never been, and yet one truth remained. This was Barry's grandmother, and Barry was the grandchild she had yearned to hold in her arms as a baby, yet she had not known about him until this past year. Barry was the grandson she had longed to see before she died.

'You all right, Ive?' George murmured in her ear, and Ivy turned, only now realising that tears were pouring down her cheeks.

'Yes. Oh, *George...*' She shook her head blindly and looked down at the bed again. 'Poor old soul. *Poor* old soul...'

The woman in the bed was old and frail, her body so small that it made scarcely a hump in the blankets that covered her. Her sallow, colourless face was gaunt. Her hair lay thin and white about her scalp, which showed through in a shade of greyish pink. Her eyes were closed and her breathing was rapid and shallow.

Konrad stepped forward and touched his mother's cheek gently with the back of one finger.

'She has been asleep all morning,' he said quietly. 'The doctor came early. He says it will not be long now.' He turned his head and met Ivy's eyes. 'You came just in time.'

Ivy looked down at her son. He was standing beside her, with George's hand on his shoulder, looking uncertainly at the old woman. She looked back at Konrad.

'I don't want him to be here when...'

'I understand that. I think she will wake in a little while, and if she knows him then, you will have done all you can.' His eyes met hers again. 'I appreciate your coming all this way, and at such a time of year. It is a great kindness you are doing.'

Ivy felt the tears brim again. She put her other hand on Barry's shoulder and drew him nearer the bed. Konrad continued to stroke the withered cheek, and the papery eyelids fluttered a little and then opened, revealing dark eyes that stared upwards in bewilderment and then moved slowly round until fastening their gaze on the face of her son.

Ivy caught her breath in shock. The eyes, which she had expected to find quite unfamiliar, were eyes she had known for years. They were Igor's eyes. Igor's, and Konrad's.

And Barry's.

Konrad spoke to his mother in their own language and the eyes moved again, their gaze drifting until settling again on Ivy's face. Ivy stared back through the gauze of tears, mesmerised. She found herself filled with an unexpected desire to talk to this woman, to tell her about the son she had lost, to tell her that she had loved him, they had loved each other, even though their love was illicit and she had been ridden with guilt ever since. She wanted to tell her about Barry, what he had been like as a baby, as a small child, as the awkward youth he was now becoming as he grew towards manhood. Perhaps, a little later, if she could be left alone with the old woman, she would be able to do that. But there was only one thing she must do now, and she knew that it must be done quickly.

'Barry,' she said quietly and pressed gently on his shoulder, 'this is your Polish granny. You can say whatever you want to her. She just wants to see you and hear your voice, even if she doesn't understand your words.'

Barry looked up at her and she saw the trepidation in his face. She smiled at him and pressed his shoulder again, and he turned his eyes reluctantly towards the bed.

'Hello, Granny,' he whispered, and the old eyes widened and looked from him to Konrad. Barry hesitated, then asked, 'What – what is the Polish word for "Granny"? I don't think she understands...'

Konrad's face was sombre as he answered. 'She knows who you are. I told her earlier and her mind is well enough to understand. She understands some English as well, but you can call her *Babcia*.' He pronounced it 'Bab-cha' and Barry nodded and repeated it.

'Hello, Bab-cha.' He moved closer, a little fearfully, and as she reached out a trembling hand, he took it in his and said, 'I'm Barry.'

Chapter Thirty-Two

Christmas in Burracombe was a little more subdued than usual that year. Everyone celebrated with presents, cards, Christmas dinners and family get-togethers with games and sing-songs, just as usual, but there was a shadow over the whole village after the death of Billy Friend. It was not until after the funeral, held on New Year's Eve, that any of the villagers felt they could move forward.

'I'm thankful we could bury the poor dear before the turn of the year,' Dottie said as she and Joe walked slowly down the church path after the service. 'I don't know why, but it wouldn't have seemed right, somehow, to have it in a different year from when he died.'

'There were plenty of people to see him go,' Joe commented. 'I don't think there's a soul in the whole of Burracombe that wasn't here, apart from the kiddies and those looking after them at home. What the vicar said was right, you know – if you can live your life not doing harm to anybody but making people happy to know you, you've lived well. Billy never harmed anyone and I reckon we all felt better for seeing his smile around the place. It just shows, Dottie, you don't have to be rich or clever to have people love you.'

'Well, that's just as well,' she said with a smile, 'because I'm not either of those things and I'd like to think folk loved me nearly as much as they did poor Billy!'

'Every bit as much,' he said, tucking her arm through his. 'The trouble is, people only talk about how much they think of you at funerals, and you're not having one of those for a good many years yet. You'll just have to take it for granted that they do.'

'There's a few that don't, all the same. Ivy Sweet, for a start. She never liked me much even when we were girls.'

'One, then,' he allowed. 'But that's all. And you

might be surprised by Ivy, if you could just see inside her mind. I reckon folk misread her, you know. She's not half as bad as you all make out.'

Ivy herself had been to the funeral, with George. They had been shocked to hear the news about Billy when they had returned to the village late on the afternoon of Christmas Eve. Ivy had gone to the Bell Inn that evening, knowing that Bernie and Rose would be busy even though they now had their second barmaid, and had found out then. Rose, who told her before they started work, was surprised to see tears in Ivy's eyes.

'Poor chap,' Ivy said, surprised herself by her own reaction. 'And poor Jeanie and Jessie too. 'Tis a shame, and just before Christmas as well. You'd have thought they could have been given that time with him.'

'He was very poorly,' Rose said. 'It was a kindness in the end, just like you said yourself it would be. Dottie says it was very peaceful.'

Ivy nodded and began to prepare the bar. She was still shaken by her visit to Nottingham, which she and George had barely had time to discuss on their own. It was obvious that the old lady herself was very close to death, but they had seen how much Barry's visit had meant to her and they were proud of him for agreeing to stay beside her until she slept again. A lot of boys wouldn't have been able to get out of the room fast enough.

Ivy too had been granted her short time alone with the woman who might have been her mother-in-law. Not quite sure whether the sick woman was awake or asleep, she had sat beside her, talking softly of the time she had known Igor, of the love they had felt for each other. 'I know we were wrong to do as we did,' she said quietly, 'but it was wartime and it all seemed different then. He told me there'd never been any other girl, and I've always been glad I could give him some happiness in those last weeks. And he gave me Barry. George and me might never have had any children if it hadn't been for Igor.'

They'd gone into Tavistock the first chance they'd had and had managed to buy Barry a new bike. A lot of the children who had passed the examination for the grammar school a few months ago had been given bikes as a reward, but most of the secondary modern children either had to wait for a hand-down from an older brother or sister, or were given a second-hand one. Ivy and George were determined that Barry's should be new and, to their relief, they found one with a bright red frame, just as they knew he would like. His face when he saw it on Christmas morning was, as Ivy said, a 'picture' and worth the expense.

Now Christmas was over and, with Billy's funeral done, they were looking ahead to the new year, like the rest of Burracombe, and hoping it would be a happier start for the whole village.

'There's so much to look forward to,' Basil said as he and a few friends sat at the dinner table at Burracombe Barton. 'I know January and February can be bitterly cold, but the days do begin to draw out quite soon and with the Organ Festival to look forward to as well, we have much to celebrate.'

'Not to mention Joyce Warren's Winter Extravaganza,' Hilary said with a smile. 'I think it was

337

a very good idea to move it from November or December to early February. There's so much going on before Christmas, it's hard to fit it all in, and it will make a bright spot in the middle of the worst weather. David and James are already starting to rehearse their duets.'

'And that's another thing to look forward to,' Basil said, his face pink with delight. 'Frances and James's wedding. What an Easter it is going to be!'

'I may have news too, soon,' Constance Bellamy said. 'My two young people have decided to stay on for another three months! I'm so pleased. They've brought a real ray of sunshine into my life.'

'Have they found anything interesting yet?' Gilbert enquired. 'Anything about your family, I mean.'

'Oh, lots of things. Old papers and documents, you know – diaries, letters, there's no end to the stuff my ancestors hoarded. Only the other day Katie unearthed a painting of one of my great-great-aunts, standing with its face to the wall, covered in dust and signed by a known artist! It's probably worth quite a bit, but of course it will never be sold. I'm going to have it professionally cleaned and it can hang in the dining room.'

'Nothing about your long-lost uncle?' Hilary asked. 'That's what they first came to find out, wasn't it?'

'I think we've almost forgotten him,' Constance said with a laugh. 'It's all been so interesting – hardly a day goes by without them appearing downstairs, covered in cobwebs, brandishing some

338

new discovery. And they've been doing a lot of redecorating too. It's all been quite wonderful.'

'It's a pity they didn't come along this evening,' Gilbert remarked. 'It can't be good for them to spend all their time rooting about in your attics, seeing nobody of their own age.'

'Oh, they do. Jackie Tozer's been helping them. Now that her leg's almost completely better she can get up the stairs quite easily and I hear peals of laughter floating down to me. And they go to London from time to time, so see other relatives on their father's side. That's where they are now. They went just after Christmas to spend the New Year. They'll be back in a day or so.'

'Has Minnie Tozer accepted their presence now?' Gilbert asked. 'I heard she was very much against them for some reason.'

Constance frowned. 'She hasn't said much to me lately, but I'm not sure she has. I think she suspected that they were after my money!' Constance gave a short bark of laughter. 'Such as it is! I'm afraid it's dwindled away considerably since the war.'

'Still, there must be some value in the house itself,' Gilbert persisted. 'And you've plenty of heirlooms – that painting, for instance, and the silver you've got on your sideboard. I dare say there's even more stored away in cupboards and up in the attic. You do need to take care, Constance.'

'I trust them completely,' the old lady retorted. 'They've lived long enough in my house now for me to know them well enough. Even if they did turn out in the end to be no relations of mine, they've been good friends and good company. Why shouldn't I leave everything to them if I feel like it? Frankly, Gilbert, I don't know what business it is of anyone else's what I do.' She gave him a sharp look. 'Not so long ago, you yourself, if I remember correctly, were ready to leave the whole of the Burracombe estate to a thirteen-year-old child you'd never even known existed!'

Hilary drew in her breath and saw Basil Harvey put his hand to his mouth. She was aware of David's amusement as the two old people glowered at each other across the polished dining table. Then Gilbert let out a bellow of laughter and Hilary let her breath go.

'You always did know your own mind, Constance, and you never took kindly to being questioned on it. Very well, have it your own way, but remember, when it all ends in tears, that we all tried to warn you. We only have your own good at heart, you know.'

'I do know, thank you, Gilbert,' the little woman replied, though there was still some acid in her tone. 'And I'll certainly remember. But I can assure you, it won't end in tears. I haven't reached the age of eighty without developing some judgement of character and I've lived long enough now with these two young people to be quite sure they're genuine. Whether or not there is blood between us, I can't know for certain, but I believe there is. I believe it very strongly. And if there isn't – why, I'll adopt them! And then it won't matter either way.'

She stared at them defiantly but there was a twinkle in her little black eyes and Hilary found herself smiling. Miss Bellamy smiled in return and in a moment the tension had evaporated and they all relaxed. Hilary got up to fetch the cheese board from the sideboard, and Gilbert offered port to go with the Stilton.

'She really is quite wonderful,' David said to Hilary later as they got ready for bed. 'I've never seen anyone stand up to your father like that, and stare him down too. But perhaps he was just being polite.'

'Father, "just being polite"?' Hilary exclaimed with a laugh. 'You surely must know him better than that by now, David. Of course, Miss Bellamy is quite a few years older than he is, and probably gave him more than one cuff round the ear when he was a boy, for scrumping apples and so forth, but I think he really does have a lot of respect for her. He sees her point about her right to decide who to leave her property to, but he is also concerned that she shouldn't be hoodwinked.'

'She's obviously not going to be easy to hoodwink,' David said, holding out his arms. 'Come to bed, darling.' He drew her under the blankets beside him and she snuggled against him. 'You know,' he went on, stroking her shoulder reflectively, 'I think this is my favourite moment of the day. You and me together, cosy and warm in our own bed, where nobody can disturb us. Who was it who said something about the deep, deep peace of the marriage bed?'

'I think it was—' Hilary began, but the sharp note of the telephone bell interrupted her. David groaned and she raised her eyebrows. 'And what were you saying about nobody being able to disturb us? Only half the village, that's all!'

David reached out and picked up the receiver, which stood on the small table close to his side of the bed.

'Dr Hunter here. Yes. No... No, it isn't.' He listened for a moment, then said wearily, 'No, I am not your friend Harry. I'm afraid you have the wrong number. Try again – and if you'll take my advice, wait until the morning before you do. You may be able to speak more clearly by then.' He replaced the receiver and turned back to Hilary, who was now convulsed with giggles. 'And you can stop laughing, too!' he ordered her, and drew her back into his arms. 'Now ... where were we?'

'So that's that,' Ivy said as George replaced the receiver and looked across the room at her. 'The poor old soul's gone. Well, it's a blessing really. She was ready, you could see that.'

'He said he was sorry to ring so late,' George said, coming to sit beside her and putting his arm across her shoulders. 'But he knows I'm always about at this time and he didn't want to risk Barry hearing. That was thoughtful of him, Ive.'

'Yes, it was. He's a nice man, George, and I reckon his mother was a nice woman when she was younger. She brought her boys up right.' She turned to meet his eyes. 'What Igor and me did was wrong, I know, but there's plenty of folk fall into that trap. Always have been and I reckon always will.'

He nodded. 'I tell you what, Ive, I don't think there's any need for us to talk about that any more.

Not between you and me, anyway. Everything's been said that needs to be said. It's different where Barry's concerned – he'll have to know the truth one day. But for now, all he needs to be told is that his Polish granny has passed away, and then we can go back to living the way we always have.'

'You don't reckon we should take him to the funeral?'

'No, I don't, and neither does Konrad. He said so. All he wanted was for the old lady to see her grandson. He wants to keep in touch – write now and then, so he knows how Barry's getting on, and maybe come to see him from time to time. He is his uncle, after all, and he'll have no other nephews of his own blood. I reckon we can put up with that. And he says there's a few bits and pieces he wants Barry to have – a watch and one or two other things that belonged to his mother and father. He'll send them down. Apart from that...' He paused, then added quietly, 'I reckon that's pretty well the end of it, Ive, don't you?'

'Yes,' she said after a moment, and looked at him with wet eyes. 'Oh, George, I feel as if a huge load I didn't even realise I was carrying has just rolled away off my shoulders. I feel a different person. It's like it's the end of a chapter for us.'

George nodded. 'The end of a chapter. And the beginning of a new one.'

Chapter Thirty-Three

Ben Mallory didn't come to Burracombe for Christmas or for New Year. He told Luke he had received an invitation from some friends to go skiing in Switzerland and wouldn't be back in England until the middle of January. Val heaved a silent sigh of relief when she heard this, and hoped that by the time he came home the attractions of the Devon countryside would have waned.

'I really like us to be a family on our own,' she said as she and Luke sat by the fire in the cottage. 'We're complete. We don't need other people.'

'I know.' He drew her closer on the little sofa. 'That's what I like too. But you won't mind him coming again, will you? Some time in the spring?'

Val sighed. 'Not if you really want him here, I suppose. But I don't expect he'll want to come again. He's had all he's likely to get here and now he's got other fish to fry.'

Luke frowned. 'That sounds rather bitter, darling.'

'It's not. I mean, he wanted the autumn colours, didn't he, and they're well and truly over now. And these new friends he's been to Switzerland with—'

'They're not new friends. He's known them longer than he's known me.'

Val moved her shoulders impatiently. 'Well, whoever they are ... he seems more interested in spending time with them than us, you have to

344

admit that.'

There was a tiny silence, then Luke said, 'If I didn't know you better, I'd say you sounded a bit jealous.'

'Jealous! Of course I'm not – why ever should I be jealous? He's welcome to his friends, whoever they are, and they're welcome to him!' She realised that her voice was rising and bit her lip. 'I've got nothing to be jealous of,' she added more quietly. 'Nothing at all.'

'No, of course not,' he said, but there was an odd note in his voice. Val wanted to turn and look at his face but didn't dare. She realised that she was a little afraid of what she might see in his eyes – or perhaps of what he might see in hers.

After a minute or two, she changed the subject. 'You will be here for the Extravaganza, won't you? It's the week after next.'

'Yes, I'm not back in London till the week after that. I'll be here until the day after St Valentine's Day.' He squeezed her shoulders gently. 'So I'll be able to give you your card in person!'

'Oh, Luke! As if that mattered.' But it did matter, and they both knew it. Luke's Valentine cards – all the cards he gave Val – were exquisite little paintings that she kept and framed and hung on the bedroom wall. She would have been bitterly disappointed if she had not been given one this year – and given it in person.

'I'm very lucky to have you,' she said quietly. 'Very lucky indeed. And I'm not jealous of any-one else in the world – except,' she added with a little smile, 'the people you see and talk to in London, people I don't know and will probably never meet.' She thought of Ben's hints that as an artist Luke would have a more free and easy approach to other women, might even enjoy the odd 'fling' himself, and she felt a tiny knot of fear deep inside her. She didn't believe those hints, she told herself angrily, not for a moment.

She trusted Luke absolutely.

The Tozers were also getting ready for the Extravaganza.

Much as they might grumble about Joyce Warren behind her back, the villagers had to admit that she did get things going and she was never short of ideas. And she did know how to put on a good show. Since Felix Copley had moved over to Little Burracombe and she'd taken over the pantomime and other Christmas productions, there had been some really good evenings in the village hall. This one looked like being as good as any of the others.

'There are six of us in the family to ring the handbells,' Minnie mused. 'Ted and Alice, Joe, Tom and Joanna, and Val. That's twelve bells and we can make some good tunes on those. I might even do one or two new harmonies.'

'I'd have thought we already had enough to fill an entire evening,' Tom remarked, sifting through the placards with their columns of figures which Minnie had written out so carefully over the years. 'Do we really need any more?'

'We have always got to have one or two new ones, to show we keep up with the times,' his grandmother declared. 'There's that new song they keep playing on the wireless – "No Other

346

Love". It's got a nice tune, and I reckon I can do something with that.'

'It's a lovely song, and Ronnie Hilton's got a lovely voice,' Alice said. 'It would go down a treat, if you can do it.'

Minnie was confident she could do it and spent several evenings listening to the record on Tom and Joanna's record player and writing down the notes she heard. After a while, she got Ted to take down the handbells that hung by their leather straps from the beam in the kitchen and hang them on a row of hooks in a wooden frame he had made her years ago for this very purpose. She then used a small hammer with a leather covering over its head to tap the tune out on the bells.

'That sounds handsome,' Ted said admiringly. 'A proper job, Mother. I can see you've not lost your touch.'

'I should hope not,' she said, frowning a little. 'I'm not too happy about that middle bit, mind. I think that needs a bit more work.' She put the record on again and Ted who, like the rest of the family, had heard more of 'No Other Love' than they had ever wanted to, retreated to the yard where Alice was feeding the hens.

'She's at it again. Says the middle bit's not right. I hope the village appreciates what we put up with here so that they can have a few minutes' entertainment.'

'At least it keeps her mind off Miss Bellamy and those two Australians,' Alice said, throwing out the last handful of corn. 'Not that our Jackie's much help, coming home day after day with tales of what they've found up in those attics.'

'I wouldn't have thought there could be much left to find by now. They must have carried down mountains of stuff to sort through and chuck out. She got Tom to take the truck round the other day and he said it was full to the top with old newspapers, and letters and diaries you could hardly read, they were so old and tattered.'

Alice straightened up. 'That's a shame, if you ask me. Old letters and diaries can be really interesting, and so can newspapers, come to that. Like taking up an old carpet or piece of lino and finding papers laid down there ten years ago. Only, these'd be even older than that. They ought to be kept.'

'I think they're reading them through, quick like, to see if there's anything interesting, but most of them's just pages about livestock sales and cattle prices and such. Nobody'd want to know about them now.'

'I wouldn't be surprised if someone would. People like to keep track of things. And there's always museums and whatnot, wanting old stuff.'

'Well, they're gone now,' Ted said. 'Is our Jackie up there again?'

'I think so. I'm beginning to wonder if she's got something else to interest her there, apart from old papers.'

Ted looked at her. 'You mean young Greg?'

'Well, it could be, couldn't it? I know it's only a few months since she lost Bryce, but she's young and young hearts mend easy. And she's grieved long enough. I'd like to see her taking an interest again.'

'You won't like it if she decides to go to Australia instead of America,' Ted pointed out, and Alice sighed.

'I don't say I'd want it to come to that. I just want to see her come to life a bit and be the girl she used to be, and there's nothing like a bit of romance to do that. Nothing serious, mind – just a boy-girl thing like she had with Roy Pettifer years ago.'

Ted had his own ideas about whether Jackie's romance with Roy had been 'just a boy-girl thing'. He'd seen them once or twice behind one of his hayricks and they'd looked more friendly than he thought they should. But they'd slipped off quick enough, hoping he hadn't seen them, and he'd never said anything to Alice. He didn't say anything now except to remark, 'That'd be the best thing, if she could take up with a local boy again and settle down in the village. But I don't suppose it'll come to that. She's a wanderer, our Jackie, and broken leg or no broken leg, I'm afraid she's not going to stop wandering just yet. Always wants to see round the next corner, she does, just like when she was a kiddy.'

Alice said nothing for a moment. She knew he was probably right but she didn't want to believe it. At last she said, 'She's seemed happy enough to stop at home these past few weeks.'

'Only while her leg's been getting better. Now it's almost back to normal, she's going to want to be off again. You got to face up to it, Alice. She's got to earn her own living again, to start with.'

'She could do that here. Bernie and Rose are looking for a new barmaid again. That one they had first hasn't turned out much good at all.'

'For goodness' sake, Alice! Jackie's not going to want to work behind the bar in the village pub. She's done better than that already. Anyway, she told me backalong that they were keeping her job open for her at the glass factory.'

Alice stared at him. 'You mean in Corning?'

'Well, I don't know of one round here.'

'There's no need to be clever!' she snapped. 'And if she told you that, why did she never say a word to me? Why didn't *you?*'

'Because we both knew you'd be upset, and anyway I hoped it'd blow over and never need be said.'

'So why say it now?' Alice demanded unreasonably. 'Has she told you anything else she's never bothered to tell me? Like, when she's going back?'

'No, of course not. I don't know any more than you do. Come on, my dear, 'tis no good getting aerated about it. Jackie'll do what she wants, just as she always has, and there's nothing much we can do about it.'

'She's still under twenty-one.'

'And how much does that mean? We couldn't stop her before and we can't stop her now.' He sighed. 'I don't like it no better than you, but 'tis no good getting all steamed up about it until we know for certain. Not that it will be any good getting steamed up then, either. We just have to take her for what she is.'

'I know,' Alice said after a pause. 'It don't make it any easier, though. I always thought we'd have all our children nearby, all our lives. Now Brian's gone up north and only comes home now and then for a visit and it looks as if Jackie's going to settle too far away even for that.'

'It's the way the world is now, Alice. Young people go away from their homes more than they did when we were young. It's two wars that have done it and I don't reckon it will ever change back. Mind you, you're a fine one to talk yourself. You left home at eighteen to come and work here as a maid.'

'I didn't come that far. I could always get home by bus or train.'

'Well, all right,' he said, still trying to avert an argument. 'Maybe we should just think ourselves lucky we've still got two children nearby, especially as Tom's working on the farm with me and bringing up his family under our roof. And Val's only a step or two away.'

'I know. And I know you're right about Jackie, too.' She brightened a little. 'I tell you what, Ted, if she did take up with this Greg, it might be all right after all. We don't *know* that he means to go back to Australia. Suppose Miss Bellamy *did* leave everything to him and his sister and he decided to stay in Burracombe. Our Jackie could end up living at the Grey House!'

Greg and Jackie were going through yet another box of old papers.

'There can't be many left,' Jackie said, brushing dust out of her hair. 'This family never seemed to throw anything away.'

'And none of it's given us any clue about Grandfather,' Greg said, sitting back on his heels. 'I'm beginning to think he couldn't have been Auntie

Con's uncle after all. You'd think, with all this, there would have been *some* clue left behind.'

'Not if they wiped him out of the family as they seem to have done. Miss Bellamy herself doesn't remember anyone mentioning him after he went away. That's not natural. People talk a lot about family members who have left home.'

'So you think they would have thrown away any letters or photos that had anything to do with him.' Greg looked despondent. 'You're probably right. It looks as if we're never going to know for sure.' He picked up yet another yellowing envelope and shook out its contents. 'More old photos, and I bet none of them's any use.'

'We'd better look at them, all the same.' Jackie slipped them back into the envelope, then looked round as Katie appeared at the top of the stairs with a tray bearing three cups of tea and a plate of biscuits. 'Oh, thank goodness. My throat's as dry as the Sahara.'

'Let's have a break,' Greg said, moving over to a battered old sofa they had dragged over to the small window. 'We deserve it – we've worked like slaves today.'

Katie carried the tray to the window and set it on a small table. 'We've made quite a cosy little den up here, haven't we? If this house was mine I think I'd take down those walls that are only partitions and open it all up to turn this whole attic into a big apartment.'

'That would be lovely,' Jackie said. 'What would you use it for?'

Katie smiled. 'Oh, I'd live up here. Or let it as a flat to someone else. There are all sorts of things you could do with a house like this.'

Jackie looked at her and thought of Minnie's suspicions that the two were after Miss Bellamy's money. She said doubtfully, 'I didn't know you wanted to stay in England.'

'I don't know if I do, really.' Katie shivered. 'It's too cold! I never knew it was *possible* to be as cold as it's been lately.'

'It's not always as cold as this, even in winter.' Jackie dropped the envelope on the table and reached for her tea. 'Oh, that's good. I was really ready for this.'

'What's in that? Anything interesting?' Katie reached for the envelope.

'Only more old photos of people we don't know. It's such a shame nobody wrote the names and dates on the backs. I suppose they knew who they were, so didn't think it was necessary.' Greg watched as Katie let the sepia photographs slide out onto the table and began to look through them. 'But all those old men in mutton-chop whiskers look the same to me.'

'Me too.' Katie glanced rapidly through them, then paused and picked one up to examine it more closely. 'Just a minute...'

'What? What have you found?'

'I don't know...' She spoke slowly, holding the photograph to the light to see more clearly. 'It's not an old man, that's for sure...' She turned to her brother, then went on in a quick, excited tone, 'Greg, look at this. What do you think?'

'Who is it?' Jackie demanded as Greg took the fragile card and gazed at it. 'Who do you think it is?'

Greg turned to his sister and she met his eyes. They stared at each other and Jackie's impatience grew. '*Tell* me!'

'It is, isn't it?' Katie asked, and Greg nodded. 'It's just like that other photo Mum has of him as a young man.' She looked at last at Jackie, her face alight with excitement. 'It's a photograph of Grandad! After all this time, and in almost the very last box, we've found a photograph of Grandad!'

Jackie caught her breath. 'Are you sure?'

'As sure as we can be. Look! Look how like Greg he is there. He must have been nearly the age Greg is now when that was taken, and somebody's kept it – or else it didn't get thrown away like others of him.' She handed the photo over and Jackie took it with trembling fingers. 'And that girl he's with – she must have been his sweetheart. Oh, how I wish we knew who she was!'

Jackie stared at the picture. It was the faded yellowish brown of all the old photos but the two people were clear enough and their faces instantly recognisable. They were, as Katie had said, a young man who looked remarkably like Greg, and a young woman, standing together. But it differed from most of the other portraits they had seen, in which the subjects stood almost at attention, stiff and unsmiling, dressed in their best clothes and looking as if they'd rather be anywhere but in a photographer's studio. These two were close together and the man had his arm around the woman's waist in a manner that would surely have been disapproved of in those days. They looked joyous and happy. They looked as if they were in love.

'I wish we knew who the girl was,' Katie said again, wistfully. 'But I don't suppose we ever will now.'

'But we do,' Jackie said slowly. 'At least, I think we do. Look' – she held the picture out for them to look at again – 'doesn't she remind you of anyone – anyone at all?' And when they hesitated, she added, 'Don't you remember what your aunt said a little while ago about me being here – that it was almost like having my granny in the house, when she was a young girl?'

Katie gasped. She looked from the photograph to Jackie, then back again. She turned to Greg and Jackie saw that they had both seen what she had seen.

'Why, it's *you*,' Katie whispered. 'At least not you, of course, but someone who looks like you. If you and Greg dressed up like this and did your hair as they've got theirs done, you'd be the exact images of these two.'

'We would,' Greg agreed. He looked and sounded as bemused as his sister. 'But what does it mean? Your grandmother has always said she knew nothing about Aunt Connie's uncle. She says she doesn't remember anything about him. So who can this be? Did she have a sister?'

'I think she knows more than she says,' Jackie said quietly. 'There was a brother, who got killed in some farm accident when he was quite young, but I never heard of any sister, apart from my Great-Aunt Ada, and she didn't look anything like Granny – she was a lot taller, for a start. Do you know what I think? I think this is Granny herself.'

The brother and sister stared at her. At last Katie said, 'But – in that photo they look like sweet-hearts. And if so...' She shook her head. 'I don't understand.'

'Don't you?' Greg asked. He looked again at Jackie. 'I know what you're thinking. You think your grandmother and my grandfather knew each other – maybe too well for the family's liking and that was part of the reason why he was sent to Australia. And the reason why your grandmother won't talk about it. And if that's the case, something must have gone very wrong.'

'Yes,' Jackie said, and her eyes filled with tears as she looked again at the photograph with its two happy, laughing faces. 'Something went very wrong, and Granny has never forgotten it.' She paused and then said, 'And whatever it was, neither of them wanted anyone ever to find out.'

Chapter Thirty-Four

None of them felt much like searching any further after that. They drank their tea and stared at the photograph and wondered what had happened to the laughing couple so obviously in love. At some time after it was taken, something so terrible had happened to tear them apart that they had lived the rest of their lives separated by the whole world, and neither had ever spoken about it.

'They – or their families – destroyed all the records,' Katie said, staring at the dusty boxes.

'Letters, diaries, everything. All except this one photograph that must have got missed. And nobody ever seems to have known the truth.'

'Except for Granny,' Jackie said from the sofa. 'And whatever it was, it's been worrying her ever since you first arrived. She's been dreading every day that you might find something.'

Katie turned to look at her. 'Jackie, I'm so sorry. We never meant to upset anyone. We would never have done it if we'd known.' She sighed. 'It's not what we wanted to discover at all.'

'But we *haven't* discovered anything,' Greg pointed out. He was sitting beside Jackie and she could feel the warmth of his body against her. 'Not really. I mean, we know now that your grandmother and our grandfather knew each other, and it does look very much as if they were in love. But photographs *can* lie, you know, whatever people say. They might just have been at some family picnic where lots of photographs were taken, and laughing at some joke. Your granny was Auntie Con's nursemaid, wasn't she? Well, I expect she went to lots of occasions like that.'

'Well, yes,' Jackie said doubtfully. 'But in that case, why has she always said she doesn't remember him? She must have known him quite well, even if they were only on a family picnic together.' She picked up the photograph and gazed at it again. 'It really does look like more than that to me.'

'I think so too,' Katie said. 'And she does look so like you, Jackie. Just as he looks like Greg. We've always noticed that in the photo Mum's got, and even when he was an old man. Stand up together, the two of you.' A little bemused, they rose and stood beside each other, looking down at her. 'Now take Jackie's hand, Greg, and look at her. And Jackie, you look at him. That's right. Now smile.' She stared at them. 'You know, you could be the same two people. It's quite uncanny.'

Jackie felt Greg's fingers warm around her wrist. She tilted her head to look up at his face and saw the smile spread slowly from his mouth to his eyes. And then his expression changed and she gasped and drew away sharply.

'I ought to go home,' she said breathlessly. 'I said I wouldn't be late.'

'It's getting dark,' he said. 'I'll walk with you.'

'There's no need. I've walked through this village in the dark since I was seven years old.'

'I will anyway.'

'Let him come, Jackie,' Katie said quietly. 'We can both see you're upset. But Greg may be right, you know. We mustn't assume too much, just from one photograph. There may be nothing in it at all.'

'Except that they knew each other,' Jackie said tonelessly. 'And Granny's always sworn she doesn't remember him at all. And she's been upset about the whole thing – and now we're going to have to tell her.'

They walked in silence for the first few minutes. Then Greg said, 'I'm sorry you're upset, Jackie. Maybe your granny's right and it's not a good idea to go searching out old family stories.'

'I don't know if it is or not,' Jackie said dismally. 'The thing is, Greg, I can't believe Granny ever did anything wrong, or bad, in her life. Whatever

358

it was that went wrong, I can't really believe it was anything to do with her. And yet, why is she so against your search? Why has she been so against you, right from the beginning? She *must* know what it was all about, but if it was nothing to do with her, why won't she say?'

'And Auntie Con was too young for it to be to do with her,' he said thoughtfully. 'Let's sit on the bench under the big oak tree for a few minutes. It's not too cold.' They walked over the green and sat down. Greg took her hand and she felt the warmth of his fingers again. 'Jackie, if you don't want us to go any further with this, we could stop now, if you like. We'll forget we ever found the photo.'

She shook her head. 'We can't do that. We have found it and we know – well, we know a little bit more. And there's Miss Bellamy, too. She has a right to find out about her uncle. She's never known what happened to him, but she must have missed him when she was little. She ought to know for certain that he had a happy life in Australia, whatever happened to him here.'

'Yes.' He stroked her fingers absently. Jackie looked down at the dim shape of their hands, entwined like those of the two young people in the photograph, and felt again that shock she had experienced when she had gazed into Greg's eyes. She tried to draw away again and he tightened his hold, though very gently, and turned to look into her face.

'When Katie said it could be us, what did you feel, Jackie?'

'I – I don't know. Surprised, I suppose.'

'Nothing else?'

'What do you mean, Greg?' Before he could reply, she added quickly, 'No – nothing else. What else could I feel?'

'I'll tell you what I felt,' he said quietly. 'I wished we *were* the two people in the photograph. Laughing and happy together.' Then he added, even more quietly, 'In love.'

Jackie caught her breath. She tried again to pull away. 'Greg, please don't. I can't... I don't want...'

'What don't you want?'

'I don't want to be in love again,' she said in a low voice. 'Ever. It hurts too much when it's taken away.' She paused for a moment. 'I really did love Bryce, you know. We would have been happy all our lives. I can't think of anyone else yet – not for a long while. Perhaps I never will.'

There was a long silence. Then he said, 'I'm sorry, Jackie. I know it's too soon. You've had a terrible loss. I wouldn't have said anything – not yet, anyway. But seeing that photo – it made me realise just how much I feel for you. And you're going back to America soon. I can't let you go without telling you – without giving us both a chance.' He had captured her hand in both of his and held it close, like a tiny fluttering bird. 'Do you really have to go back, Jackie?'

Again, there was a silence and then she said, 'Yes, I do. I have to be there again, to see if I can pick up the life I was living before – before Bryce. I was happy there, Greg. It suited me – America, Corning, the family I have there, the way of life. I felt I belonged.'

'And couldn't you belong anywhere else? Australia, for instance?'

Jackie looked up sharply and met his eyes. 'What are you asking me?'

'I don't really know,' he confessed. 'All I know is that I don't want to lose you, not without at least finding out if there could be something special for us. I believe there is, but I'm not sure you've realised it yet. I don't want you to go without thinking that you might at least give it a chance. And – well, seeing that photo, it makes me think that things might have gone wrong for those two who look so much like us, but maybe we could somehow put that right. By being happy for them, if that makes sense.'

'And maybe we couldn't. Maybe they'd go wrong for us too.'

'Unless we find out what did go wrong,' he said, 'we'll never know.'

Jackie drew in a deep, shivering sigh. 'Which brings us back to Granny. Oh, Greg...' She laid her face against his arm. 'How am I going to tell her what we've found? How am I going to ask her about it? I don't think I can.'

Greg put up one hand and stroked her cheek. 'Then don't. We'll let it go. Pretend it was never found.'

'No,' Jackie said after another pause. 'I can't do that. She's already upset and worried. We have to go through with it now.'

They got up and walked on as far as the turning into the farm track. They stopped beside the hedge and when Greg drew her into his arms Jackie did not resist. She stood quietly, waiting for his kiss, knowing she could not respond.

'About America, Jackie,' he said. 'I understand

that you want to go back. But that doesn't rule out a visit to Australia, does it? Just to see if you might even belong there too?'

She looked up and caught the shine of the moonlight in his eyes.

'No, Greg,' she said at last. 'It doesn't rule it out.'

He bent his head, and touched her lips with his. It was a gentle kiss that demanded nothing, but left her feeling comforted and consoled.

But as she walked away from him, towards the farmhouse, the anxiety and sadness she felt about her grandmother returned in full force and by the time she reached the door she knew that it would be impossible to face her until she had had more time to think it over.

'So it's settled?' Dottie asked, her eyes shining as she bustled about the kitchen making tea. 'You're really going to buy Moor View?'

'No,' Joe said, and laughed at the look on her face. '*We* are. Don't forget, I promised to endow you with all my worldly goods. That means what's mine is yours. And Moor View is going to be our very own home, that we buy and do up to-gether. Somewhere neither of us has ever lived before.'

'That's lovely, Joe. That'll make it really special. And I do like the house. I'll be sorry to leave my cottage but 'tis too small for the two of us, es-pecially with no bathroom, and we need our comforts as we get on in years.'

'Well, we're not that far gone yet!' He grinned. 'But I'll be glad to have a proper bathroom again. It's been all very well going up to the farm for our

362

baths but I like my creature comforts in the same house as I'm living in! But before we move in, I want to get the Pettifer boys in to do the re-wiring, and Johnny Dodd and his boys to do the redecorating and a few repairs here and there. The Berrymans are leaving in a couple of weeks and the solicitor says the conveyance will be straightforward, so if we get cracking on it soon, we could be in by Easter.'

'Easter! You really think so?' Dottie poured two cups of tea and brought them over to the little sofa, pushing Alfred into the corner. 'Why do cats always want the best seat? So we can have most of the summer in it, then, before we go to Corning in the autumn. You're sure you don't mind waiting that long, Joe?'

'Not as long as we can spend a few months there before coming back. I need to see my grandkids before they're grown up! It'd be good to have next Christmas with them. And now Elaine's definitely moving to Buffalo, we'll have to pay her a visit there. It's going to be pretty busy, Dottie.'

'I won't mind. I'm over that silly old stroke now and as strong as ever I was.' She sipped her tea thoughtfully for a minute, then said, 'What about Jackie? I don't think she'll want to wait that long. You know she's set on going back, don't you?'

'I do, and I know my brother and his wife ain't too pleased about it. But it's her life and we know she likes Corning – in fact, she likes America. It suits her.'

'I know, but Ted and Alice will never under-stand that, even though they've been there and seen what a nice little town it is. Well, that's for them all to decide between them. I think she'll go back quite soon – unless she takes a shine to young Greg! There's something going on there, unless I'm much mistaken.'

'I think you're right,' Joe said thoughtfully. 'But I'm not sure it's what you think it is. Whatever it is, it's not making her very happy. When I was up at the farm last night, practising the handbells for the Extravaganza, she came in with a face as long as a fiddle and went straight up to her room, hardly said a word to anyone.'

'Oh, that's a pity,' Dottie said in concern. 'Do you think they'd had a tiff?'

Joe shrugged. 'Don't ask me. We don't even know they're on that sort of footing, do we? But whatever it was, she looked real down in the mouth.'

Dottie frowned a little. 'Poor maid. I hope things aren't going to go wrong for her again. Mind, I did think it was a bit soon to be taking up with another young man, but–'

'Now then, Dottie. You don't know that she is. It could be something quite different. But I agree with you – it's time Jackie had some good luck. I don't like to see the girl unhappy, and that's a fact.'

Bob Pettifer was only too pleased to be given the job of rewiring Moor View. He and Terry went along to look at the house one evening, shown round by Mr Berryman.

'It's a bit old,' Bob said, staring at the antiquated system. 'I reckon this must have been one of the first houses in the village to be wired. They were still learning the job when they did this.'

'We've always meant to have it modernised once the war was over,' Geoffrey Berryman said apologetically. 'It's one of those things you never quite get around to.'

'Well, you should have done,' Bob said. 'I reckon some of this is pretty unsafe. Ought to have been put right years ago.'

Sonia Berryman looked alarmed. 'We're not likely to get electrocuted, are we?'

'No more likely than it's been for the past five years,' he said, not giving her much comfort. 'No, I reckon it will see you through now, as long as you're careful, but it's a good job Mr Tozer's decided to ask us to do it all proper before him and Miss Friend – I mean, Mrs Tozer – moves in.'

Sonia looked doubtful but Geoffrey smiled at the two brothers. 'You'll do a good job, I'm sure. We've heard good reports of you both. And I expect Mr Tozer will want you to start work as soon as possible, so it might help you to know that the house will be empty two weeks from tomorrow. You won't actually be able to start work until the sale has been completed, a week or so after that, but you're welcome to come in and measure up and have everything ready.'

They thanked him and walked back to the cottage where Bob still lived with their parents. On the way, Terry remarked, 'That means Miss Friend's cottage will be empty. I wonder what she's going to do with it.'

'Sell it, most like,' Bob said a little gloomily. 'Wish I had the money to buy it, nice little place like that.'

Terry turned to him in surprise. 'You thinking of moving out from home, then?' He caught Bob's look. 'Here – you're not planning to tie the knot with Kitty, are you?'

'Why not? She's a smashing girl and she seems to like me all right. I might not get another chance, with my ugly mug. "All the delicate beauty of a gargoyle", that's what my old teacher at Tavistock school said. Not that he was any oil painting himself – he looked like someone had taken a hatchet to him. Probably someone else he was rude about.'

Terry laughed. 'You got the Pettifer looks, same as me. But I managed to get a good wife just the same, so why shouldn't you? Kitty's a nice maid and you ought to snap her up quick.'

'That's what I think,' Bob said. 'But us needs somewhere to live. I know we could stop with Mum and Dad, like you and Patsy did, but it's not ideal. A little place like Dottie Friend's – well, that would suit us down to the ground, being in the middle of the village and all, and with a nice bit of garden for Kitty to grow some vegetables and soft fruit.'

'Well, why don't you ask her if you can rent it? I bet she'd rather that than sell it. She don't need the money after all, not now she's married to Joe Tozer.'

'She still might not want to keep it. It's a responsibility, after all. Or she might want it for family.'

'What family? All the family Dottie's got round here have their own places, one way or another, and there's none of the Tozers looking for a place that I know of. Val Ferris is in Jed's Cottage, that Jennifer Kellaway rents to her, Tom and Joanna live up at the farm and I don't reckon Jackie's going to be settling hereabouts. It won't do no harm to ask her, Bob. She can only say no, and you'd be no worse off than you are now.'

Bob pushed out his bottom lip thoughtfully, looking even more like one of the faces on the carved stone waterspouts at the top of the church tower. People said they were modelled years ago on village residents and when they looked at Bob and Terry they would laugh and say they knew which ones. Those looks had come down through the family for generations, but everyone knew that the Pettifers' long, crooked faces with their jutting eyebrows, lumpy noses and rubbery features belonged to the nicest folk you could wish to meet. They were living proof, Basil Harvey would declare, that you should never judge a book by its cover.

'I suppose I could just ask,' Bob said at last.

Terry blew out his lips in exasperation.

'Come on, Bob – show a bit of spirit. Do you want to marry Kitty or not?'

'Of course I do. I said so, didn't I?'

'Well, do summat about finding her a place to live! If you're not careful, Bob, you'll lose the cottage *and* the girl. She won't wait for ever.' He caught Bob's sidelong glance. 'All right, I know you can say me and Patsy had it all handed to us on a plate, going over to live on her mother's farm, but us didn't have it easy to start with. You know that.'

'All right,' Bob said, making up his mind. 'I'll

ask her tomorrow evening. I got to go and see Mr Joe about the wiring anyway, so I can kill two birds with one stone.'

'That's the stuff!' Terry applauded him. 'I bet she'll say yes. And I bet Mum and Dad'll be pleased too. They must have seen the way the wind was blowing and thought you'd probably want to bring Kitty to stop at home with them. They'll be tickled pink to get the house to themselves at last!'

'I've been thinking,' Val said, dishing up beef stew and dumplings for supper that evening. 'Now that Dottie and Uncle Joe are buying Moor View, she'll be looking to do something with her cottage.'

'I suppose she will.' Luke lifted Christopher into his high chair and tucked his bib under his chin. 'I wonder what she'll do with it.'

'Well, either rent it out or sell it, I should think. Two dumplings, or three?'

'Oh, three if there are enough. Your dumplings are the best I've ever tasted.' He watched as Val carefully spooned the fluffy mounds onto his plate and then added a small one to Christopher's bowl and another two to her own. 'I wonder who might buy it. Do you know anyone who might be interested?'

Val took the stew pan back to the stove and left it on a low heat to keep hot for second helpings. She never knew where Luke, as thin as a beanpole, put all his food and had decided long ago that he must have hollow legs. She sat down and lifted her knife and fork while Luke fed Christopher a spoonful of mashed potato soaked in gravy.

'Well, I do know two people who might be.'

Luke looked at her in surprise. 'Do you? Who are they?'

'Well, us of course! *We* could buy it!' She shook her head in mild exasperation. 'Didn't it occur to you?'

'Well no, it didn't. I thought we were quite happy here. Jennifer hasn't said she wants the cottage back, has she?'

'No, but she might do one day and then where would we be? I don't think she'll ever want to sell it. She and Travis might need it themselves when he retires.'

Luke let out a hoot of laughter. 'Travis isn't going to retire for years!'

'No, but he will one day, and then what would we do? Do we really want to be paying rent for the rest of our lives and always be afraid our home might be taken away from us? But if we bought Dottie's – well, we'd be secure. Don't you see that?'

Luke chopped up some meat for Christopher and helped him manipulate his spoon. 'Yes, I do see that. You're quite right. But I don't see how we could buy it. We'd have to get a mortgage and I don't know if we could, on an old cottage. I think you can only get them on new houses.'

'Are you sure that's right?' Val asked doubtfully. 'People must buy old houses somehow.'

'Probably because they can pay for them outright. I don't really know. But I could try to find out, if you like.'

'Yes, I think you should. If it's not Dottie's cottage, we might need to know if another one comes up for sale. But I think we ought to ask her anyway. It's a lovely little house, Luke – I've always liked it. And there's just room at the top of the stairs to put in a little bathroom. You see' – her eyes shone – 'if we had our own house, we could do things like that. Change it – add to it – make it our very own.'

He looked at her and saw the excitement in her face. 'You really do want it, don't you!'

'I do. Our own house.' She reached across the table and gripped his hand. 'Please, Luke. At least let's ask her. And let's do it quickly – tomorrow – before someone else does. A lovely little cottage like that – there'll be any number of people after it. They'll be beating a path to Dottie's door!'

Chapter Thirty-Five

'I don't know what's the matter with you today, Jackie,' Alice declared as the family sat round the kitchen table at noon next day. 'You hardly ate any breakfast, you've been stuck up in your room all morning and now you look as if you've lost a shilling and found sixpence, and not got a word to say to anyone. You're not sickening for that flu, I hope? I thought it was just about over and done with by now.'

'I'm all right.' Jackie pushed her fork listlessly at her steak and kidney pie. 'I'm just not very hungry. I feel a bit tired, that's all.'

Alice gave her a sharp look. 'And how is it you're not round at Miss Bellamy's like you usually are?

Your father and me were beginning to think you'd moved in.'

Jackie shrugged. 'I just don't feel like it. I don't *have* to be there every day.'

'I hope you've not been annoying her – out-stayed your welcome or something.' Jackie didn't reply, and after a moment Alice went on, 'Or have you had a tiff with young Gregory? Is that what it is?'

'No, it isn't!' Jackie put down her knife and fork. 'There's nothing between me and Greg to have a tiff about! Stop going on at me, Mother. I told you, I feel a bit tired and just didn't want to go this morning, that's all.'

'Leave the poor girl alone, Mum,' Tom said, helping himself to more potatoes. 'She doesn't have to explain to us what she's doing.' He grinned at his sister. 'She's probably unearthed some dark family secret that's been hidden away for years and it's upset the whole apple cart!'

To his surprise, Jackie flushed a dark red. She turned on him and said angrily, 'And you can keep your nose out too, Tom! It's nothing to do with you – it's nothing to do with *any* of you!' She looked furiously round the table and caught her grandmother's eye last. For a moment, their glances met and locked. Jackie's flush deepened and tears came into her eyes. She pushed back her chair and jumped up.

'I don't want anything to eat, Mum. I'm going upstairs – and don't anyone come after me. I just want to be by myself for a change!'

There was a startled silence. Alice half rose, as if to follow her daughter, despite her words, but

Ted laid his hand on her arm. 'Leave the maid alone, my dear. It's what she wants and you ought to know by now when she flounces out like that she's best left to herself to get over it.'

'But she seems real upset,' Alice said, almost in tears herself. 'I don't like to see her like that, when I might be able to help.'

'You can't. Whatever it is that's upset her, she's got to deal with it in her own way. She'll come to us for help if she needs it, she always has.' He patted Alice's arm and she sat down again, looking disturbed.

'It's your fault, Tom,' she accused her son. 'Saying daft things about dark secrets. What sort of secrets could she find round at the Grey House? No, it's that young man that's at the root of it, I shouldn't wonder. He likes Jackie, I could see that when he's brought her home a time or two, but he don't realise what she's been through and he's upset her. It'll be just as well if she stops going there altogether.'

Minnie said nothing. She ate a few more mouthfuls without enthusiasm, then laid down her own cutlery.

'I'm sorry, Alice, I've had enough. I don't seem to have much appetite just lately. I'll just have a bit of stewed fruit and a cup of tea and then I might go and have a lie-down for the afternoon.'

Alice herself didn't seem to want much dinner now, either. She waited until Joanna and the men had finished, then gathered up the plates and scraped the uneaten food into the pig bin. Joanna brought the big dish of stewed apples to the table and served them out, and they ate in a silence broken only by Ted and Tom discussing the winter wheat they had sown some weeks ago.

Dinner over, Alice made tea and the men drank theirs down quickly and departed. Joanna took Heather to be washed and changed, saying she was going up to Wood Cottage to spend the afternoon with Jennifer, and Alice and Minnie were left alone.

'You don't think I ought to go and have a word with Jackie?' Alice asked at last. 'Only I'm supposed to be at the Mothers' Union meeting this afternoon.'

'You leave her alone,' Minnie said. 'I might have a chat with her later on myself. She may tell me what's upset her.' She paused for a moment, looking down at her hands. 'I don't suppose it's anything much, though. I don't suppose it's anything at all...'

Jackie stayed in her room for over an hour, sitting on her bed and staring out of the window. The view she had grown up with was so familiar to her that she hardly needed to look to know exactly what she would see. The sky louring with the cold grey of a particularly bitter February, the grass in the fields almost the same lifeless colour, the trees with their stark and bare branches like pencil strokes reaching into the still air. The cows were in the barn for the winter and there seemed to be nothing living at all, while beyond the fields the moors rose bleak and brown to the forbidding granite of the tors.

I wish I'd never come home, she thought. I wish I'd stayed in Corning or even gone to Buffalo with Elaine and Earl. I wish we had never had that accident. If we'd just stayed at home that night instead of going to that party... I wish Bryce had never died...

Tears came to her eyes and spilled down her cheeks and she found a hanky and wiped her face. She had tried so hard to get over this terrible, painful grief, yet at times like this it came back just as powerfully as before, and knocked her reeling. She thought of Maddy, who had been through the same kind of loss – Sammy had been killed on the roads too, by a lorry that couldn't stop – and of the way the older girl had talked to her, never suggesting that Jackie might find the same kind of happiness she had found with Stephen, it was too soon to say that, but helping her gently to understand that time would heal the worst of the pain, that there would always be a part of her heart that belonged to Bryce, but that she would again, after a while, find pleasure and purpose in living without him.

'I was horribly selfish after Sammy died,' Maddy had told her. 'I was nasty to everyone who tried to help. It was as if I didn't care about anyone else but myself. I did really, and I hated myself for being like that, but I didn't seem able to do anything about it. I didn't have the room or the energy to feel anything but sad.'

'So how did you get out of it?' Jackie had asked, and Maddy smiled.

'Felix helped me a lot. He talked to me and made me see that just doing other things would help a lot. Filling up my time with other people – that sort of thing. It's different for all of us, but you'll find a way, Jackie, because you're a strong person. Find something to do, something that won't remind you of Bryce all the time. And you have to remember that you were quite badly hurt yourself. Your body needs to get over that too.'

That was why Jackie had started to go to the Grey House to help Katie and Greg. The two young Australians knew nothing of her, or of anyone in Burracombe. They accepted her as she was and welcomed her help, and Jackie had felt from the beginning that she had found real friends. Going to the Grey House, where there were no memories of Bryce and nobody to gaze at her with anxious eyes as her family so often seemed to do, had become the most important thing in her life.

And look where it had led. If she had never gone there, Miss Bellamy would never have commented on her likeness to her grandmother. They might still have found the photograph, but they wouldn't have known that the girl with their grandfather looked like Jackie. They wouldn't have known she was Minnie Tozer. It wouldn't even have mattered to them.

Miss Bellamy might have realised, of course, but it was quite possible that she wouldn't. The photo was old and faded, Minnie as a young girl was very different from Minnie as she was now, and without Jackie there every day to remind her, the old lady might well have passed over it without comment. It was the man who was important. She would have known it was her Uncle Bernard, and the Australians would have the proof for which they had been searching that they were indeed related to Constance Bellamy, and everyone would have been happy.

Instead...

I'll have to tell her, Jackie thought miserably. I'll have to tell Granny what we've found. She's got a right to know, and she's got a right to decide what to do about it. Whether to tell us what happened or keep it hidden as she has for all these years.

And now, just to make things even more complicated, there was Greg. If I'd never left Burracombe, Jackie thought, if I'd never met Bryce, I might have felt the same for him as he says he feels for me. But how can I, now? How can I ever love any man, after what I've had and lost?

Dark secrets, Tom had said. If only he knew how close to the truth he had been!

Minnie got up from her bed and put on her dark red woollen frock. She had taken it off to lie down, and now she was cold and needed its warmth around her. She sat on her bed, looking out at the same view that Jackie could see from her window, and rubbed her hands together, trying to ease the arthritis that plagued her these days.

What had the girl found out? Minnie had no doubt that something had come to light in the Grey House. She'd known from the start that something would, even though she had been assured years ago that no trace remained. But when Jackie came home day after day with tales of old photographs, diaries, newspapers, her heart had sunk deeper and deeper. However carefully secrets were kept, they had a way of coming to the surface eventually. It seemed that this one, the only real secret of her life, had now done just that.

Minnie had known, the moment Jackie came through the door yesterday, that it had happened. The girl's face had had a tight, pinched look that had nothing to do with the cold weather. She had pulled off her coat, dragged off her boots and walked quickly through the kitchen to the stairs without even a glance at her grandmother. She'd told her mother that she had a headache and wanted to go to bed, and Alice had taken up her tea a bit later on and come down to report that Jackie was sitting huddled up against her pillows, staring out of the window and doing nothing.

'I dare say it's just a cold. Or maybe the time of the month.' There were no men in the kitchen just then, and Joanna had nodded. They all knew how low you could feel then, though Jackie usually breezed through without any problems. It was unusual for her.

Minnie, however, had known the truth. Something had been found. What it was, she had no idea, nor whether the two Australians, or even Miss Constance herself, were aware of it. But Jackie knew – or knew something, if not the whole story. And it wasn't going to end there.

Minnie heaved a deep sigh and got up stiffly from her bed. It would have to be done, and there was no time like the present, with everyone else out of the house. It might be days before the chance came again.

She opened her bedroom door and walked the few steps to Jackie's, then raised her hand and knocked.

'I thought it must be something like that,' Minnie said as Jackie's sobs finally quietened. 'All this while, I've been afraid something would turn up. They said it had all been destroyed but I could never be quite sure. His sister, Florence – she could easily have kept something back. She was broken-hearted when he went, you see. They were so close, they were almost like twins. They very nearly *were* twins, in a way – born in the same year, her in January and him the next December. And she always looked after him.' She shook her head. 'Poor Florence. Died of the typhoid not eighteen months after he went, and I don't suppose he ever knew.'

'But what happened, Granny?' Jackie asked. She had known as soon as she heard her grandmother's knock on the door that the story would have to be told now, from all sides. Her own, when she had looked at the old photograph and seen her own face smiling out at her; Katie's and Greg's, whose grandfather they now knew must truly have been Constance's uncle; and Minnie's, whose story would reveal the truth at last of what had happened seventy years ago. And perhaps even Constance herself, although only a child of nine or ten at the time, might find some ancient memory jogged.

Too late, Jackie thought, she had understood the reasons for her grandmother's distress over the investigation. Despite all her protestations about the possibility that the Australians were common criminals, out for Miss Bellamy's money, and that she knew nothing of any old scandal, it was now clear that Minnie must have known, and that she

378

had also probably been involved. Jackie had seen very clearly how bringing it all back could cause her real pain. Whatever the truth had been, whatever had happened, it must have brought a deep unhappiness to the laughing girl in the photograph.

'I'm sorry, Granny,' she said contritely. 'I'd never have got involved if I'd known. And Katie and Greg – they would never have realised who the girl was if Miss Bellamy hadn't said how like you I am.' She turned to look into her grandmother's faded eyes. 'They're really nice people, you know. They wouldn't have wanted to hurt anyone.'

'That's just it, though,' Minnie said. 'You go raking up the past and someone is going to be hurt. It stands to reason. Bernard didn't go to Australia for a holiday. He went because he was sent. Because his family didn't want him here no more. There's bound to be someone still hurt over it.'

'And that's you,' Jackie said quietly, and her tears started again. 'Oh, Granny, I'm *so* sorry...'

Minnie held her close for a few minutes. Then she said, 'Dry your eyes, maid, and listen to me. We've got to decide what to do next.'

Jackie drew back a little and stared at her. 'What do you mean? What is there to do next?'

'Why, bring it out into the open of course. You and your two friends and Miss Constance – you all got to know what really happened. And maybe even your mother and father, and the rest of the family.' Minnie sighed. 'Might as well hold a meeting in the village hall and tell the whole village while we're at it.'

'Granny, don't be silly! Of course we don't

need to do that. You don't need to tell Mum and Dad either, I'm sure. In fact, you don't need to tell any of us if you don't want to.'

'I do,' Minnie said quietly. 'Because it's family history, and we've all got a right to know that. And that means our family as well as Miss Constance's.' She drew in a steady breath and sat up straight. 'You go back to the Grey House, my dear, when you feel ready, and ask them if they'll all come up to the farm one evening, soon as we can get the whole family together. That's Val and Luke too and Joe and Dottie, of course. Might as well get it all over in one fell swoop.'

Jackie was silent for a moment. Then she said, 'Are you really sure, Granny? That everyone needs to know, I mean? Why not just keep it to Miss Bellamy and Katie and Greg? They're the ones most involved, after all. And if it was just a – a romance between you and him, why does anyone else need to know?'

Minnie shook her head. Her lips were folded tightly and Jackie recognised the expression her face always displayed when she was at her most determined.

'It was more than that,' she said. 'And it's time the whole family knew.'

Chapter Thirty-Six

Dottie and Joe had just finished supper when their first visitor knocked on the door. Joe went to answer it and came back with Bob Pettifer, ducking his head under the beams and almost bending his long, gangling body in half to come through the doorway.

'Why, hello, Bob,' Dottie said. 'It's nice to see you. I suppose you've come to see Joe about the electrics in Moor View.'

'Well, partly,' Bob said, hovering awkwardly in the middle of the room. 'But there was summat else I wanted to ask you about too. You see–'

'Sit down, boy, do,' Dottie exclaimed. 'You're making the place look untidy! And I'll get a crick in my neck, looking up at you. Sit in that chair, by the table. Now, what is it you want to ask?'

Bob opened his mouth but Joe said quickly, 'Let's get the business settled first, shall we? What's the situation in Moor View? It all looked a bit antiquated to me.'

'It is,' Bob said, grateful to be on ground he understood. 'I reckon the place must have been wired when electricity first come to Burracombe, years ago. If you want my opinion–'

'Which we do,' Joe said with a grin, 'or we wouldn't have asked you to have a look.'

'Well, the whole place needs doing all over again. Some of it's downright dangerous. Well, not exactly dangerous, not yet, but it's not far off. Doing the job piecemeal would be like darning a sock. The rest'll wear out soon and you'll be forever having problems and calling me in. Much better to make a proper job of it from the start.' He looked at them apologetically. 'I hope you don't think I'm just saying this to get the work.'

'Of course we don't think that,' Dottie exclaimed. 'I know you better than that, Bob. And if you say that's what needs to be done, I reckon that's what we'll have done. Don't you think so, Joe?'

'I do indeed. It's what I've been thinking myself anyway. And I tell you what else, Dot – while we're at it, we'll get the plumbing overhauled as well. Bob's right – it's foolish to do half the job, and once the basic things are right we'll only have to think about redecoration now and then. And furnishing, too,' he added. 'The things you've got here will only fill a quarter of the space at Moor View!'

'Half of it will look silly anyway,' she said. 'This little settee and armchair that I got three or four years after the war ended – they're what was called Utility, shoddy sort of stuff made in a hurry because so many people had lost all they owned in the bombing and needed to get set up again. I reckon us could leave that behind for the next people, whoever they are.'

'That's what–' Bob began, but Joe was frowning a little and didn't seem to hear him.

'And that's another thing we need to think about, sweetheart. You'll need to decide what to do with the cottage once we've moved to Moor

View. You can't leave it empty.'

'Could I–' Bob began again, but this time it was Dottie who overrode him.

'Do you know, Joe, I never even thought about that! With all that's been going on lately, it never entered my mind. But you're right. I'll have to think about it.' She looked round the little room. 'My little cottage, that I've lived in ever since I was born, apart from the few years I was in London! Whatever am I going to do with it?'

'You could rent it out,' Bob said, quickly, before Joe could open his mouth. 'You could even leave the furniture in it, the bits you don't want. It's a real nice little place and–'

'Rent it out? But who to? I don't know anyone in Burracombe who's looking for a place just now – do you?'

They both looked at Bob, who turned crimson and gazed helplessly back. His voice seemed to have deserted him. Joe laughed suddenly and raised his eyebrows, then turned to his wife.

'I reckon he does know someone,' he said. 'Don't you, Bob? Someone not a million miles away from us at this very moment.'

'Who on earth be you talking about?' Dottie demanded, and then she too caught the expression on Bob's scarlet face. 'Why, Bob Pettifer! Don't tell me 'tis you! Is that what you came here to ask?'

Bob nodded and found his voice. 'Yes,' he said with a squeak, and then tried again. 'Yes, it is. I don't suppose it's any good really – I mean, why would you want to rent your cottage to me – but if you did want to let it out, and you didn't have any objection... You see, me and Kitty Pengelly from Lydford want to get wed and it would suit us fine. And with the electricity business doing quite well, I reckon I could afford the rent, so if you...' His voice trailed away and he gazed at them piteously. 'It don't matter if you don't want to,' he added after a moment. 'We can stop with Mother and Father for a while, like our Terry did when he and Patsy started. Anyway, I'd better be going now. We're having a skiffle practice tonight for the Extravaganza on Saturday and I'm going to be late...'

He began to get to his feet but Dottie put out a hand to stop him. She turned to Joe. 'What do you think, my dear? Shall we let Bob and Kitty have the cottage? It'd be in good hands, I know that.'

'I know it too.' Joe thought for a moment. 'But I don't think you should rush into anything, Dot. You haven't given it any thought at all yet and you might decide you'd rather sell it.' He looked apologetically at Bob. 'Sorry, boy, but you do see that, don't you? We can't say yes or no without giving the whole thing some proper thought.'

'No,' Bob said dejectedly. 'Of course you can't. I shouldn't have asked.'

'Now, I'm not saying that,' Joe said, standing up too. 'You know what they say, if you don't ask, you don't get, and we'd never have known you wanted the place if you hadn't said. We'll talk it over and let you know – how will that do?'

'And if I do decide to let it,' Dottie said, smiling at him, 'I'll give you and Kitty first refusal, as they say. I'd like to see you two living here, and that's the truth.'

Bob made his way towards the door and Joe

went with him. 'We'll talk about the wiring in a day or two, when I get a plumber organised. The two of you will need to work together and it'll probably be a good idea if we all go along and have a look at what needs doing. Mr Berryman's being very helpful about that.' He put his hand on the young man's shoulder. 'Now, don't you worry about the cottage. I've got a feeling it'll all work out just fine.'

He watched Bob lope away into the darkness and then turned his head as he heard other footsteps hurrying near. 'Why, Val! Whatever are you doing here at this time in the evening? Is everything all right?'

Val appeared in the light that streamed out through the cottage door. 'I wanted to see you both as soon as possible,' she said breathlessly, and followed Joe indoors, unwinding her scarf as she spoke. 'It's about your cottage, Dottie. Have you made up your mind what you're going to do with it once you've moved into Moor View? Only, Luke and I were wondering if we could buy it!'

Chapter Thirty-Seven

'She wanted to tell the whole family at once,' Jackie said as she sat in Constance Bellamy's untidy sitting room with the two old ladies and the two young Australians, 'but I think you should know first. Whatever it is,' she added, taking her grandmother's hand. 'And if you'd rather I wasn't here, I'll go now.'

'Of course I want you here, my bird. If it hadn't been for you, we would never have got to this point.' Minnie sighed. 'I don't mind telling you, I'd still rather we hadn't – but there you are, truth will out and if I hadn't lived so long nobody would ever have known. So perhaps it was meant, anyway, and at least I'll be able to go to my Maker with an easy conscience.'

'Granny!' Jackie exclaimed. 'You're not going anywhere! You've got years in you yet, and anyway, I don't believe you've ever done anything to give you a guilty conscience.'

'You wait till you hear it before you decide that,' her grandmother retorted, and Jackie smiled. She looked over at Katie.

'Shall we make a cup of tea before we start?' the Australian girl suggested. Minnie began to object but Constance lifted a hand to silence her.

'I think that's a very good idea. We'll all feel easier with a cup and saucer in front of us. And you were right, Jackie, my dear. It's better to tell the story now, quietly, so that it stays between the five of us. We might decide there's no need for anyone else to know after all, and no harm done.' As the two girls went out, she added to Minnie, 'I know you've come to feel that whatever this story is shouldn't be a secret any more, but sometimes secrets need to be kept. Especially when they might hurt other people. What's the point of doing that?'

'Well, 'tis your family most involved,' Minnie said. 'So maybe 'tis for you to decide. But I don't want to burden anyone else with having to keep it.'

386

'Let's hear it first,' Greg said. 'And then Auntie Con can be the one to say whether it should go any further.'

'That seems fair to me,' Constance agreed. There seemed to be no more to say until Jackie and Katie returned with tea and biscuits and when everyone was served, they sat down and waited. Greg moved up a little to make room for Jackie and, after a small hesitation, she took her place between him and her grandmother.

Minnie looked round. Her face was tense and Jackie once again took her hand.

'Just take your time, Granny. It's waited all these years to be told, there's no hurry now.'

'Thank you, maid, but I've always said if you got something to do you don't want to do, it's best to get on and get it over with.' She drew in a deep breath and looked at Constance. 'As you all know, I was Miss Constance's nursemaid from when her was a little baby until when her was eight years old. Then my old dad got too poorly to be left alone any more and I had to go home and look after him, Mother having died a year or two before that. There was just me, my sister Ada and my brother Edward – Ned, us called him – that your father was named after, Jackie. Ada was away from home then, in service in one of the big houses in Tavistock, so she couldn't be no help and it all fell to me. And Ned wasn't a lot of help. He was a bit wanting, you know – nothing you could put your finger on, like poor Billy Friend, but there was something the matter with his mind. He could get along pretty well but he needed a bit of looking after himself. Well, that's how things were – and still are, unless you wants to send your old folk to the workhouse – and I wasn't going to see poor old Father go there.'

'Did your brother live with you too?' Jackie asked. 'He would have been my great-uncle. I've never heard much about him – didn't he die in some farm accident?'

'Don't let's get ahead of ourselves,' Minnie said. 'Just let me tell it in my own way, there's a good maid.' She paused, then went on. 'Well, I'd been living in this house here – the Grey House – along with the family for all those years so I knew them pretty well.' She addressed the two Australians. 'You'll have found out a lot about them now, from all those papers you've been looking through and from talking to Miss Constance, so you'll know she was the youngest of the family by quite a few years. There were two sisters, eleven and fourteen years older, and two brothers – Percival and Redvers.'

She stopped again, and there was a short silence. Then Constance heaved a sigh and said, 'All gone now. That's the trouble with being the youngest – you're likely to be the only one left in your old age. We lost Redvers in the first Boer War and Percival went in the Boxer Rebellion. My eldest sister, Mary, died of typhoid and Sylvia in childbirth. The baby only lived a few hours so I didn't even have any nieces or nephews. All a long, long time ago now.'

'And Bernard?' Katie asked after a moment.

'Oh, Bernard – he was my favourite uncle. He was like me, the youngest of the family with a big gap between him and the others, and he was only twelve when I was born. He was more of an age with my brothers and sisters but he treated me as a sort of pet – he used to carry me about on his shoulders and play with me, and of course I adored him. I think everybody did.'

'Yes,' Minnie said quietly. 'And so did I.'

'Hello,' Dottie said, coming into the farm kitchen and seeing the empty rocking chair by the ingle-nook fireplace. 'Where's Minnie? Not ill, is she?'

'Not her,' Alice replied, putting the kettle on. 'Fit as a flea, same as always. No, she and Jackie have gone over to the Grey House to have a talk with Miss Bellamy and those two young Aus-tralians.' She went to the larder for a jug of milk and set it on the table, looking serious. 'There's something going on there, you mark my words, Dottie. Mother had a face on her like a funeral director and Jackie looked half scared to death. I don't know what it is, but it's to do with some-thing that happened up there last week. The maid came home white as a sheet one day and wouldn't speak to any of us. We thought she was poorly or had had a tiff with that Australian boy, but now I'm not so sure.'

'They've found something,' Dottie said, sitting down on one of the kitchen chairs and leaning her arms on the table. 'Well, 'twas bound to happen. They've been searching through all those old papers and things for long enough. They had to come up with some old skeleton rattling its bones.'

'Go on, what skeletons could there be to find there? The Bellamys have always been a good family. They had a lot of tragedy but then so have most families – it don't mean there'd be skeletons.'

'So why was there all that mystery about the uncle who went to Australia? That's what those two came to find out and it looks to me as if they've got what they came for, and it isn't good.'

'I don't see why Mother and our Jackie should be concerned though,' Alice objected. 'Mother wasn't even working for the family then, by all accounts.' She made tea and brought the pot to the table. 'I just hope they don't go upsetting her. She's too old to be pestered about old memories that don't matter any more.'

'They only don't matter when there's nobody left to be upset by them,' Dottie said. 'Anyway, Alice, I came to give you a piece of our news. You'll never guess who came to see me and Joe last night. Bob Pettifer!'

Alice stared at her. 'Well, there's nothing very strange about that, surely. Didn't Joe ask him to go and have a look at the electrics in Moor View?'

'Well, yes, he did, but that weren't what Bob wanted to see us about. At least, it was – he says they need doing right through and we're going to have the plumbing looked at too, but that's by the way – but what he came for specially was to ask me about the cottage.'

'Your cottage?'

'Well, how many cottages do we have?' Dottie asked impatiently. 'Of course it was my cottage. You see, he wants to get married to that Pengelly maid from Lydford and he asked me if he could rent it. What do you think of that?'

Alice poured the tea and passed over the sugar bowl. 'There's some of Joanna's biscuits here too,

390

if you want one. Well, it sounds a good idea, if you want to keep it. But do you? I'd have thought you wouldn't want the bother.'

'That's just it. I'm not really sure, to tell you the truth. But I like Bob and I felt a bit sorry for him, not having anywhere to start married life. They'd have to stay with Jack and Nancy and although there's more room now Terry's gone, it's not ideal. And Bob being such a handy young man, he'd look after the place. Anyway, I told him I'd think about it and then just as he was going, who else d'you think turned up?'

Alice sighed. 'Half the village, by the sound of it. Were you holding open house or something? Did you put up a notice on the village board inviting everyone round?'

'Oh, you *are* funny,' Dottie said. 'I can see where Tom gets it from. It was Val.'

'*Our* Val?'

'Well, how many–' Dottie stopped herself and said, 'Yes. And *she'd* come to ask about the cottage too.'

Alice stared at her. 'She and Luke don't want to rent it, surely? I thought they were settled in Jed's. Don't tell me Jennifer Kellaway's given them notice!'

'No, not at all.' Dottie spooned sugar into her tea and stirred. 'They want to buy it.'

There was a short silence. Alice reached out and picked up a biscuit. She broke it in half and dunked one half in her tea. At last she said, '*Buy* it? But where would they find the money?'

'That's just it, they can't. Not all of it, anyway. Luke's had some good commissions lately and he's earning quite a bit at present, but like Val says, they got to be sensible and keep some back for the times when he might not do so well. That's the trouble with his sort of work. But they've got a bit put by, and she said they'd been talking about it and they wondered if we could do a sort of private mortgage.'

'What's that, when it's at home?'

'It's the same as an ordinary mortgage – you know, a special sort of loan for buying a house – but you don't get it through a bank or one of those building societies, like Abbey National. They don't give 'em out so easy on old cottages like mine anyway. You do it privately. Someone lends the money and you sign the same sort of legal documents and then you pay so much a month until it's yours.'

'But who would lend them the money?' Alice asked, trying to grope her way through what seemed a fog of legal mysteries. 'I don't think Ted and me could help.'

'No, you wouldn't need to because *I'd* lend it to them,' Dottie explained. 'At least, I wouldn't exactly lend them the money as such, but the cottage is mine, so we'd just sign all the same papers and they'd pay the money to me, like rent. It's not as if Joe and me need the whole lot. We don't need any of it, really, but it would be nice for me to have a bit of my own, and Val and Luke would be sure of their own place that nobody could turn them out of. Where they are now, Jennifer could say any time that she wants it back.'

'But what happens if they can't pay? I mean, in any of this sort of – what did you call it, a private mortgage? – if the people can't pay, what happens?'

'Well, then they get turned out, of course. But–'

'But, Dottie, that's awful! Your own family. You couldn't do that!'

'No, of course not,' Dottie said impatiently. 'We'd never do that. But it's never going to come to it, is it. The repayments won't be any more than the rent they're paying now, and they can manage that all right.'

'Only as long as Luke's earning good money,' Alice said in a worried tone. 'It's like Ted's always said, living on those sorts of earnings is the same as living by your wits. He's doing well now, but who's to say he'll be doing well in a few years' time? I'm not sure I like it, Dottie.' She dunked the other half of the biscuit and exclaimed in annoyance. 'There! It's gone all soft and fallen in. Now there'll be crumbs all through my tea. I'd better pour it away and have another cup.' She got up and swished the cup under the tap. 'And what about young Bob?' she asked over her shoulder. 'He and Kitty are going to be disappointed.'

'Yes, but not too much,' Dottie said. She was feeling rather disappointed herself by Alice's response. Instead of being delighted that Val and Luke would have their own cottage in the village, she seemed to be bringing up nothing but objections. 'If Val and Luke move out of Jed's Cottage, that leaves it empty and Bob and Kitty might be able to rent that instead, if Jennifer's willing. I don't suppose they'll mind which one it is. They just want somewhere to live, and Jed's is really nice now, since Val and Luke have done it up.'

'Mm, I suppose so.' Alice came back to the table, 'Well, you appear to have got it all worked out. There don't seem to be anything more to say.'

'Not really,' Dottie said, still a little nettled. 'Unless you got some better ideas. Someone's got to live there, after all. It seems better to me that it's family.'

Alice nodded, and then smiled a little ruefully. 'I'm sorry, Dot. You're right, and it's a lovely chance for our Val. I suppose I'm just feeling a bit out of sorts this morning, that's all.'

Dottie was instantly concerned. 'Why, what's the matter? Is it this business at the Grey House that's worrying you? You don't think it's anything really bad, do you? I don't see how it could be.'

'Nor do I,' Alice said. 'And Ted says I should put it all aside until we know for sure what's what. But if you could have seen our Jackie's face when she came in the other night, and Mother, too – she looked as if she'd been hit by a thunderbolt. I don't like it, I tell you. I don't like it at all.'

Chapter Thirty-Eight

'You were sweethearts,' Jackie said, looking at her grandmother's pensive face. 'I knew it.'

'But is that why Grandfather was sent away?' Katie asked. 'Just because you were sweethearts? I can't believe it.'

'It was a long time ago, don't forget,' Constance told her. 'Things were different then. Minnie was our nursemaid. Bernard would have been expected to marry a girl from our own sort of background – from a family with a big house and servants.' She turned to smile at Minnie. 'We can see now how silly that is. I'd have loved to have you as a sister-in-law!'

Minnie's face relaxed a little. 'It's not all that silly. I wouldn't have fitted in. I didn't have any education to speak of, and I talked with a broad Devon accent, same as now. How could I sit at a table with a lot of people like the Bellamys and the Napiers and such? I'd have let the family down every time I opened my mouth.'

'Well, I agree with Auntie Connie,' Katie said. 'It's silly! But is that really all there was to it? You and Grandfather fell in love, and the family found out and sent him away? It's idiotic! It's *cruel*.'

'No, there was more to it than that – quite a lot more.' Minnie paused and Jackie realised that they had heard only the beginning of the story. 'You're right, Bernard and me did fall in love. We'd known each other for years, of course, all the time I worked here. His parents were out in India most of the time and he was away at school, but in the holidays he used to stay at the Grey House and, like Miss Constance says, he spent a lot of time with her. And that meant spending a lot of time with me too. We used to go out for hours, the three of us, walking on the moors and paddling about in the streams and leats. He wanted Miss Constance to learn to ride the old pony, so that meant I had to learn as well. I had Sylvia's little mare, Bluebell – Sylvia didn't care much for riding and was happy enough for me to exercise her. We roamed about all over the place and I don't think either of us realised what was happening until it came to when I had to leave to look after Father. I was just about to turn eighteen then, and Bernard was twenty and at Oxford.' She paused, as if telling the story tired her, and Jackie stroked her arm gently. 'I went home just before he came back for his summer holiday – "vac" he called it – so he didn't even know I'd gone until he went up to the nursery to look for me and found Betty Bone putting out the tea things.'

'He must have been so upset,' Katie said softly. She turned to her great-aunt. 'Don't you remember it, Auntie Con?'

Constance stirred. 'Do you know, I believe I do. I didn't know what it was all about and I'd more or less forgotten it, but I do have a faint memory of Bernard coming into the nursery one afternoon and suddenly losing his temper. He'd never done it before and I was quite frightened. But I was also upset that Minnie had had to leave, and not inclined to think about the reasons why he might be affected. I just thought it was because he was becoming a man – that was the first time I'd seen him as anything other than my uncle, but he'd changed since going to Oxford – and after that I was always a little afraid of him. Especially as he came to the nursery much less. He seemed to lose interest in me,' she said a little sadly. 'Even the riding lessons stopped.'

There was a long pause as the two old women gazed into the past as if sharing their memories of a time that had affected both their lives more than they had known.

Then Katie asked softly, 'What happened then?'

Minnie roused herself. 'He came over to see me. He told me he–' She looked down at her lap, as if too shy to say the words, then continued. 'He told me he loved me and wanted to marry me. I couldn't believe it at first. Me, nothing but a nursemaid, marry a man from the family I worked for! I told him it was daft but after he'd gone that day I lay in my bed and cried, because I knew I loved him too and it seemed right that we should be together. But only in our eyes. Nobody else would have seen it that way.'

'Not even your own family?' Greg asked. 'I would have thought they'd be proud of you!'

Minnie smiled and shook her head. 'You don't understand the ways of that time, here in England. We simple folk had our own pride. We knew our place and we kept to it, in the main. Father would have thought I'd been making up to him – taking advantage, like. He would probably have thought worse than that, and if it had been known that Bernard and me were walking out together, the whole village would have been watching to see my stomach swell up. And even if it hadn't, that wouldn't have been proof we hadn't been up to mischief. And suppose we *had* been allowed to marry – like I said before, I'd never have fitted in proper. And don't forget, his father and mother were out in India and they expected him to go out there to join them once he finished with Oxford. They'd never have accepted me.'

'I don't remember any of this,' Constance said. 'I was only a child, of course, but I would have thought I'd have heard something, if only gossip between Betty Bone and the other servants.'

'It was kept pretty quiet,' Minnie replied. 'Nobody wanted a scandal. And seeing what happened next, that was just as well.'

'Why?' Jackie asked. 'What did happen next?' She felt a tingle of apprehension and, as Greg touched her arm, knew that he sensed it too.

'We saw each other all through that summer, whenever I could leave Father. He wasn't so frail then that I couldn't slip out for an hour or two most days. We'd meet down by the river at that quiet little pool about half a mile from the bridge, and walk or sit on the bank together and talk.' Minnie's eyes misted. 'It was a lovely time. A precious time. We didn't think anyone could ever have felt the way we did, or loved anyone else as much as we loved each other.'

'But *surely* you must have wanted to get married and be together!' Jackie exclaimed. 'If you felt like that, you couldn't have borne to be parted.' She hesitated, then said, 'Did he ask you to go away with him, like Uncle Joe asked Dottie when they were young? Is that why he went to Australia?'

'I keep telling you, maid, we'll come to it all in good time,' Minnie said with a touch of impatience. 'Yes, we did want to get married, even though we both knew it would be a difficult path to tread. But after a few weeks it seemed to us both that it would be worth all the trouble it might cause.' She shivered a little. 'We didn't know then just how bad it could be. You never do know what might happen, when you start breaking the rules. Once you've done that, it's out of your control.'

Nobody spoke. The two young women sat transfixed, their eyes on the old face, while Greg was sitting forward in his chair, his eyes downcast. Constance was looking distressed.

'Don't go on if it upsets you,' she said at last. 'I think perhaps you were right – these old stories should be left in the past, where they belong.'

'No,' Minnie said. 'I've gone too far now. Well, that's where we were when I slipped out one night on a full moon, the last of the summer – harvest moon, we called it – to meet Bernard. We were going to make our final plans for telling both our families, and whatever came then we were ready to face. And although up till then we'd never gone astray, we'd made up our minds that this was to be our night. So that if we were parted afterwards, at least we'd have had that.'

'Oh, *Granny...*' Jackie whispered, and clasped the old hand in both of hers.

'We'd settled on our spot. Down by the river by the pool where we had met so often. There were some old willows there then, their branches hanging down over the bank to make a sort of shelter. I took a blanket with me, off my own bed.'

The silence was breathless. They all knew the place she spoke of, even though those willows had long gone. Younger trees had taken their place now, and in their turn made a green shelter, perhaps for other young lovers. The river ran deep and quiet, and the pool was a favourite place for trout, or even the occasional salmon, to rest.

'And now,' Minnie said, 'I got to tell you a bit about my brother, Ned.'

They looked at her in surprise, and she nodded.

'Yes, Ned comes into this story too. I told you,

he was a bit wanting but it was in a funny sort of way. In lots of ways he was more clever than anyone I've ever known. But in other ways he was like a baby. You had to look after him all the time, see that he'd done his buttons up right and so on, and he could never do any jobs round the place, other than sweep the floor. And everything had to be just the same every day, things in the same place, folk coming and going at the right times, or he'd fly into such a rage it was frightening, especially as he got bigger. He didn't like it at all when I went to work for the Bellamys, but of course you couldn't give in to him all the time. He had to get used to it. But it were never easy, not for him nor for anyone else.'

'I remember him,' Constance said. 'He used to wander about the village. The children were rather unkind to him and shouted after him and he would turn and chase them, growling like a bear. They tormented him but they were half afraid of him.'

Minnie nodded, 'Like I said, there was something wrong with his mind. It wasn't his fault but it was never easy to live with him. Still, he was one of the family and families have to look after each other – that's what they're for.' She paused, gathering her thoughts again, and went on. 'He'd learned to read at school and he liked to wander about in the graveyard, reading the epitaphs on the stones. He learned them off by heart as quick as looking at them and he could always tell you where anyone was buried. He spent so much time there, the vicar asked Father if he could help the old gravedigger a bit to keep the place tidy, and he gave him a bit of money each week as a wage. And that was where me and Bernard met our downfall.'

'In the graveyard?' Katie asked. 'But I thought you said you were down by the river?'

'That night, we were. But we used to meet in the churchyard too sometimes. It was nearer for me to slip out just before bedtime, just for a few minutes. And Ned must have known. He must have heard me go and followed me, and seen us together. And that's what he did that last night. He followed me to the river and he saw us go into our little green cave, as we called it, under the willows, and he followed us.' She took a deep breath and said in a flat voice, 'He went into the worst temper I'd ever seen on him. He flew at Bernard and attacked him, and there was nothing Bernard could do but fight back. He'd have been killed, else. And then ... then they both tumbled into the water. And when Bernard came out, Ned was floating with his face down, and although we dragged him out and Bernard tried his hardest to pump the water out of his body, 'twas no use. He was gone.'

'And that was the end of it all,' Jackie finished, to a shocked silence. 'That's why Bernard Bellamy went to Australia instead of India, and why nobody ever mentioned him again.'

Minnie had asked her to tell the story to the rest of the family, saying she didn't feel up to going through the whole thing again to a different audience. 'It was right to tell Miss Constance and the others just on their own, like you said, but I still think the rest of the family ought to know as

401

well. It's not right for others to know things about us that they don't know theirselves. But I can't do it myself. I'd rather you did it.'

Jackie had been dismayed by the task but had agreed to take it on and asked Alice to get the whole family together in the farmhouse that evening. After all, she had been instrumental, with the two Australians, in bringing to light the secret that Minnie had kept for the past seventy years. If she had not spent so long at the Grey House, helping them in their search, if Constance had not remarked on how like her grandmother she was, if she hadn't found that photograph, the only one ever taken of the couple...

'They were in Torquay,' she told her mother now, handing over the fragile scrap of card. 'Granny was still Miss Bellamy's nursemaid then and Bernard took them there for a day out. They had the photograph taken by a photographer on the prom-enade and had a copy each, but Granny destroyed hers when she married Grandad.'

'I can see the resemblance,' Alice said, studying the two laughing faces. 'And they do look proper happy.'

'I don't think they even realised they were in love then,' Jackie said, taking it back. 'They were just happy to be together and enjoying the day out. It's so sad that they were never able to get married.'

'If they had,' Ted pointed out, 'none of us would be here. In fact, apart from your mother and Joanna, none of us would even have been born. Tozers would have been a lot different then.'

'And so would Burracombe,' Val said thought-fully. 'It's amazing when you think of how much effect two people can have on the lives of people all around them. It's like a poem I learned at school – "The Road Not Taken". It ends up with the words, *"And that has made all the difference"*. Just going one way instead of another can make all the difference to dozens – maybe hundreds – of lives.'

The others stared at her. Then Joe said gruffly, 'I dare say that's right, Val, and me and Dottie knows a bit about taking different roads too, but we were lucky. Our paths came together again in the end. It didn't turn out like that for Mother and Bernard Bellamy.'

'They made good lives all the same,' Alice argued. 'Your mother and father thought the world of each other, anyone could see that, and it was as if the world had come to an end for her when he died. And by all accounts, Bernard Bellamy did well in Australia too, and brought up a happy family. Those two that have been here all these months are almost part of the village now. What goes around, comes around, that's what I say, and just because things go wrong at the start of your life, it don't mean to say they're always going to be wrong.' She gave Jackie a quick glance and added, 'I hope that goes for you too, my bird.'

'But you haven't told us all the story,' Tom said. 'What happened after Ned was drowned? How did they get away with it?'

'Get away with what?' Val asked. 'They hadn't done anything wrong. It was an accident.'

'I know what Tom means, though,' Ted said. 'It couldn't end there. Something else must have happened.'

'Well, yes, of course it did.' Jackie went on with the story. 'Once they realised he was dead, they had to tell their families. They went back to the Grey House and Bernard told his uncle what had happened and they got some of the grooms and a couple of stable boys to go and carry the body back. There was no policeman in the village so they had to go to Tavistock next day and report the death and there was an inquest. Bernard said he and Ned had been alone down there and Ned had had one of his tantrums, which everybody knew could flare up for no reason at all, which was so near the truth that nobody questioned it. He never said that Granny had been there too, or why he and Ned went there at night – he let people believe they were out catching rabbits. It wasn't even poaching, since that land belonged to the Bellamys. And then the family sent him to Australia. His parents were told about it and refused ever to have anything to do with him again – they hardly knew him, as it was – so he never went to India after all. And it wasn't long before they came back themselves.'

'Didn't he even see Granny again?' Val asked.

'No. Miss Bellamy's father, who had taken responsibility for him all those years, was furious with him and wrote to tell him that he must never, ever, return to England and he was never to communicate with Granny again. Not even write to say goodbye. He said that if it all came out, Bernard might be questioned more closely and maybe even charged with murder. He made Granny go to see him one day, after Bernard had gone, and told her the same thing and so of course she dared not say a word. In any case, she felt as guilty as him. It must have been a horrible time for her,' Jackie said sadly. 'She said she thought for a long time that life was over for her. It wasn't until she met Grandad that she began to feel at all happy again.'

'And Ned was buried up in the corner of the churchyard,' Val said. 'And we never even knew that little grave, all by itself, was our uncle. How sad.'

'And nobody would ever have known if those two young Australians hadn't come ferreting about raking it all up,' Alice said. 'Mother said from the start that they were bringing trouble, and she was right.'

'They didn't bring trouble – not really,' Jackie said. 'They certainly didn't mean to. They just wanted to know if their grandfather had come from Burracombe. They had no idea what a sad story they would unearth.'

'And I think Mother was right. These old tales are best left buried. I'm sorry to have heard it, and sorry she felt she'd got to tell it.' Alice stood up and began to bustle about the kitchen, as if she were too agitated to sit still any longer.

'Well, don't be sorry on my account,' said a voice from the doorway, and Minnie came slowly into the room and looked around the circle of faces. 'To tell you the truth, I'm glad 'tis all out in the open at last. It's been a weight on my shoulders all my life, though I got so used to it I hardly even knew I was carrying it. Now I feel as if a great load has rolled away from my back. And now you know the truth about me, and maybe that's best. I'm just a human being, same as the rest of us, and just as liable to make mistakes. And that's something we can all do well to remember.'

She walked stiffly to her rocking chair and sank into it. 'And now perhaps we can get on with the rest of our lives. We got the Extravaganza to get ready for tomorrow evening, if you remember, and since we're all here, we might as well have a last rehearsal on these old handbells.'

Chapter Thirty-Nine

It was a shock for Val when she returned to Jed's Cottage after Minnie's revelations to find Ben Mallory sitting by the fire with Luke.

Val stopped in the doorway in the act of removing her coat, and stared at him.

'What on earth are you doing here?'

Luke raised his eyebrows. 'That's a fine welcome! Perhaps you'd like to try again, darling.'

Val flashed him an angry look. 'You could have told me he was coming.'

'He didn't know,' Ben said, getting up and coming towards her. He bent to kiss her cheek and Val jerked away. 'Oh, come on, Val. I won't be a nuisance.'

'That's not the point. I don't like having unexpected visitors. Luke, why didn't you tell me?'

'Ben's just told you – I didn't know. He just turned up on the doorstep. Honestly, I didn't think you'd mind. We can soon put up the camp bed in the front room like we did before.'

'But we haven't talked about it! We haven't agreed!'

'We did talk about it, a little while ago. I told you he wanted to come again.'

'And did I say I wanted him to?' Val, flushed and angry, knew she was being rude but she couldn't help it. She'd come straight from the farm, her head spinning from the story she had just heard about her grandmother, and now Ben was here and heaven knew when she would get the chance to tell Luke about it. She pulled off her boots and took them and her coat through to the scullery, taking advantage of a moment to lean against the sink and take a deep breath to compose herself.

Luke came through and put his hands on her shoulders.

'Val, what on earth has got into you? You've never been like this with Ben before.'

'I've never had him dumped on me without notice before,' she retorted. 'It's too bad, Luke. I'm not ready for a visitor. I'll have to go shopping tomorrow for extra food, and we've got the Extravaganza in the evening – I'm supposed to be helping with that, and I'm ringing the handbells and Granny's bound to want us to have yet one more "last" rehearsal, and – oh, it's just too much!' To her annoyance, she felt tears come to her eyes and brushed them furiously away. 'On top of everything else, too!'

'What "everything else"?' he asked. 'Has something happened up at the farm? What was this sudden family meeting all about, anyway?'

'Oh, so you do remember we were having one! I thought perhaps in the excitement of having your friend arrive you might have forgotten. As a matter of fact, it was quite important, but I can't tell you now. Not with *him* here.'

Luke stared at her. 'Val, what is it? Is someone ill? You've got to tell me.'

'No! It's nothing like that. Nobody's ill. And it's waited so long, it can wait another few days. I'd just like to have been able to talk to you about it this evening, that's all. But never mind me. Let's think about Ben. We've got to make up a bed for him, that means clean sheets and those spare blankets from Chris's bedroom, oh, and a pillow or two as well ... and breakfast in the morning, I suppose, and maybe he'd like a snack tonight, before he goes to bed. And then all the rest of the weekend meals. And exactly how long is he staying anyway? The weekend? All next week? I'd like to know, if it isn't too much trouble to tell me.'

'Don't you think you're being rather silly?' Luke asked quietly. 'It's only a few days. He's been here before and knows our ways and routine, and he's fitted in perfectly well. There's no need for all this hysteria.'

'*Hysteria?*' Val glared at him and then, before she knew she was going to do it, she drew back her hand and slapped Luke's cheek. The sound was like the crack of a pistol shot.

For a moment or two, they stared at each other. She saw the marks of her fingers, first white and then an angry red. Then Luke put up his hand and touched the flaring skin.

'I'm sorry,' Val said in a small, shocked voice. 'I didn't mean to do that. Luke, I'm really, really sorry...'

'Yes,' he said slowly, looking at his hand almost as if he expected to see blood there. 'Yes, I should think you are.'

He turned and walked back into the other room, and Val put both hands to her face and began to cry.

'So what do you make of all that, Dottie?' Joe asked as they walked back to her cottage at the end of the evening.

Dottie shook her head. 'What a sad little tale. And it just goes to show, doesn't it, that you can never really know all about a person. I'd never have guessed that poor Minnie was keeping such a secret all these years. And to think what she must have felt when those two young people turned up claiming to be Miss Bellamy's relatives! No wonder she was in such a taking about it. She knew it was all likely to come out.'

'All these months, she's been hoping they wouldn't find anything. And maybe they wouldn't have, if Jackie hadn't started to help them. They'd have found the photograph and known it was their grandfather, but the full story would never have come out. It's a queer world, Dottie.'

'It is,' she agreed. 'And it makes you wonder just what secrets everyone else is hiding. It's given me quite a turn, I don't mind telling you.'

'Well, you don't need to worry about any secrets between you and me,' he said, slipping his arm round her waist. 'Because there aren't any! Not on my side, anyway. I understand you can never know all about my life in America, but I can tell you now I've done nothing I need ever be ashamed of, and

409

if there's anything you want to know, all you've got to do is ask. I'm an open book where you're concerned, Dottie.'

'I know, and I got no secrets from you either.' She reflected for a moment, then said, 'It seems to me a lot of us make mistakes when we are young, one way or another, and 'tis the natural way of things. How else can we learn? And sometimes those mistakes follow us through life, and sometimes they don't, but what it tells me is that we ought to make allowances for young people today when they make theirs, and not judge them too hasty.'

'You're a wise woman, Dottie,' Joe said, and stopped to kiss her. 'And a kind one, too. I'm a lucky, lucky man.'

'And you've not grown up yet, for all your grey hair and stubbly chin,' she reprimanded him. 'Kissing and canoodling in the middle of the village street! Whatever next, Joe Tozer?'

Alice and Ted were more shaken than they'd wanted to admit by Minnie's confession. They went to their room after the handbell rehearsal and looked at each other.

'I never want to go through another evening like that in my life,' Alice said. 'As if anyone could settle down to ring handbells after hearing a story like that! And it must be even worse for you, Ted, seeing as it's your own mother.'

'I dunno,' he said, sitting down on the side of the bed and taking off his slippers. 'It don't seem real, somehow. It's more as if it was summat that happened to someone else, someone I hardly even knew. I mean, it was so long ago – before either of us was born. I can't seem to take it in.'

'It was real, all right,' Alice said grimly. 'And there's your Uncle Ned's gravestone up in the corner of the churchyard to prove it. Died in an accident, it says, and you always thought it was a farm accident and nobody told you different.'

'There wasn't any need. Look, Alice, a lot of things happened before either of us was born. Things all down the ages. We can't pass judgement on all of them, and it isn't our place to do it anyway. I've known my mother now for getting on sixty years and to me she's always been someone to look up to, and nothing I've heard tonight has changed that. She's worked hard for nearly ninety years, got through two world wars as well as those others round the turn of the century that are pretty well forgotten now, and brought up me and Joe to be good, God-fearing citizens. She was just a young girl when all this happened, and maybe she had her head turned and it was just an early romance, or maybe it was real love – we'll never know that for sure. And what happened to Ned was an accident, whichever way you look at it.'

'But they never told the full truth. They never admitted what really happened. They never said Mother was there too.'

'And what good would that have done?' he demanded. 'Led to a full inquiry, like as not, with Bernard Bellamy up in court and maybe Mother as well, and both of them going to prison – or worse. It was an *accident*, Alice, and if ever there was a case of least said, soonest mended, this is it. They both went on to live good, honest lives, and I think that's all that matters and should be the end of it.'

Alice said nothing. She began to undress, still feeling troubled. She thought of Val, who had confessed to her that she had given birth to a baby – born dead, which might have been a blessing as things were – when she was on her way back from Egypt during the war. The baby had been Luke's but they had parted by then and not met again until a few years ago when he came to Burracombe on the advice of his godfather, Basil Harvey. Alice knew that Val regretted telling her the truth, because Alice had never quite been able to forgive her.

And there was Jackie too. Alice had had her suspicions about the girl's youthful romance with Roy Pettifer, although nothing had ever come of it and nobody had told her anything about that. But she wouldn't have been surprised if they hadn't had a scare. Her own daughters, both of them! Alice had felt betrayed and disappointed.

It wasn't that this kind of thing was all that rare. Look at Patsy Shillabeer, as she had been before marrying Terry Pettifer. They'd been quite open and brazen about it, setting out deliberately to force Percy and Ann to agree to their marriage. It was as if nobody had any morals any more.

And now this revelation about Minnie. Alice got into bed beside Ted and lay stiff and silent as he put out the light. It's made her a different person, she thought. I thought I knew her and it turns out I don't know her at all.

'Listen, my dear,' Ted said quietly in the darkness, 'you got to stop taking these things to heart.

People get things wrong sometimes. They muddle along, we all do, and most of the time we think we're acting for the best. And sometimes we're lucky and all goes right, and sometimes we're not. Mother's suffered more than any of us know over this, but she's put a brave face on it and lived a good life, and we all love her. And it seems to me that's what we got to keep hold of. That's what's important – that families stick together and love each other, no matter what.'

Alice drew in a deep sigh. She turned on her side to face him and slipped her arm across his body.

'You're a good man, Ted,' she whispered. 'And your mother's a good woman. She's always been good to me. And you're right – it all happened a long, long time ago and it's what's happened since that's important. I'm sorry if I've judged her harsh.'

'You don't need to worry about that,' he said. 'Now, give us a kiss and let's go to sleep. I reckon we have had as much to deal with today as we can manage.'

Chapter Forty

The Extravaganza was a riotous success. From the moment it opened, with a song and dance performed by the smallest children in the village, including Robin and Heather Tozer as a prince and princess and with Christopher Ferris wearing a miniature cowboy suit, the entertainment ran seamlessly – or as seamlessly as anything in Burracombe ever did, not counting the moment when all the lights went out and the audience was asked to produce shillings for the meter, the sudden descent of a large pair of window curtains on the three back rows, and Norman Tozer, who was taking part in a sketch written and performed by the bell ringers, suddenly forgetting his words and completely freezing in the middle of his most important speech. But those were the kinds of things you expected and nobody worried about them. Instead, they cheered each minor disaster with almost as much enthusiasm as they applauded James's and David's duets, the comic songs sung by the church choir, Roy Pettifer's stand-up comedy routine which even had one or two new jokes in it, and, of course, the rousing music of the skiffle group.

'That little Brenda Culliford's got a real nice voice,' Jacob said afterwards. 'I reckon her could go on the London stage.'

'Don't say that!' Hilary begged. 'She's too much use at the Barton. Mrs Ellis says she has a natural flair for cooking and she's a wonderful cleaner.'

'Don't take after her ma, then,' Jacob commented, going on his way.

Val and Luke Ferris walked away from the hall silently. Christopher had gone back to the farm to stay the night and next day with Robin and Heather, as a special treat after all the excitement. Usually, this was a special treat for Val and Luke too and they looked forward to a day to themselves. But this time was different. They had not made up their quarrel and the fact that Ben was still there made it worse. He had come to the Extravaganza with them and now walked on Val's other side, his hand on her arm. She tried to shake him off but he kept hold and she wished she had the courage to make a scene. But Luke would never forgive her for that. She wasn't even sure that he would ever forgive her for the slap she had given him.

The worst of it was, she liked the feel of Ben's hand on her arm. Even through the sleeve of her winter coat, there was a warm strength in it that made her want to close her eyes. Go away, she begged him silently, just go away and leave me alone. But she knew that he would not.

'The children were very good, weren't they?' she said, trying to distract herself from the touch on her arm. She heard footsteps behind them and turned to see George and Ivy Sweet. Val stopped, twisting herself away from Ben. 'Hello, Ivy. I was just thinking how good Barry was reciting the "Highwayman" poem. He really brought it to life. You must have been very proud.'

Ivy sighed. 'Says he wants to be an actor. He's been set on it ever since that dragon play they did at the Summer Fair. George and me want him to get a trade behind him first but you know what these boys are once they get an idea in their head.'

'I shouldn't worry,' Ben advised. 'I wanted to be half a dozen different things at that age. Fireman, engine driver, sailor – all the usual stuff. He'll probably go into the bakery with you, Mr Sweet, won't he?'

'We'll see,' George answered. 'It'll be up to him anyway. I don't believe in forcing boys to do what you think they should. It's their lives and they've got to live them long after we're gone.'

'Where is he now?' Val asked, looking round, and Ivy shrugged.

'Gone on ahead with some of his friends. Too excited and pleased with themselves to walk with old fogeys like their mothers and fathers!'

She and George passed on and Luke stopped suddenly, slapping his pockets.

'Drat! I've left my pipe in the hall.'

'Go back for it tomorrow,' Val said. 'It'll still be there.'

'It might not be. They were going to clear the hall tonight ready for the St Valentine's dance next week.'

'Someone will pick it up and look after it.'

'No, I'd better go back. It'll be less trouble all round. You two go on home. I'll only be a few minutes.'

'I'll come too–' Val began, but he flipped his hand at her.

'Don't be silly. It doesn't take two of us. Anyway, it's starting to rain. You go back and get the cocoa on.' He strode away into the darkness and Val stood looking after him, feeling helpless.

Ben took her arm more firmly. 'Come on. You heard what the man said. Come home – with me.'

Val turned and looked up into his face. He was in shadow but she knew exactly was his expression would be. Satisfied, pleased with himself – and dangerous.

'Let go of me,' she said.

His grip tightened. 'Come on, Val. We haven't

had any time alone so far. We won't have long now – let's not waste it.'

'Ben, let go. And leave me alone. I've told you before, you can't talk to me like that. I don't want you to. I don't even want you here – you know I don't. Go back to London. Go tomorrow. And don't come back again. You just cause trouble.'

'Trouble between you and Luke?' He shifted into the light from a cottage window and she saw his eyebrows lift. 'Or just with you?'

'You know what I mean.' She twisted out of his grasp and walked rapidly along the village street. 'Just leave it, Ben. Please.'

He caught up with her and took her arm again. 'There are still people about,' he murmured in her ear. 'You don't want to start a lot of talk, do you?'

'I just want you to leave me alone.'

They reached Jed's Cottage and Ben opened the front gate to usher her in. Val looked desperately along the street but there was no sign of Luke in the darkness. Ben went ahead and opened the door and after a moment's hesitation, feeling as helpless as a puppy on a lead, she followed him.

He closed the door and looked down at her.

Val tried to push past him. 'Let me get by.'

He put his hands on her shoulders and then slid them down her back, drawing her close against him. 'Don't tell me you don't want this, Val.'

Val put her hands on his chest and pushed. It was like pushing a tree. 'I don't! I've told you, I don't want you here at all. Ben – *stop*–'

He bent and covered her mouth with his and the rest of her words were lost. For a moment, she struggled and then she felt her body weaken and her head begin to spin and she crumpled against him. She felt his grunt of satisfaction and knew she was powerless.

'There,' he said, drawing away a little but still holding her close against him. 'I knew I was right.'

'No,' she whispered, 'you're not right. Ben, this can't happen. I've told you. I love Luke...'

'Just a little fling,' he murmured, tracing his lips across her cheek, down her neck, his hands pushing away her scarf and collar. 'That's all I ask. Just once, so that I can taste you and see you and love you, just to give me something of you to remember all my life. That's all I'm asking, Val. Just once. Nobody will ever know. Luke will never know.'

'I can't! Ben, let me go – he'll be here any minute. *Please!*'

Footsteps sounded outside and she gave him a wild look and twisted herself violently out of his arms. This time he let her go and by the time Luke came in she was upstairs pulling off her coat, while Ben was in the kitchen, whistling cheerfully as he filled the kettle.

'Found it!' Luke called up the stairs. 'Are you coming down for some cocoa?'

Reluctantly, Val opened the bedroom door and looked down at him.

'I don't think so,' she said. 'I feel rather tired. I'll just go straight to bed. You stay and talk to Ben.'

He nodded, and she went back and closed the door. Slowly, she undressed and went to wash. She got into bed and lay staring at the wall, knowing that she would not sleep and that as long as Ben

Mallory was in the house she would not know a moment's peace.

'So that artist from London's down here again, staying with Val Ferris,' Ivy commented as she and George sat down with their own cocoa, having finally persuaded Barry to put out his light. 'I hope her hubby knows what he's doing, having a chap like that in the house.'

'Why, you don't suppose anything's going on there, do you?' George asked. He was reading the letter that had come for them that morning. 'The Ferrises seem a happy enough couple.'

'I dare say they are, but... Reading that letter over and over again isn't going to change what's in it, George.'

'No, but we have to make up our minds what to do about it. It's a big thing for our Barry, after all.'

Ivy leaned across to look at the letter again. Like George, she had read it so many times she knew it off by heart, but she still needed to see the words written on the page to be able to believe it.

Konrad's writing was very black and rather spiky. It wasn't easy to read, and even when they had grasped the sense of it that morning, they had been unable at first to believe it. They'd read it again, passed it to each other, and then taken it back, as if the words might have changed while it changed hands. They'd still hardly been able to believe it; it had been in their minds all day.

Now Ivy said, 'What do you think, George? What are we going to do?'

'Well,' he said, speaking deliberately as he often

did when the subject was serious, 'one thing we're *not* going to do is tell him. Not yet, anyway. He don't need to know till he's a lot older than he is now.'

'He won't even get it till he's twenty-one. That's what Konrad says. It'll be "held in trust". What does that mean, George?'

'I think it means it's kept in a bank so nobody can get at it till the right time. Well, that seems a good idea. You can't give that sort of money to a youngster like Barry, and there're some parents who'd use it for themselves. *We* wouldn't, but Konrad's not to know that and nor was his mother.'

'Two thousand pounds!' Ivy marvelled. 'You can buy a house for that.'

'Two houses, probably. More, if they were just cottages. And from what Konrad says here, by the time Barry's twenty-one, it'll be even more. There'll be interest, see.'

Ivy shook her head. 'It doesn't seem possible. But – what do you really think about it yourself, George? I mean, seeing where it's come from?'

'It's come from his granny,' George said steadily. 'I don't have any problem with that, Ive. I took him for my own and I still think of him that way, but I know now about what happened with you and Igor and I've put that away from me. We went to see the old lady, remember, and I could see she was a good woman. And her two sons – well, they were heroes. I'm proud that our Barry's got that blood in him.'

'So you don't mind about the money?'

'Of course not. We never expected anything

from her but she's left it to him and it's up to us to see he makes good use of it. I just don't want it to change the way we go on bringing him up, Ive. He's still got to earn his own living and I still want him to learn a decent trade. He'll have a bit behind him to start him off, whatever he does, but otherwise I don't see that anything needs to change.'

'But what about Konrad? He wants to go on seeing Barry. Look, he says here, Barry's his only living relative now, and we know that even if he gets married he won't ever have his own kiddies because of what happened to him in the war. Do you really want him seeing Barry, regular?'

'I don't see why not. He's a decent man and he's Barry's uncle.' George took a long drink of cocoa, then turned to her. 'Ive, it seems to me we got all a couple could wish for. We got a nice home, a business, a son and we got each other. Konrad's got none of those – well, he's got a home, but to me it seemed more just a house than a real home. He's got no one to share it with. Well, I reckon we can share a bit with him and be glad to. And it'll be good for Barry too. There's a lot he can learn from a man like Konrad.'

They finished their cocoa and went to bed. George put out the light and Ivy lay in the dark, thinking over all that had happened, all that had started on a moonlit night during the war, so many years ago. Who could have believed it could lead to this?

She knew that she had been a lucky woman and that she had not always appreciated her luck. Her story could have ended very differently – in bitterness, loss and even hardship. When you start out on that path, she thought, you never know where it's going to lead.

Chapter Forty-One

'So you're welcome to buy the cottage from me, and I hope you'll be very happy there,' Dottie said to Val and Luke. 'It'll have to be done proper, mind, through a solicitor, and you've got to pay some interest, like in an ordinary mortgage, but it won't be near as much. Joe's looked into it all and as long as you're happy about it, so shall we be. And I can't tell you how pleased I am the dear little place will be going to family.' She beamed at them.

'That's marvellous,' Luke said. 'Isn't it, darling?' He turned to Val and gave her a hug. 'Our very own home!'

Val smiled but looked a little doubtful. 'Are you quite sure, Dottie? I mean, suppose we decided to – to move, or something? Wouldn't you mind it being sold to someone else?'

'Why, you're not expecting to leave Burracombe, are you? And if you're thinking about the size, you know there's space to put another room on the back. There'd be plenty of room for a little brother or sister for young Christopher.'

'I wasn't thinking of that so much,' Val said. 'I was thinking – well, suppose Luke wanted us to move to London? We couldn't afford two houses.'

Luke looked at her in surprise. 'But we went through all that months ago, when I started going up there one week a month. You said you'd never want to leave Burracombe.'

'I know, but things change, don't they? Nobody can tell what's going to happen in the future. We might not even stay together.'

Dottie gasped and Luke stared in dismay. 'Val, what are you saying? Of course we'll stay together.'

She looked at him. They had still not properly made up their quarrel. She'd apologised and he'd accepted her apology, but there was a stiffness in his tone and an awkwardness between them. She hoped that it would ease, but with Ben having made no move to leave there had been no chance for the showdown that might have cleared the air. Maybe, she thought miserably, it would never clear. Maybe this time she had gone too far.

And there was still the question of Ben himself. There, in the house – sitting across the table, lounging on the settee, sleeping on the camp bed in the front room. Never far away, never leaving her alone with Luke and always with that knowing look in his dark, sleepy eyes.

'Yes, of course we will,' she said. 'I don't know what made me say that.'

'Well, there's no need to decide anything this minute,' Dottie said, with a worried glance at them both. 'Joe wants to talk to Henry Warren about it and see if he will arrange it all. He says it's best to make it all official and go to see him properly, in his office in Tavistock, so all we need to do is fix a time to suit us all and Joe will drive us in. These things never happen all that quickly, but we won't be moving out until Easter, so there's plenty of time.'

'We'll have to tell Jennifer too,' Luke said. 'I expect she'll want to find a new tenant for Jed's Cottage.'

'She won't have to look far for that.' Dottie smiled. 'Bob Pettifer came to see me about renting this one, the very same night as you came to ask about buying it, Val. He and Kitty Pengelly want to get married and of course he wants to stay in Burracombe, so it would be ideal. I haven't told him yet, so maybe it's best if you talk to Jennifer and then she can decide.'

'It's like a game of musical chairs!' Val said with a little laugh. But her laugh sounded forced and Dottie felt a fresh twinge of worry. There was definitely something the matter there, she thought, and she could see Luke was worried too. There was an air of strain between them that had never been there before and she hoped that the idea of buying a house of their own wasn't causing it. Not everyone wanted a mortgage – a lot of people said they were a millstone round your neck – and they'd always seemed perfectly happy in Jed's Cottage. Maybe this was not such a good idea after all.

'You take your time and think it over proper before you make a decision,' she said. 'There's no hurry and it's not something you should rush into. Joe and me'll wait till you tells us for certain before we do anything else.'

Luke nodded. 'That's probably best. We've all been so busy lately, we've hardly had time to think. Anyway, we'd better be going now.' He fetched Val's coat and helped her into it. 'Ben's looking after Chris and we're not sure quite how long he can stand piling yellow bricks on top of red bricks and knocking them all down again, which is Chris's latest craze!'

Dottie laughed and saw them to the door. But after she'd watched them go, she came back in and poked the fire thoughtfully.

Things aren't right with those two, she thought, and it's a shame. They're proper fond of each other and I don't like to see them at loggerheads. But something's wrong, that's plain to see.

'Val, what's this all about?' Luke asked as they walked away. 'You were as keen as mustard on buying Dottie's cottage. It was your idea in the first place. Why have you suddenly got cold feet?'

Val shrugged. 'I don't know. It's such a big commitment, and it seems a bit unnecessary when we're already settled so nicely in Jed's. And I feel we're letting Jennifer down too – she's had a lot of work done for us, putting in the little bathroom and lavatory and everything. We'd have to do all those things for ourselves at Dottie's, which means more expense ... I'm just not sure it's the right time, that's all.'

'It's not all. We've talked about all that and decided we would do them gradually over the next few years. I'm quite happy with that, and I thought you were too.' He glanced at her. 'And Dottie's right about the space – we could add on to the back and make the cottage bigger. We could put on two rooms, one upstairs and one down – a bathroom and another bedroom.'

'So that we could have more visitors?' she burst

out. 'So that people like Ben could come and practically live with us?'

There was a small silence. Then Luke said quietly, 'No. So that we could have another baby.'

Val was silent and he waited a moment, then asked, 'Isn't that what you want? A brother or sister for Kester? We don't want him to be an only child, do we?'

'No. I don't know. It's too soon. Oh, stop *bothering* me about it, Luke. About the cottage and about a baby and – oh, *everything*. I'm just not in the mood!'

She tried to swing away from him but he grasped her arm and said seriously, 'Val, you've got to stop this. There's something wrong and you've got to tell me what it is. Please, Val. We've got to talk about it.'

Val turned and looked at him. 'Luke, there is nothing wrong! *Nothing!* But how can we talk properly about anything when we never have any time to ourselves? When Ben Mallory is always in the house, always under my feet? And if he's not in the house he's out with you. I never see you alone any more. And when is he going to go, Luke? He was supposed to be staying for the weekend but it's Monday now and he's still here. Doesn't he have a home of his own?'

'I've told you–'

'Yes, you told me he never had a proper home and family and I should be sorry for him and let him be part of ours. But he's *not* ours! He's not a little boy any more, Luke, he's a grown man and it's time he made his own family. Please.' She stopped and faced him. 'Please, just tell him to

426

go back to London. I don't want him here.'

'Val, I can't do that. That's unkind.'

Val felt her shoulders sag. She turned away and walked on, defeated. 'All right, then, I'm unkind. I hate your friends and I hit you and I'm just not a nice person any more, and you wonder why I think we may not always stay together! I'm surprised you can even say you love me, let alone buy a house for us to live in together.'

She walked on, leaving Luke staring after her. Then she turned and said, 'I'm going for a walk by myself. You go home and talk to Ben, since he's so much nicer than me. I'll see you later.' She strode rapidly away in the direction of the ford.

'Val!' he called after her. 'Val, come back...' But her head did not turn and he looked at her stiff back and knew that to follow her would only make matters worse.

Baffled and distressed, he walked slowly back to the cottage.

Ivy Sweet had been to the ford too. She didn't often go for a walk for the pleasure of it, but she wanted to pick some of the snowdrops that grew there in a mass of shimmering white. She had gathered a small basketful when she caught sight of Val, leaning over the bridge.

Ivy hesitated. She could see by the droop of Val's head and body that she was unhappy, and she had a strong suspicion why. But what was the use of saying anything? She'd only get short shrift – be told to mind her own business, keep her nose out of matters that didn't concern her. She'd have done exactly the same if anyone had approached her when she was feeling low. Best to walk on by with just a cool 'hello' and let the young woman get on with it. Tozers never thanked you anyway, always thought they were a cut above the rest of the village.

And yet ... she remembered how she had been thinking in bed that she had been lucky. Her story had ended happily. But there had been a lot of misery and guilt to get through first, and some people never had the happy ending, only the misery and guilt to haunt them throughout their lives.

And Val Tozer had never done her any harm. She'd never even spoken an unkind word to her.

Ivy stopped. She laid a hand on the young woman's shoulder and Val turned with a start. She stared at Ivy as if she had never seen her before.

'Tell me to mind my own business,' Ivy said gruffly. 'Tell me to go away if you want. But let me say my piece first.'

Val's eyes flashed and she opened her mouth. Ivy, knowing what she was about to say, hurried on.

'I know pretty well what's been going on. No, there's been no gossip, not that I've heard, and there won't be none from me, you don't need to worry about that. But I've got eyes in my head and I've seen that London chap with you, and I've seen enough of that in my time to know what he's after.'

Val drew in an angry breath, but again Ivy talked over her. 'I know what folk say about me and a lot of it's true enough. I was no better than I ought to be, back in the war. I met a lot of airmen from Harrowbeer airfield when I was working in the pub over in Horrabridge and I don't mind admitting that I liked a bit of a laugh with them. There was nothing wrong with that. People here in Burracombe don't think I can laugh, but I could then, and I could see they needed it, poor young chaps. But that's all it was – until I met Igor.'

'Igor?' Val repeated, perplexed. 'I don't remember anyone called Igor.'

'You wouldn't. He never came to Burracombe. He was a Polish pilot, just a young chap like the rest of them, hundreds of miles away from home, and he didn't know what had happened to his family. There was such awful things happened over there, people shot down in the streets and killed for no reason, that he didn't even know if he still *had* a family. I felt sorry for him, same as I did for all of them, but with him it went further than feeling sorry. And – well, you can guess what happened. And then he got killed and there I was, with my Barry on the way.'

'Mrs Sweet,' Val said, disturbed and embarrassed, 'you don't need to tell me this. I don't see what–'

'You don't see what it's got to do with you. Well, nothing. Except that I want you to see that I understand. I know what it's like, because I've been through it. Falling for a man who's not your hubby. I know what it's like.'

Val's cheeks flared with colour and she turned away abruptly. 'I think you've said enough. You'd better go now. Just leave me alone.'

'I'm sorry,' Ivy said, standing her ground, 'but I've made up my mind to speak and speak I will. You don't ever need to say a word to me again if that's the way you feel, but I've got to say this to you now.' She took a deep breath. 'I've been lucky in my life. I haven't always appreciated it but I do now. I've got Barry and I've got George, who's always stood by me. But it might not have turned out that way. He could have chucked me out and nobody would have blamed him, and then where would I be? And that's how it turns out for a lot of folk. Out on the streets with their little bundle of joy and nobody to turn to. And even if you're lucky like I am, there's a lot of grief and guilt to get through. And hiding it just makes it worse.'

Val stared at her and then felt her insides crumple. Tears came to her eyes and when she brushed them away with her hand more took their place. She said in a whisper, 'I don't know what to do. He keeps on at me and – and I'm just so afraid I'll give way. I don't *want* to, but–'

'I know just what you mean,' Ivy said quietly. 'You're fighting it but he's a nice-looking man and he's got a way with him. I've seen it when he's come into the pub. I've seen it before, time and time again. He's the sort no girl's safe with. He'll go on and on till he gets his way and then he'll be off without giving you another thought.'

'At first,' Val said, 'he said he couldn't live without me. He couldn't stop thinking about me. But now apparently it's to be "just a fling". Just the once, he says, and then he'll leave me alone.' She looked at Ivy with tear-filled eyes. 'I really don't want to betray Luke, but I'm beginning to feel it's the only way out.'

Ivy nodded. 'I know, my dear. But it isn't, you know. And you don't know it'll end there. Suppose he keeps on coming to visit you. Suppose it goes on for weeks – months. You don't know what trouble you'll be piling up.' She paused. 'There *is* another way. You could tell your man and ask him to send the chap packing.'

'But he's Luke's friend! I can't do that – he'd be terribly upset.'

'Friend?' Ivy said scornfully. 'Funny sort of friend! And wouldn't your hubby be even more upset if he found you'd let him down? I reckon I know which he'd choose to be let down by, if he was asked.' She leaned over the bridge beside Val. 'Take it from me, my dear. If you go the way this chap wants, you'll have it hanging over you all your life. It's not a burden you want to carry. I know – I carried mine for the past twelve years and it's come out in the open just the same.' She told Val, quickly and briefly, how Konrad had come looking for her, and how she had finally had to confess to George. 'I told you, I been lucky and it's turned out well, except that one day we got to tell Barry the whole truth. But it's not been easy and I don't reckon it's done me any good over the years. It's not too late for you to pull back, but that's for you to decide.'

She straightened up and Val, who had been staring down at the swirling waters of the Burra Brook, turned to meet her eyes. 'I'll say no more now,' Ivy said. 'I reckon I've said enough, and I'll not mention it again unless you mention it first. But I couldn't see what I've seen lately with my own eyes and let you go the wrong way without a word.' She picked up her basket of snowdrops, gave Val a sharp nod and walked away.

Val stared after her. She felt shaken by all she had heard, and overwhelmingly touched by the fact that it had been Ivy Sweet, of all people, who had said it. Like everyone else in Burracombe, she had always dismissed the baker's wife as a sour-tempered old harridan whose only pleasure was in making spiteful remarks to hurt other people. But now she had seen a very different side and she wondered just how much the other woman's experiences had affected her. Did guilt really do that? she wondered. Did it eat away at your heart and soul and turn you into a person you had never thought you could be, trying to ease it by taking it out on other people?

I don't want to be like that, she thought. I don't want to hurt Luke and Christopher and my family and all my friends. I don't want to live with a secret hanging over me. I want to be open and honest and free, and Ben Mallory has come close to spoiling it all.

Ben Mallory *and I,* she acknowledged. Because I was close to giving way to him, and I do have a choice. I just have to make it the right one.

Chapter Forty-Two

'Pancake Day and St Valentine's on the same day!' Hilary said to Val when they met in the village street the next day. 'That's not very romantic. Whatever kind of pancakes can we make for a romantic dinner at home?' She slipped off Beau's back to let him graze for a few minutes on the verge.

Val smiled and shrugged. 'I suppose the agony aunts on the back pages of women's magazines would tell us to make them in the shape of hearts. I'm not sure our Valentine's Day dinner is going to be very romantic anyway.'

'Why not?' Hilary looked at her friend with some concern. 'Everything's all right with you and Luke, isn't it? You've got rid of Ben at last, so he won't be playing gooseberry.'

Val laughed but it wasn't the ringing laugh that Hilary was used to hearing. 'Yes, he finally went back to London this morning and I've got Luke for the rest of the week, so I should be grateful for that. Anyway, never mind us. Did you get a lovely romantic card from David this morning?'

'Well, an unsigned card came through the post so I presume it was from him. Not that I needed one, but I haven't had that many over the years so I was really rather pleased. And he gave me a huge bunch of flowers too – went into Tavistock straight after surgery and brought them back. Lovely spring daffodils from the Scilly Isles. I told him that next year I want to go and see them actually growing. They must look wonderful.' She turned to mount the horse again. 'Anyway, I must go. Jennifer's coming over for coffee. Have you seen her lately? She's quite a size now.'

'It's only a few weeks until the baby's due,' Val said, 'Jacob's getting anxious already!' She opened her front gate to go indoors.

Hilary waved goodbye and walked Beau along the street, feeling anxious herself. Val looked rather pale, she thought, and without her usual energy. Hilary hoped her friend was not going to be ill. The flu epidemic seemed to be over, but you couldn't be sure that it wouldn't return, and Val had never quite seemed to regain her strength since her difficult pregnancy with Christopher and the panic over his birth.

After a few minutes, however, her thoughts returned to her own concerns. She and David were very happily settled and her father was as fit and well now as he had ever been, although she still liked him to take care, but Stephen and Maddy still seemed to be in a state of indecision. Stephen's stump had healed well and he was able to manage better than Hilary had ever expected with just one arm, but although she knew that her father would be happy to see them stay at the Barton permanently, she also knew that this would not do for Stephen. He had a restless energy that would not allow him to sit back and be an invalid for the rest of his life, and he was still determined to make a career of his own. But what it could be, Hilary had no idea, for no more had been said about Canada or an air-freight business, and she could not ask without feeling that she was interfering. After all, she knew very well what it was like to be searching for a direction in life. You just needed to be left alone to find your own way.

Her thoughts were disturbed by a call from across the street and she stopped Beau while Frances Kemp came across to say hello.

'Why aren't you in school?' Hilary enquired, and then laughed at herself. 'I'm talking to you as if you're a naughty girl playing truant!'

434

Frances smiled. 'It's dinner time and James is on duty so I just slipped out to buy some ingredients for pancakes. We're going to be making them in the school kitchen this afternoon – Mrs Dawe has kindly agreed to come in to do a demonstration.'

'That sounds like fun. But surely most of the children see pancakes being made at home.'

'Probably, but they love cooking and getting into a mess. I'm not sure what Mrs Purdy will have to say when she comes in to clean later on, mind you!'

'Quite a lot, probably,' Hilary said drily. 'And how are the wedding plans coming along? We've received your invitation and I'll be replying in the next few days. An Easter Day wedding will be lovely – and take my mind off what happened last Easter Day, when I almost set fire to the whole house.'

Frances looked a little anxious. 'I hope those we haven't invited to the reception won't be offended. But really, it was a case of either just close friends and family – not that either of us has much family, just a few cousins and not all of them will be able to come, although I'm pleased to say my cousin Iris is going to be here – or else everyone in the village. There are so many I've taught over the years. So I'm afraid we decided on close friends and family, with a nice lunch at the Bedford Hotel in Tavistock, and a party for the village in the Bell Inn on Monday evening, like Dottie and Joe did for theirs.'

'Which is also the day of the Organ Festival,' Hilary remarked. 'Bernie and Rose are going to be run off their feet! It's a good thing they've got that new barmaid from Tavistock, who seems to be settling in well, and Ivy Sweet will probably help too. What a weekend it's going to be. And what a happy one, for everybody.'

'Let's hope so,' Frances said. 'And now I'd better be getting back to the school before James has a nervous breakdown from being left on his own with the whole pack.'

She walked on, thinking with pleasure of her coming wedding. She had never believed, after the death of her childhood sweetheart Ralph in the First World War, that such a day would ever come for her. But James Raynor had brought her heart to life and although she'd doubted it at first, her second cousin Iris, Ralph's sister, had helped her to see that it was no betrayal of that early love to accept this new one. And Iris had given her final blessing by agreeing to attend the wedding, even though the journey from Malvern might be difficult for her and returning to Burracombe, where she and Ralph had grown up, might prove an emotional experience.

'If you can marry, after all this time,' she had said to Frances, 'I'm sure I can bear to come home again. After all, Burracombe was our home, for all those years until Ralph died in the Great War, and it's still as home that I think of it.'

It would be good to see Iris in Burracombe again, Frances thought. Few of those living here now remembered the Stannard family, even though Ralph's name was on the village memorial, and nobody had ever connected Frances herself, just a young girl back then, with those days. But for the two women who had such special memories of the past, it would be like bringing a long chapter of their story to a satisfying end, before beginning another.

She heard the school bell ring to tell the children that the dinner hour was over, and hurried towards the gate with her basketful of ingredients for pancakes.

'Thank you for the card you made me,' Val said to her husband that evening as she stood at the kitchen table beating eggs into a bowl of flour. 'It's really lovely.' She looked at him as he came through the door. 'I don't deserve it.'

'Of course you do, darling.' He came over and put his arms round her to give her a kiss. 'It's Valentine's Day and I love you. Why wouldn't I give you the best card I could make?'

Val brushed at her eyes, leaving flour all over her face. 'Because I've been so horrible to you lately. I'm really sorry, Luke. I'm sorry I've been so bad-tempered, and I'm really, really sorry I slapped you. I never meant to. I didn't even know I was going to do it until it happened.' She leaned her head against his chest and whispered, 'Can you ever forgive me?'

'Darling, I already have. It was a shock, I can't deny that, and I was upset and hurt and angry at the time. But I've got over that.' He looked down gravely at her face. 'There's still something worrying me, though. It's not like you to be so on edge. What's wrong, Val? I know there's something, and you really must tell me. We're married, remember? That means we face problems and sort them out together. Whatever they are.'

Val met his eyes and nodded. 'I know. And I will tell you, Luke. But can we make it later? I've got pancake mixture here and Kester has been looking forward to his pancakes all day. Let's wait until he's tucked up and fast asleep, and then we'll talk.'

'Promise?' he asked seriously, and she nodded again.

'Promise.'

Pancakes featured in the evening meal of almost every home in Burracombe that day. The children, who had enjoyed smothering themselves and most of the school kitchen with flour that afternoon, now considered themselves qualified to direct operations in their mothers' kitchens, to varying response. Joanna Tozer stood patiently at the kitchen table, mixing flour and eggs under Robin's critical instructions, Billy Madge's mother shooed him out, saying she'd been making pancakes all her life and didn't need his advice, and Mrs Crocker gave up altogether and let the twins make the mixture entirely by themselves. The results were surprisingly good, and she told them that, if they liked, they could take over all the cooking.

'Only if we can have pancakes every day,' George said, wolfing down the last scrap of his fourth. 'Can we go out to play now?'

Ernie Crocker watched as the boys scrambled down from their chairs and grinned at his wife. 'You'll never turn them into proper cooks. They just likes making a mess.'

Mrs Crocker sighed. 'I don't know why we

couldn't have been blessed with two little girls that I could have dressed up in pretty frocks and shown how to cook proper meals. And they're only seven years old, Ernie. Look how many more years we've got to get through before they're grown up!'

Ernie chuckled. 'You know you don't mean that, love. They're little scamps, 'tis true, but there's not an ounce of real harm in them. They'll be chaps to be proud of when they're grown.'

'I hope so,' she replied. 'I just wonder what all the mothers of little girls now will think, when our two are eyeing up the girls and still pretending to be each other!'

'Pancakes!' Stephen Napier exclaimed, as Hilary and Maddy entered the dining room at the Barton bearing a huge covered dish. 'Marvellous. I've been looking forward to these all day.'

'What I never understand,' Gilbert said as he was served with three rolls of pancake, liberally sprinkled with sugar and lemon juice, 'is why we don't have them more often. We all like them and apparently they're quite easy to make, yet we only seem to have them once a year. Can't we make it a more frequent treat, Hilary?'

She laughed. 'I don't know either, Father. All I know is, we say the same thing every year and yet it never happens. Tell you what, we'll make them a special treat on your birthday – that will help us to remember. How about that?'

'But I always have roast pork and apple pie on my birthday. I don't think I could manage pancakes as well.'

'Have them for breakfast, then,' Maddy advised,

cutting Stephen's pancakes into forkful portions for him. 'That's what they do in Canada, isn't it, Stephen?'

There was a sudden silence. Hilary glanced at her brother and then at her father. He was staring at his son from beneath lowered brows.

'Don't tell me you're still hankering after the idea of emigrating to Canada?'

Stephen put a forkful of pancake into his mouth and chewed. He cast Maddy a fleeting look, then swallowed and met his father's eyes. 'Not hankering, no,' he said equably. 'Making plans.'

'Making *plans?*' Gilbert laid down his own fork. 'What do you mean, plans? What *sort* of plans? You can't still be considering this air-freight idea you talked about.'

'Why can't I?' Stephen asked, his tone as casual as if he had been asking why he couldn't have a fourth pancake.

'I should have thought that was obvious! You were fit and well when you first had that idea. Now – well, you can't claim to be the man you were then. You're just not *able*. And you don't have to take offence at that,' Gilbert added hastily as Stephen's eyes flashed. 'You were honourably wounded in battle, nothing to be ashamed of there. But you must see how it limits you.'

'It doesn't limit me at all. I can still do a lot of things with just one arm. I can drive – you've seen me do that, you've even been in the car with me. I can fly – I've been to the airfield at Bodmin twice a week for the past month, taking Jeremy Cartledge's plane up. I can do pretty well as much as I need to do.'

'Apart from cut up your own food,' Gilbert said brutally, and Hilary gasped and began to protest. He raised his hand. 'All right, you don't need to tell me – that was out of order and I apologise. But you must see, Stephen, that this is far too big a step to take after all that's happened. It needs a great deal of thought and planning–'

'Which is where we came in,' Stephen cut in. 'Maddy and I *have* been thinking and planning. We know it won't be easy but we don't see that as being something to stop us. What else would you have us do? Stay here and be a drain on the estate? We're certainly not contributing anything at present.'

'I don't see it as being either one thing or the other, with no alternative,' Gilbert said, beginning to eat his pancake again. 'There must be a hundred and one other things you could do. You have a very good degree in mathematics, for a start. You could use your brain in that way.'

'I will be using my brain. I'll be running a business.'

'But why in Canada? Why not run a business in England? There must be opportunities here too. The same *kind* of opportunities.' Gilbert's face was red and Hilary glanced at him in alarm, then looked at David, who shook his head slightly. She sighed with impatience.

'Father, it doesn't help to get yourself worked up about it.'

'It won't help *not* to!' he retorted. 'How else is the boy to be made to see the risks he's taking – risks that aren't necessary?'

'What risks?' Stephen asked. 'All right, let's sup-

441

pose you're right and there *are* opportunities here for the kind of business I want to set up – an airfreight and ferry service from the mainland to islands that at present don't have it, except in a very limited way. Where are these islands in this country? The Scillies – yes, they might be a possibility, but apart from flowers like those over there' – he nodded towards the daffodils David had given Hilary that morning, now displayed on the sideboard – 'and a few travellers, there's not much that doesn't go over by sea on the *Scillonian*. I don't see a huge business opportunity there. Or maybe you think the Isle of Wight would be a better bet. Or the Isle of Man. But they're all well served already. The only areas that are similar to the one I want to start up in are the islands off the north of Scotland, and, as a matter of fact, I have looked at those. But I still think that Canada presents a better opportunity. There are thousands of islands in the Hudson River, for example, and that's just a start.'

Gilbert stared at him, then he turned to Maddy. 'And what do you think about all this, Madeleine? Are you ready to up sticks and go off to some isolated place on the off-chance that your husband will make a success of this scheme of his? Have you thought what it will be like for you, knowing he's risking his life every time he takes to the air in some rickety little freight plane? Suppose you start a family, as I'm sure you hope to do – have you thought what it will be like, raising children largely on your own, in the wilds of Canada?'

Maddy met his eyes. Hilary, watching, felt a slow rise of admiration for the younger woman's

442

composure as she answered simply, in a cool, level tone, 'Yes, Uncle Gil. Yes, I've thought about all those things.'

There was a short silence while Gilbert waited for her to enlarge upon her statement, then he grew tired of waiting and asked impatiently, and in a tone he had never used to her before, 'Well? Is that all you have to say?'

'Yes, it is,' she replied, then smiled at him and added, 'but if you do want me to say more, I'll just say that Stephen and I have thought about it all very carefully, we've found people who know Canada and we've talked to them, and we think it will work very well. We both want to give it a try. After all, if it doesn't work, we can always come back.' She paused, then added quietly, 'And I'm afraid, Uncle Gil, that I don't think you are arguing fairly. You say he'll be "risking his life". I don't think there's any more risk than there is in driving a car. Look what happened to Felix and Stella that night they ran into the ponies, only a few miles from here. And he won't be using a "rickety little plane". It will be a good aircraft and it will be properly maintained. We're taking one of the mechanics Stephen knew in the RAF, someone who really knows his job. And I won't be on my own in the "wilds" of Canada. Where we're going is a civilised and quite prosperous little town. With doctors, nurses, a hospital and a school,' she added. 'You don't need to have any fears about that.' She got up and walked round the table to stand beside him and bent to lay her cheek against his. 'You won't lose us, Uncle Gil,' she said softly. 'We'll come back to see you, often.' She gave him a sudden, dazzling smile. 'And we'll bring your grandchildren to visit you as well.'

Even in the Grey House, pancakes were on the menu for supper that night.

'I don't know what all the fuss is about,' Greg said, grinning as Jackie came in bearing a bowl full of fresh eggs from Alice's hens while Constance brought in a bag of flour from the larder. 'We often have pancakes at home. We don't treat them as anything special.'

'It's the beginning of Lent,' Jackie told him severely. 'It's because in olden times there wouldn't have been many eggs or much fresh food at all during the second half of winter, and people would have had to live on things like salted meat – if they had meat at all, which most of them didn't – and root vegetables like turnips. And of course they would have fasted until Easter anyway, when the hens would start to lay again, and that's why we have Easter eggs. So we make a feast of what we have now and then tighten our belts for six weeks.'

'Really, Greg!' Katie said to her brother. 'Auntie Con will think we're complete heathens. You know all this already. Or you would, if you'd paid attention in Sunday School.'

'I'm afraid I was never one for listening in church,' he said ruefully, and gave Jackie a soulful glance. 'But if you want to teach me a few lessons, I promise I'll be good.'

'I'll teach you a few lessons, all right,' she said, starting to break the eggs into a mixing bowl. 'But it may take rather a long time.'

'That's all right,' he said quietly, 'you can have all the time in the world.'

There was a sudden small silence. Jackie felt her face grow warm and glanced quickly at Katie and Miss Bellamy, but both were apparently paying attention to their own parts in pancake making. She began to beat the eggs rather more fiercely than they needed.

'You can decide what fillings you want,' she said rapidly. 'We usually have lemon and sugar but you can have jam, if you like, or stewed apples. Anything at all, only you'll need to say soon.'

'I'll have mine however you have yours,' Greg said, and put his fingers on her wrist. She stopped beating and raised her eyes to him, feeling the heat increase in her skin. 'And you can give me your first lesson now – on how to eat pancakes the English way.'

Chapter Forty-Three

'So tell me all about it,' Luke said, pouring Val a cup of tea. 'What's been bothering you so much, these past few weeks?' He sat down beside her and slipped his arm round her shoulders. 'You're not ill, are you?'

'No. Whatever made you think that?'

He sighed. 'I didn't tell you this, but someone I know in London – his wife's about your age and she's got a growth or something – here.' He touched her breast. 'It's really serious. It made me

445

wonder… It really is nothing like that?'

Val shook her head. 'No, nothing like that, I promise. I'm sorry, Luke, I wouldn't have had you worry like that for the world. And before you ask, I'm not expecting again either. I know we both want another baby some time, but it's not going to happen by accident. It'll be something we both want, at the right and proper time.'

'Well, then,' Luke said after a pause, 'since those are the two most important things out of the way, what else could be causing all this upset? Because I know that whatever it is, you think it's serious.'

'It is,' she said, then took a deep breath and spoke the words she had been dreading, the words that would bring it all out into the open. 'It's Ben.'

Luke stared at her. '*Ben?*'

'Yes. You know I haven't been happy, having him here–'

'Yes, but Val–'

'Please, Luke. Listen to me.' She took another breath. 'I know he's your friend, or you think he is – no, don't interrupt again, just listen – but you don't know what he's been doing. What he's been saying.' She met his baffled eyes. 'Luke, he's been making passes at me. He won't leave me alone. Every time you leave us together, he starts again. First of all he said he couldn't live without me. Then it was just a fling that he wanted. He said you would understand because you're an artist and – and artists do that sort of thing.' Her eyes filled with tears and she choked a little on the words. 'I told him I didn't believe him, that we loved each other, and he said that didn't make any difference. Now he's saying that if we don't – don't make love once, we'll never be able to stop wanting to. He says if I let him – just once – it will be all over and he'll leave me alone.' She was crying in earnest now. 'Luke, I've tried and tried to stop him, I've tried to tell you I don't want him here, but nothing seems to make any difference. I feel as if I'm on one of those trains in a film that you know is going to crash and you can't do a thing to stop it. Luke, you've *got* to tell him not to come here any more. *Please.*'

She stopped abruptly and covered her face with her hands. The tears dripped through her fingers and made a damp patch on her skirt. Luke, his arm still across her shoulders, sat very still, staring at her bent head. At last he spoke, his voice cracking on the words.

'Why didn't you tell me before?'

'Because he's your *friend!* Because I didn't want to upset you. Surely you can see–'

'And what did you mean when you said *"we'll never stop wanting it"*?'

'It was what *he* said. Not what I said.'

'But you say he said *"we"*,' Luke said flatly. 'Why would he say that?' He waited a moment, then added, 'Val, you have to tell me all of it. *Did* you want to?'

Val hesitated. Then she remembered Ivy Sweet's words. Secrets could bear you down over the years. She recalled her own realisation that there must be no more secrets.

'He said I did,' she said at last. 'Luke, I don't honestly know whether I did, or whether he'd just sort of mesmerised me, like a rabbit. But I think if he had kept on, I would have given in, just to get rid of him.' After another moment she added in a very small voice, 'I'm sorry.'

It was a full minute before she dared look up into his face. His eyes were dark and she could see the anger growing deep within them. Her heart seemed to twist a little. Then he drew her close against him.

'Oh, Val,' he murmured into her hair. 'My poor, poor Val. You must have been so miserable. So scared.'

'I didn't want to let you down,' she whispered. 'Truly I didn't. But' – Ivy's words came back to her again – 'I've got to be honest with you now, Luke. I *did* find him exciting, in a dangerous sort of way. I was scared of myself as much as of him. That's what I'm most sorry about.' Then she added forlornly, 'I don't expect you to understand that, but I have to tell you, even if it means you stop loving me. I want you to know all the truth.'

Luke gripped her hard against him. 'Of course I understand, darling! Do you think you're the only person this has ever happened to? Look, I meet people all the time in London, women, I mean, who make it quite plain that they'd enjoy a "fling". And sometimes I find them attractive too. But never enough to want to have a "fling" with them. And it doesn't mean I love you any the less. In fact, it's the thought of you and Christopher and all we have here that keeps me on the straight and narrow. You don't have to worry about them, Val, any more than I worry about you. We trust each other. *Don't* we?'

'I trust you. I don't see how you can trust me, after what I've told you.'

'I trust you *because* of what you've just told me.' He held her away from him a little so that they could see each other's faces. 'It's all right, darling. Ben won't be coming here any more and he won't be a friend of mine any longer. I suppose I shouldn't be surprised – I always knew he had an eye for any chance that came along, though I never thought he would see you as a "chance".' He looked grim. 'I'll be going back to London next week and the first thing I do will be to have a talk with Master Ben and set him quite straight. He won't bother you again.'

'Oh, Luke,' Val said, almost collapsing in his arms in her relief. 'Luke, I'm so glad. And things are really all right between us?'

'More than all right,' he said, and kissed her. 'In fact, I think we should make up our minds now about where we are to live in the future. Here – or in Dottie's cottage? I saw Joe this afternoon and he said he's talked to Henry Warren. All we have to do is go along to his office together some time this week, and the documents can be drawn up ready, and all the legal procedure of selling and buying a house gets started. With luck, we could be in by Easter!'

'Easter?' she exclaimed, her heart lifting. 'Luke, that's wonderful! What an Easter it's going to be. Oh – and I've just thought of something else. If we're definitely moving out of here, and if Jennifer's agreeable, Bob Pettifer could have this cottage for himself and Kitty Pengelly. It's almost as if it was meant.'

'Perhaps it was,' Luke said, and gathered her into his arms again. 'I wouldn't know about that.

But I do know something that *is* meant – and that's that you and I should have a long and very happy life together in Burracombe. And what better night to celebrate that than St Valentine's!'

'Rent it to Bob Pettifer?' Jennifer said thoughtfully as she put another log on the fire at Wood Cottage. 'Well, it's an idea. But are you really going to go ahead with buying, Val? It's a big commitment.'

'I know, but we're paying rent anyway and it won't be that much more. And we'll be paying for something that will be ours one day instead of–' She stopped and looked apologetically at her friend. 'Well, you know what I mean. It's been so kind of you to let us rent this cottage, but it's never going to be ours. And you and Travis may want it for yourselves one day. Or even for one of your children.'

'It's all right.' Jennifer smiled. 'I do understand, and it's a wonderful chance for you to buy Dottie's cottage. Are you going to give it a name or just call it Dottie's, like this one is called Jed's?'

'We haven't even thought that far! It would be nice to give it our own name, instead of always living in a house that's called after someone else, though.'

'You could blend your own names,' Jennifer offered. 'Quite a lot of people are doing that these days, with all the new houses being built. "Luval", for instance.'

Val wrinkled her nose. 'I don't think much of that. We'd be forever telling people how to spell it. And our surnames aren't much better. No, I don't think that would work. Maybe Luke would like to call it something arty, like The Studio.'

'Or The Paint Box,' Jennifer suggested with a grin. 'Or even The Ferris Wheel. What fun, to be able to name a house yourself. It's even better than naming a baby.'

'Talking of which,' Val remarked, 'it's not going to be long before you're doing that yourselves. Have you thought of any names?'

'Oh, you know what it's like – we keep making lists and adding to them or crossing names off and then putting them back. Travis likes Denise for a girl and Stuart for a boy, but I like Philip for a boy and Pauline for a girl. At least, that's what we liked yesterday – it may all have changed by tonight!'

Val laughed. 'You'll have to make up your minds soon, or the poor little thing's going to be stuck with whatever favourites you happen to have had on the day it's born.'

'Well, at least it'll be settled then.' Jennifer shifted awkwardly in her chair. 'I'm getting awfully big, though. Only seven months, and I'm the size of a house already.'

'Not really. It just feels that way. You need something new to wear, to cheer you up. A new maternity smock in a nice colour.'

'It seems a waste to spend money on something I'm only going to wear for a few weeks,' Jennifer objected. 'Although I'll want something smart for the wedding – you know, Miss Kemp and Mr Raynor. I know we're not going to be invited to the reception but we'll be going to the church and the party at the Bell on the Monday. And then there's the Organ Festival that day too. So I suppose it will be worth it.'

'Of course it will. And you're not to keep it for then, either. Buy something nice and wear it as much as you can. Or you could make a dress – they're easy enough, after all, just like sewing a tent, and you could use it as a dressing gown afterwards. Tell you what, why don't we go into Tavi one afternoon and choose some nice material and a pattern, and I'll help you make it.'

Jennifer brightened. 'That's a good idea. All right. We'll go on Friday and visit the market as well. And before that, I'll talk to Travis about Bob Pettifer and the cottage. I'd be happy for him to have it. I know he'd look after it, and Kitty seems a nice girl. It would be good to see them settled in the village.'

Val returned home feeling happier than she had for many months. Ivy Sweet was right, she thought. Secrets weighed you down and made you miserable. And in the end, she thought, they made you bitter and inward-looking, as Ivy herself had become.

I've only been keeping my secret a few weeks, she thought, and I hadn't even done anything wrong – not really – but Ivy kept hers for years and could have lost everything through what she did. No wonder she turned into such a misery. But now it's all come right for her, perhaps she'll change again – if it's not too late.

She remembered her mother's words when she'd been a child and sulking over some refusal to have her own way: *'One of these days you'll get stuck like that, Valerie Tozer, and then nobody will want to speak to you at all.'*

452

Ivy Sweet had got stuck like it and might never be able to unstick herself completely. But she had noticed what was happening to Val, and had taken the trouble to warn her, and for that, Val thought, she had found herself a friend – perhaps the first she'd had in Burracombe for years.

With Lent firmly under way, plans for the Organ Festival were now taking shape. Joyce Warren and Grace Harvey were in charge, reporting their activities to the committee headed by Gilbert Napier, with Basil, Constance Bellamy and Dorothy Doidge as willing slaves. Hilary, Alice Tozer and Dottie found themselves dragooned into helping as well, as the to-do list grew, and Minnie, who seemed to have acquired a new lease of life now that her own secrets had been told, also wanted to put her five eggs in, as she termed it.

'You want things going on in the hall as well,' she announced when Alice came home to tell them the latest developments. 'Why don't we do a few demonstrations? Pasty-making – we could bake them up and sell them as well – maybe a bit of spinning and weaving, cake decorating and the like. Pity 'tis the day after Easter, or we could have done Easter eggs too.'

'I don't see why we shouldn't, all the same,' Alice said. 'Mabel Purdy's master good at decorating eggs. But where are we going to serve the refreshments if all this is going on in the hall?'

'Chapel, of course,' Minnie declared. 'They've got a nice little kitchen and plenty of room for chairs and tables.'

'Would they want to?' Tom asked doubtfully,

coming in at that moment. 'It's for the church organ, after all, not theirs.'

'It's for the village,' Minnie said firmly. 'And church and chapel have always joined together in village things. They could have half the money from the teas and lunches anyway. They'd be pleased enough with that.'

'I think it's a good idea,' Dottie agreed. She had come back with Alice for a cup of tea. 'And you could do the pasty-making, Minnie.'

'Me? I thought you'd do that! My pasties are nothing special.'

'They're very good pasties,' Tom, who always ate at least two, interrupted. 'Go on, Gran, you'd be a great success.'

'But I don't have no proper recipe! I just use whatever comes to hand.'

'Well, isn't that what the old miners' wives would have done backalong?' Tom asked. 'They didn't have posh cookery books and probably couldn't have read them if they had! They just used whatever they had so they could send their men down the mines with something solid for their crib.'

'Same with the farmers' wives,' Alice agreed. 'Whatever pastry they happened to be able to make, and filled with potato, a bit of turnip if there was any around, and whatever scraps of meat they had in the larder, if they were lucky enough to have any at all.'

'And you know what they used to say about the pastry,' Tom added. 'You should be able to throw it down a mineshaft without breaking it! Really, in the old days it was just something to wrap the meat and potato in, not meant to be eaten at all

– especially if their hands were covered in bits of arsenic most of the time! I bet they ate it just the same, though – no wonder they all died young.'

'I hope you're not saying 'twas the pasties that killed them,' Minnie said in an affronted tone, and he laughed.

'Not unless one hit them on the head! Go on, Gran, you do the demonstration. That's the best way.'

'You seem to know a lot about cooking all of a sudden,' Alice observed. 'Perhaps you'd like to do a demonstration.'

Tom laughed. 'I'd do shearing if it was the right time of year, but the ewes won't be ready and the lambs will all be too small. We could have a pen with a few in on the green, though, just for the tackers to see and pat.'

By the time the committee met again, the idea of demonstrations in the village hall had become a firm plan and it was agreed that refreshments would be served in the chapel all day. This meant that at least two chapel members should be invited to join the committee and they, too, had their own ideas.

'We could have a few stalls on our bit of ground as well. The sort of games we bring out for the summer fair. Bowling for a pig, that would be good – Fred Wethercott's sow's due to farrow soon. He'd probably let us have one.'

'We mustn't forget what all this is really for,' Ted Tozer pointed out. 'It's to welcome the church organ back with music in the church all day. We don't want everyone outside enjoying themselves.'

'That could have been said better,' Joanna remarked. 'I think the vicar is hoping that those inside will be enjoying themselves too. But I'm sure they will be!' she added hastily. 'How are the invitations going, Mother?'

'Nearly everyone's answered already. There'll be organists here from all over the Deanery. Hilary's working out the times for each one and they're all letting her know what they'll be playing, so that we don't get the same tune played over and over again. Dorothy Doidge is getting into a proper state over it all!'

'We'll have the organ for the Easter Day services, though, won't we?' Joanna enquired.

'Oh yes, and the wedding, of course. And Dorothy will be able to practise during the week beforehand. The bishop's coming too, on Easter Day itself, to rededicate it. It's going to be a real festive weekend.'

'Everything seems to be turning out right for Burracombe this Easter,' Joanna said, but there was a wistful note in her voice and Tom moved to put his hand on her arm. 'It's all right, love. I've got over thinking of Easter as little Suzanne's anniversary. You were right, we've got to keep it separate for Robin and Heather's sake. This year, it's going to be a real happy Easter, and the whole village is going to be celebrating.'

Chapter Forty-Four

Plans for the wedding were also taking up a lot of time. Despite Frances and James's best intentions, the children in the school seemed determined to take over and organise it in their way. An afternoon of drawing and painting resulted in a display of pictures of the happy couple arrayed in everything from the regal splendour of purple robes and golden crowns (some of the smallest infants hadn't yet grasped the difference between a queen and a bride) to riding suits in hunting pink (one of the Crocker twins). There was also a lot of discussion about the party afterwards.

'My mum says it's only for grown-ups and it'll be in the pub,' Shirley Culliford complained. 'That's not right, is it, miss? Because that wouldn't be fair, and you always say us got to be fair.'

'*We* got to be fair,' Frances said automatically, and then heard what she had said. 'I mean "*we've*" got to be fair. But–'

'That's what I said,' Shirley agreed. 'But my mum says life's not fair and the sooner us learns that, the easier it'll be later on.'

Frances gazed at her. Life for the Cullifords certainly hadn't always been fair, although it was true that Maggie and Arthur had brought a lot of their difficulties upon themselves. But it seemed that there were always one or two families like that in any community – a little feckless, possibly

457

a little shady, somehow never quite capable of keeping on an even keel. You had to accept them and do what you could to help. And with the help of the entire village, the Cullifords did seem to have made an effort in the last year or so and their children were improving all the time.

Perhaps Maggie was right to warn her family about life's tendency to be unfair occasionally, but it did seem a pity that they should have to learn it so young.

'There'll be a party for the school as well,' she said. 'We'll have it at the school on the last day of term. Better still, if it's a nice day, we'll have a school picnic in the bluebell woods.'

And that's another thing to organise, she thought as the children went whooping in from the playground to their classrooms, where the infants would inform James of this latest development. Well, never mind. We should be able to organise a simple thing like a school picnic standing on our heads. And the best part is that Iris will be here too by then. She'll love it.

Frances' cousin Iris was coming down from Malvern the week before the wedding. She hadn't been back to Burracombe since her parents had left it, not long after their son Ralph had been killed in the First World War. Her father had been a pharmacist in Tavistock but they had lost heart in their business and had decided to move to the Midlands, to make a fresh start. Iris still lived in the house they had bought on the slopes of the Malvern Hills, overlooking the town and the flat, chequered plain of Worcestershire with the whaleback hump of Bredon Hill on the horizon.

'I'll stay with you until the wedding,' she'd said to Frances on the telephone, 'and then I'll move out to the Bedford Hotel for a few days until the Organ Festival is over and you and James go off on your honeymoon.'

'Why move out?' Frances asked and heard Iris chuckle at the other end of the line.

'Because James will be moving into the school-house, of course! He won't want me in the house on your wedding night.'

'Oh.' Frances felt herself blush and was glad Iris couldn't see her. 'Well, you don't need to go into Tavistock anyway. You can stay in James's cottage. Stay as long as you like – until we come home again, if you want to. We'll be able to relax more then, with the wedding and the festival over and done with.'

James was equally pleased with the idea. 'Why don't you ask her if she'd like to use my cottage, from time to time? It will be empty and I haven't decided yet what to do with it until we come to need it ourselves. It would be convenient just to keep it available for any of our friends or family who might want to visit.'

'That's not a bad idea,' Frances said thoughtfully. 'It would be good to have Iris here sometimes, if she likes the idea. She never wanted to come back before, you know – it was a bad time when Ralph was killed – but it seems that she's ready now. The only problem might be that your cottage is so cosy, we'll probably never be able to get her out of it, once she's there!'

'I'm so glad we'll be here for Easter,' Maddy said

to her sister Stella as they strolled along the Little Burracombe lane, picking primroses. 'And it's lovely to have these couple of weeks staying with you. It's nice at the Barton, and Hilary and David are dears, but with Uncle Gil I do feel I have to be on my best behaviour all the time. It's probably because I always felt that as a little girl, when I used to go there with Fenella.'

'It won't be long now before you leave for Canada,' Stella said, tying up a bunch of primroses and adding it to the pile already covering Simon's pram quilt. 'You will write every week, won't you? And come back as often as you can?'

'Of course we will. And you and Felix and Simon must come over to see us too. Stephen says air travel is going to get easier and cheaper all the time. He says it will be almost the only way to travel in ten or twenty years' time. They'll be building bigger planes and new airports – it'll change the world.'

'Not too much, I hope,' Stella said. 'I quite like the world the way it is now – when there aren't any wars going on, anyway. It's really a rather nice one.'

'It is,' Maddy said. 'And the best of it is, it's full of nice people! I expect Canada is full of new friends, ready and waiting for us. That's the good thing about moving about, Stella – you make lots of new friends and you keep the ones you leave behind too.'

'Well, don't forget your old ones when you meet all these lovely new ones,' Stella said, feeling a twinge of jealousy. 'And I'm your sister, remember – not just a friend. It took me a long time and a lot of searching to find you after we were separated during the war.'

'And here I was in Burracombe, all the time. All you had to do was wait for Fenella to bring me back from France.'

'How does she feel about you moving to Canada?' Stella asked curiously. Maddy had been adopted by the famous actress Fenella Forsyth and had travelled with her after she had left school, but she saw less of her now that Fenella lived with her husband in France. 'I don't suppose she'll ever travel to Canada, will she?'

'She might. Stephen and I will go to see her before we finally leave. She's not all that well now, you know. I think Pierre's quite worried about her. But she's told me I must go with Stephen and not worry about her. She says she borrowed me for a while, but now it's time to give me back to my family – that's Stephen, and you and Felix, and Hilary. And most of Burracombe too, when you come to think about it. So many of them were my family when I was growing up and living with Dottie.'

'That's what Burracombe is,' Stella said thoughtfully. 'A family. Full of people we know and love, some more than others, but all caring about each other. Look at what happened when Billy Friend died. Everyone was upset about that.'

'Is it the same in Little Burracombe?' Maddy asked.

'Oh yes. I think it's the same in any village, really. That's why villages are so important, and why it's so important to keep them small, so that we still have the family feeling and the caring. It

461

can't be the same in big towns and cities. Even people living in the same street hardly know each other. Felix says he thinks the ideal number of people to live near each other, to keep that village feeling, is about three or four hundred. No more. He says that's enough for people to be able to know and care about each other, yet still keep their own privacy. Once you start to get more than that, people stop saying good morning to each other when they pass in the street, and once that happens, they stop caring. And that's what civilisation is all about – caring for each other.'

'Goodness me,' Maddy said. 'What deep conversations you and Felix have! I thought it would be either all about the parishioners' little squabbles over the new church window, or Simon's new tooth.'

Stella laughed. 'We do talk about those too! And speaking of Simon, he may be fast asleep at the moment but it will soon be four o'clock and he'll be waking up demanding his next feed. So we'd better turn for home.'

'Home,' Maddy said. 'Such a comforting word. And Burracombe will always be home to me – both Burracombes, in fact. I hope you and Felix never leave, Stella.'

'He'll have to leave when he becomes a bishop,' Stella said, and laughed at Maddy's expression. 'Don't worry! Felix may have more than one bishop in his family but I don't think he'll ever be one himself. He couldn't keep his face straight long enough!'

They strolled on together along the lane. The hawthorn hedges were laced with green and violets created a dash of purple amongst the clusters of pale yellow primroses, like the robes of an emperor against the spring gown of his empress. Maddy added a few to her posy and admired the effect.

'I won't pick any more, though. I like to see them along the lane, for everyone to enjoy.' She glanced up as two more figures appeared round a bend, walking close together and deep in conversation. 'Look, there's Jackie Tozer with that nice Australian boy. Hello, you two. Isn't it a lovely day?'

The newcomers approached and stopped. Jackie was looking flushed and bright-eyed and Greg was smiling. They paused to admire the baby and Stella invited them back to the vicarage for a cup of tea.

'Well – not this time, thanks,' Jackie said, a little awkwardly. 'Mum's expecting us back at the farm and we're late already. We went for a walk along the Burra Brook and over the bridge to Little Burracombe and there was a kingfisher, so of course we stopped to watch it and – well, we forgot the time.'

'Oh yes?' Maddy said, with a lift of her eyebrows. She and Jackie had known each other as children, when Maddy had first come to Burracombe as an evacuee and had lived with Dottie Friend after being adopted by the actress Fenella Forsyth. 'I know how easy it is to forget the time when you're watching a kingfisher!'

Jackie blushed and Greg laughed. He took her arm. 'Come on, little lady. Let's get you home before your mother sends out a search party.'

'She's hardly likely to do that in broad daylight,'

Jackie protested, but she smiled at the two sisters and allowed herself to be led away. 'We'll come and see you another day,' she added. 'I want to hear all about Simon and how much weight he's put on and how many teeth he has, and all that. Not that you'd be interested,' she told her companion. 'It's women's talk, not men's.'

'You'd be surprised what might interest me,' he said, and they both laughed and walked on.

Stella and Maddy watched them go, then looked at each other. 'And what should we make of that, do you think?' Maddy enquired wickedly.

'Not too much,' Stella said reprovingly. 'Jackie's not long lost her fiancé and got over that broken leg. I don't suppose she's at all ready to start another romance. And Greg will be going back to Australia soon, I dare say.'

'I'm not so sure. I thought I'd heard he and Katie were thinking of staying here.' Maddy shrugged and walked on. 'Well, it's none of our business anyway – but I'd like to see Jackie happy again. She's had a sad and difficult time lately, and she's a nice girl.'

'She'll be all right, whichever way it goes.' They reached the vicarage and Stella opened the garden gate. 'She's not the sort to let life get her down for long. And now let's go in – Simon's going to start crying in earnest any minute and I could do with a cup of tea myself.'

'The kingfisher will be my favourite bird from today,' Greg said, pressing Jackie's arm close against his side. 'Did you know kookaburras are kingfishers, by the way? You'll see what I mean

464

when you get to see one close up.'

'Oh, will I?' Jackie felt her heart beat a little faster. The kisses she and Greg had shared on the riverbank were still warm on her lips but rather than being excited by them, she felt confused and anxious. 'And what makes you think I'll see one close up? Unless they have them in London Zoo, of course.'

'They probably do, but that wasn't what I had in mind.' He stopped and drew her into the shelter of a gateway, where they were almost invisible from the lane. 'Jackie, I want to say sorry – I think I've scared you a bit. I didn't mean to do that. I don't ever want to do anything you don't like or want.' He looked down at her, searching her eyes. 'But when I kissed you back there – I truly thought you wanted it too. Was I wrong?'

Jackie looked down. He was holding both her hands now and she stared at their entwined fingers. For a moment, she seemed to see other fingers entwined with hers, and before she could prevent it a tear fell and splashed across them. Greg made a small sound and drew away one hand to lay his arm around her shoulders and pull her close.

'Jackie... Sweetheart, don't cry. I've upset you. I've gone too fast for you. I'm sorry.'

She shook her head. 'It's all right. You haven't upset me, not really. It's just...' She lifted her eyes and looked at him again. 'You were right, Greg. I did want you to kiss me. I wanted to kiss *you*. But when it happened, it felt...'

'Wrong?'

'No, not wrong exactly. Just – too soon, I suppose. It's not very long since – since...' Her voice trembled and broke. 'I didn't think I would ever want to be kissed again,' she said in a very low tone.

'But you did. And even if it felt too soon – maybe there'll be a time when you're ready. Do you think so, Jackie?'

'Perhaps,' she whispered, looking down again.

'And will it still be me you'll want to kiss?'

'Perhaps – if you're still here.'

'I'll still be here. But will you?' He put one finger under her chin and lifted her face towards his. 'You won't have gone back to America by then?'

Jackie stirred in his arms. 'Oh, Greg, I don't know! I don't know *what* I want to do. Some days I know for certain, I want to go back and start again – and then the next day I know just as certainly that I don't. But I don't want to stay here either. I feel as if I'm on a swing, going one way and then the other and never knowing where to get off.' She rubbed her hand across her face and drew in a deep, shivering breath. 'I'm in a complete muddle.'

Greg was silent for a moment. Then he said quietly, 'How about this for an idea? Why not try something – some place – completely new? Somewhere you've never been, never even thought of going. Somewhere like...' He let his voice fade and she looked up and half smiled.

'Somewhere like Australia, perhaps?'

'Well, why not? I could take you there – show you around – let you find your feet again. There'd be no strings attached,' he hurried on. 'You'll be completely free. But if, when you're feeling

466

strong and ready to look about and take life by the horns and start living properly again – well, I'll be there. If you want me. What do you say?'

For a long minute, Jackie said nothing. Then she met his eyes and took a breath.

'I'll think about it, Greg,' she said softly. 'I can't say any more now – but I will think about it. And if I do say yes – I think I'll be glad if you're there. Very glad indeed.'

For Jennifer Kellaway, who had been born and brought up in Plymouth, Burracombe had also become home.

'Both my parents came from here,' she said to Travis as they discussed Bob Pettifer's request to rent Jed's Cottage since Val and Luke were buying Dottie's. 'So it's no wonder I feel my roots are here. But you came from Dorset and you might want to go back there one day.'

Travis shook his head. 'I don't think so. It was a good place to live, and I like going back to see my family, but this is where I've made my own place. Even more so since I found you. And you're happy here, aren't you?'

'Yes, I am.' She relaxed against him. 'That's why I want to keep Jed's Cottage. We'll have to leave this house some day, and then our own little home in the village will be waiting for us. I don't want to sell it.'

'And you're happy about letting it to Bob and Kitty?'

'Of course I am. He's a good, sensible young man and Kitty's a lovely girl. They'll look after it and enjoy living in it. I don't suppose they'll want to live there for ever – they'll probably look for a bigger house one day, and they may even want to buy their own home as more people are beginning to do now – but for the time being it would be ideal. And Jack and Nancy will be pleased to have them so near.'

'Everything seems to be coming together,' he said thoughtfully. 'You and I, settled with our little family, which will be perfect once the new baby arrives; Val and Luke buying their own house – I know you've been a bit worried about them, but they seem to have got over whatever troubles they had; both the Pettifer boys settling down and ready to start their own business once Terry finishes his apprenticeship; Hilary and David as happy as larks at the Barton; Dottie and Joe buying Moor View and looking forward to their next trip to America; Miss Bellamy as pleased as Punch to have her two young Australians with her; the schoolmistress getting married at last; and Stella and Felix settled over in Little Burracombe. All we need now is for Bob Foster to propose to Edie and the whole village will be done and dusted!'

'Hold on a minute!' Jennifer said, laughing. 'There are plenty more things to happen in Burracombe before we can say that. For a start, there's Jackie Tozer talking about going back to America, which Ted and Alice definitely don't want, and Stephen and Maddy going to Canada. There are more babies to be born and, I'm afraid, people to die. Village life is never "done and dusted".'

She paused, then added thoughtfully, 'I don't think the Burracombe story will ever truly come to an end.'

Chapter Forty-Five

Easter came at last. The last few days of March had turned cool and grey, and on Good Friday a thin, bleak little wind blew across the moor and through the lanes, bringing with it a spatter of chilly rain. Basil wore an extra jumper under his cassock as he went to the church to take the long Good Friday service and the congregation came in winter coats they had hoped were put away for the summer. They prayed almost as much for fine weather on Sunday and Monday as for their own souls and then went home to smoked cod or haddock and hot cross buns for tea.

On Saturday, the church was filled with women arranging flowers. Frances and James had requested only spring flowers for their wedding, which was to take place immediately after the morning service on Easter Sunday, and Hilary had asked David to order masses of daffodils from the Scilly Isles. They arrived in a van and it took nearly twenty minutes to unload them and bring them into the church. With the primroses picked by the schoolchildren, who had been given a picnic and games up at the Standing Stones on the last day of term, and some early bluebells and violets, the church seemed to be filled with sunshine and as Alice and Dottie and their helpers emerged at the end of the afternoon they saw the sun break through the clouds, pushing them back with its warmth to reveal a clear blue sky.

'It's going to be a lovely day,' Dottie said, pausing with her load of discarded stems and greenery to turn her face up to the sun. 'Look at the gorse all in flower up on the moor. It's like a blanket of cloth of gold thrown down from heaven. What a wedding it's going to be. And what a festival for the organ.'

The organ was to be played for the first time at tomorrow's services. Dorothy Doidge, filled with panic, had been practising all week and those passing the church had paused to listen to its majestic notes. In fact, a lot more people than usual had seemed to find reasons to pass the church that week and little knots of villagers could be seen standing in silence as their favourite hymns sounded across the green. Everyone was looking forward to Monday, when it would be played all day and organists from all over the Deanery would be in the church to show off their own skills and play music that had seldom, if ever, been heard before on the Burracombe organ.

Frances and James had their own reasons to feel nervous and excited. They were on the brink of a new adventure that neither had thought would ever come their way. They went together on the Saturday to meet Iris, who had come down from Malvern by train, and James drove slowly back through the lanes so that she could adjust to being once again in the place where she had grown up.

'Some of it hasn't changed at all,' she said quietly, gazing out of the window. 'Time seems to have stood still in this little corner.'

'It hasn't really,' Frances said, smiling. 'But perhaps the changes are just those that take place more subtly – people coming and going. Births and deaths. A farm changing hands, a different herd of cows, or breed of sheep ... the kinds of things that may not be noticeable to us all, but make a difference just the same. And the war didn't touch Burracombe in the same way as it did the cities. You'd see enormous changes in Plymouth.'

'I know. There was almost nothing left after that terrible Blitz. I saw photographs afterwards in the newspapers.' Iris shuddered, then changed the subject. 'Is our old house still here?'

'Yes, it is. A local solicitor lives there now – Henry Warren. You'll meet him and his wife Joyce – she's one of those people who have a finger in every pie but makes sure everyone else is involved too.' Frances laughed. 'Some call her a busybody and she can be very irritating, but the village would fall to pieces without her.'

'There's one in every village.' Iris smiled. 'Do you remember Elsie Wollacott, when we were children? She was like that.'

'So she was. I'd forgotten her. She must have died before I came back to teach.'

They arrived in Burracombe, still reminiscing, and James stopped at the schoolhouse and carried Iris's suitcase in. 'You'll be moving into my cottage tomorrow evening, so don't unpack too much. Someone will come and collect your case again in the morning.' He grinned. 'It won't be me, though – Frances says it's unlucky for me to see her before we meet in church!'

He left, with a kiss for each woman, and after

471

he had shut the door they looked at each other.

'Well,' Iris said. 'Here we are. Back in Burracombe together, where it all began.'

'Yes,' Frances said. 'And I can't tell you how good it is to see you here, after all this time. You won't go rushing back to Malvern afterwards, will you? You'll stay for a while? James says you can stay as long as you like and use the cottage whenever you want to come.'

'You must be careful what you say,' Iris replied with a smile. 'Now I've plucked up the courage to come back, I may decide to stay for a very long time indeed!'

The church, already full for the Easter Day service, was packed for the wedding that followed it. There was a reshuffling as the front pews, normally occupied by the Napiers and other prominent families, were freed for the guests. Frances had asked Charles Latimer to give her away, so Mary Latimer sat in the front pew with Iris, Stella and Felix and some of the others who had been closest to Frances during her years in Burracombe. On the groom's side, James was sitting nervously with his best man – a friend from his army days who had come down from London – a smattering of other friends both from the army and from the prep school where he had taught, and a few of his and his first wife's family who had come to wish him well. The rest of the congregation were Burracombe people, many of whom had been taught by Frances over the years in the little village school.

The organ, played now with more confidence by Miss Doidge, sounded out in the voluntary she had chosen, and Basil, standing at the door to receive the bride, remembered that other wedding, six months ago, when it had broken down and Felix had persuaded the congregation to hum the 'Wedding March'. There would be no such alarms today, he thought with relief, and held out both hands as Frances, accompanied by Charles Latimer, came up the path in bright spring sunshine that was almost dimmed by the radiance of her smile.

'My dear,' he said, 'you look beautiful. You have all my very best wishes for your happiness. Are you ready to go in?'

'Yes,' Frances said, holding her bouquet of spring flowers like a trophy before her. 'Yes, please. I'm quite, quite ready.'

After the joy of Easter Day and the wedding, it might have seemed that Burracombe would need a breather before the next celebration. But with the Organ Festival happening the very next day, there was no time to rest.

'At least the flowers are still looking fresh,' Basil said as he and Grace went into the church early on Monday morning. The arrangements created so carefully by Alice and her team were still as bright and glowing as when Frances had walked up the aisle to greet her groom. 'It really was a lovely day, and this festival is the best idea you've ever had.'

'Let's wait until this evening before you say that,' Grace begged. 'I feel as nervous as a bride myself. Just tell me nothing's going to go wrong!'

'Nothing's going to go wrong,' he said obediently, and gave her arm a squeeze. 'Of *course* nothing's going to go wrong, my dear! It's been planned down to the very last detail. Whatever *could* go wrong?'

Grace gave him a look. 'We said that before the children's Nativity play that they did all through the village, and look how you nearly allowed Billy Madge to bully you into letting him and the little girl playing Mary into the vicarage, donkey and all. And then there was that dragon, only last summer, running amok in the village street and nearly killing poor Dottie in her wheelchair, not to mention causing a stampede with Ted Tozer's cows. In a place like Burracombe, Basil, there is always something to go wrong.'

'Well, not today,' he said, and turned as the church door opened and a little group of men and boys entered, stamping their feet on the coir mat and talking quietly. 'And here are the bell ringers to start the proceedings off in style. Good morning to you all. And Micky and Henry too. Are you going to give us some of your new style of ringing?'

'Method.' Travis nodded. 'Or "scientific", as Devon folk like to call it. Yes, we'll be doing that as well as the call changes. In fact, we're going to do something rather special today. We're going to ring a quarter peal.'

'A quarter peal?' Basil queried.

'It lasts for three-quarters of an hour,' Henry said. 'A whole peal lasts for three hours, you see, and none of the changes are repeated. It's different all the time. It's going to be our first.'

'And the first ever rung in Burracombe,' Travis added. 'It'll be printed in the ringers' newspaper

474

– *The Ringing World* – so that everyone knows about it. We might even get a board done to hang in the ringing chamber as a record of the occasion. And if we're to finish before the first organist arrives to play at nine o'clock,' he added to his team, 'we'd better get the bells up and ready.'

Basil turned to Ted Tozer. 'Well, that sounds as if it will be very special indeed. And are you taking part too?'

Ted shook his head. 'Bless you, vicar, no. I'm not a scientific ringer. Too complicated for me. I leave it to these youngsters.' He took a step nearer. 'To be honest with you, I was a bit against it to start with but now I've heard 'em at it, when they gets it right, it do sound quite musical. But us'll be ringing good old Devon call changes the rest of the day, on and off in between the organ playing. To my mind, it don't matter how clever these scientific ringers be, there's nothing to beat Devon call changes, struck proper. Nothing at all.'

The bells were ringing out as Basil and Grace left the church and went back to the vicarage for breakfast. They paused at the door, listening to the constantly changing music, and the rosy-checked vicar looked at his wife and smiled.

'What a lovely sound. And what a lovely Easter this is turning out to be.'

Basil Harvey wasn't the only person to voice this comment as the day went on. With plenty of visitors from other parishes in the Deanery coming to hear their own organist play, the village seemed full of people from dawn to dusk. As well as enjoying the recitals, they streamed into the chapel all day long for morning coffee, lunches and cream teas. They crowded the village hall to watch Minnie making pasties (which were then baked and sent to the chapel to add to their supplies) and see George and Ivy Sweet decorate wedding, birthday and Christening cakes. They watched Luke painting, and bought instant sketches of themselves. They watched the spinners and weavers at their work, and marvelled at Mabel Purdy's skill at applying patterns to hens' eggs. The braver amongst them tried their hands at some or all of these things and went home proudly carrying their creations.

While it was mostly women and children who went to the village hall, their menfolk bowled for a pig on the village green or sat outside the Bell Inn with pint tankards before them. Many of them were also bell ringers and were invited by Ted to 'have a pull' while the organists were changing over. It was as good as Deanery Day itself, they declared, and the Burracombe bells were as good as ever.

As the day drew to a close, Dorothy Doidge and the organist from the Tavistock church itself played the last notes together in a duet, and Basil sighed with relief and smiled into his wife's eyes.

'You see? Nothing went wrong. Well, apart from Tom Tozer dropping the teapot – I don't know what he was doing with it in the first place – and Micky and Henry making off with a whole tray of pasties, which, I must say, they deserved after ringing that quarter peal of theirs, and the Crocker twins – well, I'm not sure what the Crocker twins were doing, except that there seemed to be far

476

more than two of them! But nothing serious happened and everyone has enjoyed it.'

'They certainly have. And now come along to the village hall. They're finishing the last tidying up and they want us there.'

Basil followed his wife into the hall. The whole of his congregation was there, not tidying up at all, but sitting at tables with glasses and bottles of what looked suspiciously like champagne in front of them. He stopped dead and Gilbert Napier, sitting with Hilary, David, Stephen and Maddy, rose to his feet.

David and some of the other men began to go round opening the bottles. 'We couldn't let the day go by without a proper thank-you to our vicar and his wife,' Gilbert said, 'and to all the helpers who made this day possible. And, indeed, to all those who make Burracombe the village it is. A very special place indeed.'

'The vicar!' they chorused, holding up their glasses. They drank, and then Gilbert raised his glass again.

'I want to propose another toast as well. This is to those who will soon be leaving us, perhaps for quite a long time. To Jackie Tozer, who wants to stretch her wings on the other side of the world. To Katie and Greg Kemble, who will be going back to Australia soon, although we hope they'll visit us again – they have Burracombe blood running in their veins even though they grew up almost as far away as it is possible to be. And to my own son Stephen and his wife, our dear Maddy, who will soon be off to make a new life in Canada.' He lifted his glass towards the young people and bowed slightly. 'Our love and best wishes go with you all, and we hope and pray that you will come back, as soon as you can and as often as you can, and never bid Burracombe a last goodbye.'

Maddy looked across at the next table, where Jackie was sitting with Greg and Katie, and Constance Bellamy.

'Jackie looks happier than I've seen her for a long time,' she said quietly to Stephen. 'Do you think she'll stay in America this time?'

He followed her glance and grinned. 'I'd say a visit to Australia might be on the cards. Not yet, perhaps, but in a year or two. But who knows what will happen to any of us in that time? There could be all sorts of changes that nobody's ever thought of.'

'That's what makes life so exciting,' she said. 'Even though the changes aren't always happy ones.' Her face sobered a little as she thought of the changes that had happened in her own life – the Blitz, which took her mother and baby brother from her, the loss of her father at sea, which had resulted in her separation from her sister Stella, the tragedy of her sweetheart Sammy's death... 'We're so lucky, Stephen. We've come through so much and we've been given so much. And somehow Burracombe has always been at the heart of our lives.'

She turned to look at him and reached out for his hand.

'And it's not goodbye,' she said. 'Nobody ever really leaves this village. We shall never, in our deepest hearts, say farewell to Burracombe.'

The publishers hope that this book has given you enjoyable reading. Large Print Books are especially designed to be as easy to see and hold as possible. If you wish a complete list of our books please ask at your local library or write directly to:

Magna Large Print Books
Magna House, Long Preston,
Skipton, North Yorkshire.
BD23 4ND

This Large Print Book for the partially sighted, who cannot read normal print, is published under the auspices of

THE ULVERSCROFT FOUNDATION